A
CALLER'S GAME

J. D. Barker

A Caller's Game

Published by:
Hampton Creek Press
P.O. Box 177
New Castle, NH 03854

This is a work of fiction. Names, characters, places and incidents either are products of the author's imagination or are used fictitiously. Any resemblance to actual events or locales or persons, living or dead, is entirely coincidental unless noted otherwise.

Hampton Creek Press is a registered Trademark of Hampton Creek Publishing, LLC

Cover Design by Stuart Bache
Book design and formatting by Maureen Cutajar
Author photograph by Bill Peterson of Peterson Gallery

ISBN: 978-1-7342104-4-6 (hardcover)
ISBN: 978-1-7342104-5-3 (ebook)
ISBN: 978-1-7342104-6-0 (paperback)

I'm going to offer you a choice.

For Thad McAlister, gone too soon.

Jordan

"Oh, hell no!" Jordan Briggs brought her palm down hard on the horn and held her middle finger up through the open sunroof of her Audi R8. She'd been forced to stomp the brakes, and when she shifted her foot back to the gas, her heel snapped. "These are my favorite Louboutins, you piece of shit!"

A beefy arm reached out the window of the garbage truck and gave her the finger back with a little wave.

"Who are you yelling at, Jordie?"

She made a mental note of the phone number under the *How's My Driving?* sticker on the back of the truck.

"Goddamn garbage man! Just lumbered out on 49th from Madison without stopping. Didn't even slow down. Damn near took out the front of the Audi."

She took off her shoe, examined the busted heel, and tossed it in the passenger seat footwell.

"You're driving? Why are you driving? Oh, shit, wait—you're way back at Madison? We're on the air in six minutes!"

"I'm heading out to the Hamptons when we wrap today, and it seemed stupid to take the car service in from home, then have to go all the way back out to Connecticut to get my own car in a few hours."

"Frank gets you here on time."

"Screw Frank."

Traffic lurched forward several feet, then stopped again. The garbage man completed his invasion of her personal driving space, nearly sideswiping a Lincoln SUV in the next lane over. Probably texting. Everybody was texting. No reason to pay attention to what you're doing in New York traffic. Cars practically drive themselves.

Asshole.

Jordan looked down at the car stereo. An annoying habit she couldn't get herself to break whenever she had someone on speakerphone. "Billy, put this up on the board—hashtag zero, two, two, two, two, zero, two, two."

"Okay. What is it?"

"Write this down, too." She rattled off the phone number on the truck's sticker.

"Got it. Hey, you didn't tell me your husband was coming in. They're painting your office today. I had to put him in the green-room with Senator Moretti."

"Ex-husband. And I didn't tell you because I didn't know. Did he say what he wants?"

"Nobody tells me anything, you know that," Billy replied. "He's got Charlotte with him."

"Charlotte? She should be getting ready for school."

He should be getting her ready for school.

Charlotte had missed too many days as is. She couldn't have her kid repeat the sixth grade—how would that look? The press would have a field day.

"Please tell me you're close," Billy said over the car speakers.

She'd gained at least seven more feet in the past minute. Total progress.

The clock read four minutes until six.

"I can see the building from here," she replied. And she could, nearly two blocks ahead. A digital billboard with SiriusXM light and bright at the top.

Jordan held the horn down again. Seemed like the right thing to do.

She gained another three feet.

Yay, horn.

Billy sighed. *"The Today Show* has Meghan Trainor this morning."

"Seriously?"

"That's why Rockefeller Center is all backed up. Last of their summer concert series."

"All this traffic is for Meghan Trainor?"

"Could be worse. At least they don't have Ed Sheeran."

"Why don't *we* have Ed Sheeran? I don't want to talk to another senator. Not right before the weekend. Politicians kill my buzz."

"The booking came direct from corporate. I think he's a friend of Greenstein. Maybe Goldblatt."

Jordan clucked her tongue and inched forward several more feet. "We're booking friends of corporate now? I pay you to keep shit like that from happening, Billy. I pay you to get me guests like Ed Sheeran."

"Do you want me to call *The Today Show* and have Meghan Trainor stop by when she's done there? I've got a number for her manager around here somewhere, too. I'm sure I could get her."

"I don't do sloppy seconds, Billy."

The traffic on her left was moving. Why wasn't her lane moving? She could cut over, but she'd have to merge back to the right in a block.

Worth it?

Maybe.

Maybe.

Jordan gripped the wheel, slipped her foot to the gas, and—

A bus inched up on her left and stopped. Blocked her.

Dammit.

Too late.

Billy must have covered the phone. She could still hear him, but his voice was muffled. Sounded like he was shouting at someone. He came back a moment later. "Jordie, we need a backup plan. You're not gonna make it."

"I'll make it."

The clock read three minutes until six.

She wasn't going to make it.

The bus next to her had a billboard for her show on the side. *Overdrive with Jordan Briggs* in giant two-foot letters along with a publicity shot she'd taken about this same time last year. She hated that photo. She hated all publicity photos—she kept aging while they did not. Not only that, but someone always ran them through some magic PhotoShop Malibu Barbie filter that made her look damn near perfect. She didn't look like that. It was like staring into a mirror only to have a better version of yourself glare back and mock you.

Less than two minutes to six and more than a block and a half to go. Traffic was in complete gridlock now.

Someone in the bus recognized her and was shouting her name.

Jordan powered up her window, hid behind the dark tint. She closed the sunroof, too. Last thing she needed was someone tossing their spinach smoothie down into her car.

Billy said, "If you were with Frank, he'd let you out right there. and you could hoof it."

"I'm not with Frank, am I Billy?" Jordan said flatly.

Then she had an idea.

Oh, she couldn't.

But she did anyway.

Before she could change her mind, Jordan killed the motor, jerked up the emergency brake, flicked on the flashers, and got out of the car. "Have someone meet me in the lobby with a head-set, Billy!" she shouted as she yanked off her other heel and tossed it to the floor inside next to the broken one.

Billy said something else, but she slammed the door on him and ran for the sidewalk, one hand behind her back pressing the lock button on her remote.

The Audi chirped.

2

Cole

NYPD Officer Cole Hundley stared in utter amazement at the woman from the car in front of him. He watched as she got out in the middle of 49th, locked her car, and ran off down the sidewalk, leaving the Audi in the street, in the middle of a traffic jam, blocking his patrol car and God knew how many others behind him.

WTF.

He'd really just seen that.

That happened.

He was fairly certain she took off her shoes, too, because why not?

He reached over and tapped the button for his siren, gave it three loud chirps.

When she turned toward him, he expected her to freeze, maybe give him some apologetic, embarrassed smile and climb back into the car—the kind of thing people did when they got caught with their pants down by the police. But what did she do? She smiled. Then she waved and hightailed it down the road on bare feet.

He supposed the car could be stolen. That might make sense—it was a nice car. But she didn't look like the joyride type, not dressed like that. Even without shoes, her outfit screamed money. Plus, she locked the car. Most car thieves didn't have the keys on hand. They rarely locked a vehicle before abandoning it. They certainly didn't turn on the hazard lights. She abandoned her own car, on 49th, during rush-hour traffic.

She was quick, too. Half a block away already, with the grace and form of a practiced sprinter.

There were many times Cole had reconsidered his various life choices in the twelve years since he'd joined the force. Most of those times involved bullets flying at him, sometimes knives. He'd been bitten twice, only once by a dog. Both required shots. Some people liked to spit. That was never a good way to start (or end) the day. The verbal abuse was never in short supply. He'd once been attacked by a woman wearing nothing but aluminum foil held together by a roll of duct tape who insisted times square was an elaborate landing pad constructed by aliens. A woman abandoning a hundred thousand dollar car in the middle of the street and running off should surprise him but it didn't, in New York, that meant it was Tuesday.

Cole shifted his patrol car into park, flicked on the red and blue strobes, and with a deep breath, got out of the car and went after her.

He felt several cellphone cameras shift focus from her to him as he edged past the bus, crossed in front the parked Audi, and made his way to the sidewalk with random horns blaring all around.

Ironically, of all the cameras recording at that particular moment, the only one that didn't work reliably was the two-thousand-dollar bodycam attached to his uniform.

3

Jordan

Jordan ran across sixth against the light. Didn't matter much. Traffic wasn't moving in any direction. She wasn't the only one, either—probably a dozen other people wandered across the street as she did, their heads buried in their phones, oblivious to everything and everyone around them—at least she was paying attention. The lack of vehicular movement didn't keep the several cabbies nearby from nailing their horns. Cabbies seemed to live for that shit, like they were filling some horn quota. She didn't want to live in a New York without horns. They were the song of her people.

She was half a block past 6th, nearly to the SiriusXM building, before she realized she'd left her cell phone plugged into the dash of her car. Not much she could do about that, not now. Not much she could do about the cop behind her, either, other than keep him behind her. Plausible deniability was a wonderful thing, and she was fairly certain if she didn't make eye contact with him again, she could find a way out of this. Whatever *this* turned out to be. She had bigger problems right now.

Keeping her head down, Jordan pushed through the inevitable wall of tourists taking photos outside 1221 Avenue of the Americas and managed to get into the lobby before any of them had a chance to recognize her. While that was a miracle, she then found herself caught in the thicker crowd at the security desk, slowly moving through the metal detectors. One of those damn tour groups creating a bottleneck. Real New Yorkers didn't wear NY apparel or feel the need to snap two thousand pictures of a lobby.

The large clock above the elevators read 5:59:22. She had less than forty seconds.

Jordan cupped her hands around her mouth and shouted, "Holy shit! Some cop just punched Howard Stern out on the sidewalk!"

Yeah, that did it.

Lobby forgotten, the group shifted and rushed the doors like suburban housewives outside a Walmart on Black Friday.

Jordan rounded the crowd from the outside, shoved her way past several suits she didn't recognize, and got to the front without slowing down. "Coming in hot, Bobby!"

The security guard looked up, his eyes wide, as she ran through the metal detector, setting off the alarm. "Jordie, you need to—"

She didn't hear the rest.

She slid across the marble, reached the elevators, and pressed all six up buttons.

No Billy.

Where the hell was Billy?

She went back down the line and pushed the buttons again.

The clock above her read 6:00:02.

Shit.

Shit.

Shit.

The third elevator from the left dinged, and the doors opened. A girl with shoulder-length pink hair wearing an *Overdrive with Jordan Briggs* tee-shirt stepped out, this deer-about-to-meet-bumper look on her face. She cradled a wireless Bose headset in one hand and a cell phone in the other.

Jordan didn't recognize her. "Hey!"

The girl looked up, smiled, and started toward her all slow and nonchalant. No reason to hurry. Wasn't her life on the line. Take your time, honey. Wouldn't want to trip.

Fucking interns.

Seemed like there was a new crop of them every hour and none of them worth a damn.

Jordan ran over and snatched the headset, put it on. She heard the tail end of her theme song playing in the cans.

The intern held up the phone. "Billy had me take a picture of the board in case you—"

Jordan grabbed the phone and jumped in the elevator, hit the button for the forty-third floor so hard she thought she heard the plastic break. She threw her keys at Pink Hair. "Go get my car off 49th before someone steals it!"

As the elevator doors slid shut, she caught a glimpse of the cop. He was back at the security desk, staring directly at her.

Over the music in her headphones, Jordan heard Billy's voice. "You there, Jordie?"

"Ye of little faith, Mr. Glueck. When have I ever missed work?"

"Get your breathing under control. You sound like you just got fucked by an MMA fighter."

"I just ran two blocks. How would you know what getting laid sounds like?"

"Oh, I've been there," Billy said. "Sounds a lot like my credit card getting maxed out, followed by some pointing and laughter, then maybe a little cuddle time before the car door opens and one of us has to leave."

Jordan looked up at the elevator display. Twenty-first floor and climbing. "How's the level?"

"We're good," Billy replied. "Goldblatt wants to talk to you about taking tomorrow off."

"Screw Jules. Not his call."

"We're on in five, four, three…"

Billy went silent.

Jordan looked down at the photograph of the board on Pink Hair's cell phone screen.

The music ended.

She closed her eyes for a moment, drew in a deep breath through her nose, held it, then let the air back out through her mouth, a soft, controlled blow over her lips.

There was a subtle shift in sound as her microphone went live and she began to speak. "I want all of you to write down a number," she said, her voice calm, soothing. "This will be the first of two numbers I give you today. I met a man earlier. Not the kind of man who offers to carry your groceries when you're juggling several bags or the kind of guy who might hold a door open for you. Definitely not the kind of guy who gives up his coat when he sees that you're a little chilly. This was the kind of guy who tells you to get out from in front of the television when the game is on. The type who will fart on a bus or enthusiastically scratch his nether region while in line at the checkout in plain view of anyone unfortunate enough to glance over into his space. Manscaping is as foreign a concept to him as beachwear to an Eskimo. My new friend probably thinks chivalry is a borough out in Jersey. Yes, I met *that guy*. In true form as a representative of the species, he was kind enough to give me his phone number. I didn't ask for it, he just put it out there. For all the aforementioned reasons, he assumed I would want to call him, maybe get to know him a little better. For the sake of convenience, let's go ahead and say his name was Stan. He gave off a definite *Stan* vibe."

The elevator dinged, and the doors opened on the forty-third floor. Jordan found herself looking at the same publicity shot from the bus earlier, her own face smirking back at her from a poster large enough to cover half the wall behind the large oak receptionist desk. She stepped out into the hallway, turned left, and started for her studio.

The people in the crowded hall shuffled out of her way. Several smiled and nodded, others looked away. They all knew better than to try and speak to her when she had the headset on. Not their first rodeo.

"Ya'll know I'm a nice Southern girl at heart," Jordan said with a hint of sarcasm, playing up an accent she never really had since she was born outside of Cleveland. "So I took his number with a gleeful, *awe, shucks, sir* and went about the rest of my morning counting the minutes before I could get to a phone and ring up my new beau, my Prince Charming, my lovely, Stan. Being a Southern girl, I've got a bit of a shy streak. Those of you who listen to me on the regular may not think so, but I do. When a guy gives me his phone number, I become that awkward little thirteen-year-old I was back in middle school with gleaming braces and acne that seemed to compete with my freckles for the most skin real estate. You know, with thoughts like: was it my thick glasses or my incredibly flat chest that drew him in? Maybe it was my ability to dangle a participle in English class or the way I so grace-fully missed the rim with two out of three shots in gym. Couldn't have been my personality. None of the guys really talked to me back then, so they didn't know me, not really. I was a shadow, a ghost, a fly on the wall just trying to buzz through life without getting swatted. I was never the girl the Stans wanted, not back then. Or maybe they did, and I just misread the signals. I don't know, it's hard to say. Like most guys, Stans don't always fire a shot clear across the bow when they want to say howdy-do to a gal. Sometimes they skirt the issue. Dance around a bit. My Stan, this hunk of a man I met this morning, he chose cutting me off on 49th as his little way into my life. Not the most subtle approach, not by a long shot. He pulled right out in front of me and wiggled his big truck in my face. The rules of love clearly trump the laws of traffic in Stan's world, and aren't we all so lucky to be living in Stan's world?

"I get it, it's tough to meet new people. I suppose cutting me off in traffic might have been his way of pulling my pigtails or bump-ing into me at the punch table at the big homecoming soiree—we're all shy in our unique little ways. I gotta give him kudos for at least trying to climb over his Great Wall of Bashful to say hello, but I can't help but wonder, did he *really* need to be such a dick about it? Was that the strongest trick he had tucked away deep in the bowels of his magic hat?"

Jordan rounded the corner, stepped into the small break room, and made a beeline for the coffee maker. She poured herself a cup, black, sidestepped to the espresso machine, and added two shots. Closing her eyes, she took in the wonderful aroma, that heavenly scent of caffeine, the sweet sweat of gods. Oh, how she wanted to drink it, just a sip, but she knew she couldn't, not on the air. Broadcast 101.

She carried the cup back out into the hall, gave it one more sniff, then turned right, toward her studio at the far end of the corridor. "I can forgive some Stans. I really can. Like I said, it's tough to meet people. In today's world, you gotta get creative. We're not allowed to date at work, not anymore. Just ask Bill and Monica. It's been twenty years, and people still talk about that little knob-polish and The Dress That Shall Not Be Cleaned as if their little drama played out yesterday. Workplace relationships used to be the norm, and that makes sense, right? We spend a good portion of our day at the office with those particular people, you get close. You see them at their best and their worst—you see the crap they keep in their cubicle, for God's sake! If you can see beyond *Star Wars* figurines and *My Little Pony* statues and *Garfield* word-a-day calendars and still find the object of your love, shouldn't you be allowed to act on it? Is it really so wrong to spend three minutes in heaven atop the copy machine with that special someone from accounting to break up the monotony of a Wednesday? Yep, yes sir, it is. In today's world, it most certainly is. Hell, in my case, I'm sorta the boss, so if I wanted to pursue one of my coworkers in a biblical sense, there'd be paperwork involved and several conference calls with the good folks up in legal before I could so much as offer up a smile. I'd be willing to bet there's a video we'd have to watch alone, then maybe together, probably under adult supervision. It ain't easy being sleazy—not no more. Not for the boys or the gals or those who fall somewhere in between. You wanna date in today's world, you gotta get creative. You gotta cut someone off in traffic. Right, Stan? That's how you do it. You steal their wallet in line at Starbucks, then offer to pay for their latte when they realize their credit card is MIA. You pretend to be their Uber driver and trip the child locks until they agree to a movie and a show. You follow them down a dark sidewalk in a baggy hoodie and say something funny like, 'Got a nine-volt? My stun gun's dead.'

"Of course, there's always the apps—Tinder, Grinder, Minder, Blender, or Sidewinder—you can satisfy just about any kink with a swipe these days. I don't know about you, but I've never found those particular relationships fulfilling. Maybe Stan hasn't either. Maybe that's why he cuts off the single ladies on the road. Maybe that's not so bad a way to vie for the attention of a lady in 2020."

Jordan stepped into her office. Plastic painter's tarps lined the walls and covered most of the furniture. Her mail was piled on a chair near the door. She shuffled through the small stack, found the letter she'd been expecting, and shoved it in her pocket, thankful her staff hadn't opened it.

Crossing the hall, she eyed Billy through the window. The heavy soundproof door to her studio was designed to open freely when exiting but locked from the outside automatically to prevent someone from walking in unannounced and disrupting the show. She heard the subtle click as the magnetic lock disengaged and pushed through into the room.

Billy Glueck nodded at her from his glass producer's booth to her left and pointed at the large LCD monitor on the wall—5,300,049 listeners at the moment. God, she loved satellite radio and their real-time stats.

Jordan settled into her chair, a six-thousand-dollar Herman Miller. She placed the coffee on the desk in front of her, took another whiff of the steam, and smiled. "So I'm on the fence. Do I call this guy, or do I throw him back? As a nice Southern girl, do I forgive his awkwardness and give him a peek under my petticoat? I've been flipflopping on this all morning, and frankly, I just can't decide, so I'm gonna ask you all to do me a favor. Get a pad of paper out and write this down."

Jordan looked over at the large whiteboard next to her desk, all her talking points for today, and found the phone number she'd gotten off the back of the garbage truck.

"I want each of you to give Stan a call on my behalf at 212-555-6717 extension 304, feel him out for me; I trust you. Help me determine if he's my Mr. Right and we just got off all wrong, or if my first impression was spot on and he's just some Neanderthal looking for love in all the wrong places. I can't wait to hear what you decide. I'm counting on you to help me make the right choice…we'll be right back."

In the booth, Billy held up his index finger, paused a beat, then said, "…and…we're out." He looked up at her. "You wore braces when you were a kid?"

"Nope, that was all bullshit."

"You're one cold-hearted bitch, you know that?"

Jordan wrapped her hands around the coffee, raised it to her lips, then froze, remembering her daughter.

Shit, why did Nick bring her here?

She set the coffee back down, watched it slosh over the side, and jumped up. "I'll be right back!"

"You only have two—"

She didn't hear the rest, already out the door.

4

Cole

NYPD Officer Cole Hundley remained in the elevator for a moment when the doors opened, even though he was fairly certain he had the right floor. After pushing his way through a mob at the front of the building, talking his way past several security guards who insisted he check his weapon with them before entering, then glimpsing the crazy woman who abandoned her car out on 49th Street disappear into this very elevator from the lobby, he'd watched the display tick away the floors above. Her elevator stopped on the forty-third, forty-fifth, then the fifty-second floor before finally coming back down to the lobby. He'd hit all three buttons and fully expected to ride the elevator all the way to the top and back down again, without hide nor hair of her when the doors opened and a ginormous image of Crazy Woman glared at him from the wall across the hall. The words *Overdrive with Jordan Briggs* written beneath her, followed by *Weekdays 6-10.* The entire monstrosity was blanketed in lights from LED floods in the ceiling.

The elevator doors started to close, and Cole stuck his hand out, triggering the sensor to keep them open.

"May I help you?"

This came from a woman in her late forties wearing red-rimmed glasses and a matching blazer over a white button-down blouse sitting behind a large reception desk directly under Crazy Woman's oversized photo. People buzzed up and down throughout the hallway, and someone was blabbering a little too loud from speakers lining the walls. Something about a guy named Stan.

"Can you hit lobby for me?" a UPS deliveryman said as he wheeled a hand truck past Cole and settled into the back corner of the elevator.

When Cole didn't hit the button, the man reached around him and hit the button himself, muttering *Thanks, Officer* under his breath before settling back and clicking through something on his tablet. A second later, he looked back up. "Do you mind? You're blocking the door. I've got work to do."

New Yorkers were like a ray of sunshine in the morning.

Cole stepped out of the elevator and crossed over to the reception desk, the door sliding shut behind him.

The woman in red offered him one of those nervous smiles people often used with cops, the one that said *I'm here to help as long as you're not here for me.* The same one they kept on their face a little too long as they sifted through all the wrongs they'd committed of late and wondered if any were serious enough to bring in the po-po.

Cole said, "I'm here to see Jordan Briggs."

He couldn't help but look back up at the poster.

The way she'd looked at the camera made it feel like she was looking directly at him, watching him standing there. She had one hand on her hip, the other at her side. Her head was tilted a little to the left, an inquisitive smirk on her lips.

"Ms. Briggs is on the air. Do you have an appointment?"

Cole shook his head.

"Has there been an accident?"

"Not that I know of. Not yet."

This seemed to confuse her.

Behind him, the second elevator dinged and opened. A wiry-looking man in a gray suit stepped out, gave the receptionist a curt nod, and hurried down the hallway to the left.

Cole watched him for a moment, then leaned over the reception desk slightly. He wasn't a very large guy, but he knew when he did this, particularly in uniform, it tended to throw people off-balance. "I need to talk to her, now."

"Well…" She let the word hang.

Down at the far end of the hallway, Crazy Woman pushed out through a heavy oak door with a window down the center. She looked slightly flustered.

"Jordan!" the man in gray shouted. His shuffle turned into a half run toward her.

"Not now, Jules—I'm in the middle of a show." She started further down the hall.

"You can't give out phone numbers on the air," the man shouted from behind her. "How many times do we need to talk about this?"

"None, Jules! We need to discuss it exactly none times," she shot back over her shoulder.

Cole watched her pick up her pace. It looked like she was heading toward a room down at the end. He started after her at a sprint.

"You can't go down there!" the receptionist called out from behind him. "Jordie! Visitor!"

The man in gray had closed the distance to less than five feet. "Maybe I should set up a little sit-down with you and the team in legal. That was fun the last time, wasn't it? All of us chatting about the many ways you've fucked us on the air over the past fiscal year and the resulting financial implications of said fuckings? Let's do that again."

"You're right, Jules. I was a naughty girl, and I should be punished."

"I need a spreadsheet to keep track of all the liabilities you create."

"How about a pie chart? I like pie charts. They're pretty."

"Not funny, Jordie."

"Not meant to be, Jules. You do your job, and I'll do mine."

"My job is making sure you do your job without destroying all our jobs."

"Ms. Briggs!?" Cole called out.

Crazy Woman turned and glanced back at him. If she was in the least bit surprised to see a police officer jogging down her hallway, she didn't show it. She held up her index finger at Cole, then glared at the man in gray again. "Why exactly are we taking bookings from corporate? I'm not here to push Greenstein's political agenda or help his buddies get elected."

"The senator is a friend of the show."

Crazy Woman smirked. "The senator is a tool. He's a brain-dead walking dildo in a bad hairpiece sticky from spray-tan residue."

The man in the suit looked nervously toward the room behind them. "Jesus, Jordie, keep your voice down!"

"You put him on the air with me, and I'll make him look like a fucking clown."

"You'll interview him and play nice, or we'll end up in a meeting about that too."

Cole cleared his throat.

Crazy Woman looked at him, turned and pushed through the door at her back. The sign on the door said: JORDAN BRIGGS GREENROOM.

The man in gray swore under his breath, and when he turned, he saw Cole for the first time. "Oh, Christ, what else did she do?"

"The list is growing," Cole replied, following her into the room.

He found her in the far corner, kneeling down and hugging a little girl. There was a man standing beside them holding a pink Strawberry Shortcake backpack in one hand, his other hand in his pocket. Another man was sitting on a black leather couch at the opposite end of the room, drinking coffee and talking on his cell phone. Senator Moretti. Cole recognized him from television.

Cole stood between Crazy Woman and the door. She wasn't getting out. "Ms. Briggs, we need to talk about your car."

She looked back at him, puzzled. "What about my car?"

"You left it in the middle of the street."

"No, I didn't."

"Yes, you did."

She reached around the little girl and pressed a button on the phone sitting on an end table next to a leather recliner.

"Yes?"

"Sarah? It's Jordie. Where's my car right now."

"Your car?"

"Yes, the vehicle I drove to work today."

"It's in the garage. Trixie left your keys with Billy."

"Thanks, Sarah." Crazy Woman smiled up at Cole. "Mystery solved."

Cole really wasn't in the mood for this. "There's video, Ms. Briggs. I have a dashboard camera. You parked in the middle of 49th, exited your vehicle, locked your vehicle, then ran off."

"Mommy, are you going to jail?" the little girl said.

Crazy Woman pouted and pulled the girl closer. "Are you going to arrest me in front of my child, Officer?"

"That would traumatize me," the little girl said. "I'm at a very impressionable young age and highly susceptible to society's negative imagery."

From a speaker in the wall, a voice said, *"Jordie, you're on in fifteen seconds."*

She kissed the girl on the head. "Wait for me here, okay, Charlotte?"

The girl nodded.

She got back to her feet. "Don't leave," she told the man holding the backpack. "Put that in my office and wait here." On her way out the door, she patted Cole's chest. "You, though, you can go. Thanks for looking out."

Thanks for looking out?

Cole turned, but she was already out the door, sprinting back down the hall.

5

Jordan

"Christ, Jordie, if you're going to cut it this close, take the wireless with you," Billy said as Jordan fell back into her chair. She quickly raised the cup of lukewarm coffee to her lips and chugged it down, then held the mug up over her head. An intern snatched the mug out of the air and disappeared out the door to fill it as Billy counted down in her headphones.

The red ON THE AIR indicator lit up on her desk.

"I think I made an uh oh," Jordan said into her microphone. "I ran into my boss out in the hallway, and he was quick to point out Stan may not want to hear from five million people this morning. I get that, I suppose. I don't know what kind of data plan he's got on his phone or what his schedule looks like. We don't want to overwhelm the guy. So do me a favor: If you were planning on calling him, hold off for now. Call the main switchboard here at the station instead and ask for Jules Goldblatt, our VP of Programming. He's graciously offered to take down your names and contact info and pass it on to Stan instead. We figured this way Stan can call back whomever he wants. No pressure. Jules is such a team player. Always willing to take one for the rest of us, that guy."

Jordan had three monitors on her desk. The first belonged to a computer attached to the Internet, the second listed callers currently on hold by name, and the third monitor contained a chat window that allowed her to communicate with Billy and other members of her staff while on the air. A single keyboard and mouse with a selector switch controlled all three, so she didn't have to clutter up her space with hardware. She hated clutter. A message popped up on the third screen:

BILLY: *Jules will can you*
Jordan quickly typed, *He just bought a new Jaguar F-Type, he's not canning his golden goose*
BILLY: *All lines full – go to Crystal on 2*

"Crystal, you're on the air."

"I am?"

Jordan frowned at Billy through the glass and snapped her fingers three times in the air above her head.

He shrugged his shoulders and smiled back at her apologetically.

She needed energy. Vitality. You can't wake up the world talking to people who keep one hand on the snooze button while the other flips through a coffin catalog. "Yes, Crystal. When you call a radio show, get placed on hold for ten minutes listening to commercials, more than likely you will end up on the air when the host picks up. That's how this works. Exactly how Marconi envisioned it."

"I was curious if you watched the debate last night."

"Oh, hell no. I don't do debates. I'd rather listen to an instrumental version of the Backstreet Boys' greatest hits on repeat while someone sticks toothpicks under my fingernails than watch a debate. Please tell me you didn't sit through that drivel."

"There are so many choices."

"Which one is your favorite?"

"I like Borton from Iowa."

"Is he the one that's kinda short with the beady little rat eyes who likes to wear bow ties?"

"I think he's handsome."

Jordan glanced over at the second monitor, the one listing callers on hold:

Line 1 – Stan (wants to apologize)
Line 2 – Crystal (on air)
Line 3 – Stan (this one says he dated you in high school)
Line 4 – Bernie (wants to play a game)
Line 5 – Stan (female – says the best "Stans" are women)

She blew out a breath, not sure she liked the way this morning was shaping up. "Mind if I ask you a personal question, Crystal?"

"No, go ahead."

"How old are you?"

"I'm seventy-six."

"Wow, seventy-six. And you haven't given up hope. God bless you."

"It's good to have hope."

The intern returned with her coffee and set it softly on the desk. Jordan pulled the mug close and sniffed. The rich aroma of dark roast filled her nostrils, the steam washed over her face. She would make love to that mug if it weren't illegal in New York. "When I was in the seventh grade, we held student elections, and Bobby Corbin was running for class president against Lisa Almond. Bobby had buttons and posters, and damn, was he a looker. Dark hair all slicked back and a smile that made my little knees quake. Not just me, either. He had all the girls swooning. He was no Zac Efron or Jesse Metcalfe, but he could have held his own on the cover of Teenbeat. Not Tiger Beat, but I'll give him Teenbeat. He had that special something that just caused you to nod your head and agree with whatever topic he spouted off about. He ran circles around Lisa at the first two debates. I gotta give her credit, she hung in there, I would have bolted off and hid in a locker or under the bleachers or something, especially after the second debate. Kids started chanting 'Bobby, Bobby, Bobby' every time Lisa opened her mouth to speak. She had no shot of winning. At least, we didn't think so. During the third and final debate, she pulled an ace out of her pocket. Her parents owned a vending machine company. They had machines all around the city, and she said if elected, her father would put soda and candy machines in the school. Not just in the cafeteria, but all over the school. We'd never be more than a few steps away from a Snickers bar. That got my vote; I loved me some chocolate. Apparently, I wasn't alone, because when the election came around, Lisa cleaned up. I helped count up the ballots—she won nearly five to one over Bobby Corbin. Wasn't even a contest. Oh, and were we kids excited. She had this map of the school, and we could see where each machine would go, where the prime locker real estate was for next year. She had told us her dad would fix the price at twenty-five cents, way cheaper than the store. Good times. Then a month went by, then another month. Then a third month, and no machines. Month four, nada. No vending machines. Turns out, she never cleared Project Sugar Rush with administration. Looking back, I'm not even sure her parents agreed. I do know it was a hot topic at one of the parent-teacher conference nights, and not a single adult was on board. In fact, some of them came in fists all clenched, ready to fight. I knew little Lisa pretty good, and I'm certain she didn't purposely lie to us. She just didn't tell us all the truths. I'm sure there's a difference in there somewhere if you look really hard, but when you're twelve years old you really don't care, you just want your effin' candy. Tell you what, though, Lisa was the better politician. She had us figured out. No different than all those people on the debate stage last night."

Jordan reached over to her keyboard and brought up a search window on her first monitor. "You think he's handsome, huh? That Borton. Gets your granny panties all up in a bunch? What's his first name? Brett? Seth? Something like that?"

"Rhett. Rhett Borton."

"Of course he is." She keyed in the name, and the screen filled with various publicity photos. He was a troll. A bow-tie wearing troll with teeth that were a little too white behind a smile a little too wide. "Tell me, Crystal, in all seventy-six of your years, has a politician ever actually followed through on a campaign promise? Just once. Even something small."

Before Crystal could answer, Jordan said, "They dangle vending machines in front of us, they hold out candy, they tell us exactly what we want to hear, and there's zero follow-through, zero accountability. It's never their fault. They're always quick to point out who's in their way, but they never accept responsibility. I'd love to see every elected official sign a list of their campaign promises on the morning they enter office, and if they can't put a checkmark next to each one on that final day as they're clearing out their desk and packing up their white banker box with their awards and knickknacks and photos of their trophy family, they should have to forfeit their salary. Create some accountability to keep their promises in check. That will never happen, though, because politicians are usually lawyers and lawyers are scum, and all any of them really care about is lining their own pockets. Don't be fooled by a bow tie, Crystal. He's no better than the rest."

Jordan disconnected the call and glanced at her second monitor again:

Line 1 – Stan (wants to apologize)
Line 2 – Crystal (on air)
Line 3 – Stan (this one says he dated you in high school)
Line 4 – Bernie (wants to play a game)
Line 5 – Homeless Harry

Female Stan had dropped off. Harry was a regular caller, but she wasn't ready for him yet.

Jordan clicked line 4. "Hey, Bernie, what kind of game do you have for me?"

6

Cole

"She always like that?" Cole said to the man holding the Strawberry Shortcake backpack.

He was a few years older than Cole, probably early forties, with sandy-brown hair and dark-brown eyes. He looked tired, like he hadn't gotten much sleep. He ruffled the little girl's hair. "What do you think, Char? Your mom always like that?"

The little girl looked from him to Cole, then leaned against the man's leg. "I don't think we should answer *any* of his questions without an attorney present."

Cole couldn't help but smile. He knelt down. "How old are you?"

"I am eleven."

"You are clearly your mother's daughter."

This seemed to puzzle her. "Who else's daughter would I be?"

"Don't you have school today?"

She looked up at the man beside her. "Can he arrest me too, Daddy? For playing hoagie? I don't want to go to jail. Not even with Mommy."

Her father said, "I think you mean hooky, Char. He's more likely to arrest me for that."

He offered to shake Cole's hand. "I'm Nick Briggs, Jordie's hus...ex-husband... As of last month." He smiled weakly. "I'm still trying to get used to that."

Cole shook and got back to his feet. "Sorry."

Nick placed his palms over the girl's ears. "Don't be. It feels like a doctor cut out a big ol' tumor out of my ass and declared me cancer-free."

"That's gross, Daddy."

He ruffled the girl's hair again. "Your mommy is the world's best mommy, and I was lucky to have her," he said while looking at Cole with wide eyes, shaking his head no and drawing an imaginary knife across his throat with his free hand. "Charlotte here was supposed to spend the weekend with me, but a work emergency came up and we've had to make some last-minute changes to our plans."

"I'm going to the Hamptons!"

"With homework for today *and* tomorrow," her father added, squeezing her shoulder. "That you will do each day *before* you go to the beach."

"Maybe jail would be better." She pouted.

The radio on Cole's shoulder chirped. He reached up and pressed the transmit button. "This is 5839, go ahead."

"We're getting reports of your cruiser abandoned in the middle of 49th. Are you on a stop? You didn't radio in."

Shit.

"Minor fender bender, but we're all clear now."

"Gaff's not gonna let you off traffic if you do things like abandon your cruiser in the street. Even if you're close, you gotta call it in."

"Understood."

This wasn't worth the headache. Cole gave Nick Briggs and his daughter a quick good-bye and raced out the door back to the elevator. He'd already done two weeks on traffic, had one more to go, and he really didn't want to screw it up. The dispatcher was right—Gaff would easily tack on another month to his sentence if given the chance, and Cole wanted to get back to homicide.

When he pushed out the doors of the building back onto the sidewalk, he found the traffic had barely moved. He knew it wouldn't, not until *The Today Show* wrapped and they opened up the block again. They went through this a few times each week during the summer.

He got into the squad car and pulled the door shut. Turned off his red and blue strobes.

Behind him, a taxi had attempted to inch around his bumper into the lane on his left and was now crossing both lanes with no place to go. Nobody was moving.

A bus a few car lengths up and to the left had a giant advertisement for Crazy Woman on the side. Same photo as upstairs in the SiriusXM building.

Cole rolled his fingers on his steering wheel. Left to right. Right to left. Back again. He could hit his siren and force his way out of this, but what was the point? Maybe get another block or two over and write a few parking tickets? Better off just to sit here.

He took out his phone and downloaded the satellite radio app, clicked on FREE TRIAL, and entered his e-mail address.

Research.

On-the-job research. That's what this was.

Just while he waited.

He'd turn it off when the traffic cleared.

He typed *Jordan Briggs* into the app's search box, and three channels came up under the heading of *Overdrive with Jordan Briggs*: LIVE, REPLAY YESTERDAY'S SHOW, and CLASSIC. He clicked on live. A moment later, her voice came through on his phone's speaker. "...don't be fooled by a bow tie, Crystal. He's no better than the rest."

It took a couple more clicks for Cole to connect to the patrol car's stereo via Bluetooth.

Jordan Briggs's voice filled the vehicle. "Hey, Bernie, what kind of game do you have for me?"

7

Jordan

Jordan rolled her eyes when he didn't answer. "Are you there, Bernie, or did you nod off on me?"

Several odd noises came over the line, as if the phone had been dropped, then a man's voice. Midwest accent, probably in his thirties. After a decade on the air, Jordan had gotten pretty good at attaching voices to an age, demographic, and ethnicity. She could damn near guess their hair color. He said, "I'm here. Sorry. I was looking for the coffee, and I had you on mute."

"You lost the coffee?"

"I'm visiting friends and it's so early, I beat them up. I'm rummaging through their kitchen, trying to keep quiet so I don't wake anyone. Walls are thin around here."

"Where are you calling from?"

"Their kitchen. I said that."

"Don't be a smartass, Bernie."

"Sorry, I'm in Brooklyn, Seventh Ave, near Prospect Park."

"And where do you call home?"

"Oh, no place in particular. I've never been good at planting roots."

"What do you do for a living?"

"I used to drive a truck, but ever since I got hurt, I've been on disability."

"Sorry to hear that." Jordan slumped down in her chair, got more comfortable. This guy was slowing things down a little, but sometimes that worked. Her gut told her to stick with him, and over the years she'd learned to trust her gut. Billy, on the other hand, was on her third monitor, getting antsy:

BILLY: *Captain Cornflakes tuned the mellow up to eleven. Light a fire under him or move on.*

"When did you get hurt?"

Bernie paused a moment. She imagined him ticking off the time on his fingers. "Seven years ago to the day, actually."

"You've been on disability for seven years?"

He laughed softly.

"Do you find that funny?"

"I've been listening to you for a long time, Jordan. I know you. What you're really asking is have I been sucking on the government tit for the better part of a decade, right?"

Here we go.

"Oh, we'll get to that, don't you worry. But first, I'm truly curious. I want to know. What exactly happened to you?"

"Shit."

"What's a matter?"

"I cut my finger."

"You cut your finger making coffee?"

"My friend's kitchen is a dangerous place."

"Sounds like it."

Bernie cleared his throat. "I didn't get a whole lotta sleep last night. I don't really sleep all that well anymore, but last night in particular was tough for me. All these thoughts running around in my head, competing for my attention. You know what that's like, right? When you just can't shut your brain down."

Jordan chuffed. "All those voices talking to you at once, telling you what to do. Yip-yapping and screaming. Is that what's going on, Bernie? I've heard if you make a hat out of tinfoil, you can block them out."

"Damn, you'll say anything just to hear the sound of your own voice, won't you? You must love the sound of your own voice."

"I do give sexy voice," Jordan purred.

"I'd be willing to bet you have a busy head, too," Bernie replied. "I think if I were to riffle around in your medicine cabinet, I'd find a slew of meds to knock you out—Ambien, Xanax gummies, maybe a bottle of Jameson on the nightstand to keep you warm at night now that your husband's not there anymore."

Jordan's split from Nick wasn't exactly a secret. The tabloids seemed to notice their marriage was in trouble before they noticed the signs themselves. Plastering these unflattering pictures of the two of them walking through Central Park several feet apart, angry expressions on their faces. Even on a good day, the paparazzi managed to snap at least one or two unflattering pics. They never caught them smiling or holding hands, always a scowl or eyes turned away. She'd gotten used to their relentless attacks, Nick had not. He bought into it. Let it burn him. That had been part of the problem. One of the problems. One of many. Page Six in particular covered her personal life every chance they got, running crazy headlines to try and get a rise out of her, knowing she'd go off on the air and they'd sell papers. They'd started running photos with Charlotte last fall. That's what finally pushed Nick over the edge. He could live with the press's personal attacks on her. He'd even tolerate the ones that included him. But when the press decided their daughter was fair game, he was done. He'd given Jordan a ridiculous ultimatum and filed for divorce a week later when she made it clear she couldn't walk away from her career.

None of this made it any less weird when some stranger brought up their split on the phone, on the air.

Fuck you, Bernie. Don't poke the bear.

"How about you. Is there a Mrs. Bernie, Bernie? Have you managed to rope someone in from dusk till dawn, or do you pay someone to spoon by the hour?"

Bernie went quiet. He didn't hang up, though. She could hear him breathing.

Take the bait, little man. Bite the shiny hook. Talk *to me.*

"It's just me. I'm alone. Is that what you want to hear?"

Bingo.

"Of course not, Bernie. I want nothing but the best for you. Nobody should be alone."

He let out a soft laugh. "I've been listening for a long time, remember, Jordan? I know you don't give a shit about me. All you care about are your ratings. You want me to open up, tell you something personal, give you something you can exploit. Maybe I'm overweight. Maybe I drink too much. Maybe I shut out the rest of the world. I give you something, and you'll pull on it like a loose thread on a sweater. You'll just keep tugging, unraveling, taking me apart piece by piece. You've created a career chipping away at people. I'm not going to let you chip away at me."

"You sound very bitter, Bernie."

There was a soft *ding*, sounded like a microwave completing some task. "Sure, let's go with that. I'm bitter."

"What made you that way? Was it the accident?"

"Maybe I was always that way."

Jordan said, "I don't think so. In fact, I think at one point you were anything but. I get the feeling you were an eternal optimist until that accident you mentioned, then you got hurt, lost your job, lost your self-worth, packed on a few extra pounds, took up drinking, and now you're you. That's the day you kicked Cheerful Bernie out the door and became Bitter Bernie. Does that sound about right?"

Bernie didn't reply.

Jordan purposely let the silence linger, let it grow like thickening soup on a hot, blue flame.

A loud bang came from his end of the line, followed by a crash.

Jordan glanced up at Billy in his booth, who just shrugged.

"What exactly are you making for breakfast, Bernie?"

Another loud bang, then three quick thuds. Sounded like he dropped the phone.

Then nothing.

Silence.

The sound of crickets came over her headphones.

Jordan glared up at Billy and shook her head.

On her third monitor, he typed:

BILLY: *No sound effects. Got it.*

Jordan typed back: *Let the quiet linger*

BILLY: *Not sure where you're going with this guy.*

Jordan wasn't, either.

Bernie must have retrieved the phone. The noises stopped, there was a soft shuffle, then he was back on the line. "Sorry about that."

"What happened?"

"One of my friends woke up, just startled me. I'm back now."

"How many people are there with you?"

This time, Bernie didn't reply. Not at first. When he did, his voice dropped lower. He ignored her question and asked one of his own. "Have you ever woken up in the middle of the night and wondered if this is it? If today is the day you'll die?"

"Well, that's morbid."

"It's not morbid. It's the natural way of things. From the moment we're born, the clock is ticking. We go through the motions of life—childhood, we grow up, get a job, start a family, some grow old, others don't—through all of it, that clock keeps ticking. Sometimes you get a scare, something that reminds you about the clock, your personal clock—cancer maybe, death of a friend—you know what I mean. That little wake-up call that reminds you you're mortal and the rug could get pulled out at any moment. I don't think most people realize how fragile life really is. When we get up in the morning, make breakfast, head out to work, we fully expect to come back home later. Eat dinner, maybe watch a movie with someone we love before going to sleep and starting all over. That rinse and repeat of another day. Only a handful in history have started the day knowing full well they wouldn't be around to see the end of it—suicide bombers, death-row inmates—it's a short list.

I can't help but wonder if those few people find it refreshing. Like a relief. Knowing this is it, today is the day I die. They can wipe out their bank accounts, tell their asshole neighbor to fuck off, do whatever they want, knowing they won't be around tomorrow to deal with the consequences. That's got to be like the heaviest burden lifting off your shoulders, right?"

Jordan's eyebrows furrowed. "Are you smoking pot, Bernie? This sounds a lot like the kind of thing you talk about after a hit of Augie's Special Blend out of Mexico. Or maybe that hydroponic medicinal stuff they sell in Colorado."

"No, I'm completely sober right now. I don't do drugs."

"Do we need to be worried about you hurting yourself?"

"I'm just making conversation."

"Because you sound like you might hurt yourself."

"I don't plan to hurt myself."

"But you're wondering if you'll live to see the end of the day?"

"That's not what I said."

Jordan frowned. "Sure it is."

"You love to talk, but you don't know how to listen," Bernie replied. "You're too busy focusing on your next line. You don't take the time to process what you just heard, *to listen*."

BILLY: *Wacko*

"I asked if *you've* ever woken up in the middle of the night and wondered if this is it. If today is the day *you'll* die. And if it was, if you could be absolutely certain of that, how would you live out the rest of the day?"

"Are you threatening me, Bernie? I thought we were friends."

"No. Of course not. Like I said, I'm just making conversation."

Jordan sighed. "Well, I'm getting bored, and I don't do bored." Her finger hovered over the disconnect button. She studied the list of callers on her second monitor.

"All this talk, and we nearly forgot the game," Bernie said softly. "Don't you want to play with me?"

BILLY: *Twenty seconds until commercial*

Jordan said, "Okay, I'll bite, Bernie. What's your game?"

"Simple, really. I'm going to offer you a choice, and I want you to tell which of the two you like better."

"That doesn't sound like much of a game."

"I think you'll find it fascinating."

"We're coming up on a commercial, so make it quick."

"Okay, here we go," Bernie said. "When it comes to public transportation here in New York, do you prefer Ubers or taxies?"

Jordan rolled her eyes. "Seriously?"

"As a tourist here in your city, I'm curious. Your opinion means a lot to me."

BILLY: *Ten seconds*

Jordan replied, "You've heard me talk about this before. Uber undercuts the locals in order to steal business. Their rates are unsustainable, and they're hoping to keep it up long enough to force the cabbies out of work. I stand behind the NTWA, the National Taxi Workers' Alliance, and I urge my listeners to as well. Any hardcore New Yorker wouldn't be caught dead in or under an Uber; they hurt the local economy. Only tourists call Ubers. There's my answer—I'd take a taxi over an Uber."

Bernie said nothing.

"Did I win?"

There was a soft click as he hung up the receiver. Jordan realized he had called her from a landline. She didn't know anyone who still had one of those.

8

Jordan

Jordan's theme song broke in, and they rolled into a commercial. She pressed a button to mute the feed, leaned back in her chair, and looked up at Billy in his booth. "Sorry, I thought that was going somewhere."

"You should have just run with all the *Stan* calls." He snapped his fingers three times. "Rapid fire, just hit them one after the other."

"Nick dropped off Charlotte. This was supposed to be his weekend with her."

Billy ruffled some papers. "Rule number one while locked in a custody battle for your only child—don't start telling people you don't want to spend time with your only child."

"You're not people, you're Billy," Jordan replied. "And it's not that I don't want to spend time with her, I love spending time with her, it's just I had plans."

A sly smile edged his lips. "Plans, huh? I guess you can't ask your daughter to wait out in the hall while you're banging some—"

"Not those kinds of plans," Jordan interrupted. She bit the inside of her cheek. "I'm meeting my mother for dinner."

"And Charlotte can't be around Grandma?"

"She's never met her grandmother."

"How is that possible? She's what, twelve, thirteen?"

"Eleven." Jordan took a sip of her coffee and picked at the bagel someone had left on her desk. "I haven't seen my mother in fifteen years."

"Her fault, or yours?" Billy asked.

"Yes."

"That's not a very insightful answer."

"Wasn't meant to be."

Reading as he spoke to her, Billy checked off two items on a clipboard. "Not a lot of Mother-of-the-Year trophies in your family, huh?"

Jules Goldblatt knocked on the studio door, his angry face pressed against the glass.

Billy buzzed him in.

His scowl only grew as he saw Jordan. "You realize the switchboards are completely overwhelmed right now, and IT will have to give me a new extension?"

"But nobody's calling Stan directly anymore." Jordan smiled. "How's that for problem-solving on the fly? Big atta-boy for you helping out like that!"

Somehow, his face managed to grow redder. "You're not taking tomorrow off."

She cocked her head. "No? I'm pretty sure I am." She looked up at Billy. "What's on the calendar for tomorrow?"

He set down one clipboard and picked up another, flipped to the next page. "According to the schedule, you're out for the day and we're running a highlight package with some of your best musical performances. We've got Paul Simon, Jon Bon Jovi singing The Beatles, the guys from Imagine Dragons doing a cappella…I can't wait. I've been looking forward to this one for weeks."

"Weeks," Jordan repeated, nodding at Goldblatt.

Goldblatt shook his head. "We haven't run a single commercial promoting that."

"Well, who dropped the ball? You really should have been running commercials, right? Sounds like you missed an opportunity."

"You didn't communicate it properly. Does marketing even know?"

"Nobody asked me."

"It's your job to keep the team informed."

"Nope." Jordan shook her head. "It's my job to talk on the air. The rest is all somebody else's job. You're probably in charge of that somebody, and that somebody is doing a piss-poor job, and that reflects badly on you. I hate seeing you get in trouble for the inactions of others. It burns my heart. Makes me feel all cold inside, like when those hunters killed Lassie right in front of Timmy in that old cartoon."

"That was *Bambi*," Goldblatt muttered.

"Absolutely *Bambi*."

Billy said, "She can do this all day, Mr. Goldblatt. It will make your head hurt. I learned long ago it's best to just back away slowly and be thankful nobody is watching."

Goldblatt was shaking his head. His gaze found Jordan again. "I want the senator on next."

"Soon."

"Next."

"Right. Soon. Got it. I need to talk to my daughter."

She pushed by him and out the door. Jordan found Charlotte in the greenroom, nibbling on a donut from one of the snack trays. "Oh, don't eat that, honey. That stuff's been sitting out for nearly a month."

From the couch in the corner, the senator looked up from his plate. He'd made a crude sandwich out of two bagel halves, cheese, and some kind of meat. Maybe salami.

She looked over at him and winked.

He frowned down at the sandwich and set the plate on the corner table.

Charlotte said, "Why did the policeman want to arrest you?"

Jordan hugged her. "Oh, I think he heard a little girl was walking around up here with an illegal amount of cuteness dripping off her, and he came to put a stop to it."

Charlotte narrowed her eyes and fell back on her left foot. "You're deflecting, Mother."

"Mother, huh?"

"Yep."

"Did your daddy leave?"

"He had to tinkle."

"I'm done tinkling," Nick said from the doorway.

Jordan glanced over at him, then smiled back at Charlotte. "Can you go hang out with Sarah up front for a few minutes so I can talk to your dad?"

"Are you gonna hurt him?"

"I might."

Charlotte seemed to consider this for a moment. "Okay, but not the face. I like daddy's face." On her way out the door, she reached up and patted him on the back. "Good luck, Mr. Briggs."

When she was gone, Nick let out a sigh. "I know this is short notice, Jordie, but I don't have a choice. I've got to be in Boston by this afternoon. I'll be back as soon as I can. Tomorrow night at the latest."

"You know what I'm doing tomorrow night."

"Take Charlotte with you. She deserves to meet her grand-mother."

"Her grandmother doesn't deserve to meet her," Jordan fired back.

"It's been fifteen years."

"Not a chance."

"How about a sitter?" Nick suggested.

"On a Friday night in the Hamptons, right. I've got a better shot at negotiating a truce between Palestine and Israel."

Nick shoved his hands in his pockets. "Well, I don't know what to tell you."

"Tell me you'll cancel your bullshit trip and handle your re-sponsibilities, like a big boy."

"I can't do that."

"What's so important in Boston?"

He didn't answer.

Jordan felt her face flush. "This is you being a shitty father."

"That's not fair."

"Life's not fair."

Billy's voice came over the intercom. "Jordie, on in thirty seconds."

Jordan glared at him for at least ten of her remaining seconds, then pulled the envelope she'd taken from her desk earlier out of her pocket, shoved it into his chest, and stormed out.

9

Cole

"Please get back in your car, ma'am."

Cole was doing his best to stay calm, he really was, but this woman wasn't making things any easier. He was standing on 49th about five vehicles up from his patrol car. Some guy in a Prius had let his foot slip off the brake and he rolled into her Lexus from behind. He couldn't have been doing more than one or two miles-per-hour. He'd only drifted a couple of feet.

"He rear-ended my car!" she shouted back at him.

"There's no damage," Cole said for the fourth time. "Most bumpers are designed to take a hit up to five miles an hour before they dent. He wasn't going fast enough. You need to get back in your vehicle."

Her hair was dyed this awful shade of orange, with at least half an inch of gray roots showing. Cole tried not to stare, but he kept catching himself looking down at the top of her head.

Somewhere up ahead, Meghan Trainor's band was warming up. Cole could hear someone beating on an amplified bass drum. Each hit fed the headache growing behind his eyes.

The man who bumped into the woman's car was standing next to him, not sure what to do. He'd already offered her his insurance information. She'd refused it, insisting Cole write a ticket instead.

If NYPD wrote up everyone who rolled into the car ahead of them during stalled traffic, they'd all be driving new cruisers and ticket books would be empty.

Christ, now he was starting to think like a traffic cop. He really needed to get back to homicide. Dead people didn't complain, and they certainly didn't tell him what to do.

Cole forced a smile. "How about this? I'll write him up with a warning, and if he ever does it again, the judge will send him straight to Rikers. They throw the book at repeat offenders."

Somewhere back near his patrol car, someone hit their horn and held it down for nearly ten seconds, paused a beat, then did it again. Why the hell do people do that? Traffic wasn't going anywhere.

"I want him to get a ticket," the woman insisted again. "A sizable ticket."

The man who hit her threw his hands up and started walking away. "Decide what you want to do. I'll be in my car."

Cole's cell phone rang. He held up a finger, turned his back on both of them, and took it from his pocket. It was his partner, Garrett Tresler. He tapped *ANSWER*. "Hey, what's going on?"

"I just caught a double homicide out in Brooklyn. Woman, mid-thirties. Stabbed. Husband beaten to death, according to the uniform on scene. I'm heading out there now. Can you break away, or are you stuck playing meter maid?"

Behind him, the man and woman were still arguing. Horns blared all around. Someone was tuning an electric guitar. He walked about ten more feet, put a few more cars between him and them, and pressed the phone to his ear. "No way Gaff will let me off the hook early. I've got another week."

"You're an idiot. Should have kept your mouth shut."

"I figured he'd be a little more understanding."

"About his daughter? You can play dumb all you want. We all know better than to screw with the Gaff family."

Up ahead, a tow truck eased onto 49th from 5th and stopped alongside an NYPD cruiser parked at the curb. A heavyset cop was directing other vehicles around it. Looked like they were trying to get to a late model Chevy that had overheated and stalled. When he spotted Cole, he shouted, "Hey, newbie. How 'bout you go grab me a cup of coffee?"

Cole turned away from him and started back in the opposite direction.

His patrol car was still parked in traffic, strobes flashing—he had turned them back on when he got out. He'd wandered further away from the car than he thought. The taxi was still attempting to work around his bumper. He'd managed about three more feet in the past ten minutes. He gave it about another minute before the passenger finally gave up on the ride and got out and walked.

Cole said, "Maybe you should call Gaff. Tell him you need my help on this one."

"And risk him giving it to someone else? No way," Tresler fired back. "Just skip out on traffic. He won't know."

Oh, he'd know. He had eyes everywhere.

"I get busted doing that, and he's liable to give me another month out here."

A loud boom erupted from somewhere near Rockefeller Center. Cole felt the blacktop rattle.

"What the hell was that?" Tresler asked.

"I think *The Today Show* is using pyro. They're prepping for Meghan Trainor."

Tresler laughed. "Oh man, traffic duty, and you have listen to that shit? I really hope she was worth it."

Another boom.

This one seemed closer. Definitely louder.

Cole noticed a thin line of black smoke in the air about three blocks east. He thought he heard a scream. "I…I gotta call you back." He disconnected and dropped his phone back into his pocket.

A third explosion. Not pyro. An explosion.

Very close.

The world went suddenly and completely quiet.

People on the sidewalk stopped moving. Mouths hung open as everyone looked around, trying to pinpoint the sound. Several people crouched down low. Others ducked into storefronts and alcoves in the surrounding buildings.

Cole reached for the radio on his shoulder. "Dispatch, this is 5839. I've got a possible 10-80 near Rockefeller Center, over."

"Copy. Stand by."

The heavyset cop off in the distance had his hand on his radio, too. His eyes were fixed on the growing plume of smoke.

Cole spotted another one rising behind him, about five blocks away.

The first one?

He pressed the transmit button again. "Dispatch, this is 5839. I think we've got multiple 10-80s."

A moment later—*"Copy."*

He turned and started back toward his patrol car at a run.

He was about twenty feet away when the taxi cab caught behind his cruiser exploded in a giant ball of fire. The chassis bounced up off the pavement, hovered in the air for an impossible second, then fell back down to earth, crushing the trunk of his car. Cole watched this for a split second before the pressure wave hit him and threw him backward. He cracked into the fender of a white plumber's van hard enough to send an electric pain up his back and down his right arm, then fell awkwardly to the ground a moment before another taxi exploded less than a hundred feet away.

10

Jordan

Jordan studied the board for a moment, then leaned into her microphone. "I mentioned earlier I had two numbers for you all today. The first was Stan's phone number, which none of us are allowed to call anymore, so don't call it, ever. The second one is this, I want you to write it down. I'll give you a second to find a pen." She paused and clucked her tongue several times. "Ready? It's hashtag 02 22 2022. Write it down somewhere. Write it down, *everywhere.* I really need you to commit it to memory and share it with everyone in your life because it just may be the most important number in the history of all numbers." She looked up at Billy in his booth. "Hey, Billy?"

Billy hated to go on the air with her. He preferred to be the wizard behind the curtain, pushing buttons, pulling levers, creating the magic that kept her little shit-show of a program running for four straight hours. He hated speaking in public, and the idea of an audience the size of hers terrified him. So whenever Jordan put him on the spot and made him speak live on the air, his face turned a pale green unique only to him, and he glared at her with the rage of a thousand suns. He reached to his left and pressed the button that activated his microphone. "Yes, Jordan?"

On her third monitor, text appeared:

BILLY: *Bitch!*

Jordan said, "You went to college, right?"

"Yep. I went to the wonderful Dayton School of Broadcasting in the lovely state of Ohio."

"And you graduated?"

"Eventually, yeah."

"And you currently work in your chosen field?"

His eyes narrowed, not sure where she was going. "I'm beginning to think I should have listened to my mother and become a dentist, but yeah, I work in broadcasting. My field of study."

"On your very first day, did you have student orientation?"

"Yep."

"I'm pretty sure I know how that looked," she said. "A bunch of doughy-eyed former high school students, lost and afraid, most away from home for the very first time. All of you walking up the steps of some big hall or auditorium on campus, herded and prodded toward the doors like unsuspecting calves to the slaughter. Eighteen years old, adults by the legal definition, but really still a bunch of kids looking to the adults for some kind of guidance, right?"

Billy nodded.

Jordan frowned and pointed at her microphone.

Billy rolled his eyes, leaned into his own mic. "Yep. Exactly like that."

"I bet there were tables lining all the walls leading into the auditorium, just like every other first day of college all around the country. You had the sororities and fraternities, all the various student groups, all there to try and recruit new members, that's a given, but who else was there? Who took up most of those tables?"

"The credit card companies," Billy stated flatly. "All of them— Visa, MasterCard, Discover, gas cards, department stores, online retailers…"

"How many did you sign up for?"

Billy chuffed. "All of them."

Jordan tilted her head. "Was that before or after the lecture on debt and predatory lending the school gave you?"

"Huh?" He looked confused.

"You know, where they explained interest and compound rates and annual fees and credit scores and how one impacted the other, and how both of those things will follow you around the for rest of your life like herpes. You know, where they taught you all the basics before you signed on the dotted lines."

"Did your college do that?"

"Nope," Jordan replied.

"Mine neither. I signed up and maxed out almost all of them by the end of the first semester. They told me I could pull money from my student loans to cover them if I needed to, because the interest rate would be better. I remember someone pointing that out. I wasn't able to pull enough, though. Couple weeks later, they were maxed out again. That sucked. Ended up working part-time at a place called the Steak Shack. What a shit-hole that was."

"Did you use your student loans to help pay for housing?"

Billy shrugged. "What I could."

Jordan ruffled a couple of the sheets of paper on her desk. She always liked the way that sounded. "To be clear, nobody at the school taught you the pitfalls of running up credit card debt. I suppose that's not really the school's responsibility, though, even if they did let those lenders on campus, maybe even charged them to set up shop that day. I suppose it's too much to ask for them to protect our children from that sort of thing, warn them in any way. After all, you were there to learn broadcasting, not finance. You were there to learn a particular skill...for a cost...that *they* charged. At the very least, I'm sure they explained how their fees would be applied to your student loan debt and how that would carry forward and build. The interest involved there...that sort of thing, right?"

"Ah, no."

"They didn't tell you that regardless of your future circumstances, whether or not you got a job in your chosen field, or hell, whether you got a job at all, that you would have to pay back not only every cent you borrowed for school, but the interest on that debt, and no matter what happened in your life, even if you fell into the most dire of financial woes, you couldn't get out of it? Not even with bankruptcy?"

"No."

"How much debt did you run up for school?"

Billy thought about this for a second. "Credit cards, student loans, everything?"

"Yeah."

"A little over a hundred and twenty thousand dollars."

"By what age?"

"I graduated at twenty-one."

Jordan paused a beat. "I'm sure the school helped you find a job after graduation to pay all that back?"

Billy laughed at this. "Nope. They got paid. They didn't care what happened to me after that."

"But they accepted you into their program. They charged you all that money. Surely they wouldn't have done that if they didn't think you could get a job in your chosen field and pay everyone back?"

"My loans were all on deferment until graduation day. I got the first bill about two weeks later."

"So they left you standing outside on the doorstep, with a degree in one hand and a stack of bills in the other, and sent you off into the world. Did you have a car? A place to live?"

"I had a mountain of debt and no job. No way I could get those things. I moved back in with Mom."

"Do you think your story is unique?" Jordan asked him.

Billy shook his head. "Same thing happened with everyone I know."

Jordan glanced over at the second monitor, the one listing callers on hold:

Line 1 – Robin ($200k in debt)
Line 2 – Tobin (Can't buy a house or car)

Line 3 – Stan (this one says he dated you in high school – holding on)
Line 4 – Lance (skipped college – didn't want to run up debt)
Line 5 – Amanda (worked at a strip club to avoid taking out loans)

Jordan let the silence hang for a moment longer, then said, "I've got a communications degree from Stanford, cost me a damn fortune in loans, grants, and tips from waiting tables, and you know what? It's fucking useless. I was talking shit long before I went to college, and I talk shit now. The only thing that's changed is the bank has its hand out every month to collect their vig. I tried to pay off the balance a few years back, and they wouldn't let me. I called to complain, and after thirty minutes of auto-attendants I finally got a live person incapable of forming a thought of their own. They could only read scripted replies from their computer. I finally got a supervisor, and she said I couldn't pay more than three months in advance. Each of my payments is like 80 percent interest, 20 percent principal. They're making a small fortune off me. The last thing they want is me to pay everything off. That would be bad business. They returned my check and said I couldn't pay more than two months at a time… I guess three was wrong. It all seemed like bullshit. I gave up trying to get a live person on the phone to explain that one to me. Instead, I just went back to cutting their check month after month. I wrote one out again last night, and I was about to mail it and I had a thought."

"Uh oh," Billy said.

"I decided, screw 'em. I'm done bleeding for them."

"We don't have a choice."

"We have numbers, Billy. And the only way this problem gets solved is with numbers. The government isn't going to solve it for us. *We* need to do it," Jordan said. "As of this year, more than 45 million people own a total of $1.5 trillion in student loan debt. Nearly every household in America has credit card debt, an average of $8,284. A total of $13.51 trillion. Some of that is the result of stupidity, but a good chunk is debt created by students just like you who didn't know any better when the schools and lenders dangled their candy on campus. That takes us back to my original number, *the* most important number in the history of all numbers: hashtag 02 22 2022. It means *freedom*."

Jordan cleared her throat. "We the people, of the United States of America, declare February 22nd, 2022, national student loan and predatory lending forgiveness day. On that date, and for every day that follows, we will no longer make payments on existing student loans, nor will we take out new ones. If you're a lender, feel free to keep the trillions we've already paid you in interest and use it to pay off the balances of the loans. Should you attempt to file collection activity, we, the American People, will boycott your institution. If you're a bank, this means we will close all accounts and other loans with your institution and will never do business with you again. If you are the federal government, and you attempt to file collection activity, we, the American People, will no longer pay taxes."

Billy's eyes had gone wide. "There's no way anyone will let that happen."

"If all of us stop on 02 22 2022, if we all agree to do that, they won't have a choice. They'll either need to let it happen and deal with the fallout, which could be catastrophic for our financial institutions, or they can try to come up with a solution before that date. As far as I'm concerned, the clock is ticking—hashtag 02222022 is national student loan and predatory lending forgiveness day. It must be true; it's on my calendar."

Jordan heard a loud boom.

The first thought that went through her head was *That's impossible—I'm in a soundproof room.* Then she heard another one, closer than the first. Her mug jumped on her desk, and the coffee rippled.

II

Cole

Ringing.

There was nothing in Cole's head but this shrill ring.

When his eyes opened, he caught a glimpse of fire and thick black smoke before they filled with scratchy dust and dry heat and he had to pinch them shut again.

He was on the pavement, with no real recollection of how he'd gotten there. He forced his legs to work. Wobbly and shaky, he got to his feet, nearly fell over again, and braced himself against the van at his back.

The ringing faded, replaced with screams, shouts, and the blares of dozens of horns—some steady, others in the random patterns created by drivers beating on their steering wheels.

He remembered the explosions then, the smoke, distant and right here. Explosions everywhere.

Cole wrapped his arm around his face, breathed into the crook of his elbow so his shirt could filter the air. He forced his eyes open again, just slits, just enough.

People were running.

Running everywhere. In all directions.

He wasn't sure where they were going. There was fire all around. Aside from the taxi that had exploded behind his patrol car, there were two others on this block. He remembered the two he'd seen before that, near Rockefeller Center.

"5839, respond. 5839."

Cole wasn't sure how long they had been calling. The voice from dispatch just faded in, came from nowhere, and became part of all the other chaotic sounds.

He reached for the microphone on his shoulder and pressed the transmit button. "5839, copy."

His own voice sounded a million miles away.

"Do you have visual on the 10-80s?"

He was standing in the middle of the fucking 10-80s. "Yeah, I've got visual."

"We've got three on 49th between 5th and 6th, two more on 47th, one at 6th and 48th. All in the general vicinity of Rockefeller Center. Do you have any others to report?"

Cole tried to add those up, but his brain wasn't cooperating. It felt like someone tied a band of leather around his head and was tightening it. "Dispatch, was that six total?" His finger slipped off the transmit button. He gripped his microphone again. "Six taxies?"

"Affirmative. Do you have any others to report?"

He peered through the smoke and soot hovering in the air. It seemed to be all around him. People were leaving their cars. Just running. He wasn't sure where they were going. Away from here. The air seemed hot.

"5839?"

Cole forced his mind to focus, sucked in a breath even though it made him cough. "I can confirm the three on 49th. I have line of sight. I have visual on smoke for the others, but I'm not close enough to assess damage. My patrol car is totaled—I'm not mobile." He turned back toward 5th, spotted the tow truck, but there was no sign of the heavyset officer from earlier. "I need help here. I think I'm alone."

"Copy. We've got ambulances and support inbound."

Just down the block, at Rockefeller Center, a thousand people were screaming. And when he looked in that direction, he realized many of them were running toward him. With a concert starting less than an hour away at *The Today Show*, the entire square had been packed, and at least two of the explosions came from that direction. People from this block were running in *that* direction, because three taxies had blown up right here. With the other explosions to the east and west, he was boxed in. There was no place to go. They were in complete gridlock before the explosions. *Nothing* would move now.

Cole started toward his own car, toward the taxi that had been behind him, but he could get no closer than twenty feet. It was too hot. There was no way the driver survived. If he'd lived through the initial blast, the fire and smoke had gotten him by now.

He inched closer anyway, his head turned to the side against the heat, eyes narrow slits. Dozens of people were still in their cars, most likely in shock or unsure what to do. Vehicles were three lanes deep. His patrol car was on fire, under the remains of the taxi and could explode at any time—any of these cars could.

Cole began opening random car doors, telling the occupants to take cover in the buildings. Dragging people out when they refused to move. Forcing them to the sidewalks.

He spotted the remains of the other two taxies—one up the block, the other down—they'd fared no better than the first. Both blanketed in flames, occupants and drivers had to be dead,

Reaching for the side door of a minivan, he yanked it open. A golden retriever barked and leaped out at him, scrambled on the pavement, then turned back toward the open door and barked again at the occupants—a woman and her teenage daughter. Both were staring at Cole.

"You both need to get out of here! Until those fires are out, it's not safe!"

Both were wearing a Meghan Trainor tee-shirts. Both continued to stare at him.

The dog barked.

Somehow, that snapped them out of it. The mother shifted into park, started to get out, then reached back to shut down the motor and grab her keys. They scrambled out of the van, and with the dog on their heels, ran toward a crowd of people huddled under a Starbucks awning.

Cole continued through the standing cars. He could hear distant sirens, but there was no way for emergency vehicles to actually get through. Even the sidewalks were blocked by stray cars and trucks; people who had tried to drive away and gotten stuck, then abandoned whatever they were driving to take off on foot. Even a UPS truck, the side door hanging open, flashers ticking on and off.

He'd cleared another dozen cars when he spotted another taxi. This one in the far left lane, four cars up. The driver still behind the wheel. Cole approached from behind and banged on the truck. "You need to get out!"

The driver's head shot up, found Cole in the rearview mirror.

Was he on the phone?

He was.

A cell phone pressed tight against his ear.

Cole quickly rounded the back of the car and made his way to the driver-side door. When he reached for the door handle, the driver tripped the electronic locks.

"What the hell?" Cole cracked the back of his fist against the window. "Get out of the car!"

The man glanced at Cole, shook his head, then went back to his call.

Cole hit the window again. "Hey!"

The driver looked Middle Eastern, probably in his fifties. There were pictures of his family clipped to the sun visor next to his license. He said something else into his phone, paused a beat, then glanced at Cole. His forehead and the front of his shirt were covered in sweat, his eyes wide. He reached to a button under the dash to the left of the steering wheel and pressed it.

The trunk of the cab popped up.

The taxi driver looked at Cole again, then jerked his head back, motioning toward the trunk. The phone didn't leave his ear.

Cole went to the back of the car and looked down inside.

The bomb was packed into the center of the spare tire. A mound of plastic explosives beneath a jumble of electronics and wires, all of them white.

12

Cole

Cole wasn't sure exactly what he was looking at. There were no flashing lights or a running digital countdown like in the movies. No moving parts. No antenna. He didn't know if the electronics were a timer or a receiver, but there was no mistaking the C4 under the tightly-packed mix of electronics.

Cole's breath had caught in his throat, and he reminded himself to take another, then coughed as hot air and smoke filled his lungs.

"He want to talk to you!"

The driver had rolled down his window and was holding his arm straight out with the phone clenched in his fingers, his hand shaking.

Cole reached for the transmit button on his microphone and hesitated.

What the hell was the code for an unexploded bomb?

"This is 5839, I've got a 996A on 49th…near the others. Over."

No response.

"He want to talk to you now!" the driver shouted, shaking the phone.

Cole sent the message again. Still nothing. He didn't want to leave the bomb. As if deserting it might be a trigger. With people running all around, he couldn't risk someone reaching down inside and tampering with it, possibly setting it off.

"Officer!"

Cole gently lowered the trunk lid enough to close it but not far enough to engage the lock. For all he knew, that could trigger the bomb. He rounded the car and took the phone from the driver. "What?"

"That's not a nice way to answer the phone." The voice was male, no real hint of an accent. "Who am I speaking with? What's your name?"

"Cole. Who's this?"

"You mean Officer Cole. Officer Cole what?"

"Hundley. I'm with NYPD homicide."

"Homicide? In a uniform? That's interesting. You are fast, I'll give you that. I only killed those people a few minutes ago."

Cole knew this voice. "Bernie?"

"Ah, you're a Jordan Briggs fan—that's fantastic! What a timesaver! For the sake of our friend Omar, every second is so important, so I'm sure he'll be grateful I don't have to spend precious minutes explaining."

"Explaining what?"

"The game, Detective. It is Detective, right? I can only assume the uniform is some kind of a misnomer. Most likely temporary. You said *with* homicide, not *formerly of* or *recently with*. But what does that mean, exactly? Are you being punished for something, Officer Cole Hundley of NYPD homicide? Busted down to traffic for some indiscretion? I find the inner workings of the NYPD to be an absolute mess. More drama and politics than most daytime soap operas. Maybe when we have a little more time to talk, you can tell me what exactly you did to find yourself on traffic duty for the day."

With all the noise, Cole found it hard to hear. He pressed the phone tighter against his ear and slowly looked around at the windows of the surrounding buildings. "Are you watching me right now? How do you know I'm in uniform?"

"You have far greater things to worry about right now, Officer Hundley. I suggest you focus on the problem at hand. I imagine Omar would prefer you focus. All those people running about so close to you, I'm sure they'd like you to direct all your attention like a laser. Do you think you can do that?"

"Tell me how to deactivate the bomb."

"You don't have the proper tools or the skills. Maybe you should call someone who does? I believe I interrupted you while you were phoning in your findings, didn't I? A 996...A? According to the Internet, that means *unexploded ordinance* or *bomb threat*, correct? Go ahead and make your call." He paused for a second, then sighed. "Oh wait, they can't get to you. Traffic in your little part of the Apple is horrible this morning. Worse than most days. That leaves you as the only person standing between that bomb and our friend, Omar. As a homicide detective currently working traffic, you're obviously a well-diversified employee. Any chance you spent time on the bomb squad, too? If not, things aren't looking good for Omar."

The driver was staring up at him, his face damp with sweat.

Cole reached for the taxi's door handle, then remembered Omar had locked it. He mouthed the words, *Get out of the car. Run!*

Omar shook his head.

Cole jerked up on the door handle, rattled it several times.

Omar's eyes somehow managed to grow wider. He shook his head vigorously.

"I think what the nice man is trying to tell you is that he can't get up. Before you joined the conversation, I took a moment to explain to him exactly *why* he can't get up. Since several of his friends and coworkers met their end while I was explaining his particular predicament to him, he was inclined to believe me. See how he has a foot on the brake pedal?"

Cole looked down at the footwell on the driver-side of the cab. Omar actually had *both* his feet on the brake pedal. "Yeah."

"The bomb in his trunk is attached to his brake lights with a particular type of switch. Once the bomb went active, which I did remotely, it waited for Omar to use his brakes. Pressing the pedal opened a circuit. Should he remove his foot from that pedal, the circuit will close and…well…something bad will happen to Omar and all those in his immediate vicinity, including you. I know what you're thinking, so I'm just going to go there before you do— inside the driver's seat is a pressure switch attached to the vehicle's airbag deployment system. It's designed to determine whether or not someone is in the seat. I went ahead and wired the bomb to that switch, too. I tend to be an overachiever like that. If Omar attempts to leave the car, the bomb will go off. As long as he remains in his seat with his foot on the pedal, things will be just fine. I know enough about Omar to tell you he's an incredibly hard-working individual. He's spent as long as thirty straight hours in that seat before. He's accustomed to spending *a lot* of time there. I don't think you need to worry about him getting up. Although, in his current state, he may not be so vigilant. People react so differently to stress. I guess we'll just need to wait and see. Now here's where things get interesting. See the UPS truck over on the sidewalk? The one so carelessly parked?"

Cole had noticed it already. Two wheels up on the sidewalk. Flashers on. "I see it."

"The driver of that truck is currently inside the SiriusXM building, delivering a package to the forty-third floor. Ms. Jordan Briggs's floor. Inside that package is another bomb, similar in size to the one in Omar's trunk but different in scope and design. That bomb is designed to explode the moment the box is opened. Simple enough. Aside from generous amounts of C4, I also packed the box with hundreds of steel ball bearings. If it goes off, I seriously doubt anyone on the floor will survive." He paused for a moment. Sounded like he dropped something heavy. When he came back, he was slightly out of breath. "You have a choice before you, Officer Cole Hundley. A very simple choice. You can either stay right where you are and hold Omar's hand until his foot eventually slips from that pedal, or you can try to reach the other bomb before someone opens that box. I suppose you could try to call somebody, but I think you'll find it difficult to get a working phone line, at least for a little while. Everyone calling everyone else right now, and all that. Radios are problematic too, but I think you already know that. For the next few minutes, I think you can be sure of only one certainty in life. One of those two bombs will go off shortly. Which one is entirely up to you. I've already explained the rules to Omar. He's such a sport. Welcome to the game, Officer."

Bernie hung up.

Before Cole could say anything, Omar said, "Go! Get help!"

13

Jordan

Billy's face had gone pasty. "Do we stay on the air?"

"Damn right we stay on the air." Jordan huffed.

Both of them were standing at the window in Jordan's office on one of the plastic tarps laid out by the painters. Charlotte had her arms wrapped around her mother's leg, her forehead pressed to the glass. Down below, 49th was a war zone. Jordan couldn't think of any other way to describe it. Between the explosions, the smoldering ruined vehicles, pedestrians running everywhere, it was complete chaos. They couldn't see Rockefeller Center from their building, but she could imagine what was happening there. She'd been clear across the country when the World Trade Center was attacked, just starting her sophomore year at Stanford, but, oh man, how she had wanted to be a reporter. That attack had sealed the deal for her. When she watched the coverage, that was when she knew she belonged in media—on the front line with a microphone, camera—breaking news from the thick of it. Nothing beat that rush. Nothing.

Jules Goldblatt burst into the room all flustered, like he'd vaulted down the stairs from his office on the floor above rather than taken the elevator. "When we get the channels back from Emergency Broadcast, you need to be on the air."

Jordan pulled Charlotte closer and gave Billy a smirk. "Told you."

Goldblatt said, "With the senator."

"What?" Jordan felt like he had just gut-punched her. "No way. I'm gonna take the remote headset and get down to the street. Interview people. I'm not staying up here."

"Legal won't sign off on that," he replied, shaking his head. "Our insurance would never cover it. You're too high profile. You, Stern, hell, even Dr. Laura, you're all staying put. We don't even know if this is over yet."

Jordan ignored him and looked to Billy. "What's my range on the headset? Can you pick me up away from the building? I'll need some kind of handheld to pick up whoever I talk to. We should probably have one or more of the cameras follow me around too."

Billy said, "The headset runs off Bluetooth or the building's Wi-Fi. It might work right at the doors, but I can't guarantee we wouldn't lose you if you stepped out into the street. I've got another model that can go cellular, but I imagine all the towers are jammed up right now. Maybe I could rig a—"

"Your daughter's here," Goldblatt interrupted. He glanced down at Charlotte, then back to her. "You wouldn't want her to worry about her mommy, would you?"

"Oh, that's low, Jules. Even for a shithead like you, that's low."

Charlotte's eyes narrowed. "I expect better from my elders, Mr. Goldblatt."

Goldblatt looked like he was about to say something else to Charlotte, then thought better of it. Face burning, he told Jordan, "We've got a sitting US senator at our disposal with a probable terrorist threat unfolding right outside our door. How is that not entertaining radio?"

"Send him upstairs to one of the news channels. I'm sure they're all clamoring for talking heads right now. That's not my thing, and you know it."

"Today it is." Goldblatt reached for the phone on Jordan's desk and picked up the receiver. "Do I need to call Greenstein and have him tell you to do it? Or maybe the guys in legal again to explain how contracts work? We can waste the next ten minutes doing all that again, but you already know how it will end, so just play nice and do your job."

"You don't want to put him in that room with me."

"That's exactly what I'm going to do." His cell phone buzzed, and he looked down at the screen. "We're back on in three minutes." Before she could reply, he turned to Billy and stuck a finger in his chest. "You said you could control her, control her. You, I *can* replace."

The remaining color drained from Billy's face. He held both his hands up defensively.

Goldblatt stomped out of the room.

Jordan's head swiveled. "You're going to *control* me, Billy?"

"I never said that."

Jordan crouched down next to her daughter. "Who controls your mother, Charlotte?"

"Nobody."

"Why not?"

"Because you're a strong, independent woman who takes no shit."

"That's right." She ruffled her daughter's hair. "How about you stay with me for a little while, kiddo?"

14

Jordan

Guests of *Overdrive with Jordan Briggs* sat on a plush black leather couch on the opposite side of her desk behind something that resembled a chrome spider; this contraption was designed to hold multiple microphones and spare headsets. She liked that particular couch for several reasons—it was comfortable as all get-out, could hold a large group if necessary (she'd had as many as eight on there when Maroon 5 came in last month), and because it was soft and sat lower than her own chair, occupants sunk down and found themselves looking up at her. She'd had entertainers, actors, celebrities, and her share of politicians—some of the most influential and powerful people in the world—craning their necks and looking up at her from that couch. While she wasn't exactly on a power trip—okay, maybe she was on *some* kind of power trip—she learned early on in her career when she created this particular dynamic, she became the adult in the room and her guests were reduced to seven-year-olds in the principal's office. Compliant, submissive, fearful, and respectful, they found themselves talking about things they probably swore to their handlers they'd never speak aloud. They revealed some of their darkest secrets. She got the good stuff, and their agendas were left out in the hallway.

As Billy counted down on his fingers from behind the glass of his booth on the wall opposite her, the senator shifted awkwardly on the couch. The leather let out a soft fart noise, and his face went apple red. Jordan loved it when that happened. Charlotte sat in a chair beside her, a pair of headphones looking far too large on her little head.

Senator Moretti said, "I appreciate you having me on with such short notice. I think we should start by going into my general policy on terrorism and some of the things I'm doing to get weapons off the street. I know what we have here isn't gun-related, but we can segue into that for sure. I've got a bill with Ted Mercer, the *Moretti/Mercer Bill,* we've been trying to get through to the senate—the bill would allow federal law enforcement to conduct searches of homes and vehicles for those under suspicion of terrorist involvement without the need for a warrant. *Perfect* time to talk about it."

"I can't imagine anyone abusing that," Jordan said, making no attempt to mask her sarcasm.

He didn't seem to hear her. "This *is* a tragedy, that's for sure, but we can use it to make some real change. I don't normally get the chance to talk about these things on shows like this. This is great for your ratings and good for my profile. It's a win/win. If you tee up the questions, I'll volley them right back to you." He ticked off the points on his fingers. "General terrorism policy, gun control, Moretti/Mercer bill. Feel free to go out of order. I can handle it if you need to change things up."

"Ah huh." Jordan couldn't look at him. *My God, did anyone actually believe that spray tan looked real?* She turned to her second monitor:

Line 1 – Sheila (Kansas City – watching the news)
Line 2 – Ardis (NYC – Midtown – can see the smoke)
Line 3 – Tara (Chicago – wants to know who attacked)
Line 4 – Deb (Just woke up and heard – wants to make sure you're ok)
Line 5 – Frank (He heard it was gas lines)

She wasn't sure how any of these people were even able to get a working phone line. She hadn't tried to dial out herself, but whenever a terrorist in Iraq sneezed, NY phone lines went down. She had no idea how many lines there were in the city or if current technology even used lines in the traditional sense.

As Charlotte smiled up at her, she tried not to think of the fact that they were currently forty-three stories up in a high-profile New York building with no real viable way out. For that matter, she also tried not to think about the fact that Manhattan was an island, with limited means of egress and 8.7 million other people probably having similar thoughts right now. Trapped was a word she'd rather not think about.

In her headphones, Billy told her they were on the air. She had missed the light on her desk switching to on.

Charlotte straightened her back and looked over at him, heard his voice too. She gave him a thumbs up.

The senator perked up as well. Damn, did he look excited.

Jordan said, "I have got a very special guest today. Someone I admire more than anyone else on this planet. Intelligent. Witty. The kind of person we should all strive to be. Maybe one of the best huggers in the tristate area as well."

The senator's brow scrunched together into a series of jagged lines.

"Say hello, Charlotte."

Charlotte leaned forward, got right up on her microphone. "Hi."

"Scary day, huh?"

"I'm not scared."

"No?"

"Nope."

"Shouldn't you be, though? Several cars blew up right outside our window. There were other explosions a few blocks down. We're under attack. It's okay to be scared. Are you sure you're not? Not even a little?"

"Nope."

"Why not?"

"'Cause I'm a New Yorker, and the bad guys can kiss my ass." When she said this last part, her head bopped in a defiant nod.

She reached over and squeezed Charlotte's hand. "That's my girl."

"Yep."

Jordan leaned into her own microphone. "I can't think of a single thing I'd like to add to that or a reason to say another word on the subject."

From the corner of her eye, she caught Jules Goldblatt up in Billy's booth. She hadn't seen him enter, so he couldn't have been there long. He didn't look very happy.

Fuck him.

A message popped up on her third monitor, but it wasn't from Billy. It was from her receptionist:

SARAH: *Hey, UPS just delivered a box for Charlotte to the front desk.*

Charlotte must have read the message too. She slipped off her headphones and was halfway to the door before Jordan could stop her. She'd deal with that at the next commercial break.

Glancing up at the LCD monitor on the wall, she went on, "We've got a little over 5.2 million of you out there listening right now, and the last thing I want to do is give the halfwits behind these attacks a single iota of our airtime. They haven't earned it, and they certainly don't deserve it. Talking about it only gives them a forum. Those who do are no better, in my eyes. If that's what you're looking for, I suggest you change the channel. I'm sure there's no shortage on the airwaves right now. All the news networks are tripping over each other, dusting off their favorite mouthpieces. Probably salivating over the potential ratings."

She went silent for a moment. She wanted this next bit to sink in. "People lost loved ones today. Hopefully not many were killed, but even one is too many. I'm going to respect those impacted by today's events by not talking about today's events. I'll leave that to the lesser broadcasters out there."

The couch appeared to eat the senator as he sunk down into the cushions, his face a mix of anger and confusion. He turned and glared up at Jules in Billy's booth, not sure what to do.

Jordan smiled at him. "Joining us from Buffalo today, we've got our esteemed Senator, Alonzo Moretti. Why don't you kick things off? Tell us why you're here?"

15

Cole

Jordan Briggs's voice came from every speaker in the building, even those in the elevator. As long as Cole could hear her talking, he knew the bomb hadn't gone off. The package was either still in transit to the 43rd floor or sitting on a desk somewhere. He'd tried his radio several more times but couldn't get through to dispatch. When he tried calling from his cell phone, he got the same *all circuits are busy now* message he'd received the first dozen times.

He still had Omar's cell phone.

Shit.

He'd run off so fast he didn't realize it was still in his hand. He didn't have an evidence bag. Cole dropped the phone in his pocket. That was the least of his problems right now.

The floor numbers ticked up slowly.

21.

22.

Jordan asked the senator something, and he didn't reply. There was nothing but silence, and all Cole could think about was that bomb. Then Jordan said, "You're not very talkative for a politician."

When the senator spoke up, he sounded nervous, unsure. "I'm just..."

"Just what?"

"Stunned."

Could Bernie have known the senator would be there today?

Was the senator his real target?

31.

32.

33.

"Why don't we talk about your healthcare plan."

The senator cleared his throat. "Under the circumstances, I'm not sure that's appropriate."

"Didn't I read somewhere you were proposing some kind of weight-based healthcare? How would that work? People who are overweight would have to pay more?"

Now he sounded very uncomfortable. "Well, that's an over-simplification. It's clear that as people move beyond their ideal weight, the risk for health complications tends to increase. In turn, the costs to treat those individuals increase as well. Studies have found that if we pass those added costs back to the insured as a premium, they're more likely to exercise and maintain an ideal body weight to keep their premiums low. This would put the cost of healthcare into each individual's own hands."

"So it's a fat tax."

"It's a motivator."

"You don't have a problem with fat people?"

"Of course not."

There were several clicks, and then a recording of the senator played. His voice muffled and distant: "Christ, Jonny. Don't yoga pants have a weight limit?"

The recording clicked off.

Jordan said, "Isn't that you?"

The senator didn't reply.

"It sounds a lot like you."

40.

41.

"That was a long time ago. I didn't know the mic was live. It wasn't a serious conversation, just a—"

With a *ding*, the elevator reached the 43rd floor and jolted to a stop. At first, the doors didn't open, the car just seemed to stall there. Cole's thumb hovered over the open button, about to press, when they slid aside.

There was nobody at the reception desk.

Jordan's voice echoed through the halls beneath many others. As he stepped out of the elevator, he saw a number of people huddled at the windows in the outer offices, looking down at the chaos below.

"My God, are you okay?"

A scrawny guy of maybe twenty stood frozen in the hallway, staring at him. His skin was pasty, his left cheek covered in acne. His dark hair was combed back, in need of a cut, and there was some kind of stain on the shoulder of his Metallica tee-shirt.

Cole glanced down at his own uniform and realized his sleeve was torn and he was covered in dark soot. His left palm was cut and crusted with dried blood. None of that mattered. "Where are your UPS deliveries?"

The kid didn't move, not at first. Just stared at him.

"Your...UPS...deliveries!" Cole repeated, enunciating each word.

The skinny kid nodded toward the reception desk. "Sarah signs for them and passes them out. I can try to find her for you."

Cole spotted several boxes sticking out from behind the desk down on the floor. He rushed around and looked at them—six boxes in various sizes, all from UPS. He had no idea what he was looking for. Bernie hadn't given him any kind of description.

"I'm...gonna get Sarah," the kid said.

"I need everyone to evacuate this floor!" Cole replied. But when he looked up, the kid was already gone.

He tried his radio again and got nothing. When he tried to dial dispatch from his cell phone, he got the *all circuits* bullshit again. He grabbed the cord of the phone on the reception desk and pulled it down to the floor with him, fumbled with the receiver, and punched in *9-1-1*. Got nothing. Realized he probably had to dial a *9* to get out, and hit *9-9-1-1*. This time, the line rang twice before going to a recording. *You have reached New York Emergency Services. Due to higher than normal call volume, your estimated wait time is thirteen minutes and*—Cole hung up and dialed the direct line for his lieutenant and got the *all circuits are busy* message again. He had no idea how to reach the bomb squad without going through dispatch.

And he had no idea how to disarm a bomb.

Without moving any of the boxes, he got down as low on the floor as he could and studied the labels. Three were from Amazon, one was from someone named Tawny Mulvey. Those four were all addressed to Jordan Briggs. He couldn't read the other two—one was upside down, the other might have been flipped around backward. Either way, he'd have to move it to get to the label.

"Can I help you?"

Cole looked up to see the receptionist from earlier standing over him, the skinny kid in the Metallica shirt behind her. She was holding another box under her arm.

"Did that just come in with UPS?"

When he reached up for the box, she took a quick step back and jerked away from him, the box jingling.

Cole's eyes pinched shut, and he felt his heart beat against his rib cage.

She glared at him. No doubt recognizing him from earlier.

"I need you to carefully set down that box and help me get everyone off this floor."

For a moment, she looked like she might argue with him. Then something clicked. Whether it was the knowledge of what was happening outside, his current appearance, his uniform, something in his voice—all the above, he didn't know—but her face went white and she carefully lowered the box to the floor. It was addressed to someone named Billy Glueck and came from some company in Jersey called @Home Apparel.

Her nervous eyes met his. When she spoke, her voice cracked. "There's one other box."

They found Charlotte on the floor of her mother's office, the box open in front of her.

16

Cole

Cole stopped at the door and motioned for the others to stay back. The receptionist had one hand on the wall and was peering inside. The kid remained behind her. Several others must have figured something was going on; a small crowd had built up behind them. He'd told all of them to take the stairs and leave the floor, but if anyone had listened, he couldn't tell. More people kept coming. He had no idea how many worked on this floor, and they all seemed to follow instructions about as well as their boss.

Charlotte didn't see him at first. She was frowning, staring down into the box.

"Charlotte?"

When she looked up, she appeared angry, frustrated. "It's broken," she said, before reaching down inside.

Cole dove into the room and slid across the plastic painters tarp strewn over the floor to the little girl—he grabbed both her arms, pulled her away, and somehow managed to roll so when they bounced off the side of a large oak desk, his back and right shoulder took the brunt of it, reigniting the pain felt earlier from crashing into the side of the van down on the street.

Charlotte scrambled away from him, and when her own back

found the far wall, she glared, wide-eyed and frightened at Cole, then the box. Back to him again.

Cole didn't want her to panic. He forced his best disarming smile and held one of his hands out to her. "Charlotte, I need you to get up slowly and leave the room, okay?"

She shook her head.

"Please, honey."

"No. That's mine. I'm not going anywhere without it." She folded both her arms over her chest and glared at him.

Was there something in the water up here?

Omar's cell phone was on the floor in the middle of the room. It must have come out of his pocket when he rolled Charlotte out of the way.

"Okay, then just stay there. Don't move. Promise me?"

Charlotte made no such promise. "You're all messy," she said instead. "I don't think you're a very good policeman."

Cole kept one eye on her as he edged slowly back across the floor to the open box. He could see the label on the open flap. It was addressed to Charlotte Briggs here at the station. The return listed the name Bernie Briggs, also with the station's address. Not much help, but definitely the right box.

The glimmer of thousands of small metal ball bearings caught the sun streaming in from the window. The box was packed full of them. While Cole expected to find an electronic receiver or other detonation device atop plastic explosives similar in design to the bomb in Omar's car, that's not what he found. Instead, half-buried in the ball bearings was a doll. A very old doll with a ceramic head and yellow satin dress. One of the doll's fragile hands was crushed. The doll's head had a crack starting at the hairline all the way to its neck. One eye was missing. Specks of what could only be dried blood riddled the remains of the face and stained the dress. A note in the bottom corner of the box read:

Mama's been a bad girl. —B

Not a bomb at all, but creepy as all get out.

"Can I have my doll now?"

Cole shook his head and remembered to breathe. Slowly reached into the box.

A thunderous *boom* shook the building. Cole's heart slapped against his ribs, and he yanked his hand back, expecting a fireball to erupt from the box and engulf him, the room, and all those around. That didn't happen, though. Instead, the windows rattled, the fluorescent lights in the ceiling flickered. Several people in the hallway screamed. From somewhere else on the floor, others did too. Outside the window, another black cloud lofted up from the street, and Cole knew that blast had been Omar's cab.

Against the wall, Charlotte hunched down, frightened.

Omar's phone, still on the floor between them, began to ring.

Cole felt anger, hatred, and resentment churn in the pit of his stomach. He scooped up the phone and hit the answer button. "You fucking bastard!"

At first, there was no reply and Cole thought he'd been disconnected. Considering the circumstances, it was a miracle the call had even come through in the first place. Then a hesitant voice said, "Who is this?"

"Who the hell is this?" Cole fired back.

"Detective Garrett Tresler with NYPD...Cole? Is that you?"

Cole looked down at the phone in his hand. For a brief second, he thought maybe it was his own cell and not Omar's, but no, this was an android and his was an iPhone. He patted his pants pocket and felt his phone there. "Tresler? Where did you get this number?"

Tresler's voice went muffled. Sounded like he covered the phone to speak to someone else. He came back on the line a moment later. "I'm at that double homicide I mentioned, the one in Brooklyn. I hit redial on the landline to see who these people called last. What number are *you* on?"

"When did you get there?"

"Just a few minutes ago. With everything going on—"

Cole thought back to Bernie's conversation with Jordan on the air. *Where did he say?* "Brooklyn—on Seventh Avenue near Prospect Park?"

"Yeah. How do you know that?"

"Christ, he called from the crime scene."

"Who?"

He told him.

On the air, Jordan was still berating the senator. She'd brought up his stance on disability, the subject of a number of unfavorable stories in the press lately. He started to defend himself when she said, "Rather than spout off more rhetoric, why don't you talk to someone who is actually on disability? We lost him earlier, but looks like he's back on the line. Maybe he'll weigh in. Bernie? Are you there?"

17

Jordan

The senator was fuming. His face mottled. He kept squirming on the couch, looking at the door, looking back at his buddy Jules up in the booth with Billy. The fucker had every bit of it coming. She thought he'd leave the room, just get up and go, but he must have figured out that by doing that he'd open another floodgate. Somehow, the squirming prick managed to hang in there.

Line 1 – Shannon (St. Louis – thinks this was Iran)
Line 2 – Ardis (NYC – Midtown – can see the smoke)
Line 3 – Tara (Chicago – wants to know who attacked)
Line 4 – Bernie (Wants to finish previous conversation)
Line 5 – Frank (He heard it was gas lines)

Jordan hit the button for line four. "Bernie, are you there?"

His voice was clearer this time. He must have changed phones. "Did your daughter get my present?"

"What present, Bernie?"

"A little something from me to you. A blast from the past to ring in the start of today's festivities."

"Festivities?"

"What most of your cohorts are calling a terrorist act."

"Haven't you been paying attention? We're not talking about that, Bernie."

"No? I think we should. After all, you caused it."

"I did, huh?"

"I offered you a choice, and you picked taxies."

"You mean your game?"

"It's *our* game, Jordan. Just the two of us."

BILLY: *He's probably full of shit, but reports coming in say the explosions outside were all taxies – seven of them.*

Jordan looked up at him in the booth and typed: *WTF does he mean about a present for Char?*

BILLY: *Don't know*
JORDAN: *Where is she?*
BILLY: *Not sure. Sarah's desk maybe?*
JORDAN: *How long till next commercial?*
BILLY: *Two minutes*

Jordan leaned into her microphone. "So you're going to take credit for blowing up seven cabs, is that it?"

"Credit deserved, credit due. Seven little cabbies, all gone boom."

"Wow, and you rap, too? You're a talented guy, Bernie."

"Why don't you ask Officer Cole just how talented I am? I bet he's standing right outside your door, trying to figure out how to work that lock of yours."

Jordan glanced up. Through the narrow glass window in her studio door, she saw the cop from earlier. He was covered in soot, peering in. He started to beat on the glass with the back of his fist. She heard nothing but muffled thumps.

BILLY: *Want me to buzz him in?*

Jordan nodded.

Billy reached across his console and pressed a button. An LED light above the door switched from red to green and with a near-silent click. The door swung in on the room.

The cop had a box in his hands, and as he stepped into the studio, Jordan held a finger up to her lips before going back to her microphone. "No cops here, Bernie."

"I think we both know that's a lie. That's unfortunate. I thought we were friends."

"We are, Bernie. Practically besties, you and me."

"Then tell the truth. You're sitting at your desk. Your trusty do-boy, Billy Glueck is up in his booth with your producer, Jules Goldblatt—who doesn't look very happy with you. You've got Senator Moretti on your couch across from your broadcast desk—he looks even angrier than Goldblatt. Then there's Detective Cole Hundley standing in your doorway, holding Charlotte's gift. Please tell him it's extremely rude to take a present from a child. He really should return that to her. She's certainly earned the right to keep it, having to deal with a mother like you."

In the booth across from her, Billy's mouth fell open. He looked up at the robotic cameras mounted in the ceiling of the studio, five in all. Two others were on tripods and shoved back in the far corner. They'd been installed several years ago when The Entertainment Network offered her a boatload of cash to film her daily show for their streaming service. They only filmed Monday through Wednesday, never on Thursday or Friday. She hadn't seen any of their staff today. The red blinky lights were off.

BILLY: *I've got monitors in here for all the live feeds. They're all dark right now. No signal. Maybe he's guessing?*

Jordan said, "How many fingers am I holding up, Bernie?"

He didn't miss a beat. "None, Ms. Briggs. You've got both hands down on your desk."

The cop was still standing there. Staring at her, confused. She realized he couldn't hear what was happening. She pointed at a pair of headphones on the spider mic rack in front of the senator. He reached for them and put them on.

Bernie said, "I'm sorry about Omar, Detective. He seemed like a nice man. I had a point to make, and unfortunately, he caught the sharp end of that particular stick. Attention spans in today's world are so short, everyone running at eleven from the moment they open their eyes in the morning until the second they rest their heads back down on their memory foam pillow. People don't do *subtle* anymore. You've got to smack them in the head with something heavy, or they don't take notice at all. Look out the window on any given day in a city like New York, and everyone has their head down, buried in their phones. They walk down the sidewalk like that. Cross streets like that. Step out into traffic. Oblivious. They barely realize there's a world outside their bubble. Today, we take a step toward changing that. For the first time in a long time, we're all living in the same bubble."

BILLY: *Thirty seconds until hard break*

Jordan said, "Bernie, we're coming up on a preprogrammed commercial break. I can't stop it. We're going to get cut off."

"You don't like the senator much, do you?"

Jordan looked at the man on her couch. "I think I've made it very clear, I think he's a despicable human being."

"Is Officer Cole wearing a sidearm?"

She didn't have to look at him to know he was. "Yeah, why?"

"I want you to take the officer's sidearm and put a bullet in the senator's head."

"I'm not gonna do that, Bernie."

"The correct response is, 'I'm not gonna do that now, Bernie,' because in a few hours, when I ask you to pick up a gun again, you're not going to hesitate. You're—"

The line went dead.

Billy's voice came over all their headphones. "Holy shit, that's break!"

The cop yanked off his headphones and glared up into the booth. "You hung up on him?"

Jordan shook her head. "We have hard breaks at the top and bottom of every hour. The computer cuts all broadcasts for station identification. It's an FCC thing; we can't stop it. In order to keep things fresh on the air, all our phone lines dump to give new people a chance to dial in." She took a moment to catch her breath. "What the fuck was that?"

The senator got up and threw his headphones on the floor. He jabbed at her with a finger. "You're a goddamn bitch!" Before she could reply, he stormed out the door.

Jordan threw her own headphones aside. "Where's Charlotte?"

When she tried to step past him, the cop blocked the door.

"Out of my way!"

"Charlotte's safe. She's in your office. You and I need to talk."

"I need to see my daughter."

Jules Goldblatt stormed in, his face bright red. "You are so done here!"

Jordan turned on him. "My contract clearly gives me final approval on all guests. Not you, not corporate—me. I told you I didn't want to interview him, I made that abundantly clear, and you forced him down my throat. You want to try and get me fired over that? Go ahead. I'll sue the shit out of you. I'll live-stream the whole fucking thing. I'll collect the fifty million this company owes me, and I'll retire to the Bahamas with a margarita in my hand. No more getting up at three in the morning. No more fighting traffic. No more dealing with a pussy-footed shit like you every day. Push me, Jules. See how you come out on the other side. Where do you think the person who lost Jordan Briggs ends up working when the dust clears? I hope you like paper hats, you arrogant prick, because you've seriously overestimated your worth to the world."

This time when she tried to push her way out the studio, the cop didn't stop her. Neither did Jules Goldblatt.

To Billy, who had heard all of this from the hallway, she shouted, "I want those goddamn cameras covered up!"

18

Cole

Cole found her standing at the window in her office, hugging her daughter. Without turning, she said, "Crazies call in to me all the time. This isn't anything new. Stern told me when the World Trade Center came down, he must have received a couple dozen calls from wack-jobs claiming they were behind it. What's scary to me is some of them actually believed it. This guy's no different. Had I known what he was up to, I wouldn't have let him on the air. You give these people airtime, and it's like throwing gasoline on a fire. You've got to suffocate them, choke them out. Like that asshole senator."

"He's not lying."

"How do you know that?"

Cole gave Charlotte a quick glance.

Jordan understood. She squeezed her daughter again, then knelt and got face-to-face with her, brushing a loose strand of hair from her face. "Can you give us a minute?"

"Will you tell him I want my present?"

"Yep."

Charlotte shuffled out the door, eyeing first the box in his hand, then Cole. "You, sir, are not to be trusted," she told him before disappearing around the corner.

When she was gone, Jordan got back to her feet and returned to the window, looking down on the street. "I can deal with the crazies. Most of them are harmless, but when they mention my daughter's name, it spooks me. When one of them sends her something..." She let the word linger for a moment. "It's happened before, and Sarah knows better than to give a package to her before someone's checked it. I don't know what she was thinking. Over the years, I've received everything in the mail from soiled underwear to dead rats. Even when I get something that looks good, like cookies or candy, it always goes right in the trash—no way anyone is going to eat that. Thanks to that Anthrax scare years back, even cards and letters are suspect. I like to think most people have good intentions, but in today's world, you can't bank on that. When I first got pregnant, Nick, my ex-husband, tried to convince me to hide the pregnancy from the public. Swore that would be the only way to keep her safe in this crazy world. I don't see how he thought we could hide something like that—if I walk down the street, the paparazzi circle. Always have. They pounced before we had a chance to test Nick's theory. There were photos of my baby bump online before I told half my friends I was pregnant. Just got worse from there. *Page Six* ran a full-page story when I gave birth—paid some nurse a hundred grand for a photo of me holding Char in the hospital. Couldn't have been taken more than an hour after she was born. Ran it with the headline *"Rosemary's Baby – The Spawn of Jordan Briggs."* A couple years ago, one of her classmates actually found an old copy and brought it to school, the little shit. Taped it to her locker. His parents probably put him up to it. I asked for this life, I've gotten used to it. Nick never did. To his credit, he tried. Charlotte was never given the choice, though. I'm to blame for that...Officer...Detective..." She turned to him. "What do I call you?"

"Cole. Cole's good."

She studied him. Looked him over from top to bottom.

"You're a fucking mess, Cole."

Cole looked down at his torn uniform, stained with soot and dirt. Some blood had dried on his thigh, probably from the scrape in his palm. He could see his reflection in the window glass. He was filthy.

She gave him that same inquisitive smirk from her publicity photo and gestured toward the box in his hand. "What exactly did he send? Let me see."

Cole set the box on her desk and opened the flaps as carefully as he could without gloves. "He told me it was another bomb."

Jordan looked down at the doll on its bed of ball bearings and frowned. "Huh."

"Do you recognize it?"

"Should I?"

"For a second there, you looked like you recognized it."

"Nope. Ugly little thing, though."

"What about the note? Does that mean anything?"

"Mama's been a bad girl?"

He nodded.

"No." Her eyes narrowed as she sat on the corner of the desk. "This is why you believe him? He mailed a creepy doll?"

"There's more."

Cole told her what happened outside, then about the phone call from Tresler. All of it while she was on the air.

Jordan went pale. "Bernie killed two people?"

Cole nodded.

"And set off the bombs?"

He nodded again.

"Holy shit."

She fell silent, and Cole got the impression that didn't happen very often.

The air grew thick with the quiet.

When his cell rang, they both started.

Cole glanced at the caller ID and swiped the answer button. "Hey, Tresler, I—"

"You need to get down here."

"I can't. I've gotta wait for the bomb squad, and—"

"You need to get down here now."

"What about Gaff? He's not gonna let me—"

Tresler cut him off again. "Forget about Gaff. I talked to him.

Radios are jammed up. Phone lines are fucked. I'll get a uniform to keep dialing dispatch until they get a hold of someone with bomb squad. When they have an actual person on the phone, I'll tell them what's going on and give them your contact information. This can't wait. I need you here."

Cole let out a breath and ran his hand through his ruffled hair. "How am I supposed to get there? My car's totaled. Nothing's moving in midtown. I'm stuck here."

"Brooklyn? Near Prospect Park?" Jordan said softly.

Cole nodded.

"I can get you there."

"How?"

19

Cole

At first, Cole thought she was kidding. When she made a quick phone call and set it up, he realized she was not.

The starting salary of an NYPD officer was $41,975. As a detective, Cole brought home $64,750. Peanuts, by New York standards. Most law-enforcement officers for the city couldn't afford to live in the city. Even the boroughs were out of reach.

Financially, Jordan Briggs was clearly doing a little better than him.

While she was on the phone, she covered the receiver and told him he had about fifteen minutes, then pointed toward the bathroom door in the corner of her office. "There's a shower in there, if you want to use it. I think Nick left some clothes in the closet. You're welcome to those too."

Cole had taken her up on that. The bathroom was twice the size of the one in his apartment, and after peeling off his uniform, he took a moment to inventory all the cuts, scrapes, and bruises he'd picked up in the past hour. Even before he got his shirt off, he felt the large bruise on his back where he'd hit the van. An ugly shade of black and purple, it stretched from his shoulder blade down to the small of his back. He found a bottle of ibuprofen in the medicine cabinet and took three before easing under the steaming water.

Ten minutes later, when Cole stepped back out into her office wearing a white button-down shirt, tan chinos, and his own shoes, the scrawny guy in the Metallica tee-shirt was waiting for him. "Mrs. Briggs asked me to take you up. She's back on the air."

"Why can't we hear her?"

Cole had found a duffle in the closet with Nick's clothes. He crammed his uniform inside along with his gun belt and other equipment. His shoulder rig was back at his apartment, so he put his service weapon in the bag, too. He still had his backup weapon, a Kel-Tec .380, in a concealed holster on his ankle.

The guy shrugged. "She turned off the office feed. She does that sometimes. We need to hurry."

Without further explanation, he turned and was out the door.

Cole followed him to a service elevator at the end of the hallway. He produced a key, slipped it into the control panel, and twisted it to the right, then pressed the topmost button.

The doors opened on the roof, where Cole was pelted by a burst of swirling wind, dust, and the roar of a powerful engine.

The guy held the elevator door with one hand and tried to keep his hair from flying around with the other. It wasn't working. "Follow the green painted line on the roof!" he shouted. "Go 'round those air conditioners toward the west end. Keep your head down!"

"Thanks!"

The green line was about four inches wide and looked like it had been painted at least a decade ago, all chipped and faded. That didn't matter much; Cole's destination was difficult to miss.

The helicopter was painted dark blue with yellow accents and HAMPTON AVIATION in large block letters above the tail number. The rotors were turning with a steady *whop, whop, whop.* The pilot was standing beside the helicopter, both the front and rear doors open. As Cole approached, he gestured toward the back. He helped Cole inside, then handed him a pair of headphones before closing the rear door and climbing back into the front and putting on his own headphones.

"Can you hear me okay?"

Cole nodded. "Are you sure you can do this?"

The pilot reached up and flicked several switches. The engines grew louder. "The FAA hasn't restricted air travel, not yet anyway. With 9/11, they ordered everyone out of the sky right after the second plane hit, and it still took about four hours to ground everyone. There's no aircraft involved in this morning's attack, but that doesn't mean they won't ground flights as a precaution. Until they do, we're good. That could happen at any time, so we're going to make this fast. Hang on..."

He tugged up on something that looked like an emergency brake to the side of his seat, and they rose into the air with a soft lurch. The roof of Jordan's building shrunk below them, as did the streets and the mess at ground level. Thick ribbons of black smoke drifted up from the destroyed vehicles, twisting on the air, and as they grew higher, Cole realized the extent of the damage. None of the vehicles were moving. The streets of the city looked like a giant parking lot. The sidewalks were filled with people, and from the air, it was clear they were heading toward the subways. After 9/11, there had been a mass exodus out of Manhattan as residents and those working in the city, unsure of what might happen next, all attempted to leave at once. The subways were overrun in minutes and people clogged the bridges and tunnels on foot. A sophomore at Clemson, Cole had watched this play out in the common at his dorms, he and all his friends glued to the television in stunned silence. It had looked like something out of a movie—people covered in soot, shoulder to shoulder, hurrying down Wall Street carrying their children, food, and hastily packed bags of clothing. He was seeing that all over again, this time from above.

"This is insane," the pilot said. "I feel like I'm back in Afghanistan. You were down there in that?"

Cole only nodded. He couldn't find the words to speak.

"Jesus."

The pilot hovered there for another moment before finally shaking his head and circling to the southeast toward Brooklyn.

20

Jordan

Jordan kept finding herself looking up at the ceiling, at the cameras. Someone had taken black trash bags and secured them over all the studio cameras with masking tape. That was good, that was real good, but it still felt like Bernie was watching her. During the last commercial, Billy had swept the room with some kind of handheld gizmo designed to uncover open circuits and radio signals known to cause background hum during broadcasts. He swore if Bernie had somehow managed to get a hidden camera or listening device into the studio, his little thirty-dollar Radio Shack contraption would find it, but he hadn't turned up anything. While she was thrilled he'd clearly taken notes while watching the last James Bond flick, he hadn't exactly inspired confidence, so she'd instructed one of her interns to try and track down a pro. The intern, a twenty-something with purple hair and a nose ring, rattled off some nonsense about wanting to leave early, another went off about the phone lines, while a third couldn't be bothered long enough to step away from the window. Jordan left the intern bullpen then, remembering exactly why she rarely set foot in that room to begin with.

She flicked Cole's business card and sent it spinning on her desk. He'd told her if Bernie calls back to keep him on the line. He said he'd get someone to try and trace it. She'd taken the card and was halfway back to the studio before she considered the legalities of that. Could they trace a call without a warrant? Had she inadvertently given him permission? She didn't own these particular phone lines. Was she legally allowed to give him permission if she had?

She'd asked Billy these things and he told her the answers in no particular order were: no, no, and no. He was a fantastic engineer and an even better producer, but probably not qualified to dole out legal advice.

Billy went on to tell her that even if they tried to trace the call, it would never work because of IP this and transfer that…she'd tuned him out when the techno-babble started, but she got the gist of it—their phone system was a highly complex mix of Internet-based hardware, old-school analog, and direct calls via their app. This wasn't like in the movies where some techie sets up a desk full of hardware and pulls in the phone number one digit at a time. There were a hundred different ways to spoof a phone number or trick Caller ID. They wouldn't find Bernie that way unless he wanted them to.

Charlotte was back in the greenroom with strict instructions not to leave.

She left Sarah with strict instructions to message her if and when Charlotte did decide to leave, because Charlotte was not one to sit still any more than she was.

Over her headphones, Billy said, "Back on in one minute."

He was alone again in the booth, that was good. She had no idea where Goldblatt had gone off to, but she couldn't be happier he was gone.

"You need to talk about what's happening outside," Billy said.

"I told you, I don't—"

"Look at the monitor."

"I don't wanna look at the monitor."

"Three million, two-twelve. We've lost nearly half our audience in the past hour to other networks. People who *are* talking about what's happening outside."

"We're better than they are."

"No, we're not. We're losing. We're losing right now. That's what we are. Losing. Losing losers. Do you want to be a losing loser, Jordie? You've got three Peabody Awards on a shelf in your office, and you know what they're *not* for? Hard-hitting journalism. They're for entertaining people. You're an entertainer, not a journalist."

"They're not on a shelf in my office. I gave them to Charlotte, and she buried them in our back yard to ward off evil spirits after watching *The Haunting of Hill House* on Netflix. I don't give a shit about awards, you know that."

"Then do it for me."

"I give even less a shit about you," she chided.

"Pick up one of the callers, Jordie. Talk to someone. It will get your head back in the game. When we're off the air later and Greenstein wanders down to chat with you about what you did to his friend the senator, you'll want to be able to point up at that board and tell him it was the right thing to do. And if he doesn't personally see it as the right thing, at least strong numbers will show him it was the right thing."

"How are these people even getting through? I thought phones were down."

"It's sporadic, but if you keep hitting redial you can get a line. I vote for line three."

Jordan looked over at monitor:

Line 1 – Lex (says he can see you right now too)

Line 2 – Cecillia (trying to get on subway)

Line 3 – Nora (says she knows who Bernie is – recognized his voice)

Line 4 – Russel (watching firemen moving a mailbox so they can drive on sidewalk)

Line 5 – Jeremy (it's that damn ISIS)

"No way," Jordan told him. "I'm not going there."

She looked over at the board. Not a single topic worth a shit compared to this.

Crazy sells. Crazy makes for solid radio.

Billy pressed, "We need those two million listeners back. I know you're a ratings whore—if you won't do it for me, do it for the ratings."

"You have no clue how to sweet-talk a girl. No wonder you're still single."

"Line Three, Jordie. Ten seconds…"

"I do this, I'm going all in. You know that, right?"

"I expect nothing less."

Jordan picked up a pen and tapped it on the edge of her desk.

The ON THE AIR indicator lit up in red.

Jordan leaned into her microphone. "Billy?" She stretched his name out, *Biiilllleee?* and looked up at him in his booth. If she had to go there, she certainly wasn't going to go there on her own.

"Yes, Jordie?"

"Will you hold me? I'm scared…"

"You're scared?"

"Yep."

"You. The great and wonderful, Jordan Briggs…is scared?"

"Little bit."

"Why? Bernie?"

"He's a special kind of kooky."

"Which part is freaking you out? Him saying he can see you or him saying he blew up those cars?"

"Exactly," she replied emphatically.

"That's not really an answer. It was more of a one or the other or both thing."

"Right, that's what I meant."

"The guy on line one says he can see you right now. Maybe Bernie's not the only one."

Jordan reached over and pressed the first line. "Okay, Lex. Prove it."

"Red," the voice replied.

Jordan frowned. "Red what?"

"You're wearing red panties."

"So not only can you see me, but you can see my panties…through my jeans?"

"Yep."

Jordan pressed a button on the left side of control board. A loud buzz filled the air.

"That would be negative, Lex."

"I meant blue."

Jordan hung up on him and pressed another button. "Jeremy, unless you know something the rest of us don't, it can't be ISIS. The president told us ISIS is gone, and he'd never lie to us."

"Am I on the air?"

"Yes, Jeremy."

"I'm trying to reach the Jordan Briggs show."

"This is Jordan Briggs, Jeremy."

"Seriously? Holy shit!"

"Language, Jeremy."

"Holy crap!"

"Much better."

"My neighbor got back from his second tour in the Middle East last week, and he said it's a complete shit-hole over there."

"Jeremy…"

"I mean dump. Complete dump. He said they live like animals. No running water or power. The food is terrible. The women are forced to cover up every inch of their bodies even though it's like two hundred degrees all the time, and the men do nothing but sit around and smoke opium and dream up ways to punish the West. They hate everything about us. Can't drink. Women aren't allowed to drive. They tell their kids to hate Americans. They grow up thinking we're all monsters. Meanwhile, we're blowing billions of dollars, and people like my neighbor are over there risking their lives trying to keep the peace."

"So what's your plan, Jeremy? How would you fix it? Put up a McDonald's, pump in some porn, and tell them all to calm the F down?"

"Can't fix it, that's my point. We've been there for two decades, and nothing's changed. We might as well just cut our losses and get out. We're not changing anything. They see us every day and just get angrier. Then they come over here and do this sh...stuff. Better to cut and run. Out of sight and out of mind. Then this kind of thing will stop."

"It wasn't ISIS, though. It was Bernie. He said so."

"He's full of sh—"

Jordan cut him off and pressed the button for line three. "Nora, you know who Bernie is? You told my screener you recognized his voice."

"He works at my bank. At the drive-thru."

"And you recognize his voice?"

"I'm sure of it. Been there for as long as I can remember."

"Where's your bank?"

"Next to the Walmart out on 51."

Jordan rolled her eyes. "I mean, what city?"

"Oh, Pittsburgh. Been going there for nearly ten years. I'm there a couple times each week. He's always working. Got these shifty eyes. Always knew he was a bad one. His name is Ralph—"

Jordan pressed another button, muted the woman for a second. "Sorry, Nora. I had to block the last name. We don't want the wrong people showing up at his house."

"He's not home. He's at work. I just drove by and checked."

Jordan looked up at the clock. "Your bank's open at seven-thirty in the morning?"

"No, they don't open until nine, but he's always there earlier. He stops for a breakfast sandwich and gets in around six."

"You seem to know an awful lot about Ralph's schedule, Nora."

"He drives a red Ford Focus and lives on—"

Jordan muted her again. "See how this works, Nora? No personal information."

"They need to arrest him."

BILLY: *Ex, maybe?*

Jordan nodded. "What did Ralph do to you, Nora? Why are you trying to get him in trouble?"

"He didn't do anything to me."

"Maybe that's the problem? You want him to ask you out, and he won't?"

Nora hung up.

"O…kay," Jordan said. "Cecillia, line 2."

"You called the cops, right? On Bernie? And told them what he said?"

"I didn't have to. The cops were already here. NYPD is just that good."

"Then what are they doing?"

"I don't know, cop stuff."

"Are you worried about him coming down there or something? Are they protecting you?"

"I don't need protection. I've got Billy."

"What's Billy gonna do?"

"Yeah," Billy said. "What's *Billy* gonna do?"

"Human shield, obviously."

"You think so, huh?"

"You worship me, Billy, always have. I'm absolutely certain you would gladly trade your own life in order to save mine."

"If I died for you, do you think they'd put up a statue of me in the lobby?"

"Doubt that. They might put your picture up on the fridge in the break room with a thoughtful note, though."

"That would be nice," Billy replied. "Every time you get a yogurt, you'd have to think of me."

"Ugh. Sounds creepy. I'd probably put one of those mini-fridges in my office and just stay out of there altogether."

Cecillia said, "Some psychopath is gunning for you, and you're making jokes."

"He's just another crazy guy in a long list of crazy guys who have called this show over the years. I bet he lives in his mother's basement. He's probably scribbling out his manifesto right now in red crayon on a little desk between the washer and dryer.

BILLY: *Line 5!*

Jordan looked at her second monitor:

Line 1 – Niesha (cutting through Central Park to avoid traffic)
Line 2 – Cecillia (trying to get on subway)
Line 3 – John (the cops closed down his street)
Line 4 – Russel (watching firemen moving a mailbox so they can drive on sidewalk)
Line 5 – Bernie (will only talk to Jordan)

21

Cole

The helicopter set down in Prospect Park in a small open field next to the basketball courts.

Cole wasn't exactly sure what the protocol was for something like this—should he thank the pilot? Tip him? Tell him to keep the meter running and wait?

The pilot answered that question for him when he got out and opened Cole's door.

"I'm on Ms. Briggs's account, and she told me to stay with you, take you wherever you need to go. I checked with my dispatcher on the way here, and they said the feds haven't stopped air travel yet. He's not sure that they will. He tried to get permission to land here and couldn't get through to anyone." He handed Cole a business card. "That's got my cell number and our business office on it. If I'm asked to move, call one of those numbers, and we'll figure something out."

A group of six men were standing on the basketball court, staring. They looked like they had been playing an early pick-up game.

A woman was pushing a baby stroller.

Several people were out jogging.

Brooklyn.

Cole took the pilot's card, gave him one of his own, grabbed the duffle, and jumped out onto the dewy grass. He could see the flashing lights on Seventh Avenue down near the end of Tenth Street.

Ducking down low, he ran toward them.

NYPD had half the block roped off in yellow tape. Two ambulances, six patrol cars, and three more unmarked all parked haphazardly on Seventh in front of a three-story brownstone. The front door was open, and Cole could see shadows milling about inside.

When he stepped up to the yellow tape, an officer blocked his path. "Sir, I'm sorry, but you're gonna have to stay behind the tape."

Cole reached for his ID in his back pocket and realized he didn't have his ID. Gaff had his ID, no doubt locked in his desk. "I'm Detective Hundley with homicide. Where's Detective Tresler?"

The officer took in Cole's clothes, particularly the tan chinos. He looked more like he was heading off to the country club than a crime scene. "Give me a second."

He turned his back and spoke softly into the radio on his shoulder. Apparently, they worked just fine out here.

A moment later, Tresler appeared at the front door, glanced around, and spotted him. "Cole!"

The officer lifted the yellow tape and let Cole into the yard.

On the steps, Tresler worked a toothpick absentmindedly in the corner of his mouth, a habit he picked up when he quit smoking two months ago. "She got you a fucking helicopter? I thought you were joking."

"It's waiting for me back in the park."

"What's she like in person? Is she hot, or is that all airbrushing?"

"She's attractive—"

"Does she have good breath? Nothing turns me off faster than a woman with bad breath."

"She has—"

"Hurry up, get in here."

Tresler was like that. He loved to talk but had never been very good at the listening part. He led Cole down a narrow hallway. They skirted by a small end table lying on its side. A framed photo on the floor and the remains of a shattered ceramic bowl with some car keys. Evidence tags had been placed near each item, and a CSI tech was on his knees photographing everything.

They had to turn sideways to let another CSI get by them walking in the opposite direction. When they reached the kitchen, Tresler pulled an extra pair of latex gloves from his pocket and handed them to Cole.

As Cole tugged them on, Tresler gestured into the kitchen. "Meet Mr. and Mrs. Bonfigleo."

Both were sitting at a small, square formica-covered table with collapsible metal legs in the center of the room. Both in matching metal chairs padded in torn yellow pleather with orange piping along the edges.

Both dead.

Zip ties around their ankles held their legs in place. Two on each arm—one at the wrist, the other at the elbow—bound them to the chairs. The white tile floor between them was stained with blood. Their clothing, too. Their heads lulled to the side, gags crammed into their mouths.

"Are they wearing pajamas?"

Tresler smirked. "You come upon a scene like this, and it's their choice of attire you notice first? It's morning. A lot of people are still in their jam-jams."

"Yeah, but they're wearing shoes and socks."

Tresler would never admit to not noticing that, but to Cole, it was clear he hadn't. He studied the pair for a moment before he spoke again. "We think this started sometime last night. Someone cooked breakfast—we've got eggs and pancakes on the table, but everything's cold, room temp. CSI tells me the food's been out at least six hours. Coffee's fresh, though. Three cups on the table.

One half gone. We think that's our perp—no prints. Only two place settings for the food. He put that out there for show. Not sure what it means. I think the table is staged too. This is a two-million-dollar brownstone. That rusty-ass table looks like someone pulled it out of somebody's *take me I'm free* pile on trash day. We found a pricy mahogany table in the next room with four chairs neatly stacked on top. There's scuff marks on the floor. Looks like our bad guy moved it out of here, set this up, and had a little tea party."

"Why would someone change out the table?"

Tresler ignored the question. "Ronald there's been stabbed twenty-eight times at first count, maybe more. Tara's got twenty-six. Like the food, the knife work started late last night and went on through the morning. His throat was cut about an hour and a half ago. Same with the missus. The stab wounds aren't deep. He wasn't trying to kill them with those. This was some kind of torture. There's a half-used box of smelling salt on the table there next to the syrup. He wanted them awake."

"Trying to get information?"

"Or he's just a sadistic fuck," Tresler replied. "Upstairs, we've got a struggle in the master bedroom. Nightstand drawer's open on Ronald's side. Looks like he went for a .22 but never got it. Best I can figure, he pulled these two out of bed, got them down here, rearranged the furniture, tied them to the chairs, and did what he did for as long as he needed to do it. Maybe he made them move the table, who knows. Then he cooked them breakfast between jabs. No sign of the knife. Neighbors on either side didn't hear anything, but that doesn't mean much—the walls are solid—two layers of brick. Nobody saw anything. They've got an alarm, but the monitoring company said it wasn't armed last night. Seems they only used it during the day when they were at work."

"What do they do?"

"Ronald worked in the back office at Waste Management. Tara was a law clerk downtown." Tresler nodded toward a phone hanging on the kitchen wall with a cord long enough to reach nearly every room on the first floor. "That's the phone I called you on—I just dialed *69, like I said. And that rang the cabbie?"

Cole nodded. "Yeah. And I bet when you run the lugs, you'll find he called the Jordan Briggs show from that phone too. When he was on the air, he said he was visiting, staying with friends. He was rummaging around in their kitchen while he talked to her. One or both of these two were still alive. You could hear them in the background."

"Bernie, huh?"

"That's what he said."

"I don't suppose he gave a last name? Maybe a current address? Said where he's heading next?"

Cole only half heard him. He was busy studying the room. CSI had placed several risers on the floor so they could walk around without disturbing the blood. Fingerprint powder covered about half the surfaces. Several techs were busy working on the rest.

Cole asked, "Have you found anything that might indicate he worked on the bombs here?"

Tresler shook his head. "No, nothing. I doubt we will. Even if he detonated them by remote, he would have had to get the bombs in place before he got here. The feds think if he's part of this, he's not operating alone. No easy task wiring up seven cabs like that."

"Where are the feds?"

"Busy. They've got me copying them on everything while they piece together what happened in midtown. Probably keeping their distance so they've got someone to blame if this goes sideways."

Cole saw several other detectives he recognized but not the one he was looking for. "Where's Gaff?"

Tresler replaced his toothpick with a fresh one from his pocket. "Wondering why he let me pull you off traffic purgatory?"

"Yeah."

"The answer to that's in there," he said, heading toward what looked like the living room.

22

Cole

The Bonfigleo living room wasn't exactly what Cole would call a warm place. Aside from a photo near the television of the pair taken at the Grand Canyon a long, long time ago, there was nothing that really screamed "home." No photographs of children, young or old. The few pieces of artwork on the walls were bland and uninspired. As if someone had picked them all out on the same day at a department store twenty years ago, hung them, and forgotten about them. The couch, coffee table, and two overstuffed chairs had seen better days but looked comfortable enough. Probably expensive at one point, probably the same year those paintings went up.

Tresler pointed at a small desk against the far wall. A computer and printer on top. Several small cubby holes were stuffed with envelopes. They looked like bills. A digital butterfly fluttered across the computer monitor, some screen saver.

Cole didn't see anything strange. "Okay, I give up. What am I looking at?"

Tresler crossed the room and nudged the mouse.

The butterfly vanished, and the screen filled with an image of Cole's face.

Cole stepped closer. "That's my driver's license photo."

"Yep."

As he took in the surrounding text, he grew even more confused. "That's my driver's license photo in the DMV database. Not a website or something public."

Tresler minimized the window. Another photo of Cole looked back at them.

"Is that?"

"Your file with NYPD."

Another window held Cole's current credit report, down to his latest student loan payment. Another was Cole's personal cell phone account. A call log dating back ninety days.

Cole just stared, not sure what to say.

The keyboard, printer, and desktop were covered in fingerprint dust.

"The techies tell me he printed all this stuff out and took it with him. There's some kind of log."

"How did he get into all these things?"

"You tell me. He used your log-in info."

"What?"

"He used your usernames and passwords. Department-issued for DMV, and your personal accounts on the others."

"I don't even know my passwords for half of these. I couldn't tell you the last time I logged into my cell account."

"Do you use the same username and password for all your accounts?"

Cole shook his head. "No, I use a password app called Secure-Net. I log into the app, and it logs me into whatever system or site I visit with these crazy long encrypted passwords, impossible to remember."

"How hard to remember is your username and password for the app?"

Not very.

"Where would he get that?" Cole asked. "How would he even know I use it? He had no idea who I even was up until an hour and a half ago."

"Yeah?"

"Yeah," Cole repeated flatly.

For the first time, Cole noticed the two uniformed officers following close behind them, standing in the hallway.

Cole's eyes flashed angrily back on Tresler. "You don't think I'm involved in this, do you?"

Tresler reached up and twisted the toothpick in his mouth. "I think when all this works its way up the food chain, a lot of people are going to ask me if you're involved somehow, and I sure as shit better have an answer ready."

"We're partners. You know me."

Tresler shrugged. "That's not gonna matter much when the feds put a bright light in our faces. You tell me why seven cabs blew up around you this morning, and our only suspect seems to be one of your best buds."

Cole didn't answer.

Tresler gestured around the room. "When I get back to the office and dig around, am I going to find a connection between you and these people?"

"Of course not."

"Then what?"

The two officers stepped closer. The one on the right reached for his cuffs.

Cole held a hand up. "Give me a minute!"

"Nothing personal, I'm just following orders," Tresler replied. "Gaff didn't give me much of a choice. Told me to get you here and bring you into the precinct to figure this out. Keep things quiet so the press doesn't get wind."

"Until this morning, I never heard of this guy. There's no way he knew who I was, either. The first time I talked to him was on that cabbie's phone."

'You still have it? Let me see."

Cole fished the Android phone from his pocket and handed it to Tresler.

Tresler tapped through several screens. "This is a cheap burner. How do I know you got it from the cabbie? Maybe you had this phone on you the entire time so you could talk to this Bernie guy and you made up the part about the cabbie when I called you on it, when you realized I was on the line instead of him and you needed a fast cover story. There's no cabbie to corroborate."

"That's crazy!"

"Sounds no less plausible."

Tresler's own cell rang, and he pulled it from his pocket. "It's Gaff."

He picked up and pressed the phone to his ear. "I've got him here."

Gaff spoke on the other side of the call, but Cole couldn't make out the words.

The two officers managed to ease closer, standing between him and the hallway, the only door out of the house.

Tresler's eyes remained fixed on Cole as he listened to their supervisor.

Cole's heart thudded. He'd made a fist, didn't remember doing that.

Tresler frowned and looked down at Omar's phone in his other hand. "What the fuck?"

He raised Omar's phone to get a better look. *"What the actual fuck?"*

Cole stepped closer, feeling both officers narrow the gap by another step.

Tresler said, "Sir, I've got to call you back."

He hung up before Gaff could object.

"What is it?" Cole asked.

Tresler turned the screen of Omar's phone toward him so he could see what was happening. Text and progress bars were racing across the screen. The data was moving fast, but Cole was still able to pick out several of the words, the names, the phone numbers.

"Omar's phone is cloning your phone," Cole realized. "I think it's transmitting the data somewhere."

"Pull the battery," one of the officers suggested. "Quick."

He did.

Didn't matter, though. It finished.

23

Jordan

BILLY: *Jordie, pick up – Line 5!*

Jordan's finger hovered over the button.

Silence on a talk show meant death.

Silence was like a great white circling a swimmer with a tiny cut on the bottom of their foot, death growing closer each time the water went quiet, held back only by words, by an unpredictable movement in the water. Jordan feared silence more than all else, and even just a moment's hesitation brought a prickle to her skin, an anxiety.

She felt the shark edge closer as the seconds ticked, yet she couldn't bring herself to press the button.

BILLY: *Goddammit, Jordie!*

She looked up at him. He was standing in the booth, both his hands up, fingers pointing emphatically at the phone. He leaned back down over his keyboard and typed:

BILLY: *You let him spook you, and he wins.*

Fucking Billy.

She pressed the button. "Part of me thinks I shouldn't talk to you, Bernie."

"Well, that would make me sad."

"You called into a national radio show and confessed to multiple murders, to terrorist acts, live on the air. I'm not sure if that makes you stupid, or crazy, or both, but I do know what it means for me. It means at some point, I'll have to waste a significant portion of my life either testifying or giving a deposition. Probably both. A lot of people will make me justify my reasoning for speaking with you. They're going to say I did it for attention, for ratings."

"Aren't you?"

"No."

"Isn't that why you hesitated to pick up my call just now? Not out of some moral obligation to keep me off the air but because that little brain of yours had to quickly weigh whether the ratings this would bring would be worth the attached trouble on the other side? Nobody will fault you for that."

Jordan looked up at the cameras in the ceiling, still covered with plastic.

"I'm talking to you right now because if you are behind everything that happened this morning, I want to know why you did it."

"So this is you scratching an itch? Satisfying your curiosity? Nothing more?"

"Yep. I want to hear you explain yourself before some lawyer gets your ear and tells you not to."

"I'm not worried about getting caught. I'm not worried about getting arrested. And I'm certainly not concerned with what some future attorney might say. Right now, all that matters to me is you."

"That's sweet, Bernie, but you're not the kind of guy I bring home to Mom."

"You haven't brought any of your guys home to Mom, not for a very long time. I imagine that's one of many awkward talking points on deck for your dinner with Mommy tomorrow night."

How the fuck does he know about that?

"People like you, the ones who are too busy to be bothered with the day-to-day of life, put so much off. You're like a hoarder filling your garage with things you'll do tomorrow. You never consider that there might not be a tomorrow."

"You're sounding suicidal again, Bernie. Maybe crazy wasn't the right word for you, that might have been insensitive of me. Maybe I should have said you're sick, or ill."

"I'm not crazy, or stupid, or sick, or ill."

"Too complicated for a label?"

"Something like that."

"Then just tell me why you did it."

Bernie didn't answer her. Instead, he said, "Are the feds tracing this call, or are they still trying to find your building?"

"They're probably on it. I was told they could do that remotely."

"At least you're honest."

"I'd never lie to you, Bernie."

"We'll see."

"Why seven taxies?"

"You know why."

"Because I said I'd take a taxi over an Uber?"

"You chose."

BILLY: *How would he know what you'd pick? Did he wire both?*

Jordan read Billy's message twice, weighing the implications, before she spoke again. "That's ridiculous. Does that mean there's an Uber out there somewhere with a bomb in the back?"

"Not one."

"Seven?"

Bernie didn't answer.

Jordan let the quiet hang for a moment. "How do I know you won't blow those up too?"

"Do you want me to?"

"Of course not."

"Then I won't. You've already made your decision. I have no reason to detonate them anymore. I've moved on with my life. You should too."

"Just like that?"

"Just like that," Bernie repeated.

"You sound awfully calm for someone who just killed seven people."

"Twelve," Bernie replied flatly. "The seven drivers, three passengers, and two bystanders. Twelve. So far."

"So far?"

"We've got all day, Ms. Briggs. You're in this for the long haul."

To Billy, Jordan typed: *I'm hanging up on this crazy fuck!*
BILLY: *No way! Look at the ratings board!*

Jordan wasn't about to give Billy the satisfaction of looking up at the ratings board. And she was done with this guy. "I'm hanging up, Bernie. I don't want any part of this."

Bernie clucked his tongue. "You hang up, and I might have to rethink my position on those Ubers."

"You do what you gotta do, Bernie. You're not in charge here."

"You really don't want to test me."

Jordan reached for the disconnect button. Her index finger fell on it, rolled over the edges, but she didn't push it, not yet. "Nobody tells me what to do, Bernie. Nobody."

"Not until today."

"You're not in charge here," she repeated

"You can tell yourself that, but that doesn't make it true."

Jordan hung up on him.

On the air, Billy said, "...you didn't."

Jordan smiled up at him. "I absolutely did."

"You just hung up on that guy?"

"You know how I feel about pushy men."

"What if he was telling the truth?"

"Do you think he was?"

"I think I need to change my underwear. So yeah, I kinda believed him."

Jordan glanced at her second monitor:

Line 1 – Niesha (cutting through Central Park to avoid traffic)
Line 2 – Maggie (Works at Bellevue ER, wounded coming in)
Line 3 – John (the cops closed down his street)
Line 4 – Russel (watching firemen moving a mailbox so they can drive on sidewalk)
Line 5 – NO CALLER

Jordan pressed Line 2. "Maggie, you're at Bellevue?"

The line was quiet.

"Maybe she put you on hold?" Billy offered. "Maybe she's changing her underwear too."

"Let's try John on Line 3. He's got cops on his street." She hit Line 3. "John, where exactly are you?"

Silence.

Jordan looked up at Billy. "Are our phone lines down?"

He shrugged. "Maybe. Possibly. Probably. I don't know. It's been that kind of day."

"You're a lot of help. Russel, Line 5. You're on *Overdrive with Jordan Briggs*."

Nothing.

Her second monitor now read:

Line 1 – Niesha (cutting through Central Park to avoid traffic)
Line 2 – NO CALLER
Line 3 – NO CALLER
Line 4 – NO CALLER
Line 5 – NO CALLER

Goddamn phone lines, had to be. She pressed Line 1. "Niesha, talk to me."

As her finger left the button, the screen changed to:

Line 1 – NO CALLER
Line 2 – NO CALLER
Line 3 – NO CALLER
Line 4 – NO CALLER
Line 5 – NO CALLER

"Ugh, phones are definitely down."

Jordan always switched her cell to silent at the start of each show but kept it within reach. Because of her headphones, she didn't hear it vibrate, but she saw it shuffle several inches across her desk with an incoming text message. She turned the phone over and looked at the display:

UNKNOWN CALLER: *1st Avenue and East 28th.*

Jordan looked up at Billy. He wasn't watching her, he was doing something on his board. She typed the address in on her computer, added NYC, and hit search. She got a list of business and local rental properties. Nothing else.

Her second monitor refreshed:

Line 1 – NO CALLER
Line 2 – NO CALLER
Line 3 – Bernie
Line 4 – NO CALLER
Line 5 – NO CALLER

She felt a lump grow in her throat. Billy had seen the call board update and was looking at her again, typing something.

Jordan refreshed her search and got the same results.

Her second monitor updated too:

Line 1 – NO CALLER
Line 2 – Bernie
Line 3 – Bernie
Line 4 – Bernie
Line 5 – NO CALLER

BILLY: *Click this!*

He'd sent a link via chat. When she clicked on it, an NYPD blotter came up. Some kind of real-time dispatch log:

10-80 – 484 1st Ave and E 28. ALL AREA UNITS RESPOND

She didn't need anyone to tell her what a 10-80 was.
On her second monitor, the screen updated again:

Line 1 – Bernie
Line 2 – Bernie
Line 3 – Bernie
Line 4 – Bernie
Line 5 – Bernie

She needed to say something; they were still on the air, but when she opened her mouth, nothing came out.

24

Cole

Tresler threw Omar's phone at the hardwood floor and stomped on it.

"That's evidence," Cole said quietly as more of an afterthought, knowing it was too late to stop him. Tresler often led with impulse and followed up twenty minutes later with logic.

Tresler stomped on the phone again, this time grinding his heel into what was left of the display. "How the fuck is that even possible?" He stomped again. Plastic, glass, and bits of metal crunched under his foot. "Who is this guy?"

"I have no idea."

Cole's cell buzzed in his pocket with an incoming text, and he fished it out.

484 1st Avenue!

Tresler finished his death dance on Omar's phone and was reading Cole's. "What's that?"

"I'm not sure. I don't know the number."

Cole clicked on the phone number and hit dial. A moment later, he got voice mail:

"You've reached Jordan Briggs. Leave a message, and I might call you back."

Cole hung up at the beep.

Tresler's phone began ringing. "Gaff again." His eyes narrowed at Cole. "Stay right there. We need to figure all this shit out."

He pulled the toothpick from his mouth, tossed it out the open door, and turned his back on Cole so he couldn't hear what they were saying.

Cole highlighted the address in the text message, pasted it into his web browser, and clicked search. The first headline read:

"*Nissan Sentra explodes outside Bellevue Hospital.*" (*2 minutes ago*)

There were half a dozen similar stories, all posted within the past few minutes.

Cole felt a tightening in his gut.

Still on the phone, Tresler slowly turned back around and faced him again, his face white. "Does it seem like the same kind of bomb?"

Gaff said something else, then Tresler replied, "No, I think Cole's too stupid to be part of this. This Bernie guy's playing him."

"Thanks," Cole muttered.

Another message came in from Jordan: *I've got him on hold. Should I pick up?*

"Shit!" Cole blurted out. He showed the phone to Tresler.

Tresler took a fresh toothpick from his pocket and slipped it into the corner of his mouth. "Lieutenant? That Briggs woman has our guy on hold. Does Homeland have their trace in place?" As he listened, a grin slowly spread across his face. He nodded over at Cole. "Oh, we'll get this fucker quick. Tell the six o'clock to keep a segment open for his perp walk. Call me back when you got an address."

When he hung up, he shouted over his shoulder, "Somebody get me a radio!"

"We don't need a radio," Cole told him. "There's an app."

Tresler's eyes rolled. "Of course there is."

Cole quickly typed a message back to Jordan: THEY'RE TRACING—TAKE BERNIE'S CALL AND KEEP HIM ON AS LONG AS YOU CAN! Then he loaded the SiriusXM app and clicked on her channel. It took a moment to connect, then her voice came through the speakers. The two of them leaned in closer.

"You didn't have to do that, Bernie."

"I didn't do it, you did. All of this is on you. Are the police tracing my call?"

"Of course they are. What do you think?"

Bernie went silent for a second. "You covered the cameras."

"Yep."

"Make you feel better?"

"Yep."

"Funny how the little things in life make us feel safe. The package I sent you earlier easily could have been another bomb. For all you know, I've been in and out of your offices, your studio, maybe even your home a dozen times. You don't know what I look like. I might be one floor below you right now, with a gun pointing up at your—"

"You're not scaring me, Bernie. You can spout that bullshit all you want, but you won't rattle me. I'm stronger than you. I'm smarter. You're some piece-of-shit coward hiding behind a phone. If you're in the building, come on up. Sit across from me. Let's see how tough you are face-to-face."

"You used a naughty word, Ms. Briggs. The FCC frowns on that sort of thing."

"The FCC has no jurisdiction over satellite radio. I tossed my gloves in the corner the moment you threatened my little girl. A child. That's when you showed your true colors. When someone writes this up, you'll always be the namby-pamby who hid in a hole somewhere and pressed a few buttons because he didn't have the balls to step up and face his problems head on. *Shit* is too good a word for you. Those people you killed had families. Children of their own. When the cops get you, we'll all draw numbers to see who gets to put the needle in your arm."

"The Bonfigleos said to tell you hello."

Cole and Tresler exchanged a look.

Jordan didn't respond.

"Did you hear me?"

"I heard you."

"I'm visiting someone else now."

Again, Jordan said nothing in return.

"Would you like to know where I am?"

"Sure, Bernie. What's the address?"

"I caught the husband out in the garage. Would you believe he was hitting a bottle of hooch before heading off to work? Who drinks that crap this early in the morning? He said it helps to take the edge off the day. I can't imagine hating my job so much that I have to drink each day before going in just to deal with it. He was about to climb behind the wheel. I doubt his little nip was enough to get him drunk, but you gotta wonder about a guy like that. If he starts the day with a drink back at the house, he's probably got another bottle in his desk at the office. Maybe one in the glove box of his car. Probably a little silver flask with his initials engraved on the front, probably takes that one to the bathroom and has a little party in one of the stalls." Bernie let out a soft chuckle. "Well, the good news is he won't be drinking any more today. Won't be driving, either. I left him in his car with a Cuban necktie."

"A Cuban necktie?"

"I slit his throat right below his jawline, where his chin met his neck, and pulled his tongue out through the hole."

"That's lovely, Bernie."

"That was a first for me, and it didn't go exactly the way I'd hoped. I thought I'd clip his jugular with a cut like that, but turns out, once you get down in there, the jugular is off to the side. Not really in the way, unless you're gunning for it. The carotid is closer, but I didn't even nick it. I reached his tongue long before all that, managed to get it out. Messy business, but what's done is done. That left me with a problem, though. He was still alive. I wasn't sure if I should slice open one of those veins and bleed him out or just put a bullet in him. Being all tied up and with his tongue where I left it, he wasn't much help in deciding so I just left him in the car to think things over while I went inside to have a little talk with the missus."

Tresler's phone beeped, and he checked the screen. "We've got an address—he's calling from a hardwired line in North Bergen. Another house phone, like here." He looked back up, frowning. "How the hell did he get from here to Jersey so fast? Manhattan's gridlocked right now. He'd have to cut through."

"I'm not sure how he did it, but I've got a helicopter waiting for me in Prospect Park," Cole reminded him. "We can be there in ten minutes."

Tresler nodded quickly and barked orders at the officer in charge as they raced out the door. He dialed the lieutenant while in a flat-out run toward the park, with Cole behind him.

25

Jordan

Jordan realized she was shaking. Well, shaking wasn't really the correct term—more like quivering. Her entire body. Quivering like a high school sophomore with her boyfriend's hand halfway up her skirt, and that wasn't good. She realized her left hand was gripping the edge of her desk tight enough to turn her fingers white, and she let go. She massaged the feeling back into her fingertips and eyed her coffee. The last thing she needed was more caffeine, but her throat felt like sandpaper and none of her crack-team of interns bothered to put a water bottle out for her.

BILLY: *I'm on with the cops—keep him talking—they've got an address*

"Are you inside the house right now, Bernie?"

"Just went in, yeah." His voice was low, barely above a whisper. "I hope you don't mind, but I'm using one of those Bluetooth headphone thingies. I need both my hands. Honestly, with the blood gumming them, it's hard to hold onto the phone. I'd hate to drop it and lose you. I should have brought gloves."

Jordan leaned closer to her microphone and lowered her own voice. "Just so I'm clear. You just killed a man in his garage, left his body in his car, and now you're inside their home looking for his wife?"

"He's probably still alive. I'm not sure how long, though. I'm not a doctor. But yeah, now I'm inside. I wish you could feel my heart right now. Damn thing's beating so loud I'm surprised you can't hear it."

"Don't hurt anybody else, Bernie. Just…just go outside and sit on the front stoop, wait for the police to get there. You know they're tracing your call. They'll be there soon. Why get yourself into more trouble than you already are?"

"I'm not sure if they have kids. If they do, they must be older. Somebody here collects those Hummel statues. Those creepy little porcelain figurines that look like they stepped out of a Dickens novel. They're all over this place—on the mantel, on bookshelves—the kitchen counter was covered in them. At least fifty. I don't get how someone can cook around those things. Cleanup must be a bitch, all that clutter. Maybe they don't clean up. There might be grease and dust and who knows what between them. Fucking gross. No FCC, right? It's okay to say *fuck*?"

Keep him talking, Jordan told herself. That's all she needed to do. Give the police enough time to get there.

"Tell you what, Bernie. I'll let you say *fuck* on the radio as many times as you want, as long as you do like I said and go wait outside."

"Fuck, fuck, fuck," Bernie muttered in a soft, singsong voice. "That's okay, Jordan. I think I got it out of my system, that was the last of it. The Bonfigleos sure said *fuck* a lot. 'Fuck that, fuck you,' and 'fuck no.' Over and over again, those two. Crap, I said it again, I'll stop now, I promise."

Jordan looked over at the board with her notes for today's show. All of it seemed so silly right now. She reached over, picked up the eraser, and cleared everything, then wrote BERNIE? up at the top. BONFIGLEO/BROOKLYN under that.

"Why the Bonfigleos, Bernie? Why did you kill them?"

"You know why."

Jordan looked up at Billy. Behind the glass, he was back on the phone. Probably talking to the police.

"I don't know anyone by that name."

Bernie said, "She's not downstairs, the missus. I checked the kitchen, living room, bathroom, laundry. There's nobody. I hear running water up above, sounds like maybe a shower. I guess it could be a sink, maybe someone brushing their teeth, but it's been running an awfully long time, if that's the case. Kinda wasteful, if you ask me. Even for a shower, it's on the long-end. People have no respect for resources. Ron and Tara, the Bonfigleos, they had nearly every light on in their house. All of them blazing away, even in the rooms they weren't using. Wasteful. Definitely nobody downstairs. I'm heading up."

On the board, Jordan quickly scribbled RONALD, TARA next to the last name. Then, to Billy, she quickly typed: *How long until they get there?*

BILLY: *Sounds like they're about six minutes out*

Six minutes? Christ, were they walking?

Keep him talking, Jordie.

"Bernie, if you won't tell me why you picked the Bonfigleos, tell me about these people. Why them?"

"They've got creaky steps. Parts of the floor squeak, too. You can fix that, you know. All you have to do is pour some baby powder on top and spread it down into the crevices and around the nails. It's an older house, but the hardwood is nice. Looks like maple. It's in good shape, for the most part." He paused for a second. "We've got a light on in the hall bathroom. The running water is definitely coming from the shower. Found the missus, I think. I've got two closed doors up here. I'm going to see if anyone else is home before I go say hi to her."

"Bernie, if they have kids, you better not touch them."

"Is that where you draw the line, Jordan? It's okay if I kill the adults, but children are off-limits?"

"That's not what I meant. I don't want you to hurt anyone."

"How do you feel about dogs? Are you one of those people who'd rather see a person die than an animal?"

"I don't want you to kill anyone or anything," Jordan repeated. "I want you to go downstairs and wait outside for the police."

"There's no dog. I would have found a dog by now. I did see a litter box in the laundry room, but cats are pretty good at hiding."

"Don't kill anything."

"I need to be quiet for a second. I'm at the first door. Hold on…"

Jordan wanted to reach through the phone and grab this guy by the neck, choke the life out of him. "I can't let you hurt someone live on the air. I'll hang up if you do."

"You hang up, you know what happens. I've got six more Ubers in play. Maybe I'll do two this time."

Jordan quickly said, "The police evacuated all the Ubers. They've been working on that since the bomb went off."

"My Ubers are moving, Jordan. Please don't lie to me. You're not very good at it. You stay with me, or I blow someone else up. Those are the rules. Now, give me a second, I'm opening the first door…"

BILLY: *The police said stay with him – when they get to the house, this will help them determine where he is*

"Please don't hurt—"

"Shh…"

Jordan sucked in a breath and tried to calm her nerves. She was letting him control the conversation. She *never* let a guest control the conversation. Why let him? Her show. Her rules, not his. "You made me play a game. How about if I give you one?"

The words were out before she even realized what she said, her subconscious getting the jump on her.

Bernie said nothing at first, then in a whisper, "What do you have in mind?"

Jordan licked her lips. She really needed some water. "You said there were two closed doors in the hallway. How about you're only allowed to open one. You get to pick, but whatever happens, whatever you find, you're not allowed to touch the other door. Whatever is behind the second door, stays behind the second door."

Again, Bernie fell silent, and Jordan felt the seconds tick away.

Finally, he said, "Oh, I like that. I like that a lot."

It was Jordan's turn to go quiet. She forced herself to calm down. Forced her thumping heart to settle.

Her show, her rules. Slow things down. Buy time.

"You can't hurt a child, though, Bernie. That needs to be one of the rules."

"Nope. Whoever, or whatever, I find dies. That's how we play this. If you won't agree to that, we do it my way and I go in both rooms and clean house. I need a decision. If that shower stops first, they're all dead. Bam, bam, bam."

Where the hell were the police?

Where were the goddamn police!

"Okay." She knew the moment she said it that word would haunt her for the rest of her life. That single word. Billy was watching her through the glass, his mouth hanging open.

She had just killed someone.

Bernie said, "Two closed doors with a bathroom in the middle. Lights on, but that bathroom's empty. The master bedroom is at the opposite end of the hallway. That door is open, and the shower is coming from that direction. Mom's in the shower. Who's behind door number one and door number two? I have a knife and a gun. The gun is a SIG Sauer P238, a small .380. Not very powerful, but it will get the job done. I'm going to open door number one, the closest one to me. It's time for you to make another choice, Ms. Briggs. If I find someone or something inside, should I use the knife or the gun?"

Jordan's stomach tightened. "Bernie, don't ask to me to be part of this."

"You either decide, or the game is off and I go in both rooms."

"I can't..."

"She's gotta be close to the end of that shower, don't you think? Who showers this long?"

BILLY: *Gun will make noise – warn anyone else in the house. Give them a chance to get away*

Jordan looked up at him, and he shrugged.

"Tick tock, Ms. Briggs."

She shook her head. "Gun, I guess."

Bernie huffed. "Gun it is. We'll do this on three, okay? First door in three…two…one…"

The silence that filled the studio was suffocating—Jordan felt it catch in her throat like cotton, and she found herself unable to move. Billy appeared no better, looking out at her from over the control board in his booth, his mouth hanging slightly open.

The gunshot was quick and harsh.

It might as well have struck Jordan in the gut, she jerked back in her chair so hard.

26

Cole

Even before the helicopter touched down in the grass of North Hudson County Park, on the south end of a lake, Cole had the door open. He yanked his phone from the cable attached to the chopper's audio system and dropped the last few feet to the ground at a full run in the direction of 77th Street. The address they'd been given was only a few blocks away.

Behind him, Tresler shouted into his phone, his words choppy as he ran to keep up. "We have shots fired! Repeat, shots fired!"

Cole crossed Riverview Drive and bound over a low stone wall on the opposite side, coming out on 79th. He barely saw the white Honda barreling down at him. He only turned toward it when he heard the screech of brakes. The car skidded to a halt, missed him by only a handful of inches, and Cole shot past, the muscles in his legs and calves burning.

At 77th Street, half a dozen black and white North Bergen PD cruisers flew by followed by an armored SWAT van. They had their lights on but no sirens. All of them stopped in front of a tan three-story single-family home with a brick porch and gray roof. By the time Cole and Tresler ran the last few hundred feet, they had both sides of the block cordoned off with cars, and several officers were busy putting up tape and blockades while others ushered back the neighbors and spectators gathering along the street. The back of the SWAT van opened up, and a team in full tactical gear jumped out while their commander barked orders.

"You two, find high ground, get a bead on the windows. I want one of you in front, the other in back. You three circle around to the back, prepare to breach at all ingress points. You go in first, PD behind you. Understand?"

All five nodded and hustled off. The man looked up at Cole and Tresler as they approached. "Who the hell are you?"

He looked to be in his mid-forties. Short-cropped hair a mix of black and gray. His face hard, with an old scar behind his left eye. He wore a bulletproof vest over his dark uniform. His nameplate said RYLAND.

"I'm Detective Cole Hundley, this is my partner Garrett Tresler. We're with NYPD."

"You're in Jersey, fellas. This isn't your show." Pointing at the local officers, he directed them to line up behind SWAT at the doors, weapons ready.

Cole Tried to catch his breath. "We've been on this guy all morning. He's responsible for the explosions in midtown and a double-homicide in Brooklyn. He's broadcasting from inside that house. He just fired a shot—if these people aren't already dead, they will be in a few seconds—we need to go in now."

The commander seemed confused. "Broadcasting how?"

"He dialed into Jordan Briggs's radio show." Cole set his phone down on the hood of a police cruiser and increased the volume.

Jordan Briggs's familiar voice filled the air. "Oh God, Bernie, please tell me you didn't! He's not answering. Christ, Bernie. Are you there?"

When Bernie finally spoke again, his voice was still low and far too calm. "Sorry, I'm a little jumpy. I had my finger on the trigger. It just went off. I'll have to be more careful."

"What's in the room, Bernie?"

"Looks like a sewing room or some kind of craft room, I think."

"But no people?"

"No people."

"Then you need to leave. That was the deal," Jordan replied, a confidence growing in her voice. "Go wait outside for the police."

"I think the police are already here. There's some kind of hub-bub happening outside. I don't want to get too close to the windows. They probably have sharpshooters out there."

"Just leave the gun in that room, the knife too, and go back down-stairs. Go out the front door slowly, with your hands up, so they can see you. I'm sure they're listening right now—they'll know you're not armed, they won't hurt you—not with all these people listening."

"They'll put a bullet in me the first chance they get, you know that, Jordan. That's how this works. Besides, that wasn't our deal."

"Sure, it was."

"Our deal was for the two doors. I won't touch the second one, that's what I agreed to, but I still need to have a talk with the wife."

"If you don't go outside, they'll storm the house. Then they *will* shoot you. Why give them a reason?"

"How are we doing on time?" Bernie asked.

"Time?"

"You said you have hard breaks programmed in at the top and the bottom of the hour. It's two minutes to eight. Are we going to get cut off?"

Jordan let out a frustrated huff. "Billy, any way to shut those down?"

Billy clicked into the broadcast. "Sorry, Jordie. Like you ex-plained earlier, the computer will cut us off, and all phone calls will dump. I've got no way to override it."

Bernie said, "Well, that's that, then. If we're going to get cut off, it's time I leave you with another choice. Then we'll—"

He went quiet.

Cole, Tresler, and Commander Ryland stared down at the phone.

Jordan said, "Bernie? Are you there? Billy—did he get cut off?"

"He's still on the line, Jordie. We've got forty seconds until hard break."

Bernie returned a second later and spoke so very soft, barely a whisper. "The shower turned off. I can hear her humming in there."

"Don't hurt her, Bernie!"

"I think I'll use the knife. I don't like the gun much."

"Bernie, there must be something I—"

"Here's your choice, Jordan. I need an answer before we get disconnected, so don't dilly-dally. Here we go...Holland Tunnel or the Lincoln Tunnel?"

"I'm not going to—"

"Pick one before we get disconnected, or I blow them both. Five seconds, Jordan."

"You can't ask me—"

"Pick a tunnel. Three...two..."

"Christ, I don't know! Holland or—"

"Holland it is!"

"Wait! That's not what I—"

Music and a prerecorded voice broke in with, "You're listening to Overdrive with Jordan Briggs on SiriusXM..."

Commander Ryland's eyes narrowed. "What the fuck was that?"

Cole pointed up at the house. "You need to breach! He'll kill that woman!" He turned on Tresler. "Holland Tunnel—Call Gaff and tell—"

Tresler already had his phone out and pressed to his ear. "I'm on it! I'm on it!"

Ryland said, "We can't just go in. There's protocol. We need to establish contact and attempt to negotiate."

Cole felt his face flush. "Another twenty seconds, and whoever is in that house is dead! He's got a trail of bodies behind him just this morning—this guy is not surrendering, and he's definitely not going to negotiate. You need to go in!"

Shaking his head, Ryland picked up his radio. "Are my shooters in position? Do either of you have a visual?"

"Affirmative on position. No visual, over."

"Same. No visual. Blinds closed on all windows. Over."

Ryland looked up at Cole again and must have seen something convincing in his face, because he let out a heavy breath and turned back to the house, the radio at his mouth. "Team leaders. We breach on my go. Take out the doors and deploy flash-bangs. Suspect is armed with a gun and a blade. He's on the upper level—most likely closing on a potential victim in the master bedroom. Get inside and ascend as quickly as possible. Possible friendlies inside, so watch your fire. All in position?"

His team quickly sounded off.

At the front door, Cole saw one of the SWAT officers heft up a black battering ram while the others raised their weapons and lined up behind him. On the side of the house, others squatted down under the windows.

Ryland took quick stock of all of them, then pressed the transmit button again. "Go in three...two...one...Go! Go! Go!"

The SWAT officer swung the battering ram in a high, backward arch and brought it forward. It cracked into the wooden door between the knob and the dead bolt. The wood splintered into a gaping hole, and the door swung inward. One man threw a concussion grenade into the opening, and it went off with a deep boom and blast of white smoke. The officer with the battering ram cleared out of the way with a practiced turn, and the others rushed by him through the open doorway. The second one was in the mouth of the door when a heavy explosion shook the house and ground, knocking Cole and the others to the pavement.

A fireball erupted from the interior of the home, burst through all the windows, and shot nearly twenty feet across the front lawn, enveloping those in its path. The second explosion, this one from upstairs, was worse.

27

Jordan

Jordan tried to speak and found that she couldn't. When she opened her mouth, nothing came out. Her eyes found this speck of dust on her desk, and she just stared at it, as if her mind were no longer capable of advanced thought and staring at that speck of dust gave her purpose but took every ounce of brainpower she could muster. The blood rushed through her ears with a deep *whoosh*, pushed by a heart ready to explode, fueled by air she couldn't keep in her lungs. She stared at the dust because it was all she could do to keep herself in the present, keep herself grounded. Keep herself from passing out, because that's what her body really wanted—shut down and wake sometime on the other side of this thing in the comfort of her bed, knowing it all had been a bad dream.

In her headphones, Billy said, "Jordie? I've got the police on the line. They're blocking off both ends of the Holland Tunnel and the Lincoln Tunnel as a precaution. Nothing has exploded. They said they have safeguards in place to prevent that sort of thing—bomb sniffers and counter-intelligence James Bond spy shit. They said there's no way he could get explosives into any of the tunnels without a dozen alarms going off and a ton of NYPD hell raining down on him. They think he was bluffing."

He wasn't bluffing.

He's not a bluffer.

When Jordan exhaled, the dust vanished from her desk, and she forced herself to look up.

Billy said, "None of this is your fault, Jordie. There's nothing you—"

She didn't hear the rest. She pulled off her headphones and dropped them on the desk.

Standing on wobbly legs, she crossed the studio and pushed out into the hallway, where about a million-and-a-half people were standing and staring at her and the studio door. Some scattered at the sight of her, others stood still and watched her like they were viewing a YouTube video and she was the star.

Jules Goldblatt got directly in her path.

Before he could speak, she asked, "Where's Charlotte?"

"Sarah is watching her in the greenroom. Listen Jordie, I—"

Jordan didn't hear the rest of what he said, either. She elbowed her way by him, through the crowd, down the hall, and into the greenroom.

Charlotte looked up at her with large brown eyes. "Can you tell Sarah it's okay for me to eat a Pop-Tart?"

Jordan crossed the room, dropped down to her knees, and threw her arms around her daughter. She squeezed her so tight she heard the girl deflate with an audible gasp.

Her face smothered in Jordan's chest, Charlotte muttered, "Mommy, you're squashing my personal space."

That just made her squeeze harder. She didn't want to let go. Ever. She felt everyone watching her, didn't care.

After nearly a minute, she loosened her grasp and pressed her hands against the sides of Charlotte's face. "I love you more than anything on this planet. You know that, right? I would never let anyone harm you or talk down to you or treat you like anything other than the incredible human being that you are."

Charlotte looked up at her, clearly taken aback, then said, "So...I *can* have the Pop-Tart?"

Jordan fought the urge to cry. "You can have an entire box of Pop-Tarts and wash them down with chocolate milk, if that's what you want."

She hugged her again.

Sarah was watching her with pursed lips. "I turned off the feed in here. The televisions too. Figured it better not to…"

Her voice trailed off, but Jordan understood.

She nodded and mouthed, *Thank you.*

Behind her, Goldblatt cleared his throat. "Jordan?"

"Not now, Jules. I'm having a moment with my daughter, and I'd prefer you don't muck it up."

"Jordan, people from the FBI are here to see you."

Jordan didn't budge, but Charlotte did. She pulled away slightly and looked up over Jordan's shoulder. "You're a G-man?"

"Yes, ma'am."

"You should talk to them, Mommy. They've got a bunch of guns."

Jordan's head spun around, thinking someone had a gun out, but instead she found six people in suits standing in the doorway. Four men, two women.

One of the women stepped forward and offered her hand. "Ms. Briggs? I'm Special-Agent-in-Charge Allison Varney. Is there someplace private we can speak?"

Jordan fought the urge to answer that with *Really?* Because Allison Varney didn't look like an Allison Varney. She was clearly Asian, and a tall one at that, at least five-nine, and she had green eyes. She was wearing a navy FBI windbreaker over a gray pants suit, white blouse, and a gun that looked far too large strapped to her hip. "I've got six minutes before I'll have to get back on the air. I'm not leaving my daughter."

"Okay."

Jordan ruffled Charlotte's hair. "We can go to my office."

"Someplace other than your office."

"Why?"

"We're searching your office."

Jordan felt her face go red. "You're what? Who gave you permission to go through my office?"

The look on Jules Goldblatt's face gave her the answer.

He raised his hands defensively. "Corporate said to cooperate, so we're cooperating. Nobody here has anything to hide, right, Jordie?"

"What about a warrant? Due process? We don't live in a police state."

"We do today," Allison Varney said flatly. "We could stay here. We just need a little privacy." Her head bobbed back toward the door and the dozen or so people standing beyond it.

Jordan rose to her feet. "Jules, get out. The rest of you too. Everyone out."

Goldblatt knew better than to argue. He started toward the door, ushering everyone else out first. One foot in the hallway, he paused. "Jordan there's one other thing. The senator is still here. In light of everything that's happened this morning, his staff felt it would be safer for him to stay here at the studio than attempt to get back to his office. If you see him, I expect you to act cordial. You berated him enough on the air. There's no need to add to the problems you created by acting hostile."

From the table next to the couch, Jordan picked up an empty can of Coke and threw it at him, striking the wall about a foot to the right of his shoulder. "I'm not hostile."

Goldblatt shook his head and left, pulling the door shut behind him.

Agent Varney tilted her head. "Which senator is here?"

"Moretti."

Last year, Moretti had proposed a bill to fold the FBI into Homeland Security, close nearly a dozen offices, and cut more than one thousand jobs. The bill stood no shot at passing, and many thought he'd just floated it to get his name in the papers.

"Totally justified, then." Agent Varney offered a terse nod and smiled down at Charlotte. "I understand why you want to keep your daughter close today, but it may be better if she doesn't hear this."

"I'm not a fragile little snowflake," Charlotte stated. "I can take it."

"I'm sure you are the toughest little girl on the planet, but I need to talk to your mommy alone." She glanced back over her shoulder. "How about if you wait out in the hallway with a couple of my other G-Men?"

Jordan was prepared to argue, but a quick look at the clock told her she only had five minutes. She squeezed Charlotte's arm instead. "It's okay, sweetie. I'll be right out. Stay with Sarah. Don't let the feds touch anything they're not supposed to."

Her daughter hesitated, then found Sarah in the hall. Three of the agents followed her out—the other woman and two of the men. The other two men remained in the greenroom, standing silently at the door. Jordan wasn't sure if they were there to participate in whatever this was or to keep her from running if she decided to bolt for the door. Their silence was unnerving.

Agent Varney nodded at the couch. "Why don't you take a seat."

"No," Jordan replied. "Why are you searching my office?"

"Because I don't like surprises." Agent Varney's eyes narrowed. "What is your connection to this man?"

"There isn't one."

"Sure there is. There's a reason he chose you this morning."

"I've got a large audience."

She shrugged. "Stern's got a larger one. *The Today Show* is right down the street. I can spit and hit Jimmy Kimmel's studio from your office window. Dozens of other broadcasts, with bigger audiences than you, right here. So why you?"

"I have no idea who he is."

"I don't believe you."

"I don't care." Jordan nodded up at the clock on the wall. "I've got four minutes."

Varney's gaze didn't leave Jordan's face. "I'm well aware of the time, and in light of the current circumstances, I'm going to allow you to get back on the air. Before you do, though, I want you to consider something very carefully. Right now, I'm *asking* you why this man has fixated on you. I'm giving you the opportunity to explain whatever it is that ties the two of you together. I'm giving you that courtesy. In four minutes, when you walk out that door to get back on the air, if you haven't given me that answer, and I figure it out on my own—and I *will* figure it out—you will be charged with obstruction. If I'm able to tie you to his crimes as some kind of accomplice, things will get far worse. New York is still a death penalty state, and even though they haven't used the electric chair up at Sing Sing in nearly sixty years, your buddy Bernie has given them plenty of reasons to dust off the cobwebs and inspect the wiring. You're either going to be standing right behind him in an orange jumpsuit holding up a ticket that says 'next,' or you can work with me and come out of this a hero."

"Why exactly would I be helping this guy?"

Agent Varney didn't blink. "Ratings."

"Ratings," Jordan repeated. "I don't need ratings. My audience is huge."

"But it's not the biggest. At least, it wasn't up until this morning. Now *everyone* is listening to you. I stopped up in your corporate office before I came down here. Do you have any idea how many people have signed up to listen to your program in just the past hour?"

Had Jordan taken a moment to check the board in the studio, she would have known, but she hadn't looked. The thought hadn't crossed her mind. Because it was fucking crazy. "You can't possibly be serious with this."

"Only two people are benefiting from what has happened. Bernie has fast-tracked himself on the fame train and you—your show. You've gone from *relatively* known to *the most* listened-to talk show host in the world in a matter of hours. So you tell me: Who else should I be looking at?"

Jordan took a step closer and fought the urge to hit her. "Three minutes."

"Is this related to your husband's financial troubles? Maybe some attempt to bail him out?"

"What?"

Agent Varney shifted her weight from her left foot to her right. "Are you seriously going to tell me that you're unaware of the hole he's put the two of you in? Because it looks a lot like you plan to do that. Lying to a federal officer comes with a boatload of charges all on its own. It wouldn't be unwise to consult a—"

"I have no idea what you're talking about."

"...and there she goes." Varney scratched her forehead in frustration and looked back at the two agents near the door. "Why do they always deny rather than fess up?"

One of the agents shrugged.

"Not that it's any of your business, but *my husband* and I are divorced and have been for a while now. We've always kept separate finances because he liked to spend money on stupid shit, and it frustrated me to see it. When we were married, our incomes went into a trust maintained by our accountant, and an allowance got dropped into our respective checking accounts weekly. I didn't know if he spent his cash on saving whales or Russian whores, and I honestly didn't care. Our money is completely separated now."

"You sound a little bitter."

"He's an ass, and my opinion of you is not much higher. Two minutes."

Agent Varney raised her left hand and snapped her fingers. One of the agents behind her, a pudgy man with bad teeth, produced several folded sheets of paper from his jacket pocket and dropped them into her palm.

Without looking at them, Agent Varney held them out to Jordan. "Are you familiar with the Patriot Act?"

"Of course."

"It's a nifty little tool. If there's a potential link to terrorism, the Act allows those of us in law enforcement speedy access to financial data without a warrant. Prior, it would have taken me days, maybe weeks to access your records. Thanks to George W., I was able to pull up everything I needed on the ride over, and what I found was not pretty. You're broke, Ms. Briggs. Looks like you have been for about two weeks now. Your husband's been playing a little shell game, but it caught up to him. I'll let the good people in financial crimes pick all that apart to determine if a crime has been committed. My only interest is the motive it gives you."

The phone clipped to Agent Varney's belt chirped. She unsnapped it and looked at the screen. She frowned.

"What now?"

"We've got another bomb detonation."

Jordan felt her stomach tighten. "The Holland Tunnel?"

"No...not a tunnel at all." Her voice trailed off as she read the message.

Jordan waited for her to go on. When the agent didn't, she snatched the paperwork from her hand and went to the door. "I need to get back on the air."

28

Cole

Cole was on the ground. He didn't remember going down. He hadn't seen Tresler drop, Commander Ryland, either, but all three of them were on the sidewalk across the street, a patrol car between them and the house, with air above them as hot as a furnace. The largest of the fireballs had shot through the front door and made it halfway to the street before sucking back into the house like the fiery red tongue of some beast.

Cole rolled onto his stomach, got his knees under him, got to his feet, he spotted several men down on the front lawn, two others on fire, and yet another shedding his vest and beating it against the flames of the man closest to him. When they were out, he quickly turned and went to work on the other man who had collapsed into the grass and attempted to roll before passing out.

Commander Ryland hefted himself up and took all this in in a fraction of a second before locating his radio and shouting into the microphone, "All team members, sound off! Clear the structure—we've got booby traps! Report! Everyone, report!"

His wide eyes shifted to Cole and filled with anger. "This is on you, asshole! All of it! If I lost anyone, I mean *anyone*, I will spend the rest of my career ruining yours!"

Cole knew he was right. They broke protocol and moved on his word. He should have known better.

Black smoke belched out the front door and missing windows. The roof was burning.

Ryland turned to one of the PD officers. "Get the fire department out here!"

A SWAT officer appeared in the open doorway and stumbled out. He looked like he was in shock.

Cole bolted across the street to the front stoop. He threw the man's arm over his shoulder and helped him out onto the lawn. "Is there anybody else in there?"

The officer looked at him for a moment, dazed, then shook his head. "There's nothing in there. No furniture, no people; the place is completely empty. Vacant." He turned his head and coughed, then looked back at Cole. "I breached from the back door and made it up the stairs before the bombs went. I don't know if they tripped a wire or if it went by remote, but it was rigged to the front door with a secondary detonation in the attic. I found nothing in the house but a phone on the upstairs landing, hardwired, off the hook. This was attached to it, plugged into the handset."

He held up a small wedge-shaped black box with a white LED ring around the side and Bose written across the front. "Some kind of wireless receiver. Bluetooth, I think. Maybe WiFi. I'm not sure."

"And the house is empty?"

The officer coughed again and nodded. "Nobody. Nothing at all in there," he repeated.

Cole frowned down at the box. "He blew the first floor and the attic but nothing where you found this. He wanted to keep transmitting as long as possible."

"Who?"

Tresler ran up behind him. "What the fuck are you doing? Get away from the house!"

Cole plucked the wireless receiver from the officer's hand and held it up. He looked up and down the street, then at the houses across the street, turning in a slow circle. "He's here. In one of these surrounding homes. He said he was on a Bluetooth headset. This is the receiver. I don't think these things have much of a range, maybe a hundred feet max—he's got to be close."

Cole turned slowly and froze. His finger came up and pointed at the porch of the house next door.

At first, Tresler didn't understand. Then he got it.

Sitting on the porch was an old metal chair, covered in rust. The seat and back were both padded in torn yellow pleather with orange piping. "That's identical to the ones the Bonfigleos were tied to in their kitchen."

"Can't be."

A paramedic darted across the lawn and helped Cole lower the officer to the ground so he could get a better look at him. Cole hadn't even heard the ambulance pull up; his ears were still ringing. A fire truck rounded the block followed by two other ambulances—all of them skidded to a stop as first responders flooded the street.

"You got him?" Cole asked the paramedic.

He nodded, tearing the singed sleeve of the officer's shirt away. As four other paramedics arrived, he pointed at the SWAT officers near the front door. "Check them!"

Cole placed the wireless receiver back into the officer's hand. "Make sure CSI gets this."

A moment later, he and Tresler were on the front porch of the house next door, the ratty yellow chair beside them. They found the front door slightly ajar.

29

Jordan

When the red ON THE AIR indicator lit up on her desk, Jordan waited for the words to come. That was how this typically worked for her. Other than loose topics written on the board, she didn't plan in advance. Early on in her career, she did, but those broadcasts had felt scripted, rehearsed. Like she was reading to her audience rather than talking to them. It wasn't until she changed the format to a more informal conversation that her career really took off. Those who knew her often commented on how strange that all was because she really wasn't much of a conversationalist in person. In college, she'd always been the quiet girl in the corner, watching how effortlessly everyone else spoke. When she dated, she always let the other person lead the conversation. Occasionally, they'd land on a topic that interested her and she finally *would* speak, going off on a rant that usually left them staring at her, wide-eyed and in stunned silence. She supposed those were the first glimpses of what this show would become, but she didn't know that at the time.

When she wanted to talk, when the topic interested her, the words came.

Right now, she had no words.

Her second monitor listed all lines full, none of them Bernie. All of them wanting to talk about Bernie.

The LED counter up on the wall which had told her she had a little over five million listeners when she'd first went on the air, then dipped when she refused to talk about the bombings, now indicated nearly twelve million.

Twelve million people, waiting for her to speak.

The number kept climbing. Each time she looked at it, it was higher.

So she didn't look anymore.

The printouts Special-Agent-in-Charge Allison Varney had given her were spread out on her desk. They didn't make sense. There were statements for Nick's personal checking account, her account, Charlotte's college savings, their various retirement accounts... Together, they had a combined balance of a little over six hundred dollars. The last time she'd sat down with her accountant, she had nearly thirty million in liquid assets. Then there were the cars and houses, their rental properties, Nick's boat at Martha's Vineyard—all paid for at last check, now mortgaged to the hilt. She didn't understand how this could happen without her knowing. There were safeguards in place—particularly now with the divorce—not a single dollar moved without lawyers on both sides receiving a notification.

"Goddamn it, Nick."

BILLY: *Your mic is hot, Jordie*

Jordan looked up at him, caught the shimmer of panic in his eyes. Then the words came, and she let them. "My goddamn ex-husband. You'd think on a day like today he'd take second stage, but nope, he found a way to weasel out in front of the main event and steal the spotlight. *Steal* being the operative word here. He dipped into the honeypot and wiped it clean, didn't even leave a little bit for the ants to eat."

BILLY: *I'm not sure what this is about, but a while back you told me that if you ever said anything that might come back and bite you in the divorce to put up the red flag—this is me waving the red flag*

Jordan ignored him. "I always knew my ex was like a vampire. Count Nick, sucking every ounce of lifeblood from me, then coming back for more over and over again, not willing to stop until there's nothing left of me but this dried out husk, a shell. I saw that coming from the get-go, hoped it was just me being paranoid, told myself a million times I was just being paranoid, but nope...not paranoid at all, more of a soothsayer, an oracle, an augur, a seer, a prophet, a fortune teller with good hair surrounded by a lousy support system of professionals who should have seen it long before me and kept it from happening, but again...nope. Count Nick, if you're out there somewhere sleeping it off in your coffin covered in the dirt of your homeland, if you're listening right now, I want you to know part of me understands why you might do this to me. I may not like it, but I understand it. What I don't get is how you could do it to your daughter. That's a low I didn't think even you were capable of sinking to. I guess I was wrong about that. I was as wrong about that as I was about loving you. I want you to put some thought into how you plan to explain this to our little girl, because that's on you. I'm not going to do it for you. You decided to crawl out of your grave, you need to make things right with her before you get back in that hole, tell her exactly who you are, you fucking piece-of-shit asshole. You don't want your daughter to learn who and what you are from somebody else."

Jordan sighed and looked at the callers on line:

Line 1 – Tina (Did he kill the people in that house?)
Line 2 – Becky (Is it safe to drive in the tunnel?)
Line 3 – Julie (Explosion in Jersey – is that him?)
Line 4 – Bill (Stop doing what he says!)
Line 5 – Jeff (Where are the cops?)

None of them were Bernie. She felt a pang of anxiety. And as long as he wasn't on the line, he was out there doing what he did, and that was far worse. She'd be lying if she didn't admit that part of the pang was disappointment. She hated herself for that. She told herself she didn't want to talk to him, that wasn't it at all, but she did need to know what he was doing. That's what was eating at her.

Her phone vibrated with an incoming text from Nick. It simply said, *WTF?*

She turned her phone over.

Fuck him.

"Enough of that. He's an ex for a reason, and I'm sure all of you don't want to hear about his many shortcomings," Jordan said with a heavy sigh. "We've got a lot of people on the phone with questions. Obviously, *I* have questions. We all have questions. I don't have a whole lot of answers, though. Frankly, I don't know shit. No more than the rest of you. For the record, I have no idea who this Bernie guy is. The cavalry arrived during our last break, a bunch of federal agents all freshly shaved, starched, and pressed, and in true bureaucratic fashion, they threw me under the spotlight rather than make any attempt at catching the baddie. They seem to think I'm connected to this guy in some way. Little Miss Agent-in-Charge even went so far as to say I orchestrated all this to give myself a ratings bump. Like me and Bernie are working on some masterplan, like Boris and Natasha or Bonnie and Clyde. If this bunch of yahoos represents the best the feds have to offer, I think we're all in a lot of trouble this morning. Well, everyone but Bernie. He's got nothing to worry about, with this crack team on the case."

BILLY: *We've got a visitor. Should I lower the drawbridge?*

Jordan looked up at the studio door. Agent Varney was on the other side with her hands cupped on the glass, looking in. Jordan ignored her, shook her head at Billy. Mouthed, *No*. "Becky on Line

2 wants to know if it's safe to drive in the tunnels. I have no idea. I sure as shit wouldn't. If I had a choice, I'd be camped out in my living room with a cup of coffee, a bag of Oreos, and one of the news channels on. I wouldn't step outside, period. Ex-husbands aside, I like my life, I prefer to continue living it, so I don't step out in front of buses or put myself in harm's way when it's blatantly obvious that harm is in the air. Bill on Line 4 wants me to quote 'Stop doing what he says.' Well, Bill, I haven't done what he says. He calls me, I keep him on the line so the aforementioned members of law enforcement have a shot of tracing his call. That's it. That's what's happening. No smoke and mirrors in that. No Simon Says. I could stop taking his calls, but one of two things will happen—he'll either blow a bunch of shit up, or he'll call someone else. Then the cops will have to scramble and try and set up shop at venue number two. All that does is give him more time. And more time in his world probably means more people dead in ours. So, am I doing the right thing, Bill? Hell, I don't know. I'm doing what seems right *right now*. I'm figuring this out as I go."

Jordan glanced at the callers again. "Tina wants to know if he killed the people in that house. Hell, Tina, I don't know. I heard what you heard. It's not like he's slipping me notes on the side. Let's all hope and pray that he didn't and this is all some kind twisted prank. Considering how he started his morning, though, I'm inclined to believe him. Let's hope the cops got there in time and they've got him facedown in the dirt somewhere. I'd prefer to think that's why he's not back on the line with us right now. He's preoccupied, and hopefully not with whatever was next on his checklist."

As Jordan addressed each comment, she watched the callers fall off the line only to be replaced by others. Not him, though, not Bernie.

When her phone vibrated again, she didn't even look at it. Nick could stew in his own shit for now.

30

Cole

Both Cole and Tresler took their guns out.

The lock on the door had been jimmied. The wood was splintered, and the remnants were on the porch at their feet, clearly fresh. He'd used a wide screwdriver or maybe a pry-bar.

Cole glanced back at Commander Ryland. He was surrounded by police officers and first responders barking out orders.

"We should tell him."

Tresler shook his head and spoke softly. "And piss away more time while they sort their shit out? We're in Jersey. We tell him, and they go in instead of us. I don't know about you, but I want this guy, and I'm not about to waste another second discussing it when he's probably upstairs butchering some woman. We'll sort out jurisdiction later. Watch my back…"

He nudged by Cole, crouched down, and using his elbow, pushed the door open into a narrow hallway with stairs on the left and a family room on the right. Light crept in from around thick wooden blinds, allowing splinters of twilight to line the floors, walls, and furniture. A metal TV tray was set up in front of the couch, a pizza box on top. A couple of children's toys were scattered around on the floor—foam puzzles, the kind of thing a toddler would play with.

Cole felt a fist tighten around his heart.

Please don't let us find a baby upstairs.

As a rookie, he'd seen two dead babies. In more recent years, as a homicide detective, he'd seen four more. One forgotten in his crib by his meth-head mother for nearly a week. Three others who had died from SIDS, two more where the parents tried to make it appear that way. With one, the father had fallen asleep with the baby, only three months old, and rolled over on top of her. With the other, the mother couldn't take the crying and suffocated her newborn girl with a pillow, then claimed her nanny did it. With all of them, the tiny faces remained etched in Cole's mind. Little defenseless fingers. Wide, glassy eyes. He could handle dead adults, but the children haunted him.

Tresler eased over the threshold into the room, and Cole grabbed his shoulder. "The other house was booby-trapped. Move slow."

Tresler nodded without looking back.

A thump from above. Something moved upstairs, shifted on the floorboards.

They both looked up, then started up the stairs, careful to put their feet on the left and right edges of the steps rather than in the center in an effort to avoid the ones Bernie had said squeaked. At the top landing, they found exactly what he had described on the air—a hallway running the length of the second floor with doors on either side of a bathroom on the left end, what looked like a master bedroom down the opposite end of the hallway on the right. The hall bathroom light was on but the room was empty. One of the two doors next to it stood open—some kind of sewing or craft room—the other door was still closed. A light burned from deep in the master bedroom to their right. No running shower. No running water. No other sounds.

Tresler pointed toward the master bedroom with the barrel of his gun and started in that direction.

Cole nodded and followed.

A table lamp burned on the nightstand on the far side of a king-size bed, unmade. The sheets were rumpled around a white duvet at the foot, women's clothing was scattered on top—jeans, a sweater, bra, and underwear. Light poured out of a doorway in the corner, and steam lingered in the air.

Cole silently crouched down and swept under the bed with his gun while Tresler went to an open closet door. They found nobody in the room.

Edging around the bed to the bathroom, Tresler followed the lines of the room, his back pressed against the wall between the nightstand and open door while Cole approached head-on. With the fingers of his free hand, Tresler silently counted down from three, then dropped low in the doorway and shouted, "Police!" as Cole ran forward into the room and swept the space from left to right.

Cole knew as soon as he saw the blood they were too late.

Bernie was gone.

Her naked body was draped over the side of a white bathtub, facedown, bent at the waist. In the tub, her legs were curled awkwardly under her. Her right hand was still wrapped around the shower curtain, partially torn down from the bar above. Her upper torso slumped out, and her wet hair still dripped into a pool of blood. There were three visible stab wounds—two in her back, another in her neck just under her cheek. That one had bled the most but was bleeding no longer, and Cole didn't have to check for a pulse to know she was dead.

In the steam on the mirror, Bernie had written:

naked as a babe

Cole had one singular thought then: *The kid.*

31

Cole

Cole wasted no time.

He shoved his way out past Tresler, through the bedroom, and back into the hallway. Sweeping the open spaces as he went, he glanced into the sewing room and the empty bathroom, then braced himself outside the only other closed door for what he might find on the other side.

When he reached for the doorknob, Tresler stopped him. "If he rigged something in this house to blow, it will be that door."

Cole knew he was right.

Taking out his phone, he turned on the flashlight and inspected the knob as best he could, then ran the light over the doorjamb, starting on the bottom right corner and working all the way around in a large circle.

If the door was rigged, nothing was visible from this side. He couldn't see anything through the crack at the bottom. He told Tresler, "Get back downstairs. I'll do it."

"I'm not going anywhere."

Cole understood. He wouldn't have gone, either.

Still on his knees, he flexed his fingers and reached for the doorknob, took hold of it slowly, and began to twist—half-circle, three quarters—through the thin gap, he watched the latch-bolt slid out from the strike plate in the frame. The knob stopped. End of the line.

He gave Tresler a quick look. His partner had moved as far to the side as he could, his gun up, his finger on the trigger.

Every instinct in Cole's body told him not to open the door, but he did anyway. With a gentle push, the door swung into the room on old, squeaky hinges.

He drew in a sharp breath and swept the room with his flashlight.

Behind him, Tresler muttered, "Motherfucker," turned, and bent over with his hands on his knees. "I thought for sure…"

Cole had too, and it took a moment for the relief to wash over him.

No child.

Not even a child's bedroom.

The second room, thick with dust and cobwebs, was stacked floor to ceiling with clear plastic bins loaded up with holiday decorations and clothing. Just a storage room.

Cole was still staring at all of it when the first level of the house erupted with the sound of storming boots and multiple shouts of "Police!"

Ten minutes later, they were back out front.

After a thorough search, they found no sign of Bernie—only the dead woman in the shower and her husband, dead behind the wheel of his car in the garage, throat slit.

Cole and Tresler stood around the hood of a North Bergen PD cruiser, SWAT Commander Emmett Ryland across from them, his face burning red, and Tresler's phone between them all, Lieutenant Gaff's voice pouring out. *"What good will arresting my two officers do?"*

"Your two officers caused the death of one of my men, put three others in the hospital, then illegally searched a residence with absolutely none of it taking place in your jurisdiction."

Gaff replied, "All of it in pursuit of a suspect who started here, *in our jurisdiction.* Homeland gave that address to us, same as you.

We're all after the same thing. When it comes time for you to re-hash this in front of a review board, would you rather tell them we were all working together or tell them how you slowed things down by taking key players out of the hunt? Detective Hundley there is the only member of law enforcement to actually speak to this guy. He was out in the middle of those initial explosions. There are shots of him running on the news and the web. He's the face of this thing. He saved lives—how's it going to look if you put him in a cell? How's it going to look *for you*? Those two are the only officers with firsthand knowledge of all the crime scenes. I'll be perfectly blunt—you work with them, or my next call is over your head. My next after that will be with your replacement."

This only made Ryland angrier. "You don't have the authority—"

"The hell I don't. You really think the feds will—"

"We need to focus on the kid," Cole said softly, interrupting them both.

Ryland glared up at him. "I told you. There is no kid. The house is registered to Ted and Patty Epps, 43 and 39. Both accounted for. Killed by this sadistic fuck. No children. No grandchildren. They lived alone." He pointed up at the first house. The fire was out, but the roof was still smoldering. "That place has been vacant for the better part of two years. The owner lives in Florida and kept the utilities on so the place didn't go to complete shit. Other than the phone, there's no sign of anyone going in or out. Neighbors never saw anyone."

Cole looked up at him. "He drew us here on purpose. He drew us specifically to that house so he could kill cops. He was right next door, killing those two people, while we were here. He probably watched all of it."

Tresler said, "So this is what? Some kind of vendetta thing? He's got a problem with cops?"

Cole turned back to the second house. "Partly...maybe? I don't know. I need to see the inside again."

On the phone, Gaff said, "Ryland—you're gonna let him. I hear you didn't, you know what I'm doing next. The feds are on my other line. I gotta go." He hung up then, leaving the three of them standing around the car.

A second later, Cole's phone dinged with an incoming text from Gaff: *Don't for a second think you're off the hook for what you did to Gracie, you little shit. Your balls are still in a jar. You're back to traffic when this is over. Make it* over.

Cole just shook his head and dropped the phone back in his pocket. Before Ryland could weigh in, he turned and made his way back to the house, around the crime-scene tape, and through the door. CSI was already on scene and making their way through the house; he found two of them in the living room just inside the door. "Can you give me a minute?"

They nodded and left as Tresler came in. He took a toothpick from his pocket and slipped it into his mouth. "Make this quick. He might still pull us out of here."

"He won't." From a box sitting on a bookcase at the front of the room, Cole took out a pair of latex gloves and tugged them on. He tossed a second pair to Tresler, then went over to the metal TV tray in front of the couch. "When was the last time you saw one of these?"

"I dunno. Maybe when I was a kid."

"It's all rusty. Like the table we found at the Bonfigleo house."

"Like the chair out front here."

"Yeah."

Cole knelt down and got a better look at the puzzles on the floor. Three sets in different colors—red, blue, and yellow. They were foam, about a quarter-inch thick, with simple shapes cut out. A square, diamond, triangle, circle. Meant for a young child. "None of this belongs here. It's out of place."

"The neighbors could be wrong. Maybe they had someone visiting with a kid."

"No bags in the house. No suitcases."

Cole could see into the kitchen from the living room. Someone had brewed coffee, or maybe the machine was on a timer. Other than that, nothing appeared out of the ordinary. "No cereal. No other toys. Kids are messy. There's no gate on the steps. No child-proofing on the kitchen cabinets or doors. No way a kid lived here, and other than this, there's no sign one visited."

Tresler reached over and ran his finger over the top of the metal TV tray. It left a trail in the dust. Doing the same on the coffee table, his finger came away clean. "Okay. He left all this here. He put it here for us to find. Like the chair out front, like the furniture at the Bonfigleos'. Why? This is yard-sale crap. What's the point?"

Cole had no idea.

None of this made sense.

He tapped his finger on one of foam puzzle pieces, a red triangle. "When I talked to him on that cabbie's phone, he said 'Welcome to the game.' That's what this is to him. He called that radio show and told her it was a game too. Gave her a choice. Made a game out of blowing up those cars. Then we got these murders. They've got to be connected." Cole looked up. He'd almost forgotten with everything going on. "He sent a doll to Briggs's daughter. Made me think it was another bomb. A ratty old doll, like this stuff. Those two are talking on the air, but that doll, all these things, maybe even the murders…that's them having a second, unspoken conversation. He's telling her something."

Tresler was nodding, the toothpick bobbing in the corner of his mouth. "She's holding something back. She knows him. She must. I bet there's a connection between her and all these people."

Cole got back on his feet. "I'm not waiting for him to blow something else up. We need to get in front of this thing. I gotta get back to Manhattan and talk to that woman."

For a moment, Tresler looked like he might object. Then he nodded. "I'll stay on this. No way Ryland will share with us if I don't. I'll learn what I can, then figure out how to meet back up with you in the city." A second later, Tresler's phone dinged with an incoming text message. His face went stiff, and he looked up at Cole. "It's from the lieutenant. Something's happening at the Holland Tunnel."

32

Jordan

Jordan read the message from Billy for a second time, then looked up at him in his booth at the back of her studio. He was standing, hunched over his control board, and pressing this or flipping that. He glanced at her and gave a frantic shrug before looking back down.

Her list of incoming callers read full, but none were Bernie.

She read his message on her monitor a third time. *Will that even work?* They'd never tried before.

She let out a breath and leaned into her microphone. "Folks, something's going on at the Holland Tunnel, and my puppet masters want me to play a live feed from one of our sister news channels. I'll stay on with you, so if my crack team of engineers get this right, you should be able to hear me too. If you're currently tuned into my show on the web or with the app, you should see the live video feed so you can see what's going on along with the audio."

BILLY: *You'll get the video on Monitor 1. Cutting in in 3 -*

Jordan's first monitor flickered, then switched to a shaky video. It looked like a camera was attempting to zoom in over a large distance, so the slightest movement resulted in sweeping jumps. They panned over a number of stopped cars, fizzled out of focus, then came back into focus on the far corner of a yellow van with some carpet company logo on the side. A male voice said, "...we'll just stay on him and hopefully pick him up when he comes around on the other end of that vehicle. Can you zoom back out a little bit?" The camera did, then steadied. "Okay, so he's about a hundred feet from the mouth of the tunnel, working his way through all the cars. This gridlock goes back over a mile down into Jersey. When the authorities blocked off the tunnel, everything here went to a complete standstill. With the bombing this morning, now this, nobody is moving in Manhattan unless they're on a bicycle. Or walking. Subways are a mess. The system is completely overwhelmed. Looks like most of these vehicles have been abandoned. On the chance the threat is real, NYPD forced everyone out of the area from the mouth of the tunnel back to the bend at Newport Centre. I only see a few stragglers now, and the police are making quick work of them too, attempting to keep the area clear. We're trying to find out where this guy came from, but at this point we've got nothing but speculation. The running theory is he was in one of the cars approaching the tunnel when the police shut everything down. Then he got out and proceeded on foot. I imagine someone will piece his path together from CCTV footage. That area is covered with cameras. Just looking out at this, a road I personally travel twice a day, makes me wonder how they plan to clear all these cars without drivers when this is over. I may be here in the studio for a while. Even if they ask people to return to their cars, nobody can move unless the cars around them move. I suppose they can tow some. Can't really move them off to the side. There's no room. No matter what, this is going to take a long time to unravel. Oh, there he is. He's coming around the front of the van."

Jordan watched as the camera zoomed back in slightly, shifted, and focused on a man in a long tan coat walking between all the cars at a slow shuffle. He held both arms out, away from his body.

There was something in his right hand. They must have been filming from a long distance. Even when they attempted to focus, his features were soft, blurry.

The newscaster continued. "I know it's tough to make things out from this distance, but we've been told he's holding something the police called a 'deadman's switch' in his right hand. It's wired up through the sleeve of his coat and back to the vest. If he releases his grip, the circuit is expected to close, triggering the bomb. Because of his coat, we haven't gotten a good shot of the vest itself. I'm sitting here trying to expand and zoom in on some still images provided to me, but like the video, we're too far away to make things out clearly. Only the front of the vest is visible. There's a mobile phone there, possibly for remote detonation. The explosives themselves look like small bricks, so experts are speculating they're C4 or something similar. But between each brick, he's got these thin canisters, and nobody seems to know what those are. They could be a liquid propellant or possibly gas of some kind. He's continuing to move toward the tunnel. The police have made no attempt to hide their sharpshooters. We're not going to show them, we don't want to compromise their positions, but they're moving through the cars with this man, staying back about a hundred feet or so. He made it very clear that if they got too close or attempted to stop his progress, he would detonate. Several of the police shooters have circled around and gotten ahead of him. They've positioned between him and the tunnel. I'm going to speculate here, but I don't think they'll allow this man to enter the Holland Tunnel. That's clearly his intent—to enter the tunnel and possibly detonate inside. The infrastructure damage would be substantial. For those of you not familiar with New York, the Holland Tunnel connects New Jersey on the east end to Manhattan on the west and runs under the Hudson River. Four lanes. At its deepest, it's around ninety feet below the water. A large enough explosion could take it all down. This may sound crass, but the possible financial implications may dictate if and when the police act. They've evacuated all the civilians. If the detonation of this man's bomb is a certainty, they may work to ensure that happens in the street, in a controlled environment, where damage would be less severe. The last time we had an explosion in the Holland Tunnel was 1949. A barrel of carbon disulfide broke free from a transport truck and ignited. Five hundred feet of reinforced concrete collapsed. One man died, and sixty-six others were injured. Without knowing the exact compounds in this man's bomb, I don't think the authorities will risk an explosion inside the tunnel. He's...he's shouting something now. Can anybody make that out?"

Someone off mic said something, but Jordan couldn't tell what they said.

"I'm being told they're telling him if he moves any closer, they will shoot," the newscaster said flatly. "If there are young children watching or anyone faint-of-heart, I suggest you tune out. We are not operating on a delay. We're live; if the police take action, you will see it. Speaking from experience, these kinds of things cannot be unseen. Okay, I was just handed a statement from NYPD affirming what I said. Local SWAT and sharpshooters have received authorization to take deadly force if this man attempts to enter the tunnel. Again, I'm warning all viewers, this could get graphic. The man is shouting back at someone. Our microphones are unable to pick up what he's saying. We're too far away. He is moving again. He seems undaunted by their warning. He's continuing toward the tunnel. I'd estimate he's fifty to seventy-five feet away, which is awfully close if he—oh, my God. Okay, we have shots fired. I repeat, we have shots fired, the man is down."

The camera jerked up and away, then slowly came back down and steadied. The man was on the ground, sitting in an awkward position, still alive and still holding the switch.

"He is...he is standing back up. They're telling me he was shot in the right leg and...okay, he's back up. Oh my. He's clearly been shot in the thigh. He's back on his feet but unsteady, favoring his right leg. He's reaching into his pocket now with his free hand. He appears to be moving deliberately slow. He yelled something again and...okay, he said he does not have a gun. He's taking something out of his pocket. My producer is telling me we have a second camera on-site now, with a better lens. We should be able to get a closer shot when we switch...oh, that's much better. Okay. Again, I want to caution everyone watching. This is a live feed and not suitable for all viewers, particularly children. He's unfolding a sheet of paper and holding up a sign, it says—"

Jordan let out an audible gasp and covered her mouth with her hand.

"The sign says, *On you, Jordan*."

The camera zoomed in on the sign, then panned up to the man's face. He was grimacing, obviously in a lot of pain. As he came into focus, Jordan's stomach twisted into a knot.

BILLY: *Wait, don't we know him?!?*

The newscaster cut back in. "He has been identified. I'm not sure of the source on this—we've been told we can't release his name yet, but he's a defense attorney here in Manhattan. Forty-two years of age. Unmarried. The sign, it's clear he's referring to talk show host Jordan Briggs here at SiriusXM, which would be confirmation that this is connected to the bombings earlier today in Manhattan and possibly several murders which have also taken place today in the tristate area. A man known only as *Bernie* has been..."

His voice faded away. Jordan couldn't hear him over the sound of blood rushing through her ears. On her desk, her phone vibrated again and she snatched it up. Nick again—*Call me now, dammit! Emergency! 911!*

Seriously, you shit? Right now?

Hitting the mute button on her microphone, she tapped dial on her phone and brought it to her ear, unable to look away from her monitor.

"...he's moving again, with a severe limp. He looks like he's lost a lot of blood and must be in excruciating pain, but he's continuing toward the mouth of the tunnel anyway. Ignoring police warnings. Picking up speed with each step."

Her call began to ring.

On screen, the man's eyes went wide and he froze. He looked down at the vest. The mobile phone tacked to the center of his chest above the belt of explosives lit up for a brief millisecond before a blinding flash.

Jordan's cell fell from her fingers and clattered across her desk. Another text came in, this one from an unknown caller, and it was enough to put her over the edge.

You've made your choice. Boom.

33

Cole

Cole saw the explosion from the helicopter, this flash of white light less than a mile away on his right. Either from a blast wave or a knee-jerk reaction from the pilot, the chopper pulled hard to the left. Cole slammed into the sidewall, then grabbed the edge of the seat. They quickly climbed and leveled off a moment later while Cole fumbled with his seat belt.

Through his headphones, the pilot said, "Sorry. I flew in the war. Reflex thing. That's the Holland Tunnel down there."

A giant fireball erupted near the tunnel opening, igniting several cars. A truck exploded, bounced, and landed on top of a rusty station wagon.

"Jesus."

Cole leaned against the window. "Can you get us in closer?"

The pilot hesitated, the helicopter turning slowly as it hovered. "See those news choppers to the east? I know those guys, and they're fucking crazy. I take this bird anywhere near them, and my boss will have me driving a cab by this time next week. It's too risky. NYPD will restrict the airspace, if they haven't already. Maybe the feds at this point. They'll ground all of us."

Another car exploded. Thick black smoke lofted up, making it nearly impossible to see anything. The pilot eased them even further away. "I'm sorry, but I can't risk getting caught up in the heat draft. This chopper is built more for comfort, it can't handle that sort of thing—could choke us and cause a stall."

Cole barely heard him.

This couldn't be one man, could it?

Less than three hours, and the city was on its knees. How was it even possible?

His phone started to ring.

Lieutenant Gaff.

"This is Cole."

"Where are you?"

"On my way back to the radio station to interrogate Briggs. She has to know him."

"In a chopper, though, right?"

"Yeah."

"I need you to reroute. Get over to Rikers instead."

"Rikers, why?"

"The man who just blew himself up at the tunnel was a local defense attorney named William Daly. We found a link between him and Briggs. We need a break. This could be it."

"What's the link?"

"Not a what, a *who*. They're moving her to an interview room right now. Her name is Marisa Chapman."

34

Jordan

"That is not Nick's number!"

"I don't understand," FBI agent Allison Varney replied, her eyes fixed on Jordan's.

The two of them were sitting at the conference table in Jordan's office. The painter's tarps that had been covering the table had been discarded, bunched up in the corner of the floor. The painters a no show.

Agent Varney had asked to speak to Jordan alone, and apparently *alone* meant along with the pudgy FBI agent with bad teeth because he had followed them in and made himself right at home, sitting on the corner of her desk with a cup of coffee pilfered from her greenroom. Jordan had learned his name was Fred Schulman.

Jordan pointed at her cell phone in the center of the conference table. It was resting on top of a plastic evidence bag but had yet to be placed inside. Nick's contact information was on the screen. "Somebody changed out the number I had programmed in for him!"

"And why would somebody do that?"

Jordan knew her eyes were bouncing around like a crazy person. She only half-heard this other woman as she spoke. Her heart was beating a thousand times per minute and felt like it might burst. "Did I activate that bomb?"

Agent Varney didn't reply. Instead, she sat there for a moment, watching Jordan with this look that was a mix of condescension, condolence, and pity. She reached across the table, took Jordan's phone, and slid a finger across the screen. It had timed out. "What's your passcode?"

Jordan opened her mouth to tell her, then thought better of it.

Varney tilted her head. "You can always change it. Do you want me to help you or not?"

"I'm not sure you're here to help me."

Varney shrugged. "You know I'll get in either way. The real question is whether I get in with your cooperation or without. And that's the kind of thing that will be looked at very closely in the days to come." She leaned forward. "This is how it will play out. I'll make a phone call and request a warrant. You'll call some attorney somewhere, and he or she will tell you to not do anything until he or she gets here. He or she will not be able to get here because of what's happening outside. More people will die. I'll get my warrant. I'll send your phone back to FBI HQ, probably with someone on foot until they can work through this mess and catch a cab to Tribeca—that's where we're based. That will take a while. More people will die. Your attorney will attempt to block our access. He or she won't succeed, but that will take time, too. More people will die. Eventually, though, I'll have every scrap of data from this phone printed in triplicate with a dozen people analyzing it. I'll get what I need, and you'll be hung out to dry for stalling us *while more people died*. So, do what you want, and I'll do what I have to do. We'll see where we end up."

Jordan knew she was right, but that didn't make this any more palatable. "0-3-2-4. My daughter's birthday."

Agent Varney gave her a slight smile and keyed in the code, then brought up Nick's contact information again. "According to this, he has two cell phones." She held up the phone.

"The first one is correct. Not the second. I don't know how that got in there, but that's the one his text message came in from. That's the one I dialed."

"The one you think activated the bomb." She said this as a statement, not a question.

Jordan hesitated a moment, then nodded. "Yes."

Agent Varney looked up at her again. "If I search for William Daly, am I going to find him?"

Again, Jordan went quiet.

"What little patience I have left is quickly dwindling, Ms. Briggs." Agent Varney began to stand. "Schulman, go ahead and cuff her, and read her her rights. We're going to do this the hard way."

"Okay, wait," Jordan said. "Just wait."

Agent Varney lowered herself back into her chair.

Jordan let out a slow breath. "I don't know if he's in there. I haven't spoken to him in a long time. I've probably had a dozen phones since then. He represented me on a civil thing years back, when I was first starting out."

"A civil thing?"

"It was silly, really. I'd just moved to the city. KROQ hired me away from a station outside of St. Louis. Well, Billy and me. I'd been on the air here for a little over a week. KROQ was third in the ratings, and they brought me in to take them to number one. I hit the ground running, pulling every trick I learned along the way to drum up my audience. At this point, I had a formula. I'd hit number one in every market they put me in, I knew I could do it here, and I planned to do it in record time. So I rolled out one of our go-to stunts."

"Which was?"

"Oh, it seems so stupid now. This was probably ten years ago. Times were different. I was different."

"What did you do?"

Jordan rubbed the side of her head. "This girl called in, a liberal arts student at NYU. Nineteen years old. She called me complaining about the cost of tuition, rent in the city, lack of jobs for students. She moved here from Kansas and kept her car, a beat-up Honda Accord. She didn't have the cash to park it or put it in a garage. She said she was on the verge of dropping out because she couldn't afford to stay in the city anymore, so I made her an offer. I told her if she got in her car naked and drove down Broadway from Hell's Kitchen to Washington Heights, staying on the air with me the whole time, I'd give her ten thousand dollars cash."

"You can't be serious."

"She said no," Jordan replied. "At first, anyway. She turned me down, hung up, and I thought that was the end of it, but all these calls started coming in—from other women willing to do it and from men wanting *her* to do it. At the time, I had no idea what she looked like. She might have been 300 pounds with a mole in the middle of her forehead, but she sounded cute and that's all that really mattered. That's the beauty of radio. Listeners hear a voice and conjure up this ideal image for the person behind it. Her voice had this sweet, innocent inflection to it. She had that midwestern accent. Wholesome. Small-town girl in the big city. The fact that she didn't want to do it was what made just about everyone want to see it happen even more. Everyone wants what they can't have. My new audience saw her adversity as a challenge and started calling in with pledges, donations toward the cause. Within an hour we broke twenty thousand, then twenty-five. We were at twenty-eight when she finally called back in and agreed to do it."

Agent Varney only stared at her.

"We gave her an address in Hell's Kitchen off the air. It was a parking garage near where one of my interns lived, and I sent a crew out there to meet her with a camera." Jordan waved a hand through the air. "Nothing like what we have now, it just was some piece-of-shit Sony HandyCam, something we could use to document everything, not really knowing what we were documenting it for. We weren't on television yet. She showed up, and I think everyone was relieved when we realized she was as cute as her voice—curly blonde hair, green eyes, and the kind of body that turned heads and caused men to walk into light poles. Midwest cornfed and a hundred-ten pounds soaking wet."

"Do you have any idea how sexist this all sounds?"

Jordan shrugged. "Sexist enough to sell. Sexist enough to cause a thousand strangers to throw money into a bag. I'm not proud of everything I've done to build a career, but I'm not gonna apologize for knowing what works. What's worked for a thousand years. People want what people want, and that particular morning they wanted a naked girl to drive down Broadway, so I gave them one."

"I can't imagine how nervous she was."

"You can see it on the tape, anyone would be, but she committed—she stripped down right there in the garage, handed her clothes to my staff, and got behind the wheel of that yellow Accord with my camera-toting intern in the passenger seat and another staffer in the back holding a cell phone so we could broadcast the whole thing on the air. Her clothes went into a separate car, and she was told she could pick them up at the finish line along with her cash." Jordan paused for a moment as events came back to her. "We didn't tell my audience where exactly she'd start or where specifically she'd end up; they only knew Hell's Kitchen with Washington Heights on the other end, but not addresses. What they did know was Broadway. They knew she'd take Broadway. And that was enough. The second someone spotted a yellow Accord on Broadway, they posted the location on social media with hashtag #NakedGirl. Other people spotted her and posted. Others followed in their own cars—drove alongside, some got in front. I was on the air, giving a play-by-play like I was calling some kind of sporting event. Our phones went nuts. Local TV jumped on the story, mobilized crews. People started to line the sidewalks and wait for her like some kind of fucked up parade. You couldn't actually see anything—she was short and drove hunched down in the seat, but that didn't keep anyone away. Honestly, it might have made things worse."

Jordan paused again and looked down at her hands. "7.4 miles. A twenty to thirty-minute drive on a good day. That's all this was. All it was supposed to be. There's no way I could have known what would happen."

35

Cole

Cole had made his share of trips to Rikers Island since joining NYPD but always via car—the FDR to 278. Across the bridge, through security, and into the small parking lot reserved for law enforcement. Normally about forty minutes from midtown. By air, things were very different. They shot directly over the East River, cleared prison airspace by radio, and were easing down onto one of the helipads within a handful of minutes. Behind them, thick blooms of black clouds filled the sky above Manhattan. Cole tried not to look at them.

As Cole climbed out of the helicopter and jogged toward the prison entrance, a man in his mid-fifties pushed through one of the doors and held it open with his back. He shouted over the engine noise. "I never got one of those when I was with NYPD!"

The heavy metal door closed behind them, turning the heavy *thump, thump, thump* to a dull rumble. Cole held out his hand, but the other man didn't take it. Instead, his eyes narrowed. "I'm Warden Daggett. Gracie's godfather."

Cole felt a lump form in the pit of his stomach.

"Gaff told me what you did to our little girl. You come to my prison any day but today, me knowing what you did, and I might accidentally throw you in solitary for a month. Maybe put you in the center of the yard and tell the inmates you're a cop. Maybe both."

"It's not what you think."

"It never is. That doesn't make it right." He turned and started down the hallway. "Come back when this is all over. We'll invite Gaff and talk this out like men."

A guard stood silently in an open elevator, one hand on the door. As they stepped inside, he pressed a button for one of the lower levels. The door closed, and they began to descend.

Cole said, "What can you tell me about her?"

"She's the sweetest creature ever to set foot on this planet."

"Not Gracie. Marisa Chapman."

Warden Daggett shrugged. "Not much. She's halfway through a twenty-year stretch. Due for her first parole hearing next week. Keeps her head down, or I'd probably know more. I've got about seven thousand inmates here, and I didn't know her name until Gaff called me twenty minutes ago. That's a testament to her. Place like this, you don't want to be on my radar."

The elevator doors opened onto a wide hallway with concrete floors and yellow walls. The paint was chipped and flaking. With the prison set to close in a few years, budget constraints probably put an end to most of the maintenance.

"Third interview room on the right," the warden said. "When you're done, ask one of the guards to take you back up to the helipad."

"You're not staying?"

The warden chuffed and slapped a folder into Cole's hand. "That's everything we have on her. I don't want to be anywhere near you any longer than I need to be. Return the folder to the guard when you're done."

He turned and started down the opposite end of the hall. Over his shoulder, he shouted, "You got half a ball, you'll come back when this is over so we can chat about Gracie, shithead!"

The guard from the elevator had followed them out, and a slight smile edged the corner of his mouth, but he said nothing.

He crossed the hallway and opened the door for the third interview room, waited for Cole to step in, then closed the door behind him.

She was sitting at an aluminum table in an orange jumpsuit. Her short blonde hair was pulled back. She wore no makeup and wasn't restrained. A small tattoo of a black rose covered her right wrist. It wasn't very good. She didn't say anything as Cole took the seat across from her and opened the folder.

A photo of a much younger version of the woman was clipped to the left side. She looked like she had aged twenty years rather than the actual ten.

Cole tried not to stare at it.

He said, "Thank you for meeting with me."

"Lucky for you my schedule was wide open today."

"Do you know why I'm here?"

"Not a clue."

"Do you know what's happening in the city today?"

The lines of her face tightened. "Something that's got nothing to do with me. I was watching on the TV in the rec room when they dragged me down here."

Cole flipped through the folder. There was surprisingly little. A decade summed up in only a handful of pages. Citations for her time spent working in the prison laundry. A demerit for a fight dating back nearly nine years. A summary of the charges against her—five counts of aggravated manslaughter and one count of involuntary manslaughter.

He closed the folder. "What can you tell me about William Daly?"

"Who?"

"During your trial, he represented Jordan Briggs."

She slumped in her chair. "Oh, him."

"What do you remember?"

She smirked. "What do I remember? I remember all of it. I remember how that bitch talked me into doing something I didn't want to do. I remember how she took advantage of me and my circumstance. I remember how that greasy asshole attorney of hers twisted all the facts and somehow made all of it my fault. Like that woman had nothing to do with any of it. Like I set out that day to kill six people. I remember how my court-appointed attorney sat there and did absolutely nothing to really defend me. I remember watching the two of them talk in the corner of the courtroom, voices all hushed and buddy-buddy as they figured out what to do with me before they headed off downtown for lunch in some fancy restaurant and washed their hands of me."

"They knew each other? Daly and your attorney?"

"They all *know* each other. That's one of the things you learn in here. They act like they're mortal enemies in the courtroom, then they go and play golf after. The judges too. Daly lined his pockets keeping a rich client out of trouble, and my attorney did what little work he needed to do to get my file moved from the top of his desk to a box in a basement somewhere. Just another day in the judicial system."

"Can you tell me what happened?"

"Why?" she shot back. "What's the point? You gonna make some kind of half-assed promise to get me outta here, then disappear on me after you get whatever you need?"

"I can't promise you anything."

"Then why the hell should I talk to you?"

"The man who blew himself up at the Holland Tunnel, that was Daly."

She settled back in her chair and a smile grew across her face. "They didn't say that on the news."

"SiriusXM let his name slip, but all the networks got a gag order from Homeland Security right after. They're keeping it under wraps for now."

Her smile somehow grew larger. "I'm going to get a copy of that footage and watch it every night in slow motion before I go to sleep, like a fucking bedtime story. I wish I coulda lit him up myself."

"Marisa, people are dying. Somehow, he's connected. I need to figure out how."

"On you, Jordan," Marisa said softly. "That's what his sign said. "Bitch finally getting what's hers."

"What happened, Marisa?"

Marisa blew out a long breath, and her expression softened. For a brief moment, a glint of innocence passed over her face, and Cole realized he was getting a glimpse of the woman she used to be, the one who walked through the doors of Rikers for the first time all those years ago. "I was broke and needed money to stay in NYU. I called up her show to vent, mostly. I didn't think it would actually lead to anything. Before I knew it, she was offering me close to thirty thousand dollars to take a drive naked up Broadway. She said it was totally my choice, but it wasn't much of a choice, not really, not with that much money on the line. A couple miles in my own car. Just some radio stunt for a new show I figured nobody even listened to. I'm short. I figured I slouch down in the car, nobody would see anything anyway but maybe a couple truck drivers. Not much different than a flash at Mardi Gras or spring break. How do you say no to that? At nineteen, it all makes perfect sense. Off the air, they gave me an address in Hell's Kitchen. I met some of her staff there. They seemed as nervous as me, everybody just stared at the floor all red-faced, and in a way, that made things a little easier. I was naked and back in my car in a couple minutes. One guy with a camera got in the front with me, promised to only shoot from the waist up, another guy got in back, and we called Jordan Briggs from his cell. Before I knew it, we were back live on the air and pulling out into traffic."

She fell silent a second, her eyes half-focused on some spot over Cole's shoulder as the memories came back.

"At first, nobody even noticed me, and I thought it would all be okay. I kinda thought it was funny—all these people driving around me, wrapped up in their own bubble, none of them had a clue. I guess we got about a mile before someone started beeping their horn behind us. A few more blocks, and two guys in a Ford pickup nearly caused a wreck trying to get up alongside—beeping their horn too and yelling crap out the windows. I couldn't make out what they were saying, my windows were all closed, no way I'd open them. I don't think they were listening to her show; they just saw me. Traffic was light too, for New York, anyway. We were moving along pretty good except for the lights. Every time we stopped at a light, there seemed to be more people around me that knew what was going on. More than that damn truck. Those guys were like flies on honey. They kept getting so close, swinging over, sometimes coming within a couple of inches. At about the third or fourth light, when I still wouldn't open my window, they started throwing stuff—empty beer cans, coins, an ice scraper— whatever they could find, and that's when I started getting scared. I was okay when we were moving. It was when we stopped. We were near Riverside Park, at a light, when the guy in the truck's passenger seat reached down and started pounding on my window—full fist, shaking the glass with each hit like he meant to bust it. I got a good look at him then, and I knew he was trouble, real trouble. His eyes were all crazed and red, a mix of adrenaline and who knows what. He looked like he'd been out partying all night and had no intention of winding down. When he shouted, drool ran down the corner of his lip, spittle hit my window—he either didn't notice or didn't care. I locked my doors, tried not to look at him. Man, that light took forever to change. Through all of this, Briggs was on that speakerphone, talking through some kind of play-by-play with her intern, both of them all excited. Another car pulled up alongside on my right. Four guys in that one—and they *were* listening to her show. They had it blaring loud enough for me to hear. When we stopped at the next light, I tried to inch away from the truck but couldn't, not with that other car on the opposite side. They pinned me in. I think that's when panic started to set in. Because I realized between the two of them I couldn't change lanes or move to the left or right. The car that originally beeped was still behind me, blocking me from the back. All I had left was forward, and a thought popped into my head— what if someone cuts me off from the front too? What will these guys do if they manage to stop my car? The guy with the phone in my back seat, the one talking to Jordan Briggs, he kept calling out our position, telling people exactly where we were and how much further we had to go. He was laughing, all wrapped up in things. The guy with the camera, though, I think he started to feel what I was feeling—this shift in control from *us* to *them*. Like someone flipped a big switch. I knew we were in serious trouble when we came up on Columbia University. We both did. Even the guy in back shut up. There were students all along the sidewalks. Some were even holding up signs. Others were pointing at my car, yelling out my name. It went from a few dozen to hundreds in the blink of an eye. The guy with the camera, he told me to turn, get off Broadway, but I couldn't, not with the truck and car blocking me from both sides. At the next light, I have no idea what the intersection was, my heart was beating like a fist, almost as bad as the asshole in the truck beating my window every chance he got. Seeing all those people, that only added fuel to his fire. The driver too—he got all wrapped up in the shouting from the sidewalks and sideswiped me. Not hard, just a glance along the passenger side. Then his buddy leaned out the window far enough he looked like he might fall out—he screamed at me, angry now on top of everything else, said I hit *them*! That was bullshit, but it didn't matter. He yelled for me to pull over. No way I was gonna do that. Then they slammed into my car on purpose, caused me to swerve into the car on my right side. That car hit the car next to them…all I could see were all the faces, all these people yelling at me—from the cars and trucks around me, from the sidewalk—even the guy in my passenger seat—screaming for me to take a side road. Through all this, Jordan Briggs stayed on the phone with her intern, the two of them adding this running commentary to the whole thing like they were watching some television show rather than driving through the middle of it. We…we came to another light, at the university, and all the people from the sidewalks ran out, surrounded my car, started beating on the hood, climbing over my car, screaming. So many people…"

Her voice dropped off for a moment.

Cole realized she was trembling.

When she noticed, she moved her hands under the table to her lap. "That's when I saw the gun."

"Who had a gun?"

"The asshole in the truck. He reached out and used it to smash my window. The glass shattered, rained in on me, and everything got really loud, like all those people were suddenly in the car with me. He tried to grab me. I lost my shit then. I barely remember this next part, and I wish there was a way to get what happened next out of my head, because it's there every time I close my eyes." She looked up at Cole, her gaze glossy. "I hit the gas. He was half-way out of the truck, reaching through my window, grabbing at me, and I slammed my foot down on the gas. There were people on my car, people in front of my car, people just crossing the street with the light, they were everywhere and I didn't care, I wasn't thinking anymore, I was running on pure instinct. Self-preservation. My car jumped forward and cut through them...God, I heard it—this sickening crunching, more screaming, my eyes weren't even open, I couldn't look, I'd checked out; I just kept my foot on the gas..."

Her arms came up and she wrapped them around her chest, this solitary hug. Cole wanted to comfort her, knew he couldn't.

She went on, her voice quivering. "I...I hit a building on the opposite side of the intersection. That's what finally stopped me. That's when I opened my eyes again. That's when I realized what I'd done. I wanted to shut down again and couldn't. I just started screaming. They took me away, and I don't remember much of that part either. I was in shock. I didn't come out of it for two days, and that's when they told me five people were dead and twenty-three others had been injured."

Cole wasn't sure what to say. At first, when he opened his mouth, nothing came out. Finally, he said, "I'm sorry."

She looked back up at him. "I'm the one who listened to that ignorant bitch in the first place. Let her talk me into it. She's the reason I'm here."

Cole looked back down at the list of charges in her file. "Why were you charged with five counts of aggravated manslaughter? If that guy pulled a gun on you—"

"I had an overworked public defender who didn't give two shits about me. Nobody saw the gun but me, and it was never found. You can't see it on the video. Without that, it was all on me. Briggs's attorney, that Daly guy, he saw to that. By the time all the dust settled, Briggs looked like another victim and I was on my way here."

"Who was your public defender?"

"Some wet behind-the-ears wingnut named Dan Carswell." She settled back in her chair. "I know what you're thinking. You're thinking I'm mixed up in whatever is happening today."

"Are you?"

She shook her head. "Look, it's been ten years. Do I hate that woman? Yes. I will always hate her. She took advantage of a naive girl. But I've let go what I can let go. Hating her doesn't erase the guilt I feel. Hate won't bring any of those people back. All I can do is my time. Keep my head down and hope to come out on the other side with the remnants of a life. That's all."

Cole's eyes fell away from her, drifted back down the file. He couldn't look at her. "Five counts of aggravated manslaughter and one count of involuntary...what was..."

"What was the difference?" She licked her chapped lips and looked down at her hands. "One woman was pregnant."

36

Jordan

Jordan left Agent Varney in the hallway outside the studio for the third time and sat heavily behind her microphone. Between broadcasts, she had spent the better part of the last half hour telling her what happened with that young NYU student, the remaining minutes wondering if she should get one of her attorneys in here, and her time on the air wondering when *he* would call back.

Bernie calling back wasn't an *if*. They all knew it was most definitely a *when*, but he hadn't called back. Not yet. But that possibility was probably all that kept the agent and her friends from hauling her down to some federal building for further inquisition under bright lights. Jordan had home-field advantage here and they knew it; they most certainly didn't like it.

They'd let her keep her phone and her first instinct had been to call Nick, she hated herself for that. They'd been together for fourteen years and married for twelve. For a large portion of that time, he was her rock, her soulmate, her confidant. Her only *real* confidant. He'd been there when everything happened with that girl, he was there for the trial, and he was there to help pick up the pieces. He saw her sleepless nights. Saw her on the pills. Helped her get off the pills. He saw her fall apart and held her tight so the pieces would have time to glue back together. All of it away from the public eye as best they could, because there was no way she'd give those assholes in the press something like *that* to write about.

He was the only one who knew about the letters.

There was a moment while talking to Agent Varney when Jordan considered telling her, but that moment slipped by, and once it was gone, it was gone. If she walked out to that hallway and told her now, she'd be backpedaling. If she showed her the letters, she'd be accused of withholding. And the truth was, she didn't know if they were connected, not really. Bringing them up might just muddy the waters and throw them off whatever trail they should be following.

Jordan vaguely heard Billy count her in and caught the ON THE AIR light as it flicked on from the corner of her eye. She looked up at him. "Billy, do you think I'm a good person?"

Billy scrambled for a moment, not prepared to go on the air, then pressed the button that made his microphone go live. "Absolutely not, Ms. Briggs. I think you're a self-indulgent, inconsiderate bitch who has climbed to the top on the backs of those around you. Oh crap, did I saw that out loud? I meant, you are a saint, Jordie, and if I knew how to sculpt I would spend my off-air time creating a fifty-foot statue in your likeness in the middle of Central Park so I would have someplace where I could openly worship at your feet. I might compose music. Frankly, you deserve to be the subject of a board game."

"I'm detecting a hint of sarcasm, Billy."

"You sign my checks. I'm contractually obligated to like you."

"If I didn't, would you? Do you see me as the kind of person you'd hang out with if you didn't have to?"

"I'm not sure. Are you into porn, *Game of Thrones*, and *Minecraft*?"

"Isn't everybody?"

"I sit around in my underwear a lot."

"Me too."

"Then I guess you're okay."

"Bernie hates me."

"I think Bernie has anger issues. He seems to hate a lot of people."

"Yeah, but he particularly dislikes me."

Billy said, "Maybe if he got to know you, he'd ask for adjoining rooms in hell. You never know."

"Do you think I'm going to hell?"

On her third monitor, a message popped up:

BILLY: *Where are you going with this?*

Jordan looked up at him in his booth. "I don't think I'm a bad person. I've made some mistakes in life. Some missteps, but for the most part I try to do what's right."

"For the most part?"

"Sometimes my bitch-gene takes over. Sometimes it fights with my ambition-gene. Sometimes my drive-gene stomps on them both. That's when things get a little cloudy, but I do have a conscience."

"Are you sure? Maybe there's some kind of blood test you can take to confirm the existence of said conscience."

Jordan tilted her head to the side and pushed her hair back over her shoulder. "I've been wracking my brain, trying to figure out what could possibly push someone like Bernie over the edge, and I keep coming up empty. The feds are here, they've been grilling me, looking for an answer to that too, and I think they're even further off base than when they first got here. I feel like I'm watching keystone cops run in circles. Makes me realize how fragile everything is. A Bernie goes over the edge, the world comes crashing down around us, and the people we expect to keep order swoop in, but instead of helping, instead of instilling confidence, they point their collective magnifying glasses in the wrong direction. If the people here are the best we've got, I may go hide under a bed until this is all over."

"I'm not sure if burying your head in the sand is the answer."

"Here's the thing, Billy. I go through life trying to do what's right, what's right in my mind, and that's an important distinction because what's right to me may not be to someone else. So that's got me wondering—does that mean Bernie thinks he's doing what's right? Does this all make perfect sense to him?"

Billy said, "Hitler thought he was doing the right thing. Stalin. Castro. Oprah."

"I'm not sure Oprah belongs on that list."

"Daytime talk show hosts are evil, mind-melting propaganda filth-mongers and must be stopped. Ellen may very well be the antichrist."

"I kinda like Ellen."

"Okay, maybe not Ellen. Springer, though, him for sure. I've been told never to make direct eye contact with that guy. He'll steal your soul."

"I'm not sure anyone would argue that point." She fell silent for a moment, then said, "Do you remember Naked Girl?"

Billy's eyes grew wide.

BILLY: *We're not allowed to talk about that!*

Billy's point-of-view that day had been unique, and she was certain he hadn't forgotten a single second of it. She knew for a fact he'd worked through three different psychiatrists over the years rehashing those events.

Billy had been the intern in the back seat of that girl's yellow Accord, holding the cell phone.

Jordan said, "The attorney who represented me in that case was William Daly. The same man who just blew himself up at the Holland Tunnel."

She let the words fly, knowing once she did there would be no taking them back. Not by Billy, not by the FBI. Millions of people could not unhear her words. She was on the record now.

BILLY: *Gag orders! NDAs! Settlements! DON'T DO THIS – YOU'RE PUTTING ALL OF IT AT RISK. THIS ISN'T JUST ABOUT YOU!*

Jordan's fingers wrapped around her phone. She turned it over and glanced at the display—about a dozen messages from Nick. The last one about four minutes ago. *Call me! Call me! Call me!*

She ignored all that and typed a message back to him.

Nick's reply was nearly instant: *Not until we talk!*

She typed back *Now!!!* mashing her fingers down hard with each letter, as if the added pressure would somehow emphasize her point. *I need a copy of it now!*

The seconds ticked by, and she began to think he wouldn't do it.

She wouldn't. *Why would he?*

Then it came in—a photo of the letter she'd given him this morning. Jordan read the carefully-crafted handwritten letter again and tried to ignore the knot in her belly. She knew what she needed to do.

She cleared her throat. "Billy? I'm gonna read you something."

37

Jordan

Jordan stared down at the image of the letter, sucked in a breath, and found the courage to read aloud. "'Dear Ms. Briggs, I can't believe it's been another year! The days, weeks, and months flew by so fast! I'm in the fifth grade now, and I've grown a lot since I last wrote. In fact, I'm taller than most of the boys in my class now. That seems a little weird, but all the girls are taller now and our teacher, Mrs. Dolan, says it's perfectly normal. She says the boys will catch up soon enough, but emotionally, spiritually, and intelligently we girls will always be taller than the boys, you just can't always see it. I like Mrs. Dolan. She's nice. I like writing and math. Science is a little harder, but that's fun too. Mommy says I've got a little brother on the way. I know, I'm supposed to be excited about that, but it's just been Mommy, Daddy, and me for so long, I'm not sure I want a brother. She seems to want another baby, though, so I guess I'm happy that she's happy. Daddy says we'll have to share a room for a little while, but he promised to get us a bigger place. Mommy's excited about that too. I'm not sure I want to move. All my friends are here, so I hope the new place is somewhere close. I don't want to change schools either. My best friend Valerie and I got in trouble the other day for passing notes in class. Luckily, we worked out a secret code so Mrs. Dolan couldn't read it, but still, she caught us. I'm glad she couldn't read it, though, because the note was about a boy in my class, Blake Hilley. Valerie thinks Blake is uber cute, and I guess I do too. She's mad because Blake seems to like me more than her, but she kissed him yesterday anyway and now he's not talking to either of us. I told Mommy about Blake, and she said all boys have cooties and it's dangerous to be around them until they're twenty-five. Something about a college degree and job somehow curing them. I think she made that last part up. She also told me not to tell Daddy about Blake. She said Daddy might put me in something called a convent if he found out I talked to boys. But she said I can talk to her about boys any time I want. Remember last year when I said I wanted to be a veterinarian? I've thought about it a lot in the past year, and I think I just said that because Valerie's dog died. He was old, but we tried to save him, but sometimes dogs just get too tired and need to go to sleep. I think instead of being a veterinarian, I might become a doctor and help people. People live longer than dogs or cats or gerbils. Mommy and Daddy said I can be whatever I want when I get older, but I see doctors on TV and I want to be like them. Mommy also said I don't need to decide that kind of thing yet, but I still like to think about it. Valerie has no idea what she wants to do right now. She plans to be a doctor too. Boys are stupid most times, so I didn't ask Blake.'"

Jordan paused for a second. She didn't look up at Billy, because she knew if she did, she wouldn't be able to continue. She didn't look at her monitors or whoever might be watching her through the window in the door. She didn't look at anything but the image of the letter on her phone. A tear slipped from her left eye and rolled down her cheek. She let it. When it splashed down on her desk, she found the strength to continue.

"'When you killed me ten years ago, when you killed Mommy and I was still in her belly, when you took my entire life, *everything* away from me, from all of us really, you went on as if nothing happened. Do you remember that? You took a couple days off, and then that following Monday, when you returned to your show, you went on as if nothing happened. As with the others I've sent you, this letter is a glimpse of what would have happened *if nothing happened*. If life had just gone on as you pretended it did. Daddy says he spends every waking second wishing nothing had happened. Wishing Mommy was still alive, wishing I had had the chance to be born, wishing the little brother I mentioned would have come along someday. He says you took all that away from him, from us. Does that make you sad? You don't seem like it does. And that makes me sad. How could someone have a heart so black they feel no remorse, no guilt, no shame, no responsibility for something so horrible? When you close your eyes at night, do you see me? Because I see you. I've never stopped seeing you. I've never stopped wondering *what if* you had never entered our lives. Someday soon, you're going to wonder what your life would have been if I never entered yours.'"

Jordan's voice had grown shaky and she allowed herself several breaths, then said, "The letter is signed 'Forever and ever, Kimberly,' and that's the part that always hits me the hardest because I know there never was a Kimberly, because of me. I needed...I wanted...to share this with all of you because it's something that's weighed heavily on me for a long time. I'm not allowed to talk about the specifics, there are court orders that prohibit that, but with a quick search on the Internet, I imagine most of you will put this together. I've received ten of these letters—one for each year Kimberly would have been alive. And it's not that I didn't want to talk about it. I couldn't. I guess I've never let that stop me before, but in this case, I did, probably because that made me feel better about it." This time, she did look up at Billy, his eyes were fixed on her. "Bernie, I'm sorry for what I stole from you. I've always been sorry. You deserved to hear that a long time ago."

Jordan couldn't find the words to say anything else, so she let the silence linger and looked up at her second monitor. She watched as the names of the people on hold blinked out one at a time, all replaced with the name of the man she knew she had no choice but to speak to:

Line 1 – Bernie
Line 2 – Bernie
Line 3 – Bernie
Line 4 – Bernie
Line 5 – Bernie

38

Cole

"Her name was Kourtney Bretz," Tresler said.

Cole was standing in the hallway leading back to the helicopter at Rikers, his phone pressed to his ear.

"She was six months pregnant when Marisa Chapman mowed her down. They managed to get the baby out in the ambulance before the mother died, but the child only lived for nine minutes. Little girl. Kimberly Bretz, according to the death certificate. Next of kin is listed as Bernard Bretz. That's him. We got him."

"We got a name. I need an address, Tresler."

"Working on it. We should put some kind of protective detail on Chapman, right?"

"Warden Daggett already did. He's moving her to isolation."

"You know Daggett is Gracie's godfather, right? He's liable to knife you if he gets you alone out there. Watch your back."

Cole ignored him, thinking aloud, "It's some kind of revenge thing, got to be. That's why he's focused on Jordan Briggs, that's why he targeted the attorney, Daly. This guy snapped, and he's going after all of them. But why now? Why wait ten years?"

"Crazy doesn't grow overnight. Takes time, like mold."

"Something triggered him. Pushed him over the edge."

Cole's phone dinged with an address on 136st in West Harlem.

"That's last known," Tresler said.

"Can you meet me there?"

"I'll loop in Lieutenant Gaff so he can get SWAT out there, but I'm stuck in Jersey. No way I'm getting through this traffic. Nothing's moving."

"Find a boat to get you across the Hudson, then hoof it. That address isn't far from the pier."

"Find a boat?"

"Find one. Steal one. I don't care. No traffic jams on the water."

"Shit," Tresler muttered.

"What is it?"

"I pulled up a summary of the court transcript. Ronald Bonfigleo and Patty Epps were both on the jury that let Briggs off."

"Send me a copy of every—"

Cole's phone dinged again, this time with a list of all the juror names. He began pacing. "That was ten years ago. We need to get current addresses on everyone, track them down, and get them into protective custody until this is over."

"Sure thing. Day like today, plenty of people standing around to get right on that."

"Get Gaff to bring in the feds, Homeland…doesn't have to be NYPD."

"Newsflash, partner. They're all running this case from different angles already, and I guarantee protection will be the last place any of them will deploy resources. They want everyone trying to find him."

"If we're protecting these people, Bernie has to come to us. That's how we get in front of this guy."

"No way a judge will sign off on using civilians as bait."

"Who was the judge on the Briggs case?"

Tresler paused a second. "Brenda Northrop. Southern District, second circuit."

"Can you get to her?"

"Same problem. She's in the city too."

"You need to—"

"Find a boat…yeah, yeah."

"Look, you get to her, tell her what's going on. Tell her you're there to keep her safe. She can get on the phone and help track down the other jurors probably faster than anybody. Two birds."

"Two birds—you mean use her as bait instead. Much better to use a judge than a civilian, is that how you expect me to sell this?" Tresler said flatly.

"You're protecting her, that's how you sell her on it. If Bernie happens to show up there, then you get to end this and solve the case of a lifetime."

Cole could picture him chewing on one of his toothpicks as he thought this over.

Finally, Tresler said, "I like the sound of that. Hold on a second…" The call went muffled, probably Tresler covering the phone with his hand. He came back a moment later. "Are you listening to the Briggs show right now?"

"No, why?"

39

Jordan

Agent Varney had been pounding on the door for nearly two minutes straight before Jordan finally covered the glass with a handwritten note that said, *You're not coming in*. Billy knew better than to open it, not without her permission, and apparently he locked his door too, because none of them had entered his booth.

Her third monitor still had the message from Jules on it:

J. GOLDBLATT: *OPEN THE GODDAMN DOOR, JORDIE!*

Jordan hadn't responded to him. After taping up the note, she walked back to her desk and waited for the automated commercial break to wrap up. When the hard break broke in at the top of the nine o'clock hour, all the calls had dumped, the system working as it should, but a moment later each line blinked back, no different from before:

Line 1 – Bernie
Line 2 – Bernie
Line 3 – Bernie
Line 4 – Bernie
Line 5 – Bernie

The LED counter on the wall indicated more than thirteen million people listening worldwide at that particular moment. She couldn't imagine how many people were attempting to dial in, nor did she understand how Bernie was able to bypass all of them and hijack her system, yet he made quick work of it.

She glanced up at the cameras, still covered with plastic. Then she looked around all the dark corners of her studio and wondered where else he had eyes. She knew he did. She could feel him watching her. Her skin crawled with it. Jordan opened a new chat window on her computer and typed a quick message to Sarah.

Sarah responded a moment later:

SARAH: *The feds have Charlotte locked in the greenroom with Senator Moretti. They've got two standing at the door like sentries at the castle to keep them safe. She has her books and can call me if she needs anything, so don't worry about her. I'll keep an eye on her. Probably best she stays in there anyway. There are feds in the elevators and at the stairway door too. They're checking everyone in and out of our floor. They're on other floors, too. Not sure what they're up to there.*

Jordan considered telling her she didn't want her daughter in a room with the senator, then thought better of it. As much as she hated it, it didn't make sense to divide resources by creating another room to watch. She told Sarah thanks. A message from Billy popped up on her screen:

BILLY: *They'll probably arrest us*
JORDAN: *For what happened then or what's happening now?*
BILLY: *Yes.*
JORDAN: *I need to see this through, but if you want to leave, you can. I've gotten you in enough trouble.*
BILLY: *I'm not going anywhere*
JORDAN: *Thank you, Billy. You always stand by me.*

BILLY: *No, I mean I'm* not going anywhere – *the subway is shut down, and cabs aren't running. I'm stuck here. Might as well help you.*
JORDAN: *Fuck you, Billy.*
BILLY: *Love you too, Jordie.*

A moment later, she heard his voice over her headphones, counting her in. "On the air in three, two..."

The red ON THE AIR indicator lit up.

Jordan's finger hovered over the button for Line 1. She pressed it before she could change her mind. "Hello, Bernie."

"Do you feel better now? Relieved? Like you got some great weight off your chest?"

"No. Not really."

"Good."

"I'm trying to understand why you're doing this. What happened back then, that was horrible. It was tragic, but it was an accident. On some level, you must understand that."

"That was no accident. You orchestrated it. You pulled the strings on your puppets and brought those events into being."

"I may have lit the match, but none of us knew it could lead to something like that. How could we?"

Bernie replied, "You didn't think about the consequences. You only thought about yourself. You used that girl. You ruined so many lives that day. You gave that girl a choice, and she could have said no, but she didn't think either. None of you. None of you spent even half a second wondering what could go wrong. You just did it. Consequences be damned."

"If I could take it all back, I would."

"Would you? Even if it meant the end of your career? Even if it meant your life wouldn't have worked out the way that it did? What if it meant you'd never meet your husband? Never have a daughter? What if you could go back in time, flip a switch, and undo all of it like it never happened? Fix my life by removing yours, would you do that?"

"That's not a fair question."

"You don't get to use words like *fair*."

"Tell me what I can do to stop all this."

"You can't stop it, Ms. Briggs. All you can do is make another choice."

"I'm not playing your fucking game."

Bernie didn't hesitate. "Grand Central or Penn Station?"

"I'm not doing this again."

"Pick one, or I blow them both. I'll give you three minutes to decide. That should be enough time for anyone listening to get out. And from what I can gather, there are a lot of people listening. How is Agent Varney doing? She went through a nasty divorce a few years back. Maybe she can offer you some tips."

BILLY: *How the hell does he know who's here?*

He was studying the plastic around the camera in his booth, but like the others, it was sealed tight.

Jordan said, "Why don't you just kill me?"

"No."

"Why not?"

"Because I want you to suffer, and we're just getting started."

"What happened years ago was an accident. What you're doing today isn't. You're purposely killing people. Every single one of them has a family, maybe children, some kind of life. You're taking that away."

"So my loss doesn't equal their loss? Is that what you're trying to say? I've got my thumb on the scale, and the balance is a little off?"

"There is no way to balance this. Nothing you or I can do will bring back your wife or your daughter. You need to try to—"

"Don't you dare tell me to move on. When you wake up tomorrow, when this is over and someone tells you "you need to move on," you'll understand how that feels too. There is no moving on."

"So tomorrow comes, this is all over, where will you be?"

"I'll be dead. Just like I am now. I died that morning ten years ago with my wife and daughter, so nothing changes for me. You have two minutes, Ms. Briggs."

Jordan looked over at her monitors. Although muted, the news channel was still playing on the first one. They were running a split screen with Grand Central on the left and Penn Station on the right. People were streaming out all the doors. The transit police were hurriedly putting up barricades on the sidewalks. The scrolling ticker at the bottom of the screen said they were stopping trains in the tunnels. They didn't say whether they were evacuating the passengers or keeping them in the trains. She rarely rode the subway and couldn't imagine what it would be like to be trapped in one of the tunnels.

"You're a fucking coward, Bernie. If your wife or daughter were still alive, is this how you'd want them to see you? How you'd want them to remember you?"

"Have you made your choice?"

"I'm not going to choose," Jordan told him.

"So you'd rather see me blow up both?"

"I'd rather see the feds put a bullet in your head, but nobody's offered up that choice yet."

"I'd miss talking to you."

Jordan chuffed. "I think I'd survive without you."

"Maybe that's the answer, though, a bullet to the head. Since you can't decide between the train stations, I'll just do that."

"You'd kill yourself?"

"Not me, this guy," Bernie replied.

There was a slight ruffle as Bernie shifted the phone. Then another voice came across the line. "Jordie?"

Jordan leaned into her microphone. "Nick?"

She jumped when she heard the shot. She didn't mean to.

40

Cole

The helicopter landed in St. Nicholas Park. The pilot couldn't get any closer without landing in the middle of the road, and it meant Cole had to take his own advice and hoof it the last few blocks on foot.

The address was a five-story corner brownstone, the brick long ago painted white with a narrow alley running along the left side. Cole barely noticed the building as he ran up, attempting to catch his breath. His gaze was fixed on the beat-up yellow Honda Accord parked out front.

He knew it couldn't be the same car Marisa Chapman had driven ten years ago, but he also knew it wasn't parked there by chance. As he stepped up close enough to read the license plate and the decade-old sticker in the corner, he was certain Bernie had placed the car here. By the look of the dust and grime covering the car, Bernie had placed the yellow Honda here a long time ago. But it couldn't be the same car. Marisa Chapman's Honda would have been towed to an evidence yard somewhere, probably the Erie Basin yard in Brooklyn. While there, CSI would have dismantled the vehicle, photographing every scrape, ding, and dent. Each piece then placed in evidence bins, tagged, and logged. Any vehicle involved in a homicide was unlikely to ever drive again;

one involved in a multiple homicide like the one committed by Marisa Chapman would be carefully preserved in the event an appeal was filed and the evidence would need to be reexamined.

A single Harlem PD cruiser came to a stop in the middle of 136th, and the driver-side window rolled down. "Are you Detective Hundley?"

Cole nodded and looked up and down the street? "Where's SWAT?"

The officer shifted the cruiser into park, turned on his flashers, and slowly climbed out. He looked to be in his late forties, about fifty pounds overweight, and spoke with a slight Jamaican accent. "SWAT's tied up on the east end." Reaching back inside the car, he came back out with a worn uniform cap and slipped it over his dark bald head. Leaving his door open, he approached Cole with the slow shuffle of a man who spent far too much time sitting. "This is my beat."

Cole turned back to the Honda, cupped his hands over the glass, and tried to get a better look inside. "Have you seen this car before?"

"That wreck's been parked there for as long as I can remember. Never seems to move. Neighbors complain about it all the time, parking being what it is around here. Someone keeps renewing the permit, though, so nothing I can do about it."

Cole looked at the sticker in the upper left of the windshield and realized he was right. The sticker was only a month old. "Do you have something we can use to pop the trunk?"

"You got a warrant?"

"This is a crime scene."

"How do you figure that?"

Cole knew he was right. Without some kind of probable cause, this was just another car parked in the street. "Have you ever checked the registration?"

He nodded. "One Marisa Chapman. Address comes up as the fifth-floor apartment in this building, but nobody ever answers the door."

Cole almost told him that was impossible, but that would only lead to more questions. He rounded the car and looked down into the back seat. Empty, except for an old Taco Bell bag.

At the front of the car, he knelt down and got a better look at the bumper. Most of the paint was cracked and peeled, revealing the black rubber below. The left side stuck out at an odd angle, the passenger side had a substantial dent, and the headlight on that side was missing. The little bit of metal exposed was covered in rust. "It's been in a wreck."

"Checked that too. No reports matching this vehicle."

Can't be the same car.

"How far back did you go?"

The officer shrugged. "Dunno. Few years, maybe?"

"Unreported wreck gives us probable cause to open it up."

"That's flimsy."

"What do you have in your car?"

The officer let out a sigh and shuffled back over to his cruiser. He returned a moment later with a pry bar about two feet long, black with a yellow tip. He handed it to Cole. "You'll have to do it. I'm not sure I want to get wrapped up in whatever you got brewing just yet."

Cole took the pry bar and set it on the trunk, then lay down and shimmied under the car with the flashlight from his phone on.

"What are you doing now?"

"Looking for a bomb," Cole replied.

From the corner of his eye, he saw the officer take a couple steps back. "Seriously?"

Cole ran the light along every crevice, the underside of the trunk, and around the wheel wells. "I don't see one."

"Well, yay for that. Are you qualified to identify a bomb if there was one?"

"Where's your bomb squad? Can you get them out here?"

"Not sure if you heard what's happening downtown, but all Uber drivers were ordered to take their vehicles to the nearest police station for inspection. Our bomb guys won't be free until around Thanksgiving 2029 or so. Same with every other squad in the city."

Cole crawled out from under the car, got back to his feet, and dusted off his pants. Reaching for the pry bar, he said, "Then you might want to stand back."

He slipped the pry bar under the lip of the trunk below the lock, grabbed the opposite end with both hands, and jumped, coming down on the bar with all his weight as leverage. The lock snapped, the bar clattered to the ground, and the trunk lid popped open.

The smell didn't hit him, not at first. The two of them were looking down at the large plastic garbage bags for several seconds before the odor struck.

There were two bags, the heavy-duty construction kind you might find in one of those weekend warrior depot stores. Thick black plastic, placed at either end of what could only be a body and duct-taped together where they met at the center. The tape had missed one of the edges, leaving just enough room for yellowish mucus to weep out and soak the surrounding carpet. Some had dried and congealed, and in Cole's mind, he heard the sound it would make when someone eventually lifted those bags out of the trunk.

The officer beside him stumbled back, turned far faster than a man that size probably should, and proceeded to vomit on the sidewalk.

Cole was still peering down into the trunk when his phone rang.

"Yeah?"

Tresler said, "Our judge, Brenda Northrop, hasn't been into work in nearly a month. Her office filed a missing persons on her three weeks ago. One of her clerks went by her apartment, got the doorman to let her in, and said there was no sign of her. Found something odd, though. An old metal breadbox sitting in the middle of her living room floor. Rusty thing. Half a loaf of bread inside that looked a hundred years old. Completely out of place. Like those chairs and the table."

"I think I found her."

Cole told him about the car.

"It can't possibly be Chapman's car."

"I keep telling myself that, too."

"Have you been upstairs yet?"

"Not yet."

"Is SWAT there?"

Cole looked up and down the street. A woman walking her dog. Two men jogging. Otherwise deserted. Most people were probably inside glued to their televisions. "No SWAT, just me and Officer…"

"Whimbly," the man said, wiping his mouth on his sleeve. "Clifford Whimbly."

"Just me and Officer Whimbly. This is his beat."

Tresler sighed. "Your call, but if you wait, you might be waiting a very long time."

Cole lowered the trunk lid and turned to face the building. His eyes traced the flaking white brick to the windows on the fifth floor. "I'm going up."

41

Cole

Unlike many of the old brownstones in the city, this one had never been a single-family home but instead, began its life in the early 1900s as some kind of tenement building. Five stories tall, at least eight to ten units, meant to hold as many people as possible at the lowest achievable cost. In only recent decades had this neighborhood shifted, sending real estate costs to nearly $600 per square foot, pricing out the working class who had once called these buildings home.

For Cole, this all meant one simple fact that had nothing to do with gentrification.

No elevator.

While ten flights of steps were not particularly problematic for him, he kept himself in relatively good shape, he was having second, third, and fourth thoughts about asking Officer Whimbly to follow him.

Whimbly must have had a similar thought, because he said, "Don't let my size fool you. Takes some muscle to move this kind of bulk. I played ball in high school, college, and woulda gone pro if I didn't blow out my shoulder. I've always been big. I'll keep up. I've been doing these steps and others like 'em as long as I can remember. I'm not gonna let you walk into whatever is going on up there alone."

Cole gave him a nod and checked the mailboxes.

The address he'd been given was for apartment 5A.

The nameplate on the mailbox for 5A was missing. Judging by the fresh scrapes in the surrounding paint, someone recently pried it off.

He asked Whimbly, "Does the name *Bernard Bretz* mean anything to you?"

"Nope."

"What about *Kourtney Bretz?*"

He shook his head.

Cole turned back and eyed the stairs. "Okay, stay behind me."

Not only did Whimbly keep up, but he wasn't even winded when they reached the landing for the fifth floor. He rounded the final flight of steps with his eyes locked on the door for 5A, one hand on the butt of his service pistol as his index finger unsnapped the leather with practiced ease.

Twenty minutes earlier, and Cole might have wondered about the last time Officer Clifford Whimbly had fired that gun but his opinion of the man was quickly evolving and now he got the impression he made a habit of visiting the range and keeping himself sharp.

Cole pointed first at him, then at the corner on the right side of the door for 5A, and Whimbly crossed the landing silently before pressing as tight as he could against the wall.

Cole did the same on the left side, shifted one hand to his own weapon, and knocked on the door with the other. Three quick raps. "NYPD!"

There was no answer, and as the seconds ticked by, Cole felt the eyes of a neighbor watching them through the peephole of 5B, and he wondered if Bernie was behind that other door. That's what he would do—use this one as bait and strike from the other, and when the door to 5B opened, Cole nearly drew his gun.

The woman who looked out was in her seventies, still wearing pajamas, and had curlers in her hair. Her eyes grew wide at the sight of them, but she didn't shrink back into her apartment and close the door, instead she said, "Nobody lives there."

Cole gave Whimbly a quick glance. The large man remained in position.

The woman shoved both her hands into the pockets of her heavy flannel robe. "Been vacant going on nine or ten years now."

"You haven't seen anyone go in or out?"

She shook her head.

Cole took out his phone, turned on the flashlight app, and began running the beam along the edge of the door and around the lock.

"What are you doing?"

Before Cole could respond, Whimbly said, "Go back inside your apartment, ma'am, and lock the door."

For a moment, she looked like she might argue. Then she closed the door, and several locks clicked into place.

Cole got back to his feet, braced himself, and prepared to kick the door in when Whimbly grabbed his arm. "Whoa, hold up a minute."

"You said the car is registered to this apartment. That gives us probable cause."

"That's not what I mean."

Whimbly reached around to the side of his belt, unclipped a leather pouch, and pulled out a lock-picking kit. Retrieving two picks, he lowered his large frame down on one knee in front of the door. "This is a little skill I learned before joining the force. Tends to save a lot of doorframes. Between calls from concerned neighbors and odd noises coming from abandoned properties, I've had to open my share of doors over the years."

He slipped both picks into the lock and began moving them around. Several seconds later, he twisted his grip and the lock disengaged. Rising back to his feet, he returned the picks to the case, dropped it back in his pocket, and stepped back to the side of the door, giving Cole a slight nod.

One hand still on the butt of his gun, Cole reached for the knob, gave it a twist, and pushed the door in on the apartment.

"NYPD, we're coming in!"

Judging by the dust on the hardwood floor, nobody had lived here for quite some time. But somebody had been inside—there were several tracks leading from the door down the hallway which appeared to cover the length of the apartment. Framed pictures lined the wall on the right, with several rooms were on the left. Cole took out his gun and stepped inside, carefully eyeing the floor for tripwires or anything else Bernie might have rigged. He paused at the first of many photographs.

The picture depicted a man and a woman on their wedding day—him in a tuxedo and her in a flowing white dress, both standing on the steps of the courthouse, their hands entwined. Someone had taken the time to cut out both faces some time ago. Like the floors, a thick layer of dust covered the glass. Other photographs were similar—a man and woman hiking. The two standing before a large waterfall. Another of them at a fireplace in a cozy cabin.

As Cole worked his way down the hallway, the images told a story. Several years together laid out in chronological order. Across from the first bedroom, the images shifted, became focused only on her and her growing belly. Obviously pregnant, swelling slightly from one photograph to the next. Her jeans and tank tops making way for stretch pants and roomy tunics. Her face gone from each picture.

The first bedroom contained a double-bed, nightstand, and dresser. The sheets were in a rumpled heap at the foot, and the furniture was covered in various items you'd expect to find—a hairbrush, more framed photos, some folded laundry. All of it layered in dust. In the bathroom they found two toothbrushes in a glass stained yellow with age and half-buried under a thick spider web. There were old shampoo bottles on the shower floor and rotting towels draped over the curtain rod. The water in the toilet bowl had a thick layer of mold along the outer edge—it hadn't been flushed in years.

"It's like someone just up and left. Closets are still filled with clothes."

Cole nodded and made his way back out into the hallway.

The second bedroom had faded pink paint on the walls and a white crib in the corner filled with stuffed animals, and just looking at it caused Cole's heart to pang. He knew that crib had never been used and never would be.

The end of the hallway opened on a living room with a small kitchen tucked into the corner. Couch, television, everything set up exactly as it probably had been when Bernard and Kourtney Bretz lived here. There was an empty beer bottle sitting on the coffee table. All of the furniture was old and in various states of disrepair. Nothing really matched. Cole got the impression it had been secondhand even when they did live here, pieced together over time—a young couple just starting out without much means. What wasn't there stuck out not only because of the empty space just off the kitchen but because of the square of displaced dust. To Cole, it was obvious the rusty dining table found at the Bonfigleo murder scene had come from here. The chairs found at both houses, too. Most likely the children's toys came from that bedroom.

"Why do I feel like we're being watched by ghosts?" Whimbly said softly.

That was when the phone rang, the clatter of bells on an old landline loud enough to make both of them jump.

42

Cole

Cole found the old phone hanging on the kitchen wall with a cord long enough to walk half the apartment while on a call. It was letting out the third shrill ring when he carefully removed it from the cradle.

Bernie didn't wait for him to speak. "Do you have a family, Detective?"

"No."

"Family is at the heart of all living things. I'm a simple guy; I never wanted much. A place to call my own, someone to share it with, and maybe, if I was lucky, another someone the two of us could one day pass the good things in life down to. Not much to ask. Not really, just a little piece of the dream. I met Kourtney in college. She was twenty-four, I was twenty-six. We'd both gotten to college a little later than most, so that was a bit of an icebreaker between us. Something in common. She and I against all these kids. Seems silly now to think we felt so much older than the rest back then, but when you're younger, six to eight years' difference is a lifetime. I was driving a truck back then and had to save up. Finally got my shit together enough to go to school part-time. She'd taken a couple years off to take care of her mother when she was on the tail end of a bout with pancreatic cancer. Anyway, I walked into an American lit class and there she was, the most beautiful woman I had ever seen, just sitting there all alone in the third row from the back. I had this John Cusack moment like in a movie, like she had a spotlight on her and music kicked in. She looked up at me, a quick little glance, like she got caught, then turned back to something she was scribbling in a notebook, but that's all it took. The smirk that hung on her lips for a second longer than it probably should roped me in, and I fought every nerve in my body and sat down next to her. I remember she had these dimples when she smiled, like she was trying not to smile, and that only made it brighter. And these eyes, blue as sapphires and filled with a thousand years of knowledge, like the answers to the universe's greatest questions were right there. It took me nearly a week to work up the courage to ask her out, but I think we both knew I was working up to it and she was patient. Always so patient."

Cole looked up at Whimbly and mouthed the word *trace*.

Whimbly nodded and went to the end of the hall before getting on his radio.

Bernie let out a long sigh. "We're born into this world missing something. A hole in our soul. That yin and yang business, there's something to that, and I think when we find our other half, we know it. I can't really describe that feeling, but trust me, one day you will and you'll know. There's no denying it. Kourtney was my other half, and God help her, I was hers. We both knew it from that first moment, and each day only brought more certainty. So we dated for nearly a year, long enough so people wouldn't say we were rushing into things, then we went to the courthouse and got married. Neither of us had family. I never knew mine, and Kourtney's died off with her mother, so it was just the two of us and a couple friends from school, but that's all we needed. I picked up some extra shifts, extended my routes. We scrounged our pennies and got the apartment you're standing in, some used furniture, and started our lives. It wasn't much, but it was ours and we didn't need anything else. We were two years in when we learned Kourtney was pregnant. We'd both wanted kids, that was never a question, but being in school we'd been careful. I guess not careful enough. Kourtney was a year away from finishing, and I'd fallen behind with the extra work, and we had a decision to make that wasn't really much of a decision at all. We decided I'd drop out and pick up the extra work, bulk up our savings, and then I'd stay home with the baby so she could finish up school. Then after graduation, I'd go back to work, she'd be able to find work, and we'd put the baby in daycare. We talked about me going back to school someday too, but I knew I never would. Truth was, I liked driving a truck. The pay was good, and I didn't have to answer to anybody. Not ideal, but you do what you gotta do, right? Besides, it was all worth it to see the look on Kourtney's face when I painted our daughter's room and found a crib."

Cole looked down the hall. Whimbly was on the phone now, his back to him.

Bernie continued, "There was so much love in our tiny apartment. You felt it when you walked through the door, like someone turned the heat up high and it rushed out at you. I remember coming home one morning after a night route, a little after sunup, and finding Kourtney in our daughter's room, sitting there with a hand on her belly talking to our unborn daughter, telling her about me, about us, and I'm not gonna lie...I got choked up. I almost went back out into the hall when Kourtney saw me and gestured for me to come into the room, her face beaming. She took my hand and put it on her belly next to hers, and a second later, I felt it—the baby kicked. This little bump, just enough to tell us she was there, part of the conversation, and I remember looking into Kourtney's eyes and..." His voice trailed off for a second, and he cleared his throat. "She left for school about ten minutes later. I was in the kitchen, making a sandwich. She kissed me good-bye and rushed out the door, late as usual. That's...that's the last time I saw her. You...you don't know those moments when they happen, the last time you'll see someone alive. It was just another good-bye, same as every other. I was...I was sleeping when it happened. I ate, showered, and fell asleep on the couch. I was fucking sleeping when my wife and daughter died. Taking a goddamn nap. I woke up to the news on the television. There was some reporter out in the middle of Broadway, standing in the aftermath. I remember waking up, all groggy, half-watching and hearing him talk about this girl who ran over a bunch of people at NYU. Then I saw Kourtney's backpack on the ground behind him. This gray one from L.L.Bean with a red heart in the center. I tried calling her cell phone, and right there on live television, I saw a cop follow the sound, open her backpack, and answer her phone. I heard his voice on my end, and I think I blacked out then, because the next thing I remember is waking on the couch again and someone pounding on my door."

Cole leaned back against the wall and ran his hand through his hair. Neither of them spoke for a long while. Then Cole finally said, "Bernie, if you understand what that loss feels like, why are you hurting all these other people?"

"Jordan Briggs lit the flame, Detective. She's the only one who can blow it out."

"What's that supposed to mean?"

"She still owes me an answer. She hasn't made her choice yet. I can't wait much longer."

Officer Whimbly shuffled back down the hallway, holding out a sheet of paper. He mouthed the words *we got him* and handed the note to Cole. An address written in a hasty hand.

Cole read it twice before saying, "Bernie, where are you right now?"

43

Jordan

Jordan sat across from Agent Varney at the conference table in her office again. She was still shaking.

Billy was on the air, covering for her.

She vaguely heard his voice from speakers out in the hallway.

When she opened the door to the studio, when she stumbled out in a half-daze, Jules Goldblatt had been standing there with Senator Moretti, and the two of them had hastily stepped inside. Goldblatt handed the senator a pair of headphones and got him in front of a microphone, and Billy was talking to him now on the air. She'd let it happen, she didn't have the strength to tell them no. The idea of objecting was just some far-off thought caught up in everything else shouting for attention in her mind.

Without looking up, Jordan said softly, "That couldn't have been Nick."

Agent Varney slid Jordan's phone across the table to her with the tip of her finger. "Try calling him again."

"Because he'll answer this time? Unlike the last ten tries?"

Agent Varney didn't reply, just stared.

Jordan picked up the phone, dialed Nick again, and slammed the phone down when the call went straight to voice mail. She looked up at the agent. "Can't you trace his location or something?"

"I've got people working on that."

"Well, Christ, how long does it take? Why can't they find him?"

"Calm down, Ms. Briggs."

"Don't tell me to—"

"Calm down, Ms. Briggs," Varney repeated, more forceful this time.

"I think he just shot my husband."

"Ex-husband," Varney replied.

"That doesn't make it any better."

A sly smile edged the corner of Varney's mouth. "Would it be so bad? Nick out of the picture?"

"You're sick."

Varney shrugged. "Half my people think Bernie's on your payroll and he just did you a favor. Some under-the-table, back door agreement between the two of you."

"You're out of your fucking mind."

"You wouldn't be the first ex-wife to take out her husband. Something like that happens, nine times out of ten it's the spouse. With the money thing we found this morning, the way Nick drained your bank accounts, you certainly have the motivation." She leaned forward and lowered her voice. "Between us ladies, the prick had it coming."

Jordan wasn't about to let this woman rattle her. "Money's not a motivator for me. I can always make more money. Even if he spent every penny, I know I can make it back. So you can throw whatever wild theories around you want, but all you're really doing is wasting time. You're sitting here on your hands while Bernie is out there making a fool out of all of you."

"Your buddy, Bernie."

"Give it a rest."

Although muted, the television mounted in the corner of her office was on with coverage from both Penn Station and Grand Central. Giant crowds outside both now, with police blockades at all the doors. None of the trains were running, and the last of the people had been evacuated while bomb squads searched both. Within a matter of hours, this guy shut the entire city down.

Jordan got to her feet.

"Where do you think you're going?"

"Back on the air. I can't sit here and watch this. I need to do something."

"What exactly do you plan to do?"

"I don't know. Something. Anything."

"That's not much of a plan."

"Sounds as good as yours."

"He's going to make a mistake, Ms. Briggs. They always do."

"If I waited for others to fail before I was willing to try and succeed, I'd still be a waitress."

As she turned to leave the room, Varney said, "Your phone stays here."

Jordan considered arguing with her, didn't see the point, and slid her phone across the table. "If Nick calls back, you tell me."

Before Varney could respond, she was back in the hallway heading down toward the studio.

She paused at the greenroom door and looked inside.

Charlotte was curled up in a ball, sleeping on the couch. She hadn't heard about Nick. That was good. She didn't want her to hear about it on the news or from someone else. When she woke, she'd tell her. Or maybe after she got some kind of confirmation. Maybe then. But no sooner, there was no reason to tell her sooner. Her daughter looked so small, vulnerable, this tiny thing who needed her to survive in this world.

Jordan stood there for several minutes, watching her sleep, wanting her to know nothing but that peace for as long as possible, before turning back to the hall and making her way to the studio door. The audio feed to the ceiling speakers was off, but through the window of his booth, she could see Billy speaking. Through the small window in the door, she could see the senator sitting on her couch—headphones on, leaning into a microphone, rattling on about God knew what.

Jordan knocked on Billy's glass and got his attention, then gestured to the studio door.

A look of relief washed over his face, and the lock clicked open.

The senator looked up at her as she stepped into the room, but he kept speaking.

Jordan stood there for a moment, then looked up at the ceiling, at the cameras they had covered with plastic. She reached up and grabbed the plastic from the nearest one, the camera pointed at the couch, and tore it down, then ripped the plastic from the camera that normally recorded her. Rounding the couch, she then lowered herself behind her desk, slipped on her headphones, and leaned into her microphone. "I had to take a time out, but I'm back."

Senator Moretti eyed the exposed cameras suspiciously, then looked over at her. "Billy and I were just talking about the Moretti/Mercer Bill I mentioned to you earlier. How it would allow federal law enforcement to conduct searches of homes and vehicles for those under suspicion of terrorist involvement without the need for a warrant. I think many of your listeners agree, in times like these it would give the police a valuable tool."

"Ah huh."

The third screen on her right lit up.

BILLY: *Please hurt him, Jordie. Hurt him bad.*

Instead of turning on him, she said, "Okay, Senator. I'll bite. How exactly would your bill help under today's circumstances?"

From his booth, Billy shot her a confused look.

The senator seemed taken aback as well. He'd puffed his chest out, ready for a fight, and slowly deflated as he fell into familiar rhetoric. "Well, waiting on a warrant can take up valuable time. Even if it's as little as ten or twenty minutes. In that time, a suspect could destroy evidence, flee, hurt others, a million things could go wrong…"

"*Today's circumstances,* Senator. Don't speak in generalities. If your bill was an existing law, how would it help the police *today*? I'm sure you've clearly thought this through. Studied reports and statistics. Spoken to the people in the trenches. How would you use your bill *today* to catch Bernie?"

When the senator didn't respond right away, Jordan continued, "If not a judge, who exactly determines what house the police can enter, what car they can search? Who decides it's okay to trample on someone's fourth amendment rights for the greater good?"

"The bill simplifies the process."

Jordan nodded. "Simplifies the process," she repeated. "Let's use your example. If the police feel someone is about to destroy evidence or is about to commit a crime, if probable cause exists, they are already permitted to enter a home or vehicle without a warrant. How does your bill change that?"

"My bill allows the police to conduct a search faster."

"Let's be clear. You mean without probable cause."

"Only if someone is suspected of terrorism."

"Again, if not a judge, who makes that determination?"

"The boots on the ground. Law enforcement."

"They deem someone is a 'terrorist' rather than just a criminal? They flip that switch?"

"Yes."

"And you don't think that's dangerous? To take away the checks and balances and put all that power into the hands of whoever is on the ground? Maybe one person? It's happened plenty of times throughout history. I can't think of a single instance where it worked out well. How would you prevent us from becoming a police state?"

Senator Moretti glared at her. "Don't you want to catch this guy? He may have just shot your husband."

"I'm still waiting for you to tell me how your bill would have changed anything that happened today."

"We could have gotten in front of him. Stopped him before he got started."

"How?"

"I'm sure he's in a database somewhere. Maybe he's got a record. There are a million ways somebody like this could have popped up on law enforcement radar before today, and my bill would have allowed them to zero in and stop him before he got the chance to get started."

"So somebody ticks enough boxes on your imaginary spreadsheet, and that gives you the right to storm their house. Is that how this will work?"

The senator's face turned bright red. "You're impossible, you know that?"

"I'm a realist. When given power, people like you abuse it. You're shortsighted. You're not considering all the repercussions created by a bill like yours. You're just diving in with your eyes closed. Don't get me wrong, I'm on board with what you're trying to do, in theory, but only if it can be done without stomping on our rights. That's a bridge none of us should ever cross."

"Maybe you need to place more faith in your elected officials and the people who protect you."

Jordan studied him for a moment. She didn't say a word until she saw him shift his weight on the couch. At least ten seconds of awkward silence. Guests always repositioned when they became uncomfortable, and silence had a way of doing that to the best of them.

She wanted him uncomfortable for this next part.

Jordan gave him a slight smile. "What if I told you he could see you right now?"

Senator Moretti had seen her take the plastic off the camera. He pointed up at it. "With that?"

"We think so. When he called earlier, he described what was happening here in the studio to a tee. If he's not using our cameras, then he somehow planted others in here somewhere. We looked but didn't find anything. The feds couldn't find anything either. So it's got to be our cameras, right? Like that one, pointed directly at you."

"The one you just uncovered?"

"That's right."

"Why exactly would you do that?"

"You said I need to place more faith in my elected officials. Here's your chance to talk to him, one-on-one."

"There's no reasoning with people like Bernie. I think you've seen that today."

Jordan leaned back in her chair and studied his face for a moment. "Maybe we're attempting to reason with the wrong people."

"I don't follow."

Jordan glanced up at LED counter on the wall—thirteen and half million people listening now.

Leaning into her microphone, she said, "I'm about to commit a crime with you, my elected official, as witness, Senator Moretti."

His eyes narrowed. "What kind of crime?"

"Five million dollars," she said softly. "I'd like to put up five million dollars to whoever puts a bullet in Bernie's head."

44

Jordan

"You can't do that," Senator Moretti stated.

"I just did."

"That amounts to nothing short of ordering a hit."

"I'm just trying to simplify the process. Like your bill. Maybe you can draft a bill for sanctioned hits so we can all feel a little better about it? Can't be wrong if you make it law, right?"

"You need to retract your statement immediately. Ordering a hit in the state of New York carries a penalty of up to ten years in prison and a hefty fine. You'll go jail."

"My husband may have just been murdered, I'm under duress, I'm not sure I'm of sound mind. Sweet of you to care, though." She added a wink, knowing only he could see it.

Billy looked up at his window, nodded, and reached over to the dead bolt on his door. When he disengaged it, the door to his booth burst open, and Agent Varney along with two others rushed in.

Billy dropped back into his chair, startled.

"Uh-oh, looks like the cavalry might be busting in to take me down."

The senator swiveled in the couch and looked up into Billy's booth behind him.

"I picked the wrong day to cover *all* the cameras. Federal agents just bum-rushed poor little Billy in his booth."

Varney was speaking to Billy, far more animated than she had been with Jordan. The other two agents were crowding him, one looking down at his various computer monitors, the other watching Jordan through his window.

Billy said something to Varney, then looked up and quickly typed out a message:

BILLY: *Bernie's last phone call traced here to our building. They want to move all of us to protective custody – we need to get off the air. They're evacuating. Cutting to break in five seconds -*

All of this took a moment for Jordan to process. "Folks, we'll be right back." She managed those five words as she scrambled out of her chair and dropped her headphones on the desk. The senator was halfway out of his seat when she pushed by him and out the studio door.

She heard Agent Varney come out of Billy's booth behind her, but she didn't turn. Instead, she rushed down the hall to the greenroom, where she found Charlotte still sleeping on the couch. She sat down beside her and gently stroked her daughter's hair. "Hey, sweetie. You need to get up."

Varney appeared in the doorway and seemed to choke back whatever comment she was about to make at the sight of Jordan's daughter. Instead, she turned and barked orders at several of the other agents, instructing them to double up coverage at the elevators and stairs, secure all egress points. When she turned back to Jordan, she spoke in a low, urgent voice. "When I first arrived, we cleared the floor below yours and the one above. We're emptying the rest of the building now. Most of your people have already been evacuated. We've been staging up on fifty. The ones who insisted on staying are up there. The rest were sent home. I've got a helicopter inbound. I'll personally escort you and your daughter up to fifty, and we'll evac from the roof when it arrives."

Charlotte stirred, and her eyes fluttered open. She smiled up at her. "Is it time to go?"

Jordan forced a grin and did her best to hide the mix of panic, fear, anxiety, and anger roiling in her gut. "Yep, get your stuff together. Sounds like we're going on a helicopter ride!"

Still half asleep, Charlotte didn't look impressed. She got down off the couch and began picking up her things and putting them in her backpack.

Jordan turned back to Varney. "Evac to where?"

"Federal building in Tribeca. Probably the safest place in the country. He can't touch you there."

"Don't make promises you know aren't true."

"Look, this is him making that mistake I mentioned. We *want* this. We anticipated it. I've got people all over the building. We've buttoned down every way in or out. We're searching every inch, and I'll leave a team here on your floor—in your studio, in your office..."

"You baited him with us?"

"We knew him coming here was a possibility, one of many. You're a smart woman; don't pretend it didn't cross your mind. We've got this and all the surrounding floors locked down—people at the elevators, stairwells. We've been prepping for this since we got here. He'd have to go through all of us to get to you, and that's not gonna happen. We get you and your people out and squeeze him. This will all be over in twenty minutes."

Jordan didn't like this, not at all. "He's been one step ahead of everyone from the beginning. How do you know he's not waiting for us on the roof or ready to blow that federal building of yours? He probably anticipated you going there. Can't be predictable."

"We're not—"

"You absolutely are. He knows we can't exit at ground level. That leaves the roof. The moment he thinks I'm running, that's where he'll go." Jordan looked over at Charlotte. She was picking at what was left of the food on the table. "I'm not letting you walk me or my daughter into a trap."

"It's *our* trap," Varney insisted. "It has been from the start."

Billy scrambled in from the hallway, his face flustered. "He's back on the line. What do you want me to do?"

Varney quickly turned to one of the other agents. "Kill all the building's cell phone repeaters. We need to take mobile phones out of play. If he drops off, he'll be forced to call back on a land-line. If he doesn't, we know he's already on one. Either way, isolate that call. Pin him down to a floor. Move, move, move!"

The agent nodded and vanished around the corner.

Varney turned back to Jordan. "What are we doing here, Ms. Briggs? We need to go. I can't protect you if you don't cooperate."

Jordan looked back over at Charlotte. She'd slipped her Strawberry Shortcake backpack on and was standing at the door chewing on a granola bar. She went over to her and knelt. "How would you like to meet your grandmother?"

"I have a grandmother?"

"Well, you weren't hatched. Of course you do."

Charlotte's brow creased. "What's wrong with her? Why haven't I met her before?"

"You know how when you and I have a disagreement we take a time-out to calm down? She and I had a disagreement, and we've been on a time-out."

"I'm eleven. You've been on an eleven-year time-out with your mom?"

"The time just got away from us."

Charlotte seemed to consider this. "You know all this disfunction is bad for me, right? If I get a tattoo or a nose ring when I'm fourteen, it will be all your fault."

"I promise to get you the best therapist when this is all over. And ice cream. I owe you a lot of ice cream."

Jordan kissed her forehead and stood. She dug a scrap of paper from her pocket and handed it to Varney. "Take her here. It's the bed-and-breakfast where my mother is staying in the Hamptons, completely off Bernie's radar. I'll go back on the air and talk to him, give you time to get out."

Varney glanced at the paper, considered this. "Are you sure?"

"No. The last thing I want to do is be apart from my daughter. But that's exactly why it will work. Bernie won't expect me to leave without her. As long as I'm on the air, he'll think we're all still here."

"So now you're okay with being bait?"

Jordan got right up in her face. "Me, yes. My daughter, *no*. I'm trusting you and your people with the only thing I care about on this planet. I need you to promise me she won't leave your sight. You're going to surround her with agents and shoot anyone who tries to get close. I'm trusting *you*," she said again.

Varney nodded. "You have my word. My people can protect her, but I can't leave. She'll need to go with them."

Agent Shulman came up quickly behind her and whispered something Jordan couldn't hear. Varney looked back over her shoulder, then turned to Jordan again. "The elevator is clear. We need to go."

Charlotte had heard all of this. Her upper lip stiffened. "I'll be okay, Mommy. They said I'm an honorary agent. Maybe they'll give me a gun too, and I can shoot the bad guy."

Jordan knelt again and hugged her daughter as tight as she could. She nestled her face in her hair. "I'll be right behind you, Char. I love you so much. You know that, right?"

"I love you too." When Jordan didn't release her, Charlotte added, "Don't make this weird, Mommy. I'm a big girl."

Jordan didn't want to let go but knew she had to. She forced herself to stand.

"We'll take good care of her, ma'am."

She nodded and fought every instinct to chase after them as four agents hurried Charlotte to the freight elevator at the end of the hall and whisked her away.

45

Cole

"She's not answering her phone!" Cole shouted into his cell. The cabin of the Bell helicopter was far quieter than most, but it was still difficult to hear. The handwritten note Officer Whimbly had given him was still in his palm, the ink smeared with his sweat.

The address read: 1221 Avenue of the Americas.

The SiriusXM building.

Bernie was in Jordan Briggs's building.

"We're not getting any response from the FBI agents on site," Tresler replied. "I'm not sure if it's because lines are still tied up or they're just not answering, but we can't get any of them on the phone. There's at least a half dozen already there with more on the way but no telling how long it will take. If they can reach the building at all."

"We're coming up on the building now." Cole could see it below them as they crossed over Rockefeller Center and circled in toward the roof.

Tresler said, "I just spoke to Lieutenant Gaff. They tracked down three more of the jurors, all dead. Two here in New York state, the other one in Pittsburgh. All of them dead at least a few days. The one in Pennsylvania nearly a week. They're still working on the others, but it doesn't look good. Homeland is trying to piece together where this Bernie Bretz guy has been for the past decade, retrace his steps, and from what they've learned, it's not pretty. Have you ever heard of the Sentinels?"

"The baseball team in DC?"

"No, that's the Nationals. The Sentinels is a militia group in upstate New York. When Bernie told you he was driving a truck, that's who owned the truck."

"He was in a militia?"

"Was, is, that part is a little murky. He's a ghost. The day after his wife died, he drained what little there was in the bank accounts, stopped paying all his bills, and dropped off the radar. Appeared again seven years ago when he claimed some kind of back injury and filed for disability. Looks like that money's been going into a Venmo account in Marisa Chapman's name and covered rent and utilities on the apartment ever since. A year before his wife died, he got pulled over for speeding on 87 up near Lake Placid. Registration on the truck had been flagged at some point by the FBI. They knew who owned it, so he created a blip in a database somewhere."

"What was he hauling?"

"Food, just food. But they watch everything moving in and out of those groups close. But that's all they got on him. The current thinking is he was working with the militia on the fringe in the years leading up to his wife's death, then he went full-tilt—bailed on the real world and moved up to their camp. He'd easily disappear there. They have nearly three hundred members on a thousand acres in the middle of nowhere. He couldn't possibly be doing all this on his own, but with a militia behind him, it makes sense. He's got help."

Down below, the SiriusXM building came into view. The surrounding streets were still complete gridlock with various first responders moving through the stalled vehicles on foot. Several tow trucks were attempting to clear paths, but they had very little room to maneuver.

"What's going on at Grand Central and Penn Station?" Cole asked.

"Nothing found yet, but it could take days to search everything."

The helicopter banked past the large air conditioners to the helipad on the west side of the roof, hovered for a moment, then gently touched down.

"I'm here," Cole said to Tresler. "Call me if you get anything else."

He disconnected, then fired off a text to Jordan Briggs: *He's in your building! Tell FBI to call me! I'm on roof – coming down!*

He scrambled out of the helicopter. Hunched low and shielding his face from the wind and dust, he made his way over to the elevator and pressed the call button.

Nothing happened.

He pressed it again. It didn't even light up.

He needed the key. Must be. The man who brought him up here had used a key to access the roof. It made sense he'd need one to get back inside the building.

He dialed Jordan again.

Nothing.

He ran back to the helicopter. The pilot had shut down the motor and the rotors were slowing down, the noise subsiding. He saw Cole approach and opened his door. "I can start it back up if you—"

Cole cut him off. "Can you get me to the ground level?"

The pilot shook his head. "Not in this neighborhood. The closest place we could set down would be Bryant Park. That's about seven or eight blocks away. Even that would be sketchy—the FAA is grounding all choppers in the city. My dispatch texted me and said I've got fifteen minutes to return or I need to stay put. I'm on Ms. Briggs's dime, so I figured best to wait here."

Cole could run it, but he was hesitant to have the helicopter wait in another park. People everywhere were attempting to get out of the city, and with the roads and trains cut off, anxiety was beginning to set in. On the morning of 9/11, they had multiple stolen vehicles and carjackings. Several boats were stolen. A helicopter with a pilot out in the open was too tempting of a target.

A text message came in from Jordan: *FBI coming up to let you in.*

Cole told the pilot and shot back across the roof to the elevator.

The door slid open a moment later, and a man in his mid-thirties reached out and held it still. He had a closely cropped beard, black hair, and gray eyes. His FBI windbreaker was open, and Cole could see the butt of his gun. It looked like a .44 Magnum. "We've had a hell of a time trying to get you guys on the phone," Cole told him.

The agent only stared at him for a moment, his eyes studying Cole's empty belt, looking at his ankles for a secondary weapon. Finally he said, "Are you armed?"

Cole pulled up his pant-leg. "Kel-Tec .380."

"Where's your primary?"

Cole realized he'd left the bag with his service weapon and uniform back at the Bonfigleo crime scene with one of the patrol officers. He had no doubt it would find its way back to him, but he'd hear about it from Lieutenant Gaff before this was all over. "I left it with my partner."

"Where's your partner?"

The elevator door started to close, the agent tightened his grip on it, and it slid back open. He turned his gaze on the large HVAC units toward the helicopter, as if he could see through them.

"He's at another crime scene."

"So just your pilot up here? He staying with the chopper?"

The agent had a thick Boston accent. Chopper came out as *choppa*.

Cole stepped past him into the elevator. "Yeah. Listen, I'm not sure if this has gotten to you yet, but we traced Bernie's last call. He's either somewhere in this building or redirecting his calls to make it seem that way."

The agent released the door and pressed the button for the 50th floor. "We're aware. We had this building buttoned up pretty tight before that intel came in. We've got people conducting a floor by floor." *Flaw by flaw.*

"That's the wrong floor," Cole told him. "I need to get to 43. Jordan Briggs's offices."

"We're staging on fifty. It's vacant. You'll need to debrief with my superior before you can go down there."

"I don't have time for that right now. I need to talk to Briggs." Cole reached forward and pressed the button for forty-three.

The elevator wasn't moving, and the agent realized he needed the key. He fished it out of his pocket, put it in the lock and twisted, then hit the button for 50 again.

Cole hit 43, and this time both buttons lit up.

The agent was sweating, and Cole noticed his hand was resting on the butt of the .44 Magnum on his belt. Cole fought the urge to step back. Something was wrong. Very wrong.

"I didn't know the bureau let you carry those."

When the agent looked down at his gun, his grip tightened, his finger twitched on the leather strap.

Cole rushed him. He hit him in the gut with his shoulder with as much momentum as he could muster in the confined space. They both slammed into the wall, and Cole followed through with an uppercut, catching the bottom of the man's jaw. The agent's teeth came together with a loud crunch, and his eyes rolled up into his head. Not completely unconscious but stunned, he started to slide down the wall to the floor, and Cole grabbed him under the shoulders, got behind him, and yanked the Magnum from the holster. He managed to get the barrel under the man's chin just as the elevator doors opened on the fiftieth floor.

Five people were standing there in the hallway, all of them with various weapons drawn and pointed at the elevator—waiting—ready to fire. Three in matching FBI windbreakers, two in street clothes.

Cole tightened his arm around the semiconscious man, hefting him up as a makeshift shield, the barrel of the Magnum under his chin holding up his head.

Nobody said anything.

The elevator door timed out, slowly slid closed, but not before

Cole spotted at least three bodies on the floor in that hallway behind the people who had been waiting for him.

46

Cole

Not FBI.

Cole was fairly certain FBI agents weren't allowed to have full beards. He vaguely remembered several agents complaining about the bureau's grooming policy while on a joint task force several years back. He was also pretty sure an agent wouldn't carry a .44 Magnum for the same reasons NYPD officers wouldn't. They were far too heavy to comfortably carry, and the rounds were too powerful. Standard issue for the Bureau was a Glock, either a Glock 17, Glock 19, or Glock 26, and he imagined additional weapons might be allowed if approved, but it was doubtful anyone would carry a .44 Magnum.

Those points aside, he knew for damn sure male agents weren't allowed to wear earrings on duty, and this man had a diamond stud in his left lobe.

Cole dropped the man to the floor of the elevator, then quickly reached up and pressed the button for the forty-fourth floor. He didn't know what waited for him on Briggs's floor. Then he realized whoever that was on the fiftieth floor was probably watching to see where he stopped, so he hit several more buttons at random. The doors opened next on forty-eight. A sign read DEMARCO REALTY, and all the lights were off. No doubt deserted early this morning, or more likely, employees never made it in.

Cole quickly scrambled out, pulling the man out with him. He almost forgot the elevator key and reached back in for it as the doors were sliding shut.

A quick search of the man's pockets revealed only a roll of breath mints, lighter, pack of cigarettes, and a switchblade. No wallet. No identification. No phone. He didn't have any other weapons. Cole used the knife to cut the cord from a floor lamp near the receptionist desk and bound the man's hands and legs. With the lighter, he melted the plastic so it would need to be cut away. Then he dragged him around the corner into an empty office.

He pulled out his phone to call Tresler but had no signal.

He tried the phone on the desk and got no dial tone.

There was a computer on the desk, and although it was on, when he opened an Internet browser he received an error message: offline.

On the ground at his feet, the semiconscious man was mumbling.

Cole slapped him hard on the side of the face.

His eyes opened into slits, then rolled up and closed again.

Cole hit him a second time, harder. "Who the hell are you?"

His head swiveled toward Cole, slow and lazy, then his body tensed when he realized he couldn't move. He pulled at his arms and legs, but the cord held. He glared up at Cole and licked a cut on his lip. "You're so fuckin' dead."

"Who were those people on 50?"

This time, the man only grinned. There was blood between his teeth.

"Is Bernie on 50?"

That brought on a chuckle. "You'd be lucky to meet Bernie. Someone will cap you long before that."

The accent was all wrong. This guy definitely wasn't Bernie.

"You're on borrowed time, PD."

Cole opened the switchblade and pressed the tip against the man's neck. *"Who are you people?"*

He pursed his lips, said nothing.

Cole slid the blade down and cut him. Not deep enough to kill him but enough to draw blood.

The man didn't make a sound.

Around the corner in the lobby, the elevator dinged.

"Dead man walking," the man said with a grin.

Cole hit him in the temple with the butt of the Magnum and quickly darted down the hallway as the elevator opened behind him. He heard several people shuffle out.

47

Jordan

The studio door clicked shut and locked behind her as Jordan stepped back inside.

Billy was already back up in his booth. He mouthed *thirty seconds* to her through the glass.

On the couch, Senator Moretti frowned at the screen of his phone. "What's going on out there? My call dropped, and now I've got no service."

Jordan got behind her desk and slipped on her headphones. "FBI cut cell service in the building."

Billy said, "Bernie's call *didn't* drop, so he must be on a hard line. Keep him talking. The feds said they'd tell me as soon as they know what floor he's on. We're back live in twenty."

It took a moment for this to register with the senator. When it did, the color drained from his face. "He's in the building?"

Jordan nodded at him quickly while looking at her second monitor:

Line 1 – Bernie
Line 2 – Bernie
Line 3 – Bernie
Line 4 – Bernie

Line 5 – Bernie

"Why aren't they evacuating us?" the senator asked, getting to his feet.

Jordan tried not to look up at the cameras. Not only was Bernie probably watching them, he could most likely hear them too. "They've got an armored van coming in with an escort," she lied. "They said they'll take us all out at ground level as soon as it gets here. We need to sit tight."

The senator frowned. "I thought it was complete gridlock out there?"

"Ten seconds, Jordie," Billy said.

"We can't just sit here."

Jordan said, "He's not going to blow up the building if he's in it. This might be the safest place in the city."

"If he's here, he's coming for you. You get that, right?"

"Will you stop talking, please?"

The senator stood and went to the door but found it locked. "Buzz me out," he ordered Billy.

Billy reached across his control board and hit the button.

Senator Moretti pulled on the door, but it was still locked. He glared up at Billy. "Quit screwing around."

Billy pressed the button again.

The door remained locked.

Agent Varney appeared on the other side of the door, her face inches from the glass.

Billy threw his hands up in frustration, then silently counted down from three.

On Jordan's desk, the red ON THE AIR indicator lit up. She drew in a deep breath and pictured Charlotte's face. In minutes, she'd be in a helicopter on her way to the Hamptons. All of this would be over soon, and she'd join her.

Bernie would be dead or rotting in a cell.

Good riddance.

She pressed the button for Line 1. "Bernie."

"Hey, Jordan. How are things?"

"Is Nick dead?"

"Is Nick dead," he muttered in a mocking tone. "All business with you. The polite thing to do is thank me or maybe ask me how I'm holding up after such a traumatic morning. Killing someone up close like that, watching the life leave their eyes. That takes a toll on you. You'd think you'd get used to it. I guess some people might, I'm not one of them. Maybe you are? We'll see. I did it for you, though, and I know on some level you appreciate it. You may not be willing to say it out loud, especially in your present company, but I'm sure deep down a part of you is relieved, maybe even feeling a bit giddy."

"I don't do giddy."

Jordan's first monitor was still running the local news feed with the split image of the two train stations. They were interviewing someone from the bomb squad. According to the closed captioning, nothing had been found yet.

Bernie said, "I'd like to get clarification on the bounty you put on my head. How exactly do you plan to pay for that? Aren't you broke? That's the word on the street. I heard Nick cleaned out the coffers on the way out your door. It's still flattering, though. Five million dollars is a lot of money to put up, even if you can't follow through. I appreciate you thinking of me either way. You've been in my thoughts for a long time, so it's nice to know I've got a place in your heart too."

On the other side of the window in the door, Agent Varney still stood looking in. Several times, she turned and spoke to others, but her gaze always returned to Jordan. That same calm, blank smirk.

"How's the senator holding up?"

Jordan looked over at him. He'd given up on the door and settled back into the couch. His suit jacket was off, and the pits of his shirt were dark with sweat.

"Oh, he's a pillar of strength."

"Did he tell you he has a gun?"

At the mention of this, Senator Moretti's eyes dropped away, and he folded his arms over his chest. He cleared his throat but said nothing. To Jordan, he looked like a child caught in some lie.

"It's nothing fancy, just a small snub nose .38. He keeps it in a concealed pancake holster tucked in at the small of his back. If he's shuffling around on the couch there, that's probably why. Personally, I prefer an ankle holster for those, but who am I to tell a U.S. senator how to handle his business?"

"I'm not sure I blame the guy. There are a lot of crazy people out there."

Bernie let out a soft laugh. "I'm honestly surprised you don't carry one. High-profile pretty woman like you in the city. I checked, though, nothing licensed, nothing registered with you, Nick, or most of your staff."

"Most of my staff?"

"Jules Goldblatt," Bernie replied. "He has a concealed carry permit for a SIG Sauer. We found it in a hidden compartment in his top left desk drawer. Fully loaded with one in the chamber. Your receptionist, Sarah, she had a switchblade in her purse. No permit for that. That could get her in a lot of trouble—New York City has some of the strictest weapons laws in the country. When this is all over, you may want to consider having a staff meeting to go over your stance on weapons at the workplace. I'd hate to see anyone get in trouble."

BILLY: *'We' found it?*

Jordan quickly typed messages to both Sarah and Goldblatt. Neither responded.

"Anyway, I felt it was important you knew about the senator's gun," Bernie said. "When I tell you this next part."

BILLY: *Who the fuck is we?!?*

Varney glared in from the other side of the window, her eyes fixed on Jordan. Jordan felt a knot grow in the pit of her stomach.

Bernie went on, "I made some new friends after Kourtney died, when I lost her and my baby girl. Well, not new friends—people I'd known for a while, but they tended to keep to themselves in those early years. It wasn't until after Kourtney's death that they welcomed me in, consoled me, and did their best to help me recover. Part of me had shut down, closed off—locked up, really— but they managed to open my eyes to another part of me. They helped me find purpose and love after you took those things away from me. If not for them, I'd probably be dead. When someone like you takes away everything from someone like me, the decision to end your own life goes from some distant near-impossible thing to something that feels right, feels logical, feels like the only cure for the heartache. These people, my new friends, they understood that. They talked me down, kept me off that ledge. Many of them suffered losses of their own. The woman you know as Agent Allison Varney, her husband was killed by a mugger on the subway heading out of midtown a few years back, left her alone to raise three boys. And one of the guys with her, I think he told you his name was Fred Schulman, he was taking his boy to soccer practice when some highway-hero let his rage get the best of him and cut them off, sent them into the guardrail. His eight-year-old was in a car seat, but that was no match for the steel that sliced through the side of their Toyota. If you talk to the people I have in your office today, the people I have *throughout your building today*, you'll find they all lost someone close and in every one of their cases the law, the lawyers, the system did little or nothing to make things right. There are so many broken things in this world, but we depend on that system to hold it all together and that system is broken now too. There are people like the senator there, the ones we expect to fix it, who are only making things worse. Senator Moretti and his ridiculous bill. He wants to take guns out of the hands of my new friends. Under the guise of justice, he wants to take power away from the many and give it to the few.

We, as Americans, can't let that happen. My friends came to the city today to not only help me find justice for my wife and child but to prove a point—the system cannot protect anyone. The system is an illusion. The system is dead. It's been killed by those in office."

Charlotte.

These people had Charlotte.

The image of her daughter walking down the hallway to the freight elevator with men and women dressed as FBI agents came rushing back.

How could she be so stupid?

She hadn't asked to see a single ID.

A couple windbreakers, visible guns, and carefully chosen words…*how could she be so stupid?*

Jordan tried to speak and found that she couldn't. She couldn't catch her breath. It was as if every breath she sucked in held little or no oxygen and she was drowning. She fumbled with the mute button on her microphone so it wouldn't pick up the sound. She wouldn't give Bernie the satisfaction of hearing it.

The senator was staring at her.

Billy too.

She wanted to turn away but had no place to go.

Bernie went on, "There's something I need to say right now, because if I don't, I think this situation may escalate far faster than necessary, and we wouldn't want that. This is for all the members of law enforcement listening—my people have killed your people. Anyone you had in this building is now dead. There is nothing you can do to help them, so it's best you don't try. If you do, if you attempt to enter this building, shut off the power, hinder me in any way, I'll detonate the bombs you have been unable to find at Penn Station and Grand Central. If that doesn't deter you, I'll detonate others. And *I have* others, including some in this very building. We've had ten years to prepare for today. We've infiltrated your systems, your ranks. Don't for a second believe you can get in front of this—if you try, many more people will die today. As it stands, only one more needs to die. Who that person is, Jordan, will be left up to you and the people in your studio. *Your final choice.* Do you remember what I asked you to do when Officer Cole entered your studio earlier today?"

Jordan's microphone was still on mute. She wouldn't have been able to answer him even if she wanted to.

Bernie didn't give her the chance to respond before speaking again. "It's only been a few hours, but so much has happened I understand if you forgot, so I'll remind you. I told you you were going to put a bullet in the senator's head. I told you when I asked you to pick up a gun again, you wouldn't hesitate to do exactly that. So here is your final choice, the last thing you need to do to make things right today. You need to shoot the senator. If you don't, my people will kill your daughter."

Jordan tried not to, but she found herself looking at the senator anyway, and he was looking back at her, his arms still folded over his chest but clenched tight now, his face this awful shade of pale. Sweat beaded on his forehead; he made no effort to wipe it away. He didn't move at all.

"Of course," Bernie added, "I suppose the senator may decide to shoot you first. He *does* have the gun. I'll let the two of you work that out amongst yourselves. You've got one hour to figure things out. If the senator is still breathing at ten-thirty, Charlotte will die."

"You're fucking insane," Jordan managed to spit out, and even though her microphone was still on mute, he managed to hear her.

"Maybe," he replied. "I'm what you made me. Today we settle up."

48

Cole

The first two office doors he tried were both locked, the third—this one on the left side of the hallway just beyond a small break room—was not. Cole slipped inside, quickly closed the door, and locked it.

He heard two voices.

One male, one female.

The male said, "Goddamn Pugliesi. I told you I should have went. Should have shot the cop on the roof and been done with him."

"Bernie's not finished with him," the woman replied. "Wanted him alive. Can't blame that on Pugliesi."

"Well, what the fuck is Bernie thinking? What do we need a cop for?"

"Not my place to second-guess Bernie."

"Maybe somebody should. He's on the air right now telling the world we're here. No turning back now, and he hasn't explained how we're all going to get out of here."

"He's got a plan."

The man smirked. "I'm not so sure about that. I don't think he cares if he dies today. If he doesn't expect to walk out of here, do you think he gives a shit if the rest of us do?"

"Just hurry up and check this floor," she told him. "You take the left, I'll take the right."

"He'll go to 43."

"Well, he's not there now. Varney said nobody was in the elevator."

"Should have capped him on the roof," the man repeated. "When we go back up, we need to—"

Both voices dropped off.

Cole pressed against the wall and tightened his grip on the Magnum, his finger on the trigger guard.

They were still speaking, but low, muffled.

They found the other one.

Pugliesi.

Cole made a mental note of the name.

Windows in the wall separated the office from the hallway, but they were covered in white blinds, all closed. Without knowing where those people were, Cole couldn't risk looking out, and without looking out, he couldn't determine where they were.

He crossed the office to the desk and tried the phone.

Dead.

The office had no exterior window. No other door. No other way out.

His radio was in the bag he'd left with Tresler.

A loud bang.

They'd kicked open one of the locked office doors.

Cole got down behind the desk and faced toward the knee well. He held the Magnum with both hands.

From the hallway, the man said, "Hey, Detective Hundley, if you come out, we won't hurt you. You got my word. We're just here to take you up to see Bernie, that's all. No reason for anyone to get hurt. You probably heard us talking, right? He wants you alive. That was the truth. We're on your side here. I know it may not seem like that, but we are. Give Bernie a chance to explain things to you, you'll get it. You'll understand."

Another bang as they kicked open the second door.

Silence again as they searched the room.

"Do you have a gun, Cole?"

This came from the woman.

She sounded close. Back out in the hallway.

"I imagine you do. Thanks for not using it to kill our friend. I get why you cut him. Under the circumstances, I would have probably done the same, but you didn't kill him and that's good for you. It says a lot about the kind of person you are. You're honestly not that different from us. I know that may seem completely off-base, but that's why you need to talk to Bernie. I guarantee, what you think this is…what you think we're doing here…you're wrong. We stand for the same things you do. He'll tell you. I think you'll find a lot of your coworkers are on board with us too. Do you think we could have pulled all this off today without help? Your partner, Garrett Tresler…your Lieutenant…Gaff, I think his name is…they're all working with us. Not just them, hundreds more, all levels. It's best you just come with us, Detective, before you do something rash. Something you can't take back. Hear Bernie out and better understand your place in all this, then decide which side you fall on."

Cole heard someone twist the knob on his door.

Quietly.

Just enough to determine whether or not it was locked.

The next several seconds ticked by in a long silence.

They kicked the door hard enough to crack the frame. The door flipped open and slammed against the wall.

Cole pressed the barrel of the Magnum against the wood knee well of the desk and pulled the trigger.

The report was deafening.

His ears filled with a high-pitched shrill ring.

He didn't mean to close his eyes, but they shut anyway, and when he opened them most of the knee well was gone. Through the gaping hole, he could see the open office door. Nobody stood there. The woman was on the ground, sitting up, her eyes fixed on her missing left leg—the blast had severed the limb below her knee, leaving a ragged stump in a pool of blood. Her face was white, and she stared in disbelief. With a shaky hand, she reached down and felt the empty space where her ankle should have been. The pain came a moment later. Cole saw it hit about the same time she spotted him.

Her lips moved, but the words were lost to the ringing in Cole's ears and she fell back, unconscious.

At first, Cole didn't see the other man. He only saw the man's shadow on the opposite wall of the hallway. The shadow dropped low and to the left of the doorway. Cole fired the Magnum two more times in that general direction—the glass wall shattered, and the blinds blew out. The glass across the hall vanished too. The outer window went with it, and a gush of cool air rushed inside.

The man fired back—Cole saw the three quick muzzle flashes, barely heard the reports, and forced himself to move. He crawled out from beneath the desk, carefully avoided the slippery blood on the floor, and dove through the open doorway to the office across the hall, firing again in the direction the shadow had moved.

The man had taken cover behind a copy machine, and the bullet from the Magnum hit the wall directly above him, destroying the interior windows and metal frame, sending shards of glass spraying back and down.

Even before the last of it fell, an arm reached out from around the copy machine, holding a semiautomatic, and fired three more shots blindly. Cole fired back once—the corner of the copy machine vanished. The hand that had been holding the gun disappeared in a mist of red and bone as the man bounced back against what was left of the wall behind him screaming.

Cole shot him again. Like the blast from a cannon, the Magnum blew open his chest and took out the rest of the wall. The man went still.

Cole tossed the empty Magnum aside, dropped to the ground and sucked in a breath. He tugged the .380 from his ankle holster and looked back down the hallway toward the empty office where he'd left the first man bound. He was no longer on the ground.

Cole caught a glimpse of the elevator doors sliding shut and watched the digital numbers above tick away as the car rose back to the fiftieth floor and stopped.

49

Jordan

Jordan's eyes were locked on the senator's, and his wide eyes were fixed on her. His arms, still wrapped around his chest, inched slightly as he slowly tried to unfurl them.

"Don't you dare," she told him.

This only made him move faster.

Jordan jumped up, threw off her headphones, and rounded her desk, but not before he managed to tug the gun out from the holster at his back and point it at her. She froze midstep and stared at the barrel, quivering in his sweaty hand.

"Don't make me!" Senator Moretti said. "Just get back. Get back in your seat. Behind your desk."

In the booth behind them both, Billy was on his feet, but there was nothing he could do. He didn't have a door into the studio— he'd have to exit into the hallway and come around to the studio door where Varney still stood, watching them all intently.

Billy raised both his hands, palms forward, and then slowly motioned for her to do as the senator said. He pointed at his chat computer and collapsed into his own chair.

"Alright." Jordan nodded, both to Billy and the senator, and put up both her hands in a similar gesture, then backed up and around her desk again, settled into her chair, and put her headphones back on. She realized Bernie had dropped off the line, but they were still on the air.

> BILLY: *Calm the senator. Get gun later. Disarm him when he's less jumpy. I'm working on an outside line. Keep everyone talking so the police know what's going on. Charlotte will be okay. He's bluffing. He lost a child. No way he'd hurt a child.*

Jordan wasn't so sure about that, and she had even less faith in the senator's ability to not shoot everyone in order to protect himself. What she did know is she had no other options right now.

Still pointing the gun at her, Senator Moretti turned quickly to get a look at Billy, then swiveled in the opposite direction to get a look at the studio door and Varney on the other side. "Just…nobody move."

Jordan said, "The way you're shaking, you're going to shoot me on accident. Can you point that thing at the floor?"

He seemed to consider this, then shook his head. "I don't trust you. Put both your hands on top of your desk, palms down."

Jordan did as he asked. "Okay."

"Do you have any weapons in that desk? Anywhere in this studio?"

This time, Jordan didn't respond. She only stared at him.

"Goddammit, Jordan, don't make me ask again!" His face flushed red, his grip tightened on the gun.

"Put the gun down."

"You're not in charge—"

"Okay, then shoot me if you're going to shoot me."

"You would," he replied. "If you had the gun, you'd shoot me in a second."

"I guess we're all lucky it's in your capable hands then, huh?"

"Do you have any weapons?" he asked again.

"No."

Jordan looked up at Billy. Her eyes must have lingered there a little too long, because Senator Moretti swiveled back around. "What about you? Do you have anything in that booth?"

Billy shook his head.

"See," Jordan said, "just you. You're clearly in control. Nobody is going to try and take the gun away from you. Nobody is shooting anybody. Bernie wants us to fight, so we're not going to do that." She nodded up at the LED counter on the wall—nearly fourteen million people listening. "You came here for an audience, you've got one. You're going to show your constituents what kind of man you really are, because they're listening."

The senator must have forgotten they were broadcasting, because he looked up at the board, then at one of the ON THE AIR signs lit up on the wall. He swallowed, then lowered the gun to his lap. He kept his finger on the trigger, though.

Jordan silently mouthed the word *good*.

Reaching forward, she unmuted her microphone. "Bernie, I know you're listening. I need to know my daughter is okay. I'm sure she's frightened. You've got to let me speak to her."

As she said this, a confused look washed across Billy's face. He was looking down at his board. He glanced at her and typed another message:

BILLY: *Mute your microphone and speak again*

Jordan clicked the button again, her eyes on Billy. "Bernie, are you listening?"

BILLY: *Shit. You're broadcasting whether your mic is on or off. Not just at your desk but out on the floor. He must have wired the studio for sound somehow when he rigged whatever he's using to watch us.*

Jordan typed back: *He's probably monitoring this chat network too.*

Billy grabbed a notepad, scribbled a message with a black marker, and pressed it against the glass of his booth:

Go old school with paper?

He must have realized that wouldn't work either before Jordan even had a chance to respond. He tossed the notepad aside. If he's watching them, he'd see whatever they wrote. Without knowing exactly how he was watching and listening, there was no way to hide from him.

The news broadcast was still playing on Jordan's other monitor, but rather than video from the two train stations, there was a camera trained on the front entrance of her building now. It slowly panned up to the top, then back down again, focusing on a reporter. Jordan didn't recognize her. The caption read: TERRORISTS SEIZE SIRIUSXM BUILDING—SENATOR HOSTAGE—THREATENS TO KILL FAMED TALK-SHOW HOST'S DAUGHTER.

Below the headline was a timer counting down from one hour. Jordan couldn't look at that.

She minimized the window and opened a browser, then realized she was no longer connected to the Internet. Bernie had cut that, too. The building's internal network still seemed to be live, only outside access was down.

She reached across her desk and picked up the wireless headphones she'd worn up from the lobby at the start of the show. The indicator on the side showed a full wireless signal and a battery at 78 percent. Billy was watching her intently, a curious look on his face.

BILLY: *What are you thinking?*

Jordan looked at him, sitting calmly in his booth, watching her and the senator. Her tech guru. Her producer and partner for so many years. She pulled her microphone closer. "I'll tell you what I'm thinking, Billy. I'm wondering why Bernie hasn't threatened you. You were in the car with Marisa Chapman that day. You pushed her harder than any of us. Why hasn't Bernie made any kind of move against you?"

50

Cole

Cole had no idea how much time he had, so he moved fast.

He didn't find any identification on either body. Neither had a phone or any kind of radio. He knew these people had to be staying in touch somehow, but he didn't know how. Both were carrying guns, 9mms. Glock nineteens. He put his .380 back in his ankle holster, took the dead woman's gun, and two spare clips he found on the man.

He ran back to the office lobby, pressed the upper call button on the elevator to hopefully buy a little time, then bolted down the hall to the emergency stairs before either car had a chance to arrive. With the Glock at the ready, he eased open the metal door as quietly as he could. The landing was deserted, but he heard voices and footsteps descending from above, most likely from fifty only two floors up. Cole quickly went in the opposite direction, down two flights, and pushed through the door onto the 47th floor.

Some kind of financial firm—Murdock and Brenville Investments.

The firm took up the entire floor. The main space was wide open, some kind of bullpen with dozens of desks set up facing each other in pairs. There were cubicles along the outer edge and individual offices lining the outside walls to take advantage of the windows.

The floor had been evacuated. He wouldn't be surprised if they cleared the entire building.

By the looks of things, people had been rushed out. As Cole ran through the office, he spotted a half-eaten sandwich on one desk, cups of coffee on others. Only a few employees had bothered to shut down their computers before leaving; most were still running, although some had defaulted to password screens. He tried several machines, but none seemed to have access to the Internet. E-mails failed and browser windows only displayed error messages. Muted television monitors on the walls played various news channels. Half of them were running stories about this building, the other half were tuned to financial networks and stock market reports—apparently down heavy at the open.

Cole pulled open random desk drawers and rifled through the contents—staples, pens, paper clips, cough drops, alcohol stashes, snacks, company memos stuffed away and forgotten—nothing useful.

He stood in the middle of the room surrounded by tan berber carpet and fake rosewood trim.

His left sleeve was stained with somebody else's blood.

Christ, he just killed two people.

He was breathing too hard.

Needed to calm down.

Reacting rather than acting.

They had said Tresler, Lieutenant Gaff, and others were involved.

That had to be bullshit.

How did they even know those names?

Cole remembered how the cab driver's phone had somehow accessed Tresler's cell and downloaded data. The computer at the Bonfigleo crime scene had been used to access Cole's employee file, credit report, utility bills... Cole knew nothing about this group, the Sentinels, but they clearly had someone with seasoned tech skills. His own phone was probably compromised.

They'd thrown the names out there to rattle him. That had to be it. Names they'd picked up monitoring the investigation or stole from his phone.

Or not. Could it be true?

New York had its share of crooked cops, but Tresler and Gaff? Tresler was his partner. Had been so for years. Had he missed it?

He needed to think.

Jordan was four floors below him. Bernie was three above. Bernie had either killed or incapacitated the real FBI agents and replaced them with his own people, most likely when they first arrived. Before they had a chance to properly deploy. He took the time to evacuate most of the building's occupants.

Smart?

Maybe.

Probably.

Hostages created unknowns. Too many were a problem.

The headline on one of the news channels read: TERRORISTS SEIZE SIRIUSXM BUILDING—SENATOR HOSTAGE— THREATENS TO KILL FAMED TALK-SHOW HOST'S DAUGHTER.

Cole couldn't read the closed-captioning from where he stood, but he was able to make out a countdown timer below the headline, currently at fifty-five minutes and ticking down.

What the hell was happening? Did Bernie have Charlotte?

Bernie evacuated most of the building because he had who he needed. Anybody else would just get in the way.

Cole needed to get in the way.

He took out his phone and tried the app he'd been using to listen to Briggs's show but got an error message. With the cellular network blocked, he had no signal.

Maybe at a window?

Most of the outer office doors were closed. Several had been left open. He ran to the largest office, twice the size of the others, in the northeast corner. A nameplate on the door said the office belonged to someone called Chunhua Mei, Vice President Capital Development.

The office wasn't locked, and although there were blinds on the outside windows, none were drawn.

At the glass, Cole looked down.

Traffic remained at a complete standstill, although several emergency vehicles had managed to get through. He spotted a firetruck, several ambulances, three patrol cars. They looked like toys from this height. They'd taped off the front of the building, the immediate sidewalk was clear. Several news trucks were down there. Dozens of people milled about the various stalled vehicles. Thin wisps of smoke continued to trail up from the destroyed taxi cabs, which had yet to be removed.

He held up his phone and looked at the screen again.

Still no signal.

He clicked through his settings and realized the building's WiFi network was still active, but when he attempted to join, he was prompted for a password he did not have.

Cole went to the desk and tried that phone.

Dead.

Next to a large Apple monitor was a framed photo of an Asian woman holding a girl of maybe two or three. Both were smiling. There was nothing else on the desk but a keyboard and mouse.

He tugged open one of the drawers. Unlike the desks out on the main floor, the contents here were sparse. He did find a lighter, some paperclips, and a letter opener—he shoved it all in his pocket.

He looked under the keyboard, hoping for the building's WiFi password on a Post-it note, but found nothing there, either.

When the desk phone rang, a harsh sound cutting through the otherwise silent office, Cole's heart threatened to jump up into his throat. He found himself staring down at it, at the blinking green light next to the second line.

Apparently, whoever turned them off could also turn them back on.

Cole tightened his grip on the 9mm, picked up the receiver, and brought it to his ear.

"You didn't have to kill them."

Bernie's voice was calm, eerily so. As if he'd placed the call while preparing dinner or watching his favorite television program.

"I didn't want to," Cole told him.

"Come up to 50. Let me explain what's happening to you, your role in things, before anyone else gets hurt."

"My *role* in things?"

"I knew you'd trace my call back at my old apartment. I stayed on the line more than long enough for a trace. I drew you here. I allowed you back into the building. You're standing in that office right now, still alive, because that's precisely where I want you to be. If I didn't, I could easily send someone down there to kill you, but I haven't, because you have a part to play today, the *role* I've prepared for you."

For the first time, Cole looked up at the ceiling, and while there were no cameras in this particular office, there was one right outside the door—this round, black bubble looking down at him. He spotted at least half a dozen others just like it spread out around the office space.

"Those aren't the only cameras, Detective. This building is filled with them, and my people added more of our own. The hallways, the elevators, the stairwells. You haven't been alone since you left the helicopter. Frankly, I've been following you all morning. People will know your name after today, I can promise you that. Your memory will live on long after you're gone."

If this phone was live, were the others in the office? Cole couldn't imagine Bernie had the ability to single out one phone on a system without activating the others.

Lifting the phone base from the desk, he examined the cord. It was long, maybe long enough to reach the desk just outside this office's door. He quickly shuffled in that direction. "Is this how you want your wife to be remembered? Is this how Kourtney would want to be remembered?"

"Don't say her name, Detective, not like that. You haven't earned the right to speak her name."

"If she saw what you did today, what you're currently doing, all the people you've hurt, she'd be disgusted with you. Are you too far gone to see that?"

Cole had to set the phone base down on the floor, but with the cord on the handset, he just made it to the closest desk. He picked up the second receiver, heard a dial tone, and quickly dialed Tresler's cell. His partner answered on the second ring. "Detective Tresler. Who is this?"

Into the first receiver, but loud enough for Tresler to hear, Cole said, "If you know I'm on 47, Bernie, why don't you come down here from 50? Just you."

"I'm a little busy."

"How many people do you have here? You don't seem like the kind of person who plays well with others."

"The Sentinels are a means to an end, Detective. I couldn't do what I needed to do today without them, and they needed me for other reasons." Bernie paused for a second, then said, "If it makes things easier for Detective Tresler, I could provide him with a list of the people I have here and their exact locations within the building. It's probably tough for him to hear me like that. Maybe you should put me on speakerphone?"

Cole looked up at the camera above him. He couldn't see the lens behind the tinted glass, but he could feel Bernie watching him.

"Nothing has or will take place in this building without my knowledge, Detective. Get those thoughts out of your head. I've already told NYPD and all the other members of law enforcement what I'll do if they try anything at all. I like to think they believe me at this point, but who knows, time will tell. You, though, you're along for the ride, so stop making waves. Come up to 50. If anything, we can talk about Gracie."

The line went dead, and Cole realized Tresler had dropped off, too. All the phones were dead again.

51

Jordan

"You can't be serious?" Billy replied. "You think I'm working with this guy?"

Jordan shrugged. "I don't know what to think right now."

"Well, I'm not."

"Okay."

"You don't sound very convinced."

Again, Jordan shrugged. Her eyes drifted back to the ceiling. To the cameras. One uncovered, the others with trash bags still over them. She knew the permanent studio cameras were all hardwired. They had to be to ensure the best quality signal for broadcasts, but aside from the camera focused on the senator and the one on her, all the others were covered—even if Bernie managed to tap into the feed, they'd be useless. Yet, he could still see them. He could still hear them, in a room that was otherwise soundproof and cut off from all others.

Her eyes fell back to the wireless headset on her desk, the signal strength indicator reading full.

"He's using WiFi, he must be," she said softly.

Billy was angry, only half-heard her. He frowned through the window. "What?"

"Think about it. If he managed to get his own cameras and

microphones in here, or someplace else in the building, for that matter, he wouldn't have had time to hardwire anything. If he tried to run wires, someone would have noticed. Whatever he's using must be running on WiFi." She reached for her phone and remembered that Varney still had it. "Check your phone. Do you see any WiFi networks active in here right now other than the building?"

Although he was still holding the gun, the senator took his phone out with his free hand and clicked through several screens. "I see two—SiriusXM and one called 1221."

"1221 is the building. It's the one I usually use because they have repeaters everywhere. The SiriusXM WiFi only covers this floor and the one above. It's not as reliable."

Billy said, "At the risk of getting technical, it's possible to have a hidden WiFi signal. If he's using WiFi, we may not be able to see it."

"How would that work?"

"Most networks broadcast their name, that's called an SSID. That's what you see on your phone when you try to connect. But it's possible to turn that broadcast off. The network is still there, just not visible, so you'd need to know the name in order to connect to it. Otherwise, it works the same."

"Can the building's repeaters carry more than one signal? The one we see and a hidden one?"

It was Billy's turn to shrug. "I don't know."

"He'd be using the repeaters, though, right? In a building this size, he couldn't set up his own wireless network. It wouldn't get more than a floor or two. He'd have the same problem we do with the office WiFi—too much metal, too much interference."

"Why does any of that even matter?" Senator Moretti nodded up at the lit sign on the wall. "We're live on the air. Everyone can hear us."

As he spoke the words, he seemed to understand. Everyone could hear them no matter what, but if they managed to cut the WiFi signal, Bernie would no longer be able to watch them.

Jordan wasn't sure yet how exactly that would help them, but she was fairly certain it could, if they came up with some kind of plan.

Taking several sheets of paper from her desk and a roll of tape, she got up and went over to the window in the studio door. Varney was still there, staring in. She hadn't moved since they'd been locked in. No doubt on some kind of sentry duty.

Jordan began taping the paper over the glass.

Varney's eyes remained on her until the last opening was sealed up.

In his booth, Billy did the same with his window.

Jordan reached up to the camera above the senator and yanked all the wires out of the back.

Moretti's grip on the gun tightened as she moved around near him, but he didn't say anything.

She moved around the room and hit the other cameras, too. Billy got the two in his booth. They left the plastic over the lenses for good measure.

When Jordan settled back in her chair, she said into her microphone, "Bernie, I need to know my daughter is okay. Let me talk to her."

Line 1 – Error
Line 2 – Error
Line 3 – Error
Line 4 – Error
Line 5 – Error

She stared at the monitor for nearly thirty seconds, waiting for Charlotte's name to appear, but nothing changed. When she tried to dial out, she got no dial tone. None of the office extensions worked, either.

"Do you seriously expect us to just sit here as your arbitrary clocks ticks down? How do I know you haven't already killed my daughter? Where did you put all my staff? How do I know they're all okay? If the senator shoots me, then what? What do you plan to do with him? I shoot him, then what? You kill me anyway? I can't speak for the senator, but I'm not a killer."

Jordan wanted to beg.

She wanted to get down on her hands and knees and tell Bernie she would do absolutely anything to get her daughter back, but she also knew that's what he wanted. He wanted to break her, make her fold. She knew the second she did that, the *second* she gave in, this was over.

There was an audible *click* in her headphones, and Jordan's second monitor refreshed:

Line 1 – Aaron
Line 2 – Eilene
Line 3 – Robin
Line 4 – Paula
Line 5 – Ivan

"Billy? Was that you?"

He shook his head.

"What happened?" Senator Moretti asked.

Billy studied one of his monitors a sullen look on his face. "We're receiving incoming calls again. I'm not sure how. Outgoing lines are still down."

"Who typed in their names?"

"Wasn't me. I don't know."

Normally, the phones were answered by her interns. They'd prescreen each call and type the caller's name and a brief description of what they wanted to talk about into the system. Jordan had passed the intern room the last time she sat down with Varney, and it had been empty. She'd been told most of her staff had been sent home and only a handful remained.

If her staff hadn't entered the names, who did?

She reached for a button on her control board. "Robin? This is Jordan Briggs. You're on the air."

"Holy shit, are you serious? I got through?"

"Where are you calling from, Robin?"

"Suzy! I got through! This is Jordan! She's actually on the phone!" the woman shouted to someone else, her voice slightly muffled. Then she was back. "I'm in Tulsa. Tulsa, Oklahoma. You're on the news right now. I can't believe I got through!"

Robin's voice took on an echo, and feedback started to build on the line.

"Robin, can you turn your radio down? We're getting interference."

"It's not my radio—I can hear us on the television—the news—they're live. Suzy, how cool is this?!?"

Jordan hung up on her and pressed line five. "Ivan, you're on the air."

"Ms. Briggs, it's an honor to talk to you."

"I'm absolutely thrilled to finally speak to you, Ivan," Jordan replied mockingly. She simply couldn't help it. It honestly felt good, doing something as ordinary as taking callers helped get her mind off the ticking clock she could no longer see but now felt in that minimized window.

"I'll kill him for you, if you want me to."

"That's awfully nice of you, Ivan."

"All you have to do is get me in the building. I'm right down the street at Rockefeller Center. The police won't let us through."

"Just to be clear, are you going to kill the senator for me, or Bernie?"

"I'll kill them both, if you want me to. There's a bunch of us down here. We won't let that crazy fuck hurt your little girl, and the senator is a scumbag. I voted for Gleason, what good that did me. The only thing worse than an attorney in this world is a politician, and Senator Moretti is an attorney *and* a politician. You pop him, I pop him, I don't think anyone is going to cry."

Jordan hung up on him, too. "Eilene, you're on the air."

"Kill him, Jordan."

On the couch, the senator squirmed. His shirt was soaked in

sweat, and he kept moving the gun from his right hand to his left to wipe his palms.

"Put a bullet in him and be done with it." Eilene had a thick Brooklyn accent and sounded about a hundred years old.

Jordan looked up at the senator. "Even the world's grandmothers hate you."

"They're your goddamn fans, not mine." He stood and went over to the door. He pulled on it and still found it to be locked.

In his booth, Billy mashed the button down several times before shaking his head.

The senator peeled the corner back from one of the sheets of paper Jordan had taped up. Varney wasn't standing there anymore; it was some guy Jordan didn't recognize.

Raising the gun, Senator Moretti pointed the barrel at the man on the other side and pulled the trigger.

52

Cole

Gracie's name coming from Bernie's mouth echoed in Cole's head, lingered, and was finally lost behind the silence of the dead receiver in his hand, and for a moment Cole wasn't sure he had heard her name at all. He stared down at the phone, both phones, and wished it all away because this guy couldn't possibly know her name, he had no right to know her name, yet he clearly did. He'd pulled all that personal information on Cole and left it at the Bonfigleo house, knowing Cole would see it. He probably wanted him to see it because he knew when he finally did say Gracie's name, he knew Cole would have no choice but to know he was serious about whatever he said after that.

Come up to 50. If anything, we can talk about Gracie.

There was no way Cole would go up to 50.

He couldn't stay here, either.

Cole darted back to the stairwell, listened but heard no one, then descended two more floors to 45.

Five floors below Bernie.

Two above Jordan Briggs.

Unlike 48 and 47, this floor was broken up into many smaller offices—eleven, according to the directory on the wall.

With his phone, Cole took a photo of not only that directory but the one below it listing all the other floors of the building, then ducked into the men's restroom where he knew there wouldn't be any cameras.

Unless, of course, Bernie had added one.

He pushed that thought out of his head. He couldn't let paranoia get the better of him.

He needed to talk to someone outside this building.

Tresler.

The real FBI.

Homeland.

Somebody.

He wasn't going to find a working phone in the bathroom.

He checked the walls of each stall, hoping to find the WiFi password written with a Sharpie, but no such luck. Unlike the bathrooms at NYPD, these walls were spotless. There was a janitor's closet in the far corner, but he found nothing in there but various cleaning supplies, overalls, and an old Yankees cap stained with sweat around the rim.

On the opposite side of the bathroom, there was a ventilation duct near the ceiling.

In the movies, the grill popped right off and the hero found convenient tunnels leading from point A to point B and anywhere else they needed to go, this intricate patchwork of highways and byways linking every inch of the skyscraper, which not only provided access but allowed for eavesdropping from one floor to another.

Movies were bullshit.

This grill looked like it was welded in place, and unless he managed to shrink to half his size, there was no way he'd fit in there. They'd find him a week from now, stuck at the shoulders with his ass hanging out. Even if he did fit, ductwork wasn't designed to hold the weight of a grown man—he'd be lucky if got five feet before he crashed down through the ceiling.

He turned back around and looked out over the bathroom.

Think, Cole.

Think.

He went back to the closet.

Reaching for the overalls, he rifled through the pockets, found a pack of gum and a set of keys. The keys were on a ring with a belt clip. None were marked, but he took them anyway.

Tucked in some worn boots under the overalls, he spotted a pair of earbuds. The earbuds were plugged into an old iPod Touch.

Bingo.

The iPod's battery was at 73 percent, and not only was it set up on the building's WiFi, but Cole found the SiriusXM app on the home screen. He loaded it up, found the Jordan Briggs show in the janitor's favorites, and hit play. He only put one earbud in and reduced the volume to as low as he could tolerate—he couldn't risk not hearing someone approach. Briggs's voice filled his ear. She wasn't talking to Bernie but was somehow taking phone calls.

Cole brought up FaceTime and entered Tresler's phone number.

Call Failed – Check Network Connection

Shit.

He tried again and got the same error.

He knew many public WiFi networks blocked phone calls and video transmissions in an effort to limit bandwidth usage. He had no idea if that's what was happening here or if this was related to all the other problems this morning.

He keyed in Jordan's number, expected to get the same error, but instead it rang twice, connected, and the face of an Asian woman with green eyes filled the screen.

At first, she stared at him, then some kind of recognition set in. Her voice dropped low, and she spoke with urgency. "Detective Hundley? Thank God. We've been trying to reach you. I'm Special-Agent-in-Charge Allison Varney, with the FBI. Where are you?"

I'm on 32," he lied. "Where are you?"

"43, guarding the Briggs woman and her daughter. We established a command center on 50. Can you get up there unnoticed?"

Come up to 50. If anything, we can talk about Gracie.

The dead bodies he had seen earlier when the elevator doors opened on 50 flashed back in his mind—no doubt the agents originally dispatched here. She couldn't be FBI. The real FBI agents were dead.

"I need to talk to Jordan Briggs. Why do you have her phone?"

"She's on the air. We know Bernie is in the building—we're trying to force him to call in on a landline so we can pinpoint his exact location. If you report to 50, you'll be debriefed. We could use your help."

Either she hadn't spoken to Bernie recently, or she didn't realize Cole had.

"Put Jordan's daughter on the phone."

"She's sleeping."

Varney's eyes danced nervously off to the side, then came back. "Is there anyone else with you?"

"I've got a SWAT team coming in through access tunnels in the basement," Cole lied again. "They're spreading out and working their way up from the lower floors."

"You need to get up to 50 before someone spots you. They have people all over this building, and some of them are dressed like us."

Looking down at the cleaning supplies, Cole had an idea. "I'm heading up there now."

53

Jordan

Although the walls of the studio were covered in sound-dampening foam, the shot from the senator's gun was horribly loud. Jordan jumped in her chair, and Billy nearly fell out of his, not because of the explosive noise, but because the bullet ricocheted off the metal door and cracked through the top corner of his booth's window and embedded in the ceiling. His window didn't shatter, not completely, but the bullet left a hole about a half-inch in diameter less than a foot from his head and a large spiderweb of cracks through the rest of the glass.

"Holy fuck!" he cried out, ducking down. "What the hell are you doing?"

The senator's eyes jumped from the smoking gun in his hand to the dent in the door, the man still watching him from the other side, and finally back to Billy. He seemed to consider all of this for a second, then raised the gun to the window in the door, ready to fire again.

"Don't!" Billy shouted. "That glass is more than an inch thick! It's the equivalent of ballistic glass. You can't shoot through it! You'll get another—"

The senator fired anyway. This shot left a small divot in the center of the window but didn't come close to penetrating. The bullet bounced down and vanished into the floor.

"You're going to hit one of us!" Jordan said, ducking behind her desk. "Knock it off!"

For a moment, Jordan thought the senator might fire again, but he finally lowered the gun. "We can't just sit in here and wait," he said under his breath.

Jordan got back up and eyed Billy up in his booth. She typed a quick message to him. He answered her question a few seconds later.

BILLY: *Most .38s hold five or six shots, but some models can go up to eight. No way to know what he has left without a closer look at the gun. Maybe if you ask nice, he'll point it at you again and you can check out the cylinder up close. You've got it coming after accusing me of working with that psycho.*

On the other side of the glass in the door, the man was looking in, studying the minute damage left by the bullet. His face went from a tight scowl to a grin as he raised an index finger and slowly shook it back and forth. The senator folded the paper back down so he could no longer see into the studio. "Asshole."

"Please put the gun away and sit back down," Jordan told him.

She tried to sound calm, but there was no masking the break in her voice. Every time her eyes blinked shut, she saw Charlotte's face. She saw that damn ticking clock.

At first, she thought the senator would argue with her again, but instead he blew out a breath and went back to the couch. "The national guard needs to storm this building."

Jordan knew that wasn't going to happen. There was no way they would risk Bernie setting off another bomb. This was a numbers game. "Would you authorize something like that?"

The senator, lost in his own thoughts, looked up at her. "What?"

"Think about it. Somewhere, right now, there's a room crowded with government employees with various security clearances, law enforcement, and local politicians. Somebody in that room has been tasked with totaling up the number of people most likely still in this building, added up the dollar value of damage somebody like Bernie could do based on his existing threat, and weighed that against bombs going off at Grand Central, or Penn Station, possibly both, maybe others. If you were in charge, would you tell the national guard to storm this building, or would it make more sense to keep at a distance and let this play out?"

"They're not going to let us die."

"Risk management is a bitch. I'd bet that decision has already been made. To the people in charge, this is a numbers game, and no matter how you add things up, we're on the losing side of the equation."

"People aren't that cold."

"They sure as shit are. You or I die, it's a headline for a couple days, maybe a week, but people *will* forget. They'll move on. This will all become a blip on the Internet. If there's substantial infrastructure damage, though, something that impacts people for months, maybe even years, costs them money, adds an hour to someone's daily commute, a lot of someones, people like you—the politicians—will answer for it at the polls. Somebody will have to pay for the repairs, taxes will no doubt go up. Politicians will have to answer for that too. The people standing in that room I mentioned, none of them will allow that. Nobody is coming for us."

"My God, you are cynical."

Jordan looked up at Billy in his booth, hoping he might weigh in, but he wasn't even paying attention. He was busy tracing the cracks in the glass of his window with the tip of his finger. He reached for something down on the floor, came up with one of his shoes, and slammed it into the center. The spiderweb of cracks grew larger but didn't give. He hit it several more times in frustration, then put the shoe back on his foot.

Jordan turned back to the senator. "You can't tell me if you were in charge, if you were running that room I mentioned, that you would do anything different."

Moretti went quiet for a moment. "I know the people who are probably standing in your hypothetical room, and they'll find a way."

Jordan shook her head. "The only person who can save my daughter is me."

"By shooting me."

It was Jordan's turn to fall silent.

Billy was next to speak. "Jordie, look at your caller board."

Jordan glanced over at her second monitor, expecting to see Bernie's name listed. It wasn't his name that caused a lump to rise in her throat. it was another name, on Line 5:

Line 1 – Mattie
Line 2 – Ella
Line 3 – Carl
Line 4 – Ren
Line 5 – Nick

There were a million Nicks in the world. There was no reason to believe it was him, but as she stared at the name, she somehow knew that it was. A little voice in the back of her mind told her as long as she didn't pick up, it *could* be him. That same voice told her she had to pick up. She needed to pick up before he dropped off.

Jordan's quivering finger went to the button and pressed. An asterisk appeared on her monitor next to his name. "Nick, you're on the air."

"Jordie?" he whispered, barely audible. "It's me."

54

Cole

If Varney was fake, that meant Bernie had people on Briggs's floor. He probably had people on the floors above and below Cole's current location. The truth was, Cole didn't know where Bernie's people were. He only knew where he needed to be. And he knew he had to move fast, and he couldn't do much of anything as long as Bernie had cameras; they all needed to go.

Running back out into the elevator lobby, he yanked the wires out of each camera he encountered and smashed the lens with the butt of his gun. When satisfied there were no others, he returned to the janitor's closet in the men's bathroom where he took two gallons of bleach, two gallons of ammonia, several bottles of acetone, a rolling mop bucket, and wheeled it all over to the elevators. From the women's restroom, he found two more bottles of each along with another mop bucket, and he wheeled all that out too.

Cole then tried several office doors until he found one unlocked—some insurance company—and went inside where he grabbed several wooden chairs and four plastic trash cans. He dragged everything out into the hallway, smashed the chairs against the wall, and divided the pieces between the trash containers. He poured the acetone on top and saturated the wood.

Cole filled both mop buckets halfway with bleach, then pressed the elevator call button.

When the first car arrived, he destroyed the camera inside and used the key he'd taken from the fake FBI agent who had first met him up on the roof—Pugliesi—and quickly switched the elevator's control panel to the off position, then hit the call button again. He repeated this until he had all six cars locked down with the doors open.

He stepped inside the first car and studied the panel.

50 floors total, but like most skyscrapers, there was no 13th.

Bernie was on 50.

Briggs, her staff, and possible hostages, were on 43.

He studied the controls, used the key to switch the car to emergency mode, and pulled the key back out.

Thankfully, that worked. He'd been concerned the elevator would require him to leave the key in there, and he only had one.

If his idea worked, and that was a big *if*, he'd need to move fast.

He grabbed one of the trash cans and set it inside the first elevator, as close to the door as he could. With the lighter, he set it ablaze. Before the smoke could enter the hallway, he pressed all the buttons for floors 1 through 14 so the car would be forced to stop at each, beginning with the closest and stopping at ground level. He quickly stepped out when the doors started to slide shut.

He did the same in the next car, sending it to floors 15 through 28.

He sent the third elevator to 29 through 42.

Skipping Briggs's floor, he sent the fourth car up to 44 through 49, skipping the floor he was on—45.

That left only the floor Bernie was using as a base.

Cole quickly wheeled one of the mop buckets filled with bleach into the fifth elevator, again, positioning it near the door. He then retrieved two of the ammonia bottles, removed the caps, and dumped them into the bleach. Immediately, a thick white mist began to rise from the bucket.

Chlorine gas.

Toxic.

He'd learned about the lethal mixture during a course on hazardous response years ago at the academy. Apparently homeowners regularly mixed the two chemicals in hopes of a stronger cleaning solution, unaware of the dangers.

Even as he pressed the button for the 50th floor—Bernie's floor—and stepped out into the hallway, he felt this throat constrict and his eyes begin to water.

With the second mop bucket filled with bleach, he grabbed the remaining bottles of ammonia and did the same with the final elevator, sending this one to 50, too.

Because the elevators were in emergency mode, when they reached their final floor, he knew they'd remain there with the doors open. Unless someone was standing by with another elevator key and gas mask, there was no way anyone would get inside to close it.

Again, he had to hurry.

Cole ran to the stairwell, and before slipping through the door, he raised his lighter to the smoke detector and lit the flame. At first, nothing happened, then there was an audible *pop!*—the fire alarm squealed from speakers in the wall, and water began to rain down from above.

He could only hope the same was occurring on the floors below each time the smoke-filled elevators opened their doors. He wouldn't have time to check.

Cole drew the 9mm in one hand and his .380 in the other and started up the steps, ready to shoot any of Bernie's people as they fled from above.

55

Jordan

Jordan didn't much like Nick.

Not recently.

But she didn't want him dead, and hearing his voice brought to life a flutter within her chest she hadn't felt in a very long time. "My God, I thought he shot you."

"No," Nick replied in a slow drawl. "He didn't shoot me."

"What did he do to you? You sound hurt."

"They…they roughed me up a little. I think one or two of my ribs might be broken."

Jordan gasped. She didn't want to, but it just slipped out. She looked up at the senator, at Billy in his booth, both watching her, and suddenly felt very self-conscious. Silly, considering there were millions listening. "Nick, they have our little girl."

"I know."

"Where are you? Have you seen her? Do you know where they have her?"

Someone else spoke in a muffled tone, someone near Nick, but Jordan couldn't make out the words. Nick said, "They're letting me use one of their satellite phones to talk to you, but they're right here, listening." His voice grew urgent, "Four of them, Jordan—there are four of them up here with us! They have—"

He broke off, and she heard what sounded like the rush of air as someone punched him in the gut. Nick made the most horrible sound, and she could only imagine the pain of someone hitting you when you had broken ribs. When he came back, he struggled to speak but he did anyway, pain coating every word. "They...took me in the elevator...right after I left your office. Sucker punched me, then used a stun-gun. Someone put a hood over my head so I couldn't see where they were taking me. We didn't leave the building, though. I'm somewhere in the building. Not just me. I recognize some of your staff here. Maybe people from other offices too, I really don't know. There's about thirty of us...all together. They evacuated everyone else. Only kept some of us."

Nick coughed, then sucked in a quick breath. He wheezed slightly, as if attempting not to breathe at all. She felt the pain in her own chest, as if someone stabbed at her gut with a rusty blade and was slowly pulling it back out, the serrated edges catching on her flesh. "They told me they took Charlotte, but she's not here with us. I don't know where they're holding her." He coughed again, and a moment passed before he spoke again. "They're...allowing me to talk to you because they want the authorities to know they have us. That we're here in the building...somewhere. If they try to breach the building, there's a good chance us...civilians...hostages...there's a good chance we'll be in the middle of it. I was told to tell you they need to stay out of the building. If they're working on some kind of plan, they need to stop. I guess there are snipers in some of the surrounding buildings. They wanted me to mention those too. They said if any of them act, if they fire one shot, they'll kill five of us and set off more bombs. I was told you need to kill the senator, or they'll kill...or they'll kill Charlotte."

"Nick, this is—"

"I was just told to remind you that there are forty-nine minutes left to make your choice. Jordan, you can't let them hurt—"

Nick's voice broke off, and Jordan realized they'd been disconnected.

She stared at her microphone. The tiny holes seemed to grow larger, like hundreds of mouths on some beast ready to devour her. She knew the senator and Billy were staring at her, and she couldn't look up at them. She knew millions of people were listening, and she couldn't think about them either. In her mind, all she saw was her daughter. She heard her daughter's voice, the sound of her giggling, and felt the weight of her when she held her against her chest. She heard the small noises she made when she slept and the shuffle of her feet across the hardwood in their apartment. She thought of the moment Charlotte was born and she first held her, and she thought about Charlotte's eventual graduation from high school, college, her wedding day, her daughter's first child. She thought of every day behind and all those to come.

Jordan thought of the gun.

God help her, she thought of that gun and knew if it was in her hand at that very moment, she wouldn't hesitate to kill the man sitting in front of her. She knew that if she looked up at Billy or Senator Moretti, they would immediately see that in her eyes. She knew if she looked at anything other than her microphone, they would fully understand what she had become and how quickly she'd gotten there.

Nobody would fault her if she did it.

Forty-nine minutes.

Not a single person would say she was in the wrong.

"I'm gonna swallow the bullets."

This came from the senator in a weak voice, unsure.

This time, Jordan did look up. "You're what?"

Senator Moretti had both hands wrapped around the gun as it sat in his lap. His fingers were nervously twisting and turning over the metal, the black metal shimmering with his sweat. "If I swallow the bullets, I can't shoot you and I don't have to worry about you trying to get the gun and shooting me."

"How many bullets are there?" Billy asked.

"Four left."

Billy looked over at Jordan. At least they had the answer to that now.

"You swallow the bullets, and they'll just bring in another gun. Or tell me I have to strangle you or stab you with a letter opener or chew your throat out or smash your head in or…" Her voice trailed off. She couldn't think straight, and she needed to.

What if they did bring in another gun?

They'd hand it directly to her, right? Cocked and loaded and ready to go.

Maybe that was exactly what needed to happen.

Maybe that was exactly what she should let happen.

"You could just shoot yourself," Jordan said softly.

He shrunk back at this, seemed to disappear a little in the couch. "I'm not going to kill myself."

"Are you a religious man, Senator?"

"No, that's not—"

"So you're just selfish? You'd rather protect your own skin than save a child and the other people in this building?"

"That's unfair. I—"

"Given a choice," Jordan interrupted, "I would step out into traffic in a heartbeat if it meant saving a life."

"She's your child. Of course you would. Would you step in front of a truck for someone you don't know?" he fired back.

"For a child? Absolutely. I've lived an incredible life. I wouldn't be sad if it ended today. If me ending my life meant a child got to fulfill hers, I would."

"I don't believe that. You say it. You may even believe it yourself. But if presented with the actual opportunity, you wouldn't go through with it. Nobody would. Self-preservation is one of our core instincts."

"Sacrifice for the greater good is one of the things that separates us from animals."

"Discussing this is pointless."

"You're selfish."

"I've got faith in the men and woman of law enforcement. They'll end this."

"Spineless."

Billy interrupted both of them. "Hey, according to the news, we've got fire alarms going off all over the building."

Jordan loaded the news channel back on her first monitor, doing her best to ignore the countdown clock in the corner that now read forty-seven minutes and twelve seconds. The headline on the screen said: fdny confirms fires detected on more than 30 floors of the siriusxm building and appears to be spreading.

"Do we know what floors?" Jordan asked of no one in particular.

Billy pointed up at one of the sprinkler heads in the studio above her. "Nothing on ours, or we'd be getting soaked right now."

"I smell smoke."

This came from Senator Moretti. He had his head cocked slightly to the side.

"I don't," Jordan replied.

"Me either." Billy was standing in his booth, studying the cracks in his window again. "But in a building like this, the lower floors could burn for hours before there were any signs up here. I'm not staying in this box."

Placing one hand on his wall for leverage and the other on his desk, he kicked at the glass with his right leg. There was an audible crunch, but the glass held.

He kicked it again.

Again.

With a fevered fury, he beat against the glass with the heel of his shoe.

Five kicks.

Ten.

When the thick glass finally broke, it came apart in large chunks. Several pieces fell from above. Billy's leg came through to nearly his knee. "Ugh, fuck me!" He pulled his leg back out, taking more glass with him, fell against the back wall of his booth, and vanished down below.

Jordan stood up. "Shit, are you okay?"

Billy's hand popped back into view, his thumb up. "Peachy. I think I filleted my leg. I'm bleeding."

Jordan tugged off her headphones and started toward him.

Senator Moretti stood and pointed the gun at her. "Don't. Stay there. Behind your desk."

"He's hurt!"

"Don't fucking move!" He was shaking again. His nerves taking over. He was going to shoot someone on accident long before he did it intentionally.

She raised both her hands and held her palms out to the Senator. "Billy? How bad is it?"

"I think I nicked something. Something bad. There's a lot of blood."

Jordan turned back to the senator, her eyes pleading. "There's a first aid kit on the wall over there near the door. Just let me get it and help him."

He held the gun on her and quickly glanced off to the side, where she indicated.

Now.

A voice in the back of her head told her.

Jump him now.

He turned back, though, the moment gone too fast. "You get back behind your desk. I'll get the kit." Over his shoulder, he said, "Billy? If I pass you the first aid kit, can you bandage yourself up?"

"Yeah. I think so," Billy replied, his voice quivering.

Jordan nodded softly and sat on the edge of her chair.

The senator crossed the room, keeping the gun on Jordan, tugged the first aid kit from the wall, and brought it to the hole where Billy's window had been at the back of the studio. "Here."

"I can't reach it." He didn't sound good at all. He sounded like he might pass out. "I can't get up. Slide it across the desk."

Senator Moretti reached through the opening with the box and slid it across Billy's desk on the other side. "Here, take it—"

Billy reached up with both arms and grabbed the senator's wrist. He pulled him up and through the window.

The senator fell forward.

The gun in his other hand went off, and Jordan felt a sharp burn.

56

Cole

When Cole had first arrived at this building and taken the elevator down with the fake FBI agent, he had counted five people standing in the hallway when the doors had opened briefly on the 50th floor. He'd killed two on 47, one had escaped, and through the single earbud in his left ear, he just heard Jordan's husband tell her there were at least four on whatever floor he was being held, with approximately thirty hostages. That meant Bernie had a minimum of seven people in the building, possibly more. Possibly many more.

As Cole reached the landing for 49, he paused to smash the camera above and take stock. The Glock 19 in his right hand had one bullet in the chamber and fifteen in the clip. He had two spare clips in his back pocket, but one only contained ten rounds. In his left hand, he had his .380. Six rounds in the clip, one in the chamber. Forty-three shots total.

He wore no vest. That was in his missing bag, along with the rest of his gear.

From the opposite side of the door on 49, Cole heard the shrill sound of the fire alarm go off. He nudged the door open, and water sprayed out from around the edges and started to pool at his feet.

It was working.

He had no idea how long the sprinklers would run, but it shouldn't take much to short out not only the building's security cameras on each floor but whatever Bernie managed to place. Because the stairwells were all concrete and metal and meant for escape, there were no sprinklers, but he'd destroyed every camera he found and would keep that up too until Bernie was blind.

He eased the door shut, leaned back against the wall, pointed both his guns up toward the next level, and forced his ears to hear beyond the alarms and rushing water.

Cole hoped to hear yelling. Angry shouts. Panic. Bernie's people pushing through the emergency door and running toward him.

He heard none of that. Only the alarms and water.

If the elevator with the fire already reached 49, the two with chlorine gas most certainly made it to 50—doors wide open, gas seeping out into the floor.

From the brief glance Cole got of fifty, the floor was a construction zone—concrete floors and metal stud walls wide open awaiting Sheetrock. Behind the people standing in ambush at the elevator door when he arrived, he remembered seeing all the way through the floor to the windows on the far side. Few, if any, places to hide.

Hugging the wall, Cole eased up several steps, his heart pounding in his chest, knowing the door above could open at any moment as Bernie's people pushed through like rats fleeing a sinking ship. He paused when he reached the corner, just before the landing.

Listened.

Heard nothing.

He flexed his grip on the nine-millimeter and .380, both slick with his sweat.

Counting silently down from three, Cole sucked in a breath, dropped low, and rounded the bend, ready to fire.

The stairwell was empty, the door to 50 closed.

Cole stood there.

Waited.

The alarm below continued to scream.

Nobody came out.

Bernie was a smart man. There was a very good chance he came prepared with gas masks and they were standing on the opposite side of that door waiting for Cole, the feds, SWAT, somebody, to come rushing through. An ambush to the ambush.

Cole counted to one hundred.

Nothing.

Come up to 50. If anything, we can talk about Gracie.

Fuck.

Cole shuffled up several more steps, got about halfway to the door. Stopped again.

If Bernie wanted him dead, he already had several opportunities to kill him.

Or, taunting him to come up to 50 might have just been a way to save the trouble of chasing him down somewhere else in the building.

Like the other floors, the emergency door at 50 was metal with cinderblock walls on either side. Approximately five feet on the left, a little less on the right. Concrete steps with metal railings leading both up and down from there.

Cole moved up the several remaining steps at a snail's pace, ready to fire if the door moved, but it didn't. When he reached it, he put his ear against the cold metal but couldn't hear anything.

He crouched down low again, his left side pressed against the cinderblock wall to the side of the door's hinges. He drew in several breaths through his nose, held them, and let them out through his mouth. This did absolutely nothing to calm him. His heart was beating so hard he thought he could hear it over the alarms on the floors below.

With his right hand, the one holding the 9mm, he reached up to the metal bar on the door and gave it a gentle push until the latch bolt disengaged and the door started to swing.

He didn't open it much, no more than an inch. He expected gunfire, but none came. He expected chlorine gas to drift out, but that didn't happen either.

No sound.

No movement.

Cole gave the door a hard push, sending it swinging in. He dove through the opening, landed on his stomach with both guns held out, then flipped over onto his back and sat up when didn't see anyone. Pivoting as quickly as he could, he spun around, ready to fire on anyone, but there was nobody.

The floor was deserted.

Off to his far right, he spotted the elevator doors. Each had some kind of metal bar across the front, welded in place, holding them closed. Cole had no idea what that meant for the chlorine gas—the elevator car was either stuck on the opposite side of the barricaded door or had went on to another floor, there was no way to be sure.

Cole got to his feet and turned in a slow circle, both guns held at arm's length, carefully eyeing every shadow.

The bodies he'd spotted earlier were still on the floor in pools of drying blood. Three near the elevators, a fourth about ten feet away. He went over to the nearest one, a woman. He didn't recognize her. Her ID was gone, she didn't have a badge, but Cole recognized the FBI academy ring on her right hand. Two of the men near the elevators were wearing them too. Bernie and his people must have ambushed them, somehow taken over and impersonated them. Each had neat bullet wounds in their heads, shot before they probably had a chance to draw their own weapons. None had phones. Not that it mattered—every time Cole checked his phone, he had no signal, even near the windows.

He left the bodies as he found them and continued to scout the floor in silence.

In the center of the open space, there was a large pile of cardboard boxes, at least eight feet wide and nearly to the ceiling. With both guns at the ready, Cole slowly approached it and began to circle clockwise. Because he couldn't see over the top, when he reached the midway point, he doubled back counterclockwise—on the off chance there was someone else here also circling the boxes, he hoped to surprise them.

Aside from his own, he didn't hear any footsteps.

Didn't hear anyone breathing.

Cole didn't hear the little girl's voice coming from within the boxes until he had nearly completed the circle.

57

Jordan

Jordan saw the gun go off, this bright flash. A fraction of a second later, something slammed into her right shoulder, came out the back, and tore into her chair and the wall behind her. These things all happened before she heard the gun go off, as if her brain had shifted into some higher gear and somehow became hypersensitive to all around her.

The pain came a moment later, about the same time she saw Billy pull the senator through his window and disappear behind the desk in his booth.

"I've been...shot."

Jordan heard the words, words spoken in her voice, *with* her voice, yet she seemed to be observing that happening too, like a spectator rather than a participant, and something in the back of her mind told her she may just be in shock.

"Billy..."

She heard them struggling, but the world had taken on a slight tilt to the left and it was difficult to watch them, there was a blur coating her vision, a fire burst of white light.

She lost time.

Not much (at least, she didn't think so), but when she blinked Billy was now standing in his booth, the gun in his right hand pointing down at the floor, as he flexed the fingers of his left. He looked over at her, his face white. "Jordan? Are you okay?!?"

It was weird hearing his voice directly as he stood in his booth, no headphones or microphones, only Billy. He had a nice voice.

Jordan liked his voice.

Her headphones were lying on her desktop. *Had she taken them off, or did they fall off?*

"Jordan!"

The world tilted back. She fought the urge to slip sideways with it, and instead watched in awe as the white mist in her vision began to dissolve and vanish.

"Goddammit, Jordan!"

"Why are you shouting?" she replied.

"How bad are you hit?"

"Hit?"

"Your shoulder. He shot you!"

All that happened replayed in her mind like a bad movie, and when she reached the end, she seemed to drop back into her body. Her vision cleared. Billy came into focus, and the sharp pain in her shoulder seemed to emphasize his words.

Billy's head swiveled back toward the floor. "Stay the fuck down!"

Jordan reached up and tentatively touched her shoulder.

Still pointing the gun at the floor, Billy shuffled through his broken window into the studio, reached back into his booth for the first aid kit, and moved past the couch and around her desk. "Try not to move."

"Okay."

"You're in—"

"I was in shock. I think I'm all right now."

"Yeah, you're wonderful. First time you've been quiet in ten years. I think I like it."

"Fuck you."

Billy smiled. "This is gonna hurt."

Before she could answer, he grabbed the sleeve of her shirt and tore it away.

Jordan pulled in a quick breath and fought the urge to scream. "Are we still on the air?"

Billy nodded. "Everything in this room is broadcasting. Somehow he even found a way to override the automated breaks at the top and bottom of the hour. I don't know how to shut it down."

"Lovely." She looked down at Billy's jeans. He hadn't gotten cut at all. "Nice bluff."

He glanced down, then at the gun in his hand. He placed it carefully on the desk in front of her. "If he tries to get out of my booth, shoot him. I'm not kidding, Jordan. Just shoot him."

She looked at the gun. There was still a thin trail of smoke coming from the barrel.

Billy blew out a breath. "I don't think he hit any bone. Can you lean forward?"

Jordan did, and it hurt like hell. Like wasps were taking turns to see who could get their stinger deepest.

"The good news is the bullet is in the wall behind you. Bad news is you have a hole in your shoulder that isn't supposed to be there." He fished around in the first aid kit and took out a package of something called *QuickClot*, tore the package open, and pressed what looked like thick gauze against both sides of the wound. They must have had some kind of adhesive, because they both stuck. He reached back into the box, fished out some elastic tape, and began to wrap it tight.

"Aren't you supposed to disinfect that?"

"Sure, if we had something for that. I'm going to advise you to see your primary care physician when this is over. My medical training comes from watching reruns of *Chicago Fire*; I'm really not qualified for this."

"No co-pay for you."

"At least there's that."

In Billy's booth, the senator rose to his feet, one hand on his nose. The right side of his face was red and swelling. His eyes jumped around nervously, finally landing on the gun. Jordan glared back at him, reached for it, and drew the small weapon closer across her desk. From the corner of her eye, she glanced at the newsfeed on her monitor, at the ticking clock.

Thirty-one minutes, four seconds remaining.

Billy finished wrapping her shoulder and leaned in close to her ear, his voice so low she barely heard him. "The studio door has a magnetic lock. They're controlling it from the outside somehow. The one in my booth is just a dead bolt. We can get out that way. The senator knows. I told him when he was on the ground."

Jordan considered this. "They'll see us."

"Maybe."

"Even if they don't, the second we stop broadcasting, they'll know."

Billy's eyes went to the pair of wireless headphones still on her desk. The ones she'd used when she first started the broadcast. Still showing a full WiFi signal.

"What about the man guarding the door? He's right out in the hallway.

Billy's eyes moved from the headphones to the gun, then to her, and Jordan understood.

She nodded, doing her best to ignore the pain.

They both saw her second monitor update. All the calls dropped, replaced with a single name:

Line 1 – Bernie
Line 2 – Bernie
Line 3 – Bernie
Line 4 – Bernie
Line 5 – Bernie

58

Cole

Cole wasn't sure he had heard her, not at first. The voice was so soft and muffled. But when he stopped moving and listened, there was this faint whimper, a near-silent cry.

"Charlotte?"

He wasn't exactly sure how he knew it was her, but he did, and that made this all the worse.

She didn't reply.

There was no response at all.

He tucked both guns under his belt and began tugging away the boxes, moving them aside carefully in case this was some kind of trap. They varied in size from about ten inches square to several feet. Some inside others. Some flattened, most still intact, all were empty. Far more than he initially thought.

As he neared the center, her voice grew louder. This frantic breathing.

He called out her name several more times, but she still didn't respond, and that only made him move faster.

The light caught rusted metal.

Black cloth.

Wheels.

Cole had nearly a third of it uncovered before he realized he was looking at an antique baby carriage, the hood drawn partially closed over a musty pink blanket. He snatched up the blanket and threw it aside, expecting to find Charlotte somehow stuffed inside, but she wasn't there at all. Instead, there was a baby monitor. White plastic with the image of a cartoon baby etched in the bottom corner and a stubby antenna on top.

As Charlotte cried softly, a series of blue LEDs danced across the face of the device above the round speaker in sync with her voice.

Cole looked up at the ceiling, the walls—suddenly feeling as if he were being watched. He saw nothing, though.

Reaching into the carriage, he scooped up the monitor, studied it for a moment, and pressed a talk button he found on the side. "Charlotte? Can you hear me?"

The girl sucked in a deep breath, startled. "Who is this?"

"Detective Cole Hundley. The police officer you met this morning. Do you know where you are?"

"It's dark in here."

Again, Cole looked around. A baby monitor couldn't have much range. She had to be near. As he looked closer at the device, though, he saw *WiFi-enabled* stamped proudly across the base by the manufacturer and realized she could be anywhere. He also realized if his little stunt with the elevator fires and sprinklers knocked out the building's WiFi, he might lose contact with her completely.

He tried not to think about that. "What can you see?"

"Only the clock."

"The clock?"

"Well, not really a clock. It's counting backward," she said. "Right now it's at twenty-eight minutes and four seconds."

Cole felt his heart thump. "Charlotte? Is the clock attached to anything?"

"I can't see. It's too dark. Can you get me out? They tied me to a chair, and I can't move."

"Do you know what floor you're on?"

She sniffled. "No. They…they put a bag over my head in the elevator. They said if I took it off, they'd hurt me."

"From your mom's floor?"

"Yeah. Is she with you? Can I talk to her?"

Cole closed his eyes for a moment. He tried not to think about the girl he'd met this morning, tied up and all alone somewhere in this skyscraper. He couldn't imagine how strong she must be to hold it together as well as she was. "I'm sorry, honey, she's not with me right now. She has to stay in contact with the people behind this."

"They said some mean things about her," Charlotte said softly. "They told me she did something very bad and this was all her fault."

"You know that was a lie, right? Your mom is a good person."

At first she said nothing, then her voice came back sounding so small. "Yeah, I know."

"Charlotte, this is important, because I want to help you. What *can* you tell me about wherever you are? Anything at all will be helpful."

She went quiet again, then, "I think it might be a closet. They tied my hands and my legs to a chair, but it's got wheels and if I slide side-to-side I can touch two walls. When I talk, there's an echo, like when I play in my closet at home."

"That's good, that's really good," he told her. "What else?"

"There's carpet on the floor. I think the door is on my left. I can see a little light coming in from underneath but not much. Like the lights in the room with the closet are off, and the light is maybe coming from a window somewhere."

Christ. This wasn't helping at all. There were fifty floors in this building.

She could be anywhere.

Then he remembered the elevators. "Charlotte, do you hear running water at all?"

"Water?"

"From the sprinkler system. Or how about a fire alarm?"

Her voice shot up an octave. "There's a fire?"

"Not a real one. Do you hear either of those things?"

Her voice dropped off again for several seconds. "I don't hear any water, but I think I can hear the fire alarm. Barely, though."

If his trick with the elevators worked, and that was a big if, Cole had set off the smoke detectors on every floor but this one, where he sent the—

Oh, shit. Maybe it went to the wrong floor?

"Charlotte, do you smell anything? Anything really strong? It might make your eyes water or hurt your throat. Anything like that?"

"No."

"Nothing like cleaning products? Bleach or ammonia?"

"No, I don't smell anything weird."

He looked around the floor again. There were no walls, no closets. This was basically a blank slate for future offices. She wasn't on this level.

Cole's finger began to tap nervously against the side of the monitor.

Think.

"Let's try to walk through exactly what happened when they took you, can you do that with me?"

"Okay."

"You said they put a bag on your head in the elevator on your mom's floor. Before you got in the elevator, did you see which button they pushed? Did you go up or down?"

"Up."

"You're sure?"

"Yeah. I felt it in my stomach, too. These elevators go fast."

"Good. That's very good," Cole replied. "When the doors opened and you got off, did you go right or left?"

"We didn't get off the first time. The doors opened, and a few more people got in. Then we went to another floor."

"Do you know how many?"

"No. I couldn't see. At least two, though. I felt people on both sides of me, and the man who took me from Mommy's floor was standing behind me with his hand on my shoulder."

"Okay. Think hard about this before you answer. You said you could feel it with your stomach—when the doors closed again, did you go up or down?"

Charlotte was quiet for a few seconds. "I think we went down, but I don't know for sure."

"That's all right, we'll figure it out," Cole assured her. "When you stopped again, is that when you got off?"

"Yeah."

"Did you go to the right or the left?"

"The left."

"Good. Again, think hard about this. Do you know how many steps you took? Before you answer, I want you to close your eyes, try not to think about anything, try to remember it as if it were a movie playing in your head and you're watching now."

When she spoke again, she sounded unsure. "I guess around twenty. Then we turned left again."

"Did you hear anything as you were walking? Any voices or anything?"

"No. It was quiet," she said. "But I don't think the other people from the elevator followed us. I think they went the opposite way when they got out. The floor was tile or something, and I could only hear the one man walking behind me." Charlotte paused, then added, "I couldn't hear his shoes anymore after we turned left. We were on carpet then, I think. We made another left and went four or five steps. Then he made me stop and sit in a chair. That's when he tied me up. He used those plastic zip-tie things on my wrists and my ankles so I couldn't move. I know they were zip ties because I heard them click when he pulled them tight. Then he pushed me and the chair in here and closed the door."

"Did you see anything when he took the hood off?"

"He didn't take the hood off," she replied. "When he left, I kept moving my head around until it fell off on its own. That was right before I heard you talking to me."

"Can you get either of your hands out of the zip ties?"

"I've been trying, but they're too tight."

Off the elevator, left turn down a tile hallway, another left turn into a carpeted space—most likely an office—then into a closet.

On one of fifty floors.

"I'll find you, Charlotte. I promise. The sprinklers are running on nearly every floor. If there's no water around you, that narrows it down a lot."

If they really went off on all the floors as they were supposed to.

He glanced over at the elevators, welded shut on this floor.

Where else had they done that?

He had to start somewhere.

"Charlotte, are you still there?"

"No, I went to McDonald's."

For the first time today, Cole smiled. "Grab me a Big Mac, will ya? I don't want these guys to hear me coming, so I'm going to turn down the volume on my end. As soon as I know I'm someplace I can talk, I'll be back, okay?"

"Okay."

As he was lowering the volume, he heard her ask one more question. One he couldn't answer.

"What happens when that clock hits zero?"

59

Jordan

Bernie's name flashed at Jordan from her monitor, on all five lines again.

She looked over at Billy. He finished working on her shoulder, nodded at the wireless headphones again, and bolted back to his booth.

With her good arm, Jordan removed her other headphones and put on the wireless.

Reaching up through the broken window in his booth, Billy hit several buttons, grabbed his own phone, and typed something on the small screen.

BILLY: *I'm switching everything to remote. Picking up in three, two...*

Jordan nodded and said, "Bernie?"

He cleared his throat. "I really thought we all had an understanding."

Jordan gave Billy a quick thumbs up and moved the headphone's built-in microphone a little closer to her mouth. "What are you talking about?"

"I told you and everyone listening under no circumstance was a member of a law enforcement agency permitted to enter this building."

"Have they?"

"Your friend, Detective Cole, landed on the roof in a helicopter you paid for, killed several of my people, and is currently running around the building like a hungry rat in a stocked pantry. He's setting fires. Trying to gas us. He's a serious nuisance."

"Maybe he's not a fan of my show and didn't hear your little announcement. Two demerits for Officer Cole, I guess."

"His superiors already bumped him down to traffic. I'm not sure how much further down the food chain he can go."

"Luckily, he's not one of my employees, so he's not my problem," Jordan told him.

"Today he is, Ms. Briggs. It's time to make another choice. Would you like me to kill him or a member of your staff?"

"My staff? Bernie, this needs to stop. All of it. Let my daughter go, my husband, the people who work for me—they have nothing to do with this. Deactivate the bombs. You know the police will come in. They'll kill you and whoever else you have here. That's how these things work. That's how they *always* end. Turn yourself in," Jordan pleaded. "Your wife was taken from you, your daughter. Any parent out there will understand what that must be like, just the thought…"

Her voice choked off, and even though she wanted to be strong, her body wouldn't let her. She was shaking. Her heart was grappling with the effort to keep up with all the emotions trying to chew their way out from the inside.

"You don't understand, not yet. In twenty-six minutes, you will. If the senator is still standing, if you force me to kill your daughter, then you'll know the emptiness you created in me. Then you and I can talk. How many bullets does he have left? Have you figured that out yet?"

Billy had come back to Jordan's desk and was standing beside her. The two of them looked at each other, then Billy quickly scribbled on her notepad—*I don't think he knows you have the gun. He may not be able to see us anymore! Could be the fires?*

Jordan said, "I've asked Senator Moretti to hand the gun over to me several times, but he's not big on sharing."

"How bad did he shoot you?"

"The bullet went through my shoulder, my chair, and is buried in the wall behind me somewhere. It hurts like hell, but Billy has seen every episode of *Nurse Jackie* and managed to stop the bleeding. Knowing the folks at SiriusXM, I'll probably get a bill for the damage to their studio next week." She looked over at the senator, still standing in Billy's booth. "I don't think Moretti has ever shot anyone before. It seemed to seriously spook him. He's huddled in the corner of the studio, with this wild look in his eyes. His lips are moving, but I can't hear what he's saying, like he's arguing with himself. Poor man is broken."

Senator Moretti mouthed *fuck you* back at her.

Bernie said, "Maybe now's the time to wrestle the gun away from him, while he's still wrapped up in a blanket of shock. You're a tough woman, I bet you could take him."

Billy crossed over to the studio door and peeled back the corner of the paper covering the window. He pressed his face up against the glass and looked in both directions, then returned to her desk and wrote another note—*Nobody there right now. If we're going to try and get out, we need to do it now before they come back. Do you want the gun, or should I take it? There's a good chance we'll need to shoot someone.*

Jordan reached across her desk and pulled the gun closer, wincing as pain shot out from her injured shoulder. Below Billy's writing, she wrote, *Where are we going to go? I can't leave Charlotte!*

We get help—find her—something. You've always been a disrupter, now's the time to disrupt. We stay in here and we're doing what he wants. We leave, and maybe we find a way to take control.

Jordan knew he was right. Goddamn Billy was always right. She nodded quickly, took the gun in her good hand, stood, and rounded her desk. "Tell me about Kourtney, Bernie. What kind of person was she?"

"You're just trying to buy time."

Jordan froze in her steps halfway to Billy's booth. "What do you mean?"

"You haven't made your choice yet," he replied. "Detective Cole, or one of your employees?"

"What good will doing either of those things accomplish? If you tell me about Kourtney, you might actually find some people to sympathize with you. My audience is listening. Once the police have you in custody, you'll never get in front of a group this large again. Right now, they just know you as this crazy person destroying their city. Tell them who you really are. Who she was. Convince them you're just another human who got hurt."

"They're not my jury."

Billy crawled through the broken window back into his booth, then turned and helped Jordan turn and slide in on the face of his desk. She did her best to hide the fact that she was moving from her voice. "Don't kid yourself, Bernie. Twelve people in a locked room aren't going to decide what happens to you. It will be people around the world on FaceBook, Twitter, TikTok, and God knows what else. Social media is the new judge, jury, and executioner. The 21st-century hangman."

As Jordan turned on the desk and got one leg back down on the floor, Billy held her steady. Senator Moretti took a step closer, and her grip tightened on the gun—more of an involuntary action than a conscious one, but he noticed and froze anyway.

"I'm not sure if this will help you make your decision, but Detective Cole is talking to your daughter right now. She sounds scared. Not as bad as she was, but still frightened. If he dies while they're speaking, if a bullet takes his head off, what do you think something like that will do to her in the long term? Providing she has a *long term*, that is. Traumatic events can have a serious impact on a person, children in particular, and she's at such an impressionable age."

Cole found Charlotte?

Both feet on the floor, Jordan followed Billy over to his door. Like the studio door, his window was also covered in paper, and he pulled a corner aside and took another look.

Nobody.

His hand went to the dead bolt. He twisted it slowly, until it clicked in place. Unlocked.

Bernie continued, "You need to make your decision, Ms. Briggs. Do I tell my people to kill Detective Cole, or do we pick someone from your group?"

"What happened to the train station? All these decisions, I'm getting confused."

Billy mouthed, *what the fuck?*

"I said I would blow one up, I didn't say when. Be patient. All good things, and all that…"

"Come on Bernie, tell me about Kourtney."

"How about I tell you about Detective Cole instead? Maybe knowing a little about him will help you make your decision."

Jordan watched as Billy twisted the doorknob and carefully opened it on the hallway. She raised the gun, ready to kill anyone standing between her and her daughter. "I'd love to hear about Detective Cole," she said softly.

60

Cole

Cole listened at the emergency exit door for nearly thirty seconds before pushing on the metal bar and stepping back into the stairwell. He had both guns out again, and the baby monitor tucked into his back pocket with the volume all the way down. That didn't seem to stop Charlotte's last question from echoing in his head.

What happens when that clock hits zero?

Bernie had proven repeatedly he had no problem killing today, and Cole had no doubt he would kill Jordan's daughter as a final knife in Jordan's back for the wrongs he felt she brought upon him and his family. What didn't make sense to Cole was his use of a bomb to do it. With everything today, Bernie had made a show of it. From going on the air to the explosions around the city, the murders of the people associated with the Marisa Chapman trial—everything planned out meticulously to create maximum exposure. If taking Charlotte from her mother was his final act, why would he hide her in a dark room and kill her with a bomb, something nobody would really see? Cole was by no means a profiler, but he'd worked with enough of them to know this was out of character. What he didn't know was why. He understood enough about Bernie to know everything happening today was meant to happen, at least in Bernie's eyes. So even something out of character had its place.

Your role in things.

Cole forced these thoughts out of his head so he could focus. Allowing his mind to wander right now could easily get him killed.

He started up the steps and was halfway to the next landing when he heard footsteps and voices from above.

"...is he already up on the roof?"

"Who knows, but I'm not waiting around to see how this clusterfuck ends. If he's not up there, I say we hijack the chopper and get the fuck out of here. If the others don't want to, we shoot 'em. He ain't walking away from this, and I don't think he cares if he does. This isn't what I signed on for. I don't know about you, but I don't have a death wish. What good is all of this if we don't walk away? We shouldn't wait on him. This is too far gone for that shit."

Two people.

Male voices.

"Quit jabbering, and help me with this stuff," the first one said.

A second later, Cole heard something drop against the concrete floor, something heavy.

"Goddamn it, be careful."

"Why don't we just leave it? Who gives a shit if someone finds it now?"

"Bernie said—"

"Bernie said, Bernie said. Fuck Bernie."

"Look, if you don't want to help, just go back down and send someone else to give me a hand."

"No way. I'm staying near the helicopter."

"Then quit bitching and lift. We don't get up there soon, they might leave without us."

Moving slowly, pressed tight against the wall with both guns at the ready, Cole went up several more steps.

The footfalls above were moving up, toward the roof. Heavy steps, as if carrying something large.

"We shouldn't have brought so many if we didn't need them all," the second voice said.

"Will you please stop complaining? We're almost there."

"Why not just shoot them all? What's the difference?"

"My God, you are an ass. This is why nobody ever talks to you."

"Shush."

They stopped moving. Cole did too. He was close, maybe too close. He could see one of their shadows on the wall just above the next landing.

"Do you hear that?" the second voice said.

"I don't hear…" He paused. "Wait, is that?"

"Crap, I told you! That's the chopper. They're leaving without us!"

Cole heard them drop whatever it was they were carrying. It cracked against the concrete floor with an echoing thump.

If there were more on the roof, he needed to stop these two before they got there.

Thrusting the guns out in front of him, he bounded up the several steps, rounded the corner, and shouted, "Hey!"

Both men froze and stared at him. They were on the final landing, the access door to the roof at their backs. The one on the left had a gun tucked under his belt in the front. He couldn't be more than twenty-five. His brown hair was clipped short and he wore a red tee-shirt and jeans. If the second guy had a gun, Cole couldn't see it. He was older, probably in his fifties, shaved head and gray goatee. "Neither of you move; I'm NYPD."

The younger man flexed the fingers of his right hand but didn't make a move for the gun. "Don't do anything stupid," he told Cole.

Second voice. The ass.

There was a large plastic case on the floor in front of them. Nearly four feet long and about eighteen inches on each side. Hard shell with thick metal clasps, meant to take a beating.

Cole kept a gun trained on each man. To the younger one, he said, "I want you to pinch the butt of that gun with your thumb and index finger, take it out slowly, and drop it in front of that box, on my side. You do anything other than that and I will shoot you." To the older man, he said, "I know you have one somewhere.

I don't want you moving at all."

"It's behind my back, under my belt."

"We'll get to it in a second."

The man nodded.

The man on the left did as Cole asked. Moving deliberately slow, he reached for his gun, pulled it from his pants, then held his arm out straight—extending up and over the plastic case—then bent at his knees and dropped the gun the last foot to the concrete floor. A chrome-plated 9mm. It clattered but didn't go off.

"On your knees," Cole instructed. "Place both palms flat on top of the case."

He did, grunting softly as he got down.

Cole turned to the older man. "You're going to do the same thing. Reach behind your back, and take the gun out with two fingers. Bring it around real slow and drop it right next to this one."

He nodded. "You'll get no trouble out of me, so don't get jumpy. No reason to shoot anyone."

Cole tightened his grip on the Glock, his finger on the trigger. "Slow."

The older man held his right arm out to the side, between him and the younger guy, his palm out so Cole could see it was empty, then reached behind his back with his left. As Cole instructed, he took out the gun gently between two fingers, brought it around to his front with an extremely slow and careful movement, then held it straight out as the other man had. When he started to bend at his knees, he grimaced. "My knees ain't what they used to be."

With audible pops at the joints, he managed to get himself down.

Cole watched the gun drop to the ground, a Glock identical to the one he held.

As the gun fell, the older man reached behind the back of the younger man with his right arm and grabbed at something—the younger man rolled to his right, getting out of the way. The older man tried to drop behind the plastic case as his hand came up holding another Glock.

Cole fired at both of them.

He hit the older man above his left eyebrow. The bullet exited the back of his head and struck the metal door behind him. Two shots hit the younger guy—one in his thigh, the other near his elbow, as he tried to drop out of the way. He fell hard against the floor and tried to scramble away while reaching for something in his boot with his good arm.

Cole scrambled over the case and stepped on his forearm, pinning his wrist to the ground. A short blade fell from his fingers, and the guy cried out. Cole pressed the barrel of the Glock against his temple. "That was really stupid!"

"Fuck you! You're dead anyway." The pain hit him then, and his eyes fell on what was left of his elbow—bone, cartilage, and exposed muscle. His face went white as shock started to settle in. A dark red stain was growing at his thigh. "I think I need a doctor."

Cole tucked the .380 behind his belt and pressed his index finger down into the man's destroyed elbow. "Where does Bernie have the girl?"

The man screamed. A shriek loud enough to echo down the stairwell.

Cole released his grip before he passed out and gave him a second to recuperate. "I can do this all day. Where is she?"

His eyes rolled back forward and settled on Cole. "Whoa, calm down." He grimaced. "I don't give a shit about these guys. Let me go, and I'll take you right to her."

"Where does he have her?" Cole repeated for the third time, his hand moving back toward his elbow.

"You want me to help you, you need to help me. Better hurry, though. We're both running out of time."

On the opposite side of the metal door, Cole heard the helicopter, the heavy thump of rotor blades. He'd spent enough time in it today to know it was near take-off. "Is he taking her out of here?"

"We hurry, you can trade me for her," he said. "Bernie'll do it, I know too much."

Cole grabbed him by his belt, yanked him to his feet, and shoved him toward the metal door. The man fell forward, nearly toppled over, but managed to stay on his feet by grabbing the door's push bar. The bullet in his thigh must have lodged in there. There was no exit wound, his jeans were soaked in blood. He staggered and put his weight on the opposite leg, sucked in some air, then pushed through the door, nearly toppling again as it swung open.

There was a deafening roar. Wind from the helicopter swirled through the doorway, whipping dust into Cole's eyes. He blinked it away, pointed his Glock at the back of the man's head, and pushed the man forward. "Move!"

He took several more steps and stopped. He'd never make it to the helicopter.

Cole came up behind him, grabbed him by the belt again and kneed the back of his injured leg. He nearly dropped to the ground when the pain hit him, but that was followed by a rush of adrenaline, enough to keep him moving. Dragging his injured leg, he crossed the roof and rounded the large air conditioners.

The helicopter was about six feet off the rooftop and rising.

The man shouted something, but Cole couldn't make it out over the noise.

The glare of the sun on the windows made it hard to see, but Cole thought he spotted at least four people inside, including the pilot. None of the shadows looked like a child, but he couldn't be sure.

Raising his gun, Cole pointed it at the back of the man's head.

Barely able to stand, the man raised his good arm and waved up at the helicopter. When it stopped rising and hovered in place, his waves became frantic, he stumbled closer.

A small window slid open on the passenger side of the helicopter and a long barrel came out, pointed at the injured man, and fired. He dropped to the ground, dead.

Cole pointed his gun at the shadow on the other side of the rifle, but before he could shoot, a fireball erupted from the tail of the helicopter, quickly crawled across the metal, and engulfed the chopper. He dove behind the large air conditioners and felt heat rip over his skin as the chopper exploded in a fiery rain of debris and steel.

61

Jordan

A deep rumble shook the building, and Jordan, Billy, and the senator froze.

With eyes wide, Jordan said, "Bernie, what was that?"

"It doesn't concern you."

"It sounded like an explosion."

"An explosion that doesn't concern you. We're discussing Detective Cole."

Billy gave Jordan an uneasy look, then started forward again. She followed him out into the hallway, with the senator several paces back just enough so the senator couldn't reach her if he decided to make some kind of play for the gun, but close enough so they could remain together.

Nobody was guarding Billy's door.

Nobody was guarding the studio door, not anymore.

The hallway was deserted.

Billy turned toward her and said in barely a whisper, "Which way?"

Jordan pointed toward the greenroom.

Bernie said, "Your boy Detective Cole is recently engaged."

"He is?"

"It's the reason he was in uniform when we all met him today. Apparently, he took up with the wrong girl. Her name is Gracie

Gaff—she's his lieutenant's daughter. I've gotten to know her a little bit—clearly a daddy's girl. Her mother died when she was only four, so it's been just the two of them all these years. Well, and a half-dozen of his closest cop friends—they all stepped up to help him raise her when Gracie's mother passed. Kinda touching, to have friends like that. She's a pretty thing—long blonde hair, vegan, a bit of a health nut. She just turned thirty a couple weeks ago. Hard to believe she's still single, but I guess when your father is a police lieutenant and you were raised by a bunch of very protective cops, it can be hard to get the suitors to stick around. None of that seemed to dissuade Detective Cole, though. I guess they managed to keep their relationship secret for nearly two years, but they let the cat out of the bag a few weeks ago at some cop bar in Queens. Cole, being the old-fashioned kid that he is, first asked Lieutenant Gaff for his daughter's hand in marriage. When he vehemently said no, Cole then stood up on a stool in front of the entire group and announced they were getting married anyway. That didn't go over very well with the lieutenant or his buddies in the crowd—Gracie's surrogate fathers. I suppose things could have went worse—a group like that knows how to hide a body—but they didn't hurt him. Instead, he got bumped down to traffic duty on some trumped-up disciplinary charge. At last check, those two were still engaged, so he hasn't backed down. Young love is so exciting."

The greenroom door was closed.

Billy reached for the knob and silently counted to three with his fingers while Jordan stood back with the gun. Senator Moretti had gone several steps down the hallway and was craning his neck, trying to see into one of the open office doors.

As Billy opened the door, he stepped aside to give Jordan a clear shot. She wanted to tell him she had no idea what she was doing, not really. She didn't like guns, and aside from a trip to the range with an old boyfriend, she hadn't fired one since. From what she could tell, the .38 was simple enough to operate, just point and pull the trigger, but aiming, holding her arms steady against the force of the shot, proper stance, all those things were a distant memory for her. She knew nothing beyond that one time and what she'd seen in the movies.

The door opened on an empty room.

Someone had turned the television back on, and one of the news channels was running a shot up the front of her building focused on a black cloud of smoke near the roof along with the headline HELICOPTER EXPLODES ABOVE SIRIUSXM BUILDING across the top. The sound was muted. In a small window off to the side was another shot, this one of the building's lobby. Clearly zoomed in from a distance, the camera was shaky.

"Bernie, did you blow up a helicopter?"

He clucked his tongue impatiently. "I've already told you—"

"It doesn't concern me. Okay, okay. I get it." Jordan looked around the empty room, then said, "How do you know all that? About the detective, his girlfriend, her background?"

"The same way I know things about you, your buddy Billy, the senator…my new friends have friends, and some of those friends are really good with computers. Nothing is private anymore. You know that better than anyone. The minute you sneeze, there's a record of it up in the cloud and your friends have either liked that record or shared it with *their* friends. The same people who complain about privacy issues are the ones who post pictures of their morning coffee or their children on Instagram, they put out their vacation pics in real time, then wonder how the bad guys knew they weren't home. When Detective Cole made his announcement, half the people there, the ones who weren't busy grumbling, took pictures with their phones and had them out in the world before the foam on their beer had a chance to settle."

"Is he still talking to Charlotte?"

Bernie let out a soft sigh. "I can appreciate your need to prolong this conversation, to try and put your decision off as long as possible, but I'm on a pretty tight timetable. I'm afraid I couldn't wait on you, so I went ahead and decided for you."

Do I tell my people to kill Detective Cole, or do we pick someone from your group?

Her gut clenched.

"What exactly did you decide?"

"Pick up Line 4," Bernie instructed.

Billy took out his phone, studied the display for a moment, then clicked something on his remote dashboard.

Jordan heard a soft click in her headphones and said, "You're on live with Jordan Briggs. Who is this?"

There was a momentary shuffling, then a gruff voice replied, "How the hell did you get this number?"

Jordan's eyes narrowed. "I...I didn't. You called me."

"No, I didn't. You called me."

She shook her head in frustration. "Who is this?"

"Detective Garrett Tresler, with NYPD. I know who you are, Ms. Briggs. I'm well aware of the current situation."

"I'm not exactly sure what's happening," Jordan told him. "Bernie connected us somehow. He wanted me to speak to you. Where are you?"

He hesitated, maybe not sure he wanted to tell her, then he said, "I'm outside your building with members of SWAT and the FBI."

Billy tapped her on the shoulder and pointed up at the television. One of the cameras quickly panned a large crowd of law enforcement officers on the sidewalk across the street, moved back and forth several times, and settled on a man with a toothpick in his mouth and a phone pressed to his ear. When he spoke again, Jordan noticed a slight delay between the image on the screen and the voice in her headphones, but it had to be him. "We were just told he's sending down one of the hostages."

In the corner of the television, the camera trained on her lobby zoomed in even further. The image went out of focus for a moment, then cleared—a wobbly shot of the elevators. The text changed to: WE'VE BEEN TOLD THE TERRORISTS ARE SENDING DOWN ONE OR MORE HOSTAGES. The two images swapped—the lobby image took up the main screen with the detective now in the smaller shot. Jordan didn't unmute the television. She knew they were probably carrying a live feed of her right now. Whatever she said.

On the screen, one of the elevator doors slid open.

Off to the left was what looked like a melted plastic trash can, the surrounding floor stained black.

He's setting fires. Trying to gas us. He's a serious nuisance.

Detective Cole, had to be.

She gave it very little thought, because at the center of the elevator was a wheeled office chair draped in a pink baby blanket, the outline of a small body beneath.

62

Cole

Cole had pointed his gun up at the helicopter, but he hadn't shot, he was certain of that. Even now, as he huddled behind the large air conditioner, hot air rippling over and around him, the index finger of his right hand pressed against the outside of the trigger guard, *not* the trigger itself. Even if he had shot, his aim had been on the man with the rifle in the passenger compartment, not the tail. Not the fuel tank, and he was sure the blast started there. If he closed his eyes, he saw it in slow motion, the flames flaring in the back and creeping forward, the explosion.

He saw the face of the man holding the other end of that rifle, the shock and surprise in his eyes. Then his mind jumped to one singular thought—

Was Charlotte on that chopper?

Cole got to his feet, padded the pockets of his pants, and found the baby monitor. He pulled it out and jammed down the talk button. "Charlotte? Can you hear me?"

Nothing.

He felt a sharp pain from his left back pocket, and when he reached back there, he realized the iPod had gotten crushed when he fell. It was cracked down the middle, the screen shattered. Useless. He tossed it aside.

Parts of the helicopter littered the roof, some still on fire, others smoldering. The bulk of the machine had gone over the edge, and as Cole quickly crossed the roof and looked down, he realized most of the helicopter had fallen and crashed on the roof of the building next door, at least twenty stories down from where he stood. There was no way anyone survived—if the explosion and flames didn't kill them, the fall surely would have.

"Charlotte! Goddammit, answer me!"

It was then he remembered turning the volume all the way down. As he fumbled with the control, turning it back up, her voice came from the speaker. "...not supposed to use that kind of language around a child. We're very impressionable you know."

Cole felt the air leave his lungs and mix with the acrid, heated air around him. "Thank God, you're okay."

"I've been better," she replied. "Why haven't you found me yet? I thought you were a detective?"

Cole ran his hand through his hair, his eyes drifting over the carnage on the roof. "I'm working on it."

"I know I'm only eleven, but I'm smart. If bad guys tie you to a chair in a room with a countdown timer, whatever happens when it reaches zero isn't going to be good. You need to step up your game."

"Where's the timer at now?"

"Seventeen minutes and four seconds."

The body of the first man Cole shot, then shot and killed by presumably one of his own, was sprawled out on the asphalt roof, the top corner of his head missing. About twenty feet behind him, stacked against the wall rounding the edge of the roof, were about half a dozen plastic crates like the one he'd been carrying up to the roof with the older man.

"Where do you go to school, Charlotte?" Stepping over debris, Cole crossed the roof and made his way over.

"Is this the part where you try to keep me talking so I don't focus too much on the timer and freak out?"

"Yep."

"I almost have my left hand out of the zip tie. I think it would be better if I focused on that."

The cases weren't locked. Large silver clasps held them closed. One on either end.

"Do you think you can get out?" he asked her.

"Well, that's a silly question. I wouldn't be wasting time trying if I didn't think I could. I'd try something else instead."

Cole snapped open both clasps on the topmost case and carefully opened the lid. "What the hell?"

"That's another of those words you're not supposed to use around me, Detective. You're not very good with kids."

Cole stared down at the case's contents.

Parachutes.

Six, all new.

He opened the rest of the cases and found more of the same.

Thirty-six in total.

"Oh, that's not good," Charlotte said.

"What's not good?" Cole went back across the roof, toward the door to check the case they had been carrying up.

"There's something dripping on my head from the ceiling. Like, dripping a lot. Almost like a faucet."

"I set off the sprinklers on nearly every floor."

"Somebody is going to be very mad at you."

"Probably."

Cole pushed back through the door, stepped over the body of the other man, and opened the case.

It did not contain parachutes.

"What's wrong?" Charlotte asked him.

"Huh?"

"You sighed. Not a good sigh, either."

"You heard that?"

"You must have pressed the button or something."

Cole realized the talk button on the monitor had locked down into the talk position; some kind of feature to allow two-way conversation. He set it down for a moment and went back to the case.

At one point it had probably been full, and the fact that the case was nearly empty was almost as worrisome as the items he found inside—several bricks of C-4 and a handful of timers. Judging by the empty spots and discarded packaging also inside the case, at least thirty bricks of C-4 were missing. Equal amounts of timers were gone too.

Someone had been busy.

"Um. I think the water might be coming in from under the closet door too."

"Do you still hear a fire alarm?"

"No, it turned off a few minutes ago."

Cole scooped up the monitor and slipped it in his pocket. He closed the case and looked around the stairwell. He needed to hide the explosives somewhere. There was no place here. He tried to lift it, but even partially full, the case was too heavy. He'd have to go down.

He lifted one end and dragged it as gently as he could to the edge of the step and pulled it forward, cringing as the case cracked against the concrete. It didn't explode, though, and Cole was fairly certain plastic explosive was stable without some sort of ignitor to set it off. When he reached the platform for the fiftieth floor, he tugged open the door, held it with his foot, and started to slide the case through.

"Hey!" A male voice shouted from the landing below.

Cole looked down just as the man's gun came up and fired. The bullet hit the cinderblock above Cole's left shoulder and sent shards of concrete into the air.

He'd have to drop the box to return fire, and with the gun tucked under his belt, he didn't have time for that. Instead, he yanked the heavy case through the opening and slammed the heavy metal door behind him. Another bullet hit the frame on the opposite side with a loud clank. As an emergency exit, there was no lock. Cole fished the switchblade from his pocket, extended the blade, and crammed it down behind the push-bar a moment before a heavy body slammed into the door from the stairwell.

"Open the goddamn door!" A muffled voice shouted.

Cole took several steps back. The door shook but held.

He dragged the case of explosives deeper into the room.

"We need to get to the fucking roof!"

He thought of Charlotte's ticking clock. He didn't have time for this. She wasn't on this floor or the roof. That meant she was on one of the forty-nine floors below him. He needed to get down. He couldn't take the stairs, and the elevator doors on this floor were welded shut.

"Think, Cole. Think," he muttered.

"Now you're talking to yourself?" Charlotte replied through the monitor.

"Adults do that."

"Only the wacky ones."

His eyes fell on the bodies near the elevators. The welded doors.

He went over and took a closer look.

They'd been thorough. The weld started about an inch from the top and sealed the opening nearly to the floor.

No way he could open those without—

His gaze dropped to the plastic case back by the door.

"That would be crazy," Cole muttered.

"You're still doing it. Talking to yourself like a nut job."

"Sorry."

It would work, though.

He went back to the case, opened it, and took out one of the bricks of plastic explosive, felt the weight of it in his hand. Then he took out one of the timers and studied it for a moment. It wasn't complicated. Some kind of military issue meant to be quick and easy to use. There were two metal pins sticking out the back of the timer and a couple buttons on the front to set the device, a large green button to start it, and a red one to stop it.

If he did this, he had no idea how much explosive to actually use.

He also had no time for anything else.

Cole had sent the fourth elevator for floors 44 through 49. If it completed the entire trip, it was currently one floor below him. He carried one brick of explosive and a timer over to that door, peeled the packaging off the explosive, and began rolling it between his palms. It was more pliable than he expected, and when he had it shaped into a single long cord about a quarter-inch in diameter, he pressed it against the weld in the door, covering as much of it as he could. He positioned the timer near the center and pressed it in place. The pins held tight, and it stayed. He then set it for ten seconds.

"Charlotte? You might hear a bang."

"Why?"

Cole didn't answer her.

He pressed the green button, and when the timer ticked down from ten seconds to nine, he ran for the opposite corner of the floor and crouched down behind a metal support pole and several bags of concrete.

63

Jordan

"Ms. Briggs, stay on the line. Okay?" Tresler told her.

Jordan only half heard him through the sound of blood thumping in her ears. "Yeah, okay." She took several steps closer to the television, reached up, and traced the person under the blanket in the chair. "Is that my daughter?"

"Stand by, Ms. Briggs."

"Fuck you and your stand by bullshit. Is that my daughter!?"

Tresler spoke to someone else for a second, then came back on the line. "We've got a robot going in. You need to give us a moment to get in position."

The smaller image on the screen changed from a shot of the detective to one of four police officers lifting a large robot out the back of a bomb squad van and setting it on the ground. It had treads like a tank with various pieces of hardware attached to the top—cameras, two arms; one small, one long with several joints, and a metal box of some sort, like a sample container. The moment it was on the ground, one of the officers climbed back up into the van and sat down at a workstation. He reached for two joysticks and looked up at what was presumably some kind of feed from the cameras.

The robot swiveled, turned toward her building, and began to roll across 47th Street. The steel treads had no trouble climbing up and over the curb, and when it reached the entrance, the glass doors slid open automatically.

Jordan realized she was squeezing the gun so tight she couldn't feel her index finger anymore. She moved the gun to her other hand and wiped the sweat off her palm on her jeans.

She had no idea how loud the robot was, but it must have made some kind of noise because the head of the person under the pink blanket bobbed up and turned toward the doors of the lobby.

The robot inched along, one of the cameras on top panning back and forth. It rolled through one of the metal detectors, barely fit, maybe an inch of clearance on either side. On the opposite side of the security desk, it paused, sat still for a moment, then continued again.

Christ, why was that damn thing so slow?

Jordan's free hand went to her mouth and bumped against the microphone hanging down from her headphones. She realized she was about to chew on her knuckle, something she hadn't done since she was a kid. She shoved the hand into her pocket.

She didn't think the robot could move any slower, but somehow it did. When it came into frame with the person in the chair, the news channel dropped the picture-in-picture and let the image of the lobby fill the screen.

The robot stopped about two feet away from the chair, and the larger arm mounted to the top unfolded at its various joints and extended forward with a three-fingered claw, opening wide at the end. The claw turned in a half-circle, closed on a corner of the pink blanket, and reversed, pulling it off.

Jordan forced herself to breathe as the blanket dropped away.

Not Charlotte.

Her receptionist, Sarah Delange, looked at the robot with horror. There was tape covering her mouth. Her wrists were zip-tied to the arms of the chair, her legs were bent back, and her ankles were attached to the base of the chair. She jerked in place, tried to move, but couldn't.

Unlike the vest strapped to William Daly at the Holland Tunnel, the one on Sarah didn't have a dead man's switch or a cell phone, not one she could see, anyway.

Jordan felt as if someone punched her in the gut.

Billy looked no better.

The senator said, "Is that your receptionist?"

Detective Tresler was still on the line with her. He was speaking to someone else, and she couldn't make out the words. When he came back on the line, his voice had taken on an edge. "Ms. Briggs, do you recognize that woman?"

"Her name is Sarah Delange. She works for me."

"We're going to do what we can to help her, Ms. Briggs."

On the robot, one of the cameras rose off its back, swiveled toward Sarah, and inched closer on an arm similar to the large one. It panned the vest in a slow, methodical pattern—up, down, then the robot rolled slightly, no more than an inch, edging around her, and repeated. Probably creating some kind of stitched-together image. Nearly two minutes passed before it made a complete circle.

Barely audible, someone near Tresler said, "Looks like military-grade C-4. Twelve bricks—two inches, by one-and-a-half, eleven inches long. If it is C-4, that gives us fifteen pounds of explosive. Possibly more behind her back—can't see. There's no visible trigger, but we do have wires trailing under her, so it may be a compression switch."

"What's a compression switch?" Jordan heard herself ask.

"She may be sitting on the trigger," Tresler replied. "She gets up and it goes off."

"So what do you do? How do you disarm it?"

Tresler didn't answer.

"Detective?"

"Ms. Briggs, can we speak privately? Off the air?"

Jordan looked at Billy, who shook his head. She said, "We have no way to do that. We're not even sure how Bernie connected the two of us."

On the television, the picture-in-picture returned. The camera was on a woman next to the bomb squad van. Two other officers were helping her into a bulky suit.

"We're sending someone in to disarm it."

The two officers lifted a large helmet over the woman's head, slipped it on, and began fastening straps all around. One of them disappeared into the van and came out with a pair of thick gloves. The woman waved him off.

"Shouldn't she wear those?"

Tresler said, "Some techs opt not to. They're too restrictive. Limited dexterity."

The woman in the blast suit gave the two officers a thumbs up and started across the street with a slow, lumbering gait.

She was halfway there when a thundering blast rocked the building.

64

Cole

Cole chocked back the dust and forced himself to stand.

If the men on the other side of the door were still yelling, he couldn't hear them over the ringing in his ears.

The entire floor was filled with hazy white and the acrid scent of burnt metal. Cold wind whirled around him from several broken windows on the opposite side of the level. The boxes that had been stacked around the baby carriage were strewn about, several on fire, others smoldering. The carriage itself hadn't moved; it stood defiantly at the center of the room amid the smoke, dust, and fire, and looked like it could only belong to the devil among the red glow.

Cole took several steps forward, toward the elevators. The door of the fourth car was no longer welded shut. Instead, a ragged gash had appeared where the weld had been, both doors folded partially inward, into the shaft, creating an opening about two feet wide. He could see the cables beyond, the metal tracks along the back and side walls.

The plastic case containing the explosive equipment was still near the door where he'd left it, and he was grateful for that—for the first time, he realized if the contents of that case had ignited, it might have killed him.

"Are you okay?" Charlotte asked, her voice shaking. "That *was* loud!"

He wondered if that meant she was on a floor near him or if the sound had traveled through the entire building. "Yeah, I'm all right."

The case was warm to the touch but not so hot that he couldn't move it. He dragged it over to the open elevator and looked down into the shaft. He could see the top of the car below him, one floor down. There was a ladder built into the side of the elevator shaft. He could use that, but the case was far too heavy to carry down. He'd have to drop it.

Behind him, one of the men was beating on the metal door again. "What the hell did you do?"

Cole opened the case and broke off a quarter-piece from one of the last explosive bricks and grabbed another timer. He set both off to the side, then closed the latches on the case. He slid it across the floor to the damaged elevator door, watched it teeter on the edge, then shoved it over. The heavy case crashed down onto the elevator roof hard enough to partially cave it in, but it didn't break through.

Scooping up the explosive and timer, he ran back over to the emergency exit door.

Another fist thudded on the opposite side.

Cole pressed the plastic explosive into the gap above the metal push bar, behind the switchblade, and pressed the timer down into it. He set the small device for sixty seconds, hit the start button, and ran back to the elevators when it started to tick down. Emptying his lungs, he turned sideways and squeezed through the jagged opening, careful not to touch the hot metal of the doors. There was a small metal lip on the inside, and he got one foot on it, then the other, before leaning over and grabbing a rung of the ladder. From the ladder, he quickly scuttled down to the roof, yanked open the access door on top of the elevator, and looked down inside.

Empty.

He considered dropping the case down inside, then thought better of it. At least it was hidden on the roof. He could always get it later. At the very least, they probably wouldn't find it.

He pushed it aside and lowered himself through the opening.

When Cole started the timer, he tried counting backward in his head, hoping to keep track, but he'd lost count somewhere along the way. He reached over and pressed the button for the 44th floor—the SiriusXM corporate offices, one level above the Jordan Briggs show.

Nothing happened.

He remembered he had locked the elevators with the key, fumbled through his pocket, found it, jammed it into the panel, and twisted. All the buttons flashed, and he pressed 44 again. This time the car started to move down. He took out both guns and pressed into the corner.

Cole heard the smaller explosion above as the elevator descended, as the floor numbers ticked down. He wondered just how close those two guys had been standing to the door when it went off.

65

Jordan

With the first explosion, Jordan grabbed the table next to her and immediately regretted the movement as pain radiated out from the bullet wound in her shoulder down her arm, past her elbow, and into her fingertips like someone forcing a knife with a two-inch wide blade down a one-inch wide garden hose. She found herself looking at Billy as Tresler called out to someone else over the open line, his voice distant again in her headphones.

"What the hell was that?" Tresler repeated when nobody answered him.

Jordan forced herself to look back up at the television—the woman in the bomb suit was still standing at the center of 47th Street, unmoving, and for a second Jordan thought the picture had frozen when the bomb went off, but then she moved. She turned slightly to look back the way she'd come. The other image was still trained on Sarah Delange, tied to the chair near the elevators, the robot continuing to circle her as someone tried to maneuver its camera to get a shot from below.

A female voice near Tresler shouted, "We've got smoke and broken windows near the top floor!"

A new image immediately filled the television monitor, sweeping up the outside of the building to the top floor and focusing on four broken windows with dark smoke billowing out.

"Some kind of secondary explosion," Tresler said. "Any idea what's up there?"

"The top floor is vacant," Jordan heard herself say. "That FBI woman said they were staging up there. She also said that's where they moved my staff."

"What FBI woman?"

"She said her name was Allison Varney," Jordan told him. "She wasn't real, though. None of them were. That was all part of Bernie's…they're not really up there, right?"

"Hold on a second." He fell away again.

Who the hell was he talking to?

"I've been told we have eyes on that floor and your staff is not up there."

A flood of relief washed over her, but it only lasted a second. On the television, the shot of the smoke on the top floor had been relegated to the smaller window, and the main frame was again focused on Sarah Delange in the chair, the robot, and the bomb tech stepping into the shot.

"What's her name?" Jordan asked Tresler.

"Who?"

"The woman in the bomb suit."

"I'm not sure I should disclose—"

Jordan cut him off. "A person does something this dangerous, they deserve recognition. What's her name?"

She let the silence linger until Tresler finally sighed and said, "Bernita Valla."

"Tell me about her."

Tresler hesitated, and at first, she thought he wouldn't give her any more than a name, but he went on, "She's one of the bravest people I've ever met. She signed up for the Marines right out of high school, ended up in Iraq and Afghanistan, where she spent countless tours, nearly ten years, diffusing dozens of bombs. She doesn't talk about it a lot. She's a quiet person, but she's probably saved more lives than most of us on the force combined. For what it's worth, she also listens to your show."

"Well, everyone has their faults, right?"

On the television monitor, Bernita Valla crouched down next to Sarah, and using a small mirror was studying several wires that started somewhere inside the vest and disappeared below the chair, under the seat. Whoever was in control of the robot had moved it back several feet to give her space to work. A compartment was open on the robot's side, and Valla reached in and came out with a small screwdriver. Then she laid down on the ground, on her back, and slid partially under the chair. The camera operator tried to zoom in closer for a better shot, but their angle was off.

"Sarah's been with me for a little over seven years now," Jordan said. "She's a lot more than my receptionist. She's an office manager, referee, guest-wrangler, defacto-babysitter, she's…a friend. I don't have many of those. She's one of the few people I trust."

From behind the tape, Sarah's mouth twitched. Her head was turned to the side, watching Valla work. Her mascara had left long streaks down the side of her face, still glistening with tears.

Valla slipped out from under the chair, retrieved a small pair of scissors from the compartment of the robot, then went back under.

Jordan stepped closer to the television. "What is that? On Sarah's lap? Do you see it? Between her knees?"

Almost immediately, the camera zoomed in a little closer and panned down, but again, they were limited by the angle.

"I think it's a baby bottle," Billy said.

He was right. Only a little of the bottle was visible, pinched between her knees.

Under the chair, Valla repositioned, following the wires. She too was looking at the bottle now. When the bomb tech leaned in closer, Sarah started shaking her head, shouting behind the tape. Valla was talking to someone; there must be some kind of microphone in her helmet.

"Detective Tresler, are you still there? What's happening?"

"I've been told the bomb has three different triggers. Your receptionist is sitting on one—if she stands, the bomb will go off. There is a wireless receiver under the chair—"

"Is it attached to a phone? We have no service in the building right now. That wouldn't work."

"No, it's on a radio signal. The robot has a broad-spectrum frequency blocker built in. The bomb can no longer be activated remotely. If it could, I wouldn't be telling you any of this. Then there's this final switch, attached to the baby bottle. Valla is still trying to figure that one out."

Valla had retrieved what looked like a black tube and was fishing one end under Sarah's leg while peering into the other side.

"Is that some kind of camera?"

Billy tapped Jordan on the shoulder. "Where's the senator?"

The senator was no longer in the greenroom. They were so focused on the television, neither of them had seen him leave.

Tresler said, "Yeah, a camera. Infrared with magnification. The bottle is about half-filled with milk and the switch is floating inside. It seems to be operating under the same principals as a mercury switch in a thermostat. If it touches—"

The blast was far more powerful than the other one. On the television, all the windows in the lobby exploded out. A fireball shot out across 47th Street and engulfed the air. Sarah and Bernita Valla vanished behind a wall of red and black.

66

Jordan

Jordan watched in horror as first the lobby of her building, her friend, the bomb technician, and several emergency vehicles parked on 47th Street were engulfed in a giant fireball, but then the windows of the second floor blew out with a similar explosion and the third floor after that. With all three, dark smoke belched out into the air as the building coughed and shuddered. The rumbles of each explosion reached her, rattled the floor, the pictures on the walls, her teeth, and then settled into a calmness she knew was false; nothing more than a mask created by their height, their distance from the carnage below.

Billy was first to speak, his eyes glued to the television. "We need to move. We need to find a way out."

The line with Detective Tresler was still active, and Jordan could hear dozens of voices begin to shout—fire, police, spectators—too many to pick out what was being said.

Billy gripped her arm. "Jordan…"

"We need to find Charlotte."

"The senators gone," he repeated.

"Fuck the senator."

He nodded at the gun, still in Jordan's hand. "We need him."

—*to get Charlotte back*

a whisper in the back of her mind finished for him.

You'll need to shoot that man if you want your daughter back.

"Ms. Briggs, can you still hear me!?"

This was Tresler again. He was shouting, his words punctuated by a cough.

Billy mouthed *Come on*, and pulled her toward the door.

"I'm here," she replied.

"What floor are you on?"

"43."

"Your husband said he was with at least thirty other hostages. Are they with you?"

Jordan looked to Billy, and he knew what she was thinking—she couldn't tell him the truth. Not without tipping off Bernie. "I don't know where they are. They've got us locked in my studio."

Following Billy, they edged down the hallway, peering into each office and open doorway as they went. Nobody was here. The entire floor seemed deserted. "We can't see anyone through the windows. I don't think they're on my floor," she told Tresler. Not the full truth, but something.

They checked three more offices. Then Billy froze, staring at the display of his phone. He held it up for Jordan.

Bernie was on Line One.

Jordan said, "Detective, I'll be right back."

Billy clicked several buttons, then nodded.

Bernie didn't wait for her to speak first. "I know you've left your studio, Ms. Briggs; there's no reason to keep up that pretense. I also know Senator Moretti managed to slip away from you too. That's unfortunate, with only about thirteen minutes left. But all things happen for a reason, right? You're a resourceful woman. Here's hoping you find him in time."

"You didn't have to kill Sarah. She was a good person."

"I didn't kill her, you did. You and Detective Cole. He's running around the building, causing all kinds of trouble. I've had to adapt my initial plans."

"By blowing up three floors?"

"For now, yes."

"What's that supposed to mean?"

"It means the friends I told you about earlier spent a good portion of their morning placing explosives on many floors. It's a big building, but they were pretty thorough. I'm going to blow one floor every minute."

"How do you expect us to get out?"

"All you have to do is follow the rules."

"Do you know where the senator is?"

"Yes."

Jordan's fingers flexed on the gun. "Tell me."

"Where's the fun in that?"

"You're a sadistic prick."

They rounded the corner and came upon her office. The door was open. Painters tarps, plastic, and supplies strewn about. The ugly doll from this morning was sitting on her desk.

Was that where she'd left it?

Where Cole had left it?

So much had happened, she couldn't remember.

She crossed the room and picked it up. The ceramic head bobbed to the side, the doll's single eye glared up at her—faded blue and cloudy as if riddled with cataracts. She ran her finger over the crack in the doll's head, held in place by black stitching into the crumbling fabric of the doll's yellow satin dress. The stitching wasn't right. Specifically, the thread wasn't right. The doll looked older than dirt, but the threat seemed new, recent.

Removing the headphones from her right ear, she lifted the doll and shook it. She heard something rattling around inside its head.

She looked over at Billy, but he was out in the hallway again with his back to her.

With a firm grip around the doll's face, she slammed the back of its head into the corner of her desk. The old ceramic shattered into a dozen pieces, crumbled, and spilled out over the floor.

At the noise, Billy turned back around, realized what she'd done, and looked down at the mess on the floor.

Amidst the rubble was a silver key. Shiny and new.

He scooped it up and shoved it in his pocket. "We don't have time for this! Let's go—"

Jordan watched him run back out into the hall and disappear around the corner.

She said, "If I shoot the senator, you'll let my daughter go."

"Yes."

"What about the rest of my staff? My husband? All the people still in this building?"

"One bullet, and they all go free."

On the television in the corner of her office, the bottom three floors of her building were engulfed in flames, reaching for the upper levels. Several fire trucks had already been on scene after somehow managing to get through the gridlock, and dozens of FDNY first responders were busy unfurling hoses, but it almost seemed pointless. The fire was growing too fast.

"If you were to speak to the police again, they'd probably tell you to stay put, but I assure you, nobody is coming to help you. With the senator on the move, the longer you stand there the more distance he'll manage to put between the two of you. You only have about twelve minutes left now. That's not a lot of time, and there are so many places to hide."

Jordan wasn't sure where Billy had gone off to, but he came back around the corner into her office fast, an urgent look on his face.

He gestured for her to follow him, then ran off again.

Jordan found him standing at the stairwell near the end of the hallway, holding the door open.

When she looked down at the floor, she realized why.

The woman they knew as Special Agent in Charge Allison Varney was on the ground, legs splayed out, back against the wall, one hand pressed to a bloody wound in her abdomen.

As Jordan walked up, she realized the woman wasn't dead. Varney's eyes drifted up and met hers, slow and listless. Her breathing came in short, pained gasps. "That fucker shot me," she managed.

"Cole?"

"No," she coughed. "Bernie. We were supposed to all meet on the roof to get out. The helicopter. He shot me. Blew up the helicopter. Killed everyone in it. Killed at least two more a few floors up. He's killing all of us. Not letting us leave. Anyone who's seen his face. Fucker used us. Lied."

With each word, blood seeped from between her fingers, dripped down her clothing, and added to the puddle around her.

Another explosion rattled through the building.

Fourth floor.

67

Cole

As the elevator doors opened on the SiriusXM corporate offices, water sprayed in from the sprinklers, and a heavy explosion rocked the building, shaking the car, nearly knocking Cole off his feet. He was thankful for that, because when those doors opened, a man holding an AR-15 assault rifle was standing there soaking wet, and the sudden shock bought Cole the half-second he needed to fire his 9mm, put a bullet through the man's throat, and watch him drop to the ground, dead.

Cole crouched low, quickly scanned left and right, but didn't see anyone else.

Some kind of secondary explosion hit, and he held the elevator wall to steady himself, then stumbled out of the car into the lobby, water raining down on him. He shoved the 9mm back into his belt, took the AR-15 from the dead man, and checked the extended clip—twenty rounds.

Fire alarm strobes flickered on all the walls, but the shrill alarm itself had silenced, most likely timed out.

A third explosion came, this deep rumble from somewhere down below.

Cole nearly dropped the baby monitor, slick with water, and shouted into the microphone. "Charlotte?!?"

Oh God, please don't let that have been her.

"Charlotte?!"

"What was that?" her voice came back, filled with fright.

He forced himself to breathe.

Not you. That's what it was.

He said, "Did it feel like it came from below you or above?"

"Below for sure. Are you coming? Please tell me you're close!"

"Do you smell smoke or anything?"

"You're scaring me."

"I'm sure it was nothing, Charlotte."

"Where are you? Is he blowing up the building?"

Yes.

"I don't know. I don't think he'd do that."

"There's a lot of water in here now. If I stretch, I can reach it with the tip of my shoes. Enough to splash. You need to hurry!"

"There's water here too," he told her.

There was, a lot. Nearly half an inch on the floor. Cole wondered how long the sprinklers would run. If Bernie was setting off bombs in the building, would all the water slow down the fire? If he damaged the structure itself, would that even matter?

"Where are you right now? Do you think you're close to me? I hear water by you too, so maybe you're close."

Cole looked around the deserted lobby. "I'd rather not say, Charlotte."

"You don't know who's listening? Is that it?"

"Yeah."

The design of the floor appeared similar to the one the Briggs show was on. Marble floor with a large reception desk to greet people as they came off the elevator and hallways splitting off in both directions.

Cole remembered the directions Charlotte had given him and followed the hallway to the left for twenty paces, trying to keep his steps small to mimic someone her size. At twenty, he turned left and stepped into a vacant office. There was no closet, though. No other door. He checked the other nearby offices as well, but there was no sign of her.

This wasn't the right floor.

He found nine more offices in the hallway, all empty. Several had been ransacked, though—drawers open, contents spilled out on the floor.

Leading with the barrel of the assault rifle, he turned and went back the way he'd come, past the elevator, and down the other side.

He found two more empty offices before he came upon a closed door.

Cole pressed his ear against the wood but couldn't hear anything over the spraying water. He tested the knob and found it unlocked. Ready to fire, he twisted the knob and kicked the door in.

A large conference room.

The hostages were lined up against the walls, sitting on the floor, their wrists bound behind them with zip ties. Their ankles were tied too, some to chairs, some to the person next to them, all of them immobile.

At least three dozen heads all bobbed up in his general direction from beneath black cloth bags.

Several shouted out in surprise, their voices muffled by the material.

Cole reached for the person nearest him and tugged off the bag.

Nick Briggs.

The left side of his face was horribly bruised. His eye was swollen shut. He'd taken a nasty beating.

He looked up at Cole, the rifle in his hand, and didn't recognize him at first. Then something clicked. "You."

"Me," Cole replied softly. He glanced back out into the hallway. "I killed one at the elevator. Are there any others?"

Nick shook his head. "It's been just the one for at least thirty minutes now. I don't know where the rest went."

"How many? Any idea?"

"Two. They left to carry something up to the roof."

The first two men Cole killed in the stairwell up near fifty. "I shot them. I think I killed at least two others a few minutes ago with an explosive."

"That was you? It shook the entire building."

"That was something else on one of the lower floors."

Nick coughed, and pain lined his face. "Ribs," he told Cole before he had a chance to ask. "Any idea how many are left?"

Cole wasn't sure. "Three, maybe? Hard to say."

"We need to get everyone out of here, before someone comes back."

"Daddy?" Charlotte breathed from the monitor in Cole's pocket.

At the sound of his daughter's voice, Nick's one good eye lit up. "Where is she? Do you have her?"

Cole shook his head and said, "Charlotte? Give me a second to talk to your daddy, okay?" He switched off the open microphone, knelt down beside Nick, and told him what little he knew.

When he finished, the spark had left Nick's eyes again. "Can I talk to her?"

Cole toggled the microphone back on and set the monitor in his lap. "Your daughter has been incredibly brave," he said, loud enough for her to hear.

"Detective Cole talks to himself, Daddy. I'm not sure he can be trusted."

Another explosion, many floors down.

Above them, the steady spray from the sprinklers abruptly stopped. The hiss of water ceased. The room became horribly quiet.

Had someone shut the system down? Was it the explosions? Could the water have run out?

Cole had no idea and didn't have time to think about it.

He pointed at the ties on Nick's wrists. "Talk to Charlotte for a second. I need to find something we can use to cut those."

68

Jordan

"You're still alive, Allison? I'm sorry. I liked you. I wanted to make it fast, but you ran off before I could finish. I hate to think you're out there somewhere suffering," Bernie said. "Maybe Ms. Briggs will finish things for me."

For a brief second, Jordan had forgotten that he was still on the line, that all of this was being broadcast. "You're killing your own people?"

"They tried to leave before the job was done. Couldn't have that. Not with the ticking clock. Start a job, you gotta finish the job. Can't cut and run when things get dicey. Dependability is a must in today's workforce."

At the mention of time, Jordan couldn't help but look back over her shoulder at one of the wall-mounted televisions in her offices, at the news channels countdown. The camera showed a wide-angle shot of her building, the bottom engulfed in dark smoke. The ticker read: multiple explosions at siriusxm – bottom six floors decimated – hostages still inside.

Eleven minutes.

"Is he on that thing? Can you hear him?" Varney spat out, looking up at Jordan's headphones. "Tell him he's a fucking dead man. The Sentinels will hunt him down like a goddamn mangy dog."

"Wow, she's a feisty one," Bernie replied. "Always was. You've got enough bullets left to finish her and still take out the senator, right? Nobody will fault you for that. You probably should. She's the one who got your daughter out of there in the first place. Took her from you. She tied her up and locked her in a small room to die alone. I guess I still owe her for that, but you certainly don't. If you hurry, you've got time to kill her and still find Moretti."

Jordan reached up to the side of her headphones and jammed down the mute button. Crouching, she pressed her index finger into the center of the bloody mess in Varney's abdomen and twisted.

Varney cried out and tried to shrink away but had nowhere to go.

Jordan said, "Do you know where Charlotte is?"

Varney blinked the wetness from her eyes and looked up at her. "I know exactly where she is. Your daughter is tied to a chair in a closet sitting next to a very large bomb set to go off soon. You want me to tell you where, you need to get me to the roof. Get me out of here."

"Why the roof?" Billy asked from over Jordan's shoulder, eyeing the stairs leading up. "You said he blew up the helicopter. How, exactly, do we get out from there? He's not going to let anyone rescue us."

Varney coughed, pinched her eyes shut for a moment against the pain, then said, "Can't go down. Bernie saw to that with the bombs he's been setting off. I was there when he planned this. Those explosives were placed to cut us off, to ensure first responders can't get in from the ground. We need to go up, not down. Go down, and we're dead. We'll run right into the next bomb."

"So what's on the roof?" Billy asked again.

She ignored him and looked at Jordan. "You want to save your daughter, we need to go. Now."

Jordan twisted her finger again. "You want us to haul you up to the roof, you take us to Charlotte first."

"No." Varney pinched her lips shut and stared defiantly like a child unwilling to take their medicine.

In her headphones, Bernie cleared his throat. "Where did you go, Ms. Briggs? Do I need to add a no-muting stipulation to our agreement? I want everything on the air. No secrets between the two of us."

Jordan glared at Varney.

She wanted to kick this woman's face in and stomp on her.

Nothing appealed to her more right now than using one of the remaining bullets to end her right here.

She wouldn't regret it. Not for a second.

Instead, she bit all that back and said, "Can you walk?"

Varney nodded.

Jordan dug her finger in again. "Anything happens to my daughter before we get to her, and I'll throw you off that fucking roof myself, you piece of shit."

Before Varney could respond, Jordan stood and started up the steps toward the 44th floor. "Help her, Billy."

She unmuted her microphone. "Sorry, Bernie. Girl talk."

69

Cole

Cole handed the scissors he'd found to one of Jordan's interns, the scrawny guy in the stained Metallica tee-shirt from earlier, and told him to hurry up and cut the rest of the zip ties—free everyone else. About two-thirds of the crowd were standing around the conference table, rubbing their wrists and ankles. Nick was off in the corner, talking to Charlotte on the baby monitor, trying to get anything out of her that might help them find her.

Jules Goldblatt came rushing through the conference room door. His frightened eyes landed on Cole. "Somebody's trying to get through the stairwell door."

They'd jammed the release handle with a letter opener, ensuring the lock couldn't disengage.

AR-15 in hand, Cole ran back out into the hall to the emergency exit, with Goldblatt behind him.

The door rattled as someone shook it from the other side. Then there were three loud thumps, someone's fist beating on the metal.

Careful not to slip on the wet tile, Cole crouched down on one knee and pointed the barrel of the assault rifle at the doorway, his finger on the trigger. He nodded at Goldblatt, who reached over and pulled out the letter opener before ducking down against the wall.

At first, nothing happened, then the door crashed open, slammed against the wall missing Goldblatt by less than an inch, and Jordan Briggs came around the corner talking to someone in a pair of bulky headphones while also pointing a .38 in Cole's direction.

Cole rolled to the side a half-second before she pulled the trigger. The bullet cracked against the tile, ricocheted, and embedded in the wall to his right.

She recognized him, and her face went white.

"What the—"

She held a finger to her lips and shushed him as Billy came up behind her and stumbled through the doorway holding a woman covered in blood. The two of them collapsed next to Goldblatt, who looked horrified. Jordan spotted some of her staff near the conference room door, quickly turned her back, and walked swiftly in the opposite direction toward the empty offices, still talking.

Out of breath, Billy said, "She's got Bernie on the air. I'm guessing she doesn't want him to hear any of you or know we found you."

Cole frowned. "She's still broadcasting?"

"He won't let her stop." He looked up at Goldblatt, the people at the other end of the hallway. "You found everyone?"

Cole nodded. "Everyone but Charlotte."

He told him about the baby monitor and went over to the bleeding woman. At first, he didn't recognize her. Then it clicked. Varney. The FBI agent who had called him on the iPod. "What happened?"

Billy quickly explained. "Not only is Bernie killing off his own people, but this piece-of-shit just told me they wired all the floors to explode. Not just the first three."

The woman groaned. Her eyes fluttered and rolled up into her head.

Billy slapped her, brought her back. *"Where the hell is Charlotte?"*

She didn't answer aloud, only mouthed, *Roof.*

"How much blood has she lost?" Cole asked.

He started to peel up her soaked shirt when Jordan came stomping back down the hallway. "He hung up on me again."

"Are you still on the air?"

She nodded. "I don't even think the mute button is working. Everything is going out live, whether we want it to or not."

Jordan saw Nick then, standing in the hallway.

He looked up from the baby monitor and shuffled over, one hand pressing against his hurt ribs. Without taking his eyes off Jordan, he said into the device, "Do you want to talk to Mommy?"

Jordan's eyes grew bright, and she took the monitor from him with a quivering hand. "Char?"

"Mommy?"

Tears welled in Jordan's eyes. She tilted her head back and forced herself to breathe. "Hey baby, we're coming to help you!"

"The timer says there's only ten minutes minutes left, Mommy. I think I smell smoke. Are the sprinklers still on?"

Jordan's grip flexed on the gun in her hand.

She dropped down next to the woman on the ground and pressed the barrel against her temple. "Where the fuck is my daughter!?"

"Roof," the woman muttered, half-conscious.

Cole tried to take the gun from Jordan's hand, but she yanked away. She got back to her feet, studying all the faces staring back at her—her boss, her staff, her coworkers. "Where's Senator Moretti? Is he here? Did he come up here?"

Her grip flexed on the gun again, and Cole didn't like that. He didn't like it one bit.

"He's not here," he told her.

She turned from him, walking in a slow circle. "Shit, shit, shit…"

She was growing hysterical.

Waving the gun again, she glowered down at the woman on the ground. "We need to get that bitch up to the roof before she dies. We need to—"

Nick placed a hand on her shoulder.

She fell into him and began to sob.

Goldblatt said, "He's destroying the lower floors, forcing us to go up."

"Like fucking rats in a sinking ship," Billy said.

"I found parachutes on the roof," Cole told them. "Dozens of them. Enough for everyone."

Goldblatt's voice went flat. "He wants us to jump?"

"Are we even high enough for something like that?" Billy asked.

"I didn't take a close look, but I think they were base-jumping chutes, designed to deploy automatically from low altitudes," Cole told him. "Bernie's planned every second of this."

Goldblatt pointed at the television in the corner of the office. The news channel countdown said a little over nine minutes. "Whatever we do, we need to do it fast."

To Billy, Cole asked quietly, "Can you get that gun away from Jordan?"

"No way. Not even gonna try."

"We can't let her shoot the senator."

Nobody replied to that.

They didn't have a chance.

Jordan shot at Varney instead.

70

Jordan

The shot struck the wall inches from Varney's head. All those who had been speaking fell silent.

Jordan crouched over the woman, thin smoke drifting up from the barrel of her gun. When Cole ran up, she quickly pointed the weapon at him. "Don't."

He froze.

Jordan was too unpredictable. He couldn't risk trying to wrestle the gun from her.

Jordan pressed the gun against Varney's forehead. "I've got two shots left. One for Senator Moretti, and one more for you. Tell me where Charlotte is right now, or I'll kill you. Don't think I won't." She waved a hand at one of the televisions. "We don't have enough time to get you to the roof and come back down for her. Not if that's accurate. I've got nothing left to lose by killing you right here."

Varney sucked in a breath between clenched teeth. "Fuck you. Shoot me."

Jordan shrugged, pulled the hammer back with her thumb, and—

"Don't!" Billy shouted out. "Don't. Not yet. I've got an idea."

Jordan pressed the gun hard enough into the woman's skin to leave a dent in her flesh. "What?"

Billy took out his phone and clicked through to his remote switchboard app. "I need to get that detective back on the line."

He pointed at a button on the wall and told Cole, "Hit that switch so we can all hear."

Cole did.

The amplified sound of Jordan's breathing came from a speaker in the ceiling.

Billy pressed a button on the screen of his phone and leaned in closer to Jordan so her microphone would pick him up. "Detective Tresler, can you hear me?"

"Yeah, I'm here. We've been listening. What do you need me to do?"

"Every floor of this building has WiFi repeaters. When I tell you to, I need your tech people to start switching them off, one floor at a time. Give it a five-count, then turn it back on. Like a rolling blackout from the top of the building down. Call out the floors as you go. Can you do that?"

"Hold on a second."

Jordan was frowning. "Bernie won't let us do that."

Billy began ticking off points on his fingers. "He said the first responders can't enter the building. They're not. He said we need to stay on the air, we are. He said we can't shut down the building's power, we're not. We're not breaking any rules."

Another explosion.

Goldblatt looked down at the floor. "How much of this can the building take before the whole thing comes down?"

Nobody had an answer for that.

Tresler came back. "Okay, we're ready."

Billy reached a hand out to Nick. "I need the monitor."

Nick whispered something to Charlotte, then handed it over.

Into the monitor, Billy asked," Charlotte? What's your favorite song?"

Without hesitating, she said, "'Don't Stop Believing' by Journey."

"I need you to sing it for me."

"Are we on the air?"

"Please, Charlotte. It's important."

She went quiet for a moment, then said, "Okay, but I'm not very good."

When she started singing, Billy told Tresler, "Okay, start with the top floor and work your way down. Kill the WiFi for five seconds, turn it back on, and repeat until I tell you to stop. Skip our floor. We're on 44."

"Copy," Tresler replied.

As Charlotte sang, he began calling out floors.

When he reached 37, Charlotte's voice dropped out mid-phrase.

"Stop!"

Five seconds passed, and her voice didn't come back.

Jordan eyed Billy, worried and confused. "Does that mean she's on 37?"

"She should have come back," he replied. Into the baby monitor, he said, "Charlotte? Can you hear me?"

She didn't answer.

"Detective Tresler? Did something happen on your end?"

He didn't respond either, and when Billy looked down at the remote app on his phone, he realized the detective was no longer on the line. All five lines read Bernie again. "Shit, he's back."

Another explosion came.

Another lower floor destroyed.

Jordan took in another breath. "Okay, put him on."

Bernie must have heard the line click over. "That was smart, Billy, but it was riding the edge of cheating, so I had to shut it down. I turned off WiFi on all the floors below you. I didn't want to do that. I think being able to speak to her parents was important to Charlotte, particularly in these final minutes, but I can't have you breaking the rules."

"You fucking bastard!" Jordan shouted. "Where is she?"

"The question you should really be asking is where is the senator. Every second you stand around there, he's getting further away."

"He's got to be going up," Billy said.

If Bernie heard him, he didn't answer. Jordan seemed to consider this. Her fingers were opening and closing on the gun as she thought about it. She was looking at the timer on the corner of one of the televisions.

Cole found himself watching it too, and when it clicked over from seven minutes to six minutes, fifty-nine seconds, another explosion rolled through the building. The ticker quickly adjusted: TENTH FLOOR OF SIRIUSXM BUILDING DETONATES.

The last bomb had gone off when the timer had exactly eight minutes left.

From a desk against the wall, Cole grabbed a pad of paper and a pen. He quickly scribbled out a message and showed it to Jordan and Billy:

He's setting off one bomb per minute, going floor by floor. They're all on timers. Must be. This last one went off on the tenth floor with seven minutes left on the countdown. If Charlotte's bomb is set to go off at ten-thirty—with the countdown—that means she's on the eighteenth floor.

"What are you guys talking about?" Bernie asked. "You make me all nervous when you huddle together like that."

Billy looked around the room and spotted a camera up in the corner. He went over and yanked it down, tore the wires right out.

"Well, that wasn't nice," Bernie said.

On the paper, Jordan scribbled:

I'm going!

Cole quickly shook his head and wrote:

No. No WiFi below. You need to keep him talking. Keep him on the air. You get everyone else to the roof.

Billy's eyes met Jordan's for a second, then dropped to the gun in her hand in an unspoken comment that couldn't have been louder if he had shouted it—*the senator went up*. He's your Plan B if that timer gets too close to zero.

Cole handed the AR-15 to Goldblatt. He couldn't trust Billy with it—he was just as likely to shoot the senator as Jordan was. He expected Goldblatt to shy away from the weapon, but instead, he checked the chamber and the clip and clicked the safety off and back on again. When he caught everyone looking at him, he said, "I was in the reserves back in my twenties. I'm at the range at least once a month."

Jordan was watching all of them, her mouth open slightly, her eyes quickly darting around. She clearly wasn't sure about this, and Cole was about to say something to convince her when Nick leaned over, slid the headphone cup from her left ear, and whispered. When he pulled away, she looked him in the eyes and nodded.

She put the headphones back on and raised the microphone to her lips. "You win, Bernie. We're going to the roof. Tell the senator to sit tight."

Yet another bomb went off then.

Cole looked up at the television as the timer ticked over to five-minutes, fifty-nine seconds, then bolted back down the hall. Nick followed after him—broken ribs or not, he wasn't about to abandon his daughter.

71

Jordan

Cole only had one elevator key, and without a key, the elevators no longer worked.

Jordan and the others weren't sure if that was because of the fire or Bernie or something else, and they didn't have time to stand around and think about it. Cole had to take the key—they needed to get down far faster than she and the others needed to get up, and there was no way Nick could make it down all those steps with broken ribs.

Jordan found herself paralyzed.

Every ounce of her being wanted to chase after Cole and Nick and get to her daughter, wrap her arms around her, and never let her go again. But she also knew Cole had been right—with the WiFi turned off on the lower floors, the cameras and whatever else Bernie had been using to track them were probably off. He wouldn't know what they were doing, and that was probably their only chance at getting Charlotte out alive.

Unless you shoot Senator Moretti.

She knew she could. To save her daughter.

Jordan wasn't sure when that particular switch had flipped in her head, but knowing her daughter had less than six minutes left unless she shot him made that decision far easier to make than it had been even thirty minutes ago. It wasn't even a question. If she saw him, she'd kill him.

And Bernie would stop the bomb and let her daughter go.

He would, right? Stop the bomb and let her daughter go?

While it was clear he was crazy, he hadn't lied.

He gave her a decision to make.

She made her choice.

She'd kill the senator.

Jordan would find a way to live with that, and she knew she could *if* Charlotte was with her. If she lost Charlotte there was no more living, there would be nothing…she pushed the thought out of her head.

She *wouldn't* lose Charlotte.

Bernie was rambling in her headphones, she hadn't heard a word of it.

Jordan watched in somewhat confused shock as Goldblatt took charge and started rushing everyone to the stairwell and up the steps, the assault rifle hanging over his shoulder on a strap. The half-conscious body of "Special Agent in Charge" Allison Varney dangled between two of her staffers, hopping on one leg as they carried her. Given a choice, Jordan would have left her to bleed out right there in the hallway. Given additional bullets, she would have *ensured* she bled out right there in the hallway. She'd managed to hold onto the gun, and with only two shots left, she couldn't waste them.

Jordan watched the last of them disappear into the stairwell, took one last look at the timer on the television, and forced herself to follow after them.

She smelled smoke in the stairwell.

Not a lot, just a hint of it, but it was there, and knowing she was more than thirty floors above the fire didn't help to settle the hairs on the back of her neck, some instinctual thing telling her to get out.

"There's something you should know, Ms. Briggs. About the senator," Bernie said.

If you can smell it here, what's it like on Charlotte's floor?

Focus, Jordan.

Keep him distracted.

"What's that, Bernie?"

"Today's not the first day the senator has had interaction with The Sentinels."

"What do you mean?"

"I mean, he's been to their compound. He's met with them."

"What, like a sleepover?"

"I've told you why I'm in your life today. Has anyone told you why Senator Moretti had to be on the air with you today of all days? I'd be willing to bet someone was very insistent that he be on with you today."

As Jordan followed the others up the steps, lagging back one flight so her microphone didn't pick up their voices, she recalled how Goldblatt had pushed her this morning. How he had insisted she interview the senator whether she wanted to or not. She hadn't wanted to; she had made that abundantly clear. All of that seemed like a lifetime ago, yet it had only been a handful of hours.

Bernie went on. "You berated him, and he stayed on the air. You made him look like a complete fool, and he put up with it, just to stay on the air. Doesn't that strike you as a little odd? Not the berating part—you do that all the time to your guests—but the staying part? How many of your guests have walked out after just a fraction of that kind of abuse? Not him, though. Not Senator Moretti. He stayed. He took each hit and shrugged it away. And what did he do when the bombs started going off? He brought up that bill of his. How his bill could have saved the day, prevented all of this."

Jordan paused for a moment, on the landing for the 46th floor, as this sunk in. "Are you saying Moretti was somehow in on this?"

"I'm saying he's knee-deep in it. From the planning stage until the first taxi blew up this morning, he's been following along, ticking off boxes on some mental checklist with each explosion."

Jordan had fallen behind and started moving again. "No way."

"Way."

"Hypothetically, let's say I believed you. Why would The Sentinels ever go along with that? A bill like that would make their lives miserable. Law enforcement could walk right into their compound anytime they wanted to, no warrant necessary, search whatever they wanted to. That goes against everything those groups stand for."

"And that's exactly *why* they went along with it."

"I don't follow."

"Have you ever spent time in a place like that?"

Jordan rounded the landing for the 48th floor. "Some walled-off compound in the middle of Nowhere, USA, with a bunch of crazies holding guns in one hand and mixing Kool-Aid with the other? Nope. Not my first destination when I get a day or two off."

"Well, they're a powder keg looking for a spark. *Waiting* for a spark. Imagine a group of like-minded individuals who spend every waking moment preparing for war—gathering supplies, training, recruiting—only to realize that war is unlikely to ever come. They've watched their founding members grow old and die...waiting. They give speeches, get fired up, get ready, and find themselves only waiting some more. They preach hatred for government, talk about how the hand of that government is at their throat, squeezing, but they do nothing. They do nothing because they know if they make the first move, if they trigger some kind of war, the general public will see them as the bad guys. But if the government starts things...if the government tramples on their rights, on the rights of every citizen, that puts them on the defensive. That puts them in the right."

"So you're saying—"

"I'm saying, their relationship was mutually beneficial. Senator Moretti needed a day like today to help push his bill over the finish line, and The Sentinels know if that bill goes through, some government agency will eventually do something stupid and set off a reason to start the war they've been preparing for. Not just

The Sentinels, you can be sure other militias around the country would join in too. What's happened today in New York isn't the end, it's just the beginning."

72

Cole

Cole had the 9mm ready as the elevator doors slid open on the eighteenth floor. Nick stood off in the corner near the control panel, hunched over slightly, his left arm wrapped around his chest, pressing against his damaged ribs.

In his right hand, Nick held the baby monitor, but that had proven useless since Bernie cut the WiFi. Although they still had a signal on the 44th floor, the moment the elevator began to descend, the signal vanished. Cole tried not to think about Charlotte alone in the dark, still singing, unaware she was now completely alone.

As the door opened, a ripple cascaded across the otherwise still tile floor, rolled into the far wall, and came back again. Water rolled over the elevator's metal threshold from the hallway and fell through the crack down into the shaft. The only visible movement. The sprinklers were no longer on. A smoky haze filled the air, no doubt coming up from the floors below. A single emergency light flickered near the ceiling, a flashing red light beside it. A large gold sign mounted into the wall opposite the elevator doors read: *Tierney, Lubbock, and Holton, Attorneys At Law*.

Cole glanced over at Nick, held a finger to his lips, and slowly stepped out of the elevator. He quickly swept the gun to the left and right, but with nearly a half-inch of water on the tile floor, there was no way anyone was nearby unless they were perfectly still and had been long enough for the water to settle.

Cole motioned for Nick to follow behind him and turned to the left, leading with the gun as he recalled Charlotte's directions.

He followed the hallway for twenty short, child-size paces, then turned left and found himself facing a closed office door. A small metal nameplate identified the office as belonging to Gary Tierney, Attorney. Cole tried the knob—locked.

With the butt of his gun, he smashed the glass on a side panel next to the door, then reached inside and unlocked it.

Unlike the hallways, the office had no sprinklers, but enough water had come in from under the door to soak the thin, gray carpet. As Cole stepped inside, each footfall sloshed; the carpet sucked at his shoes.

A thin, child voice said, "Is someone there?"

Nick nearly pushed past, but Cole held up his free arm and held him back. "Bernie may have booby-trapped the room. Stay behind me."

As if to remind them of how little time they had left, another explosion boomed from below. The entire floor shook with it, and Cole found himself reaching for the doorframe to stay on his feet. On a desk at the opposite side of the office, a cup holder filled with pens toppled over and a painting dropped from the wall and clattered to the ground. Surely the building couldn't take much more of this.

With the explosion, Charlotte yelped, recovered, then said, "Who's out there?"

"Charlotte, it's Daddy," Nick said from behind Cole and again tried to get by, but Cole held him back. "Sit tight. We're right outside your door."

"The timer says three minutes and forty-eight seconds, Daddy!"

"That's plenty of time, honey. We just want to make sure it's safe to come in."

He pushed at Cole's back, tried to shove him deeper into the office, but Cole didn't budge. Instead, he pointed.

The closet door was on the left, a chair positioned in front of it. On the chair, wrapped in a length of barbed wire, was a stuffed bunny—white with pink ears and nose. The toy seemed to stare back them from its beady black eyes. Its fur was matted with dust, stiff looking.

Cautiously edging closer, Cole got a better look. It smelled of rot.

"I don't see any wires," Nick said from behind him.

"He could have planted something inside, or maybe some kind of pressure switch," Cole replied, crouching down, trying to see under it.

"We don't have time for this," Nick shot back impatiently. "We need to get her out."

"Daddy? What's happening out there? I know I shouldn't be, but I'm really scared."

"It's okay to be scared. I'm scared too."

"Are you scared right now?"

"Yes."

Charlotte fell silent for a second. "Well, that's not good. You're the adult. You're supposed to exude confidence."

"Ha ha."

If the stuffed animal was rigged to somehow explode, Cole didn't see how. Nothing was visible. He nudged it with his finger.

The building rocked with another explosion.

Cole fell back, tried to break the fall with his hand and slipped on the damp carpet.

Charlotte yelped.

Nick had gripped both sides of the doorway and managed to stay on his feet. "That felt like it was right below us."

That was the fifteenth floor. Three floors down, three minutes left.

"Daddy?"

Nick had had enough. Before Cole could get back up, he rushed by him, threw the chair and stuffed animal aside, and yanked open the closet door.

The bunny rolled to the far corner and came to a stop. The chair cracked against the side of the desk.

Cole waited for another explosion, but none came.

From inside the closet, Charlotte's head jerked up and stared at them both, her face filled with surprise. Her cheeks were red, streaked with tears. When she saw the bruises on her father's face, his swollen eye, her mouth fell open. "Oh, you didn't win, did you…"

This came out as more of a statement than a question.

Nick tried to smile. "I'm here with you. Of course I won."

Charlotte was tied to an office chair with the same plastic zip ties Bernie's people had used on Nick and the others—her wrists were bound to the chair arms, her legs were bent under the seat and fixed to the center bar, above the wheels. A black cloth hood was on the floor beside her.

The bomb was on the opposite wall of the closet.

The timer read: two minutes, twenty-four seconds.

"Find something to cut the zip ties," Cole told Nick.

He wanted the man out of the closet before he noticed the second bomb, this one wrapped around Charlotte's waist, held in place by a steel cable and fastened to the back of the chair with a heavy silver padlock.

73

Jordan

Jordan continued up the steps. "Bernie, Where is the senator now?"

"Close. Real close."

Her fingers twitched against the gun.

"When you shoot him, go for the head. You've only got about two minutes left, and he needs to be dead in order for you to fulfill your part of the bargain. I'd hate to see Charlotte die just because you winged him with some errant shot. I don't think anyone appreciates technicalities this late in the game."

Fuck him. Cole and Nick will find her. Probably already found her. Charlotte's will be fine. Charlotte is fine. They're all going to be fine.

Up ahead, a scream tore through the stairwell.

"Well, that didn't sound good," Bernie said.

A moment later, Billy came bounding down the stairs from the 50th floor, his face this odd shade of white and green. "There are two dead people up there, on the landing. It looks like someone blew the door open from the other side while they were standing there."

"Two of our people?" Jordan asked.

"Two of *my* people," Bernie replied before Billy could. "Well, two of The Sentinel's people. That was Detective Cole's doing. I guess he did me a favor; two less for me to deal with. That sounds awfully messy, though. I bet it stinks, too. That's the kind of smell that gets in your clothes and doesn't wash out. It's best to throw them out."

Billy turned, resolute, and started back up the steps.

Jordan followed.

She tried to prepare herself, but the smell hit her. Then she saw it, and her breakfast scurried up her throat. She choked it back down, barely.

"I told you," Bernie said. "A bomb is a horrible way to die. The obscene things it does to the human body. We're really fragile when it comes to things like that. Balloons filled with water and guts."

Billy took Jordan by the arm, held her steady. He put himself between her and what was left of the two men against the wall of the landing. "Try not to look; I'll guide you. Just look straight ahead."

Jordan wasn't much for chivalry, but this time she wasn't saying no. She kept her eyes trained forward, and she and Billy hugged the opposite wall, stepped by the twisted remains of the 50th floor's metal door, around several piles of things she wouldn't allow her mind to identify on the concrete steps and walls, and onward toward the final two flights of stairs that would lead them up to the roof. The door at the top was open, and a cool wind crawled over her skin, helped mask the heavy odor in the air. She was grateful for that. Morning light streamed down from above, and something about that light told her everything was going to be okay. This would all be over soon.

As Jordan and Billy stepped out onto the roof, she realized that was all an illusion.

While she could see daylight above, when she looked over toward the sides of the building, she was met by a wall of black smoke, a thick living thing, breathing, undulating, creeping up the outer walls from all the burning floors below, drifting up toward the heavens as if someone above lifted them on heavy cords, a curtain isolating them from the rest of the world. The air held a dry heat, specs of soot drifted about, and Jordan understood this was where she would die.

Another explosion came, and she just stood there as the rumble rose up through the structure, a belch from down below. She stood there as others screamed, as the rooftop rocked under their feet. She stood there as all eyes began to fall on her, their boss, their leader, all these people looking to her to save them. They would die too, right beside her.

"You have less than two minutes, Ms. Briggs," Bernie told her. "What are you going to do?"

"If I shoot the senator, will the bombs stop?"

As she said this, Billy released her arm. She expected him to say something in protest, but he didn't. He didn't say anything.

"You shoot the senator, everything stops."

"Where is he?"

Jordan looked out over the roof, at all the faces, but she didn't see him. He had to be up here. There was no place else to go. She supposed he might have hidden on one of the floors below, but those floors were a death trap. More bombs, smoke within the building, structural integrity of the building itself. Then there was Bernie. Bernie wanted her to shoot him. He was watching all of this far too close to let that man cower in a corner somewhere and hide from that. He wanted the senator in her sights. Bernie would have found some way to drive him up here as surely as he had driven them. She was under no illusion now that they had found their way to this roof under any semblance of free will. She was standing exactly where Bernie wanted her to be.

Whoever had carried Varney up had left her on the ground, slumped against the western wall. Her lifeless eyes looked out across the rooftop. Jordan had no idea when she died but she was clearly gone.

Jules Goldblatt came running out from behind several of the HVAC units with the assault rifle bouncing against his back, holding two white bundles in his hands. "We found the parachutes. Boxes of them. Ruban from accounting said that detective was right—they're called SOS chutes, designed for escaping high-rises like this in an emergency. According to the instruction card, they deploy automatically in under a hundred feet. He jumped. I don't know where or if he landed, can't see through all the smoke, but he cleared the building, I saw that much. We're all going. These are for you—"

He handed one chute to Billy and tried to give the second to Jordan, but she made no effort to take it. Instead, she asked Goldblatt, "Where is the senator?"

"There." Billy was pointing to the northwest corner, toward a cluster of about a dozen people hovering over large plastic crates, passing out parachutes similar to the ones Goldblatt had.

The senator was fastening the last of the buckles.

"No!..." Jordan raised the gun, her feet stumbling into a run. "Don't let him jump!"

She shouted this to nobody in particular, and with the gun pointing in their direction, everyone began to move away from the senator, out of Jordan's range. "Don't let him jump, goddammit!" She fired a round, and the bullet cracked into the concrete safety wall several feet to the senator's left.

Jordan was too far.

She ran.

Senator Moretti raised both hands and started to blindly shuffle backward. "You don't want to do this, Jordan!"

Only one shot left.

She squinted as she ran—lined the senator's chest up in her site. Bernie had said to go for the head, but she knew she'd never hit him from this distance if she tried that. She aimed at the center of his chest, at the biggest mass.

The back of the senator's legs knocked against the roof wall, nothing but smoke and rising soot behind him. Shaking his head, he reached behind himself, used his hands to leverage himself up onto the wall. He scrambled back to his feet, balanced precariously on the ledge. He held his hands up again, between them, inched back toward the edge.

Jordan, close now, pulled the trigger.

Her final shot left the barrel.

74

Cole

"It's not a bomb. The man who tied me to the chair said it *wasn't* a bomb. I'm supposed to give it to Mommy," Charlotte insisted as Cole studied the silver box in her lap.

The steel cable wrapped around her waist, around the base of the chair, through the arms, and fastened behind the chair with a padlock weaved through to heavy clasps welded to the metal box, one on either side. Without the key, they'd have to cut the cable.

Charlotte's right wrist was bleeding where she tried to pull it out of the plastic ties. He took a closer look at that too. It was superficial but had to hurt. She hid it well, though. She looked him dead in the eye, as if staring down the pain itself. In that instant, Cole saw her as an adult. As the woman she would become.

He had to get her out of this.

Nick returned with a pair of scissors and went to work on the zip ties, his fingers moving fast as he spotted the metal box for the first time. "What the hell is that?"

"Stop," Cole told him.

"Why?" Nick didn't. He clipped the ties on Charlotte's left wrist, then started on her ankles.

"That cable is twisted around everything, including her.

Without the key, we can't get it off. That means even if you cut all those ties, she's still stuck in the chair."

Nick only seemed to half-hear him; he was working feverishly. He didn't reply. Instead, he tried to force the tip of the scissors into one of the welds of the box, between the side and the clasp. He got the tip in but when he pried forward, the scissors snapped. "Fuck!" he cried out.

The outburst caused him to cough, and red drops of spittle appeared on Charlotte's shirt.

He'd been wheezing, but Cole hadn't said anything. Now he did, though. "It's not just your ribs, is it? How bad did they beat you?"

Nick looked first at Cole, then at his daughter, before wiping his lips on his sleeve. "Doesn't matter." He squeezed deeper into the closet and looked behind Charlotte's chair. "She's tied to the chair with the cable, but I don't see anything keeping this chair in the closet. We can wheel her out."

On the opposite side of the closet, the timer ticked down from one minute, one second, to one minute and everything shook as the deep boom of another explosion shook the building. This one clearly only one floor below them. Several ceiling tiles broke from above and crashed down onto the office floor. One of the windows burst, and a rush of smoke-filled air choked the room, dark and gray.

Cole's eyes began to water as the acidic heat washed over him. Across from him, Nick fought the urge to cough again. Charlotte sat still in the chair, her eyes fixed on the timer, both hands resting on the box in her lap.

Cole didn't want to move her. If that box did contain a bomb, it would certainly go off either as they moved her from this closet or at some other point before he was able to get her to someone who could disarm it. This could easily be Bernie's failsafe—if they managed to get Charlotte back to her mother before she shot the senator, he might just pull out a remote and detonate whatever was inside. It could even be triggered by altitude or location and go off automatically as Charlotte left the building. There were a million ways to set off a bomb. One thing was certain, though—if they stayed in this closet, they'd be dead in less than a minute from the other one. They had no choice.

"It's not a bomb," Charlotte insisted again, looking down at the box.

Cole got to his feet and helped Nick stand.

Without looking back at the bomb ticking down behind them, they wheeled Charlotte out of the closet, out of the office, and down the hallway to the elevator.

Once inside the car, Nick coughed, one hand on his ribs, bent over to ease the pain. There was a wetness to the cough Cole hadn't heard the last time, and although Nick had covered his mouth with the back of his hand and wiped his lips again, he missed a bit of blood on one of his teeth.

Cole pressed the button for the 50th floor and nothing happened.

He twisted the key first to the off position, then back to emergency, and pressed the button again.

Nothing happened.

"Try another floor," Nick suggested.

He didn't wait for Cole. He reached over and mashed in the buttons for 44, 46, and 48.

Nothing happened at first. Then the doors lumbered shut, and they began to rise.

"Must be some kind of malfunction from—"

Nick's words were cut off as the bomb on the 18th floor went off.

The pressure smacked into the bottom of the elevator with a heavy jolt.

The car jumped up.

The lights flickered and went off, and they came to a hard stop.

75

Jordan

The bullet missed.

It went wide and to the senator's right.

She'd reached him and with all her strength, Jordan grabbed him and hauled him back off the ledge before he could deploy his chute.

"I shot him!" Jordan shouted into her microphone staring down at the senator's frightened face. "He's dead!"

Her words came as the explosion on 18 lumbered up the building, shattered more glass, shook the rooftop, and nearly knocked her to her feet.

"NO! NO! NO! Goddammit, Bernie, I shot him!"

He didn't answer.

"He's dead, Bernie!"

"No, Ms. Briggs. He's not. I'm afraid you failed. Your daughter is gone. For what it's worth, I'm sorry."

Jordan was shaking her head. "No, she's not. I'd know. I'd feel it."

"I think you do feel it. That hole in your heart. The sinking emptiness in your gut. You know it's true. The senator's alive. Therefore, Charlotte is dead."

Jordan leaned over the edge of the roof, her hands pressing down on the ledge. She was met with the heavy smoke, renewed again by the latest explosion.

On 18.

On Charlotte's floor.

On the ground at her feet, the senator looked up at the empty gun in her hand, groaned and rolled onto his side, turned away from her.

"I know what comes next," Bernie said. "You're going to play the 'what if' game. What if I shot him when we were still in the studio. What if I shot him back when he was still on the couch. What if I didn't let him get away...you know you did, right? You could have tied him up. You could have kept the gun on him. Kept him close. You didn't, though. You let him scamper off. I imagine that was your subconscious trying to give you some kind of out. Your mind offering up an excuse so you wouldn't have to live with another death on your hands. What good that did. It's still your fault. You can break it down in a million different ways, but in the end, you let that scumbag live, sacrificed your daughter for him."

"No."

"Do you think her last thoughts were about how alone she was? Sitting in the dark, tied to a chair, watching the numbers beside her tick down like some meter that measures her mother's love? At what point did she realize nobody would come for her? I wonder if she thought of you in those final seconds. How she came in second in your eyes, always a few steps behind your career."

"That's not true."

"Sure it is. Just look at today," Bernie said. "Those first bombs went off, and what little comfort you gave her, you did on the air. Then you pawned her off on someone else and went back on the air. As you and I started talking today, got to know each other, you locked her off in a room somewhere, got her out of your hair."

"That's bullshit."

"Even after you learned I was in the building, you jumped at the chance to send her away with Ms. Varney and her friends. The last thing you wanted was to be saddled with a child through all this. Charlotte was a thorn to you."

Jordan's eyes welled up with tears. She tried to stifle the sobs forcing their way out. "They said they were FBI! They were supposed to take her someplace safe! I was trying to protect her!"

"All your daughter wanted was a hug. She wanted her mother to hold her close and tell her everything was going to be okay. Nothing more. Instead, you pushed her away. Think about that last moment, Ms. Briggs, when you handed her off and they led her out of your studio, think about the look on Charlotte's face. She wore this forced mask of confidence, tried to show you how strong she was, but all she really wanted was her mother. All you *really* wanted was to be rid of her so you could get back to me, your audience, your show—the things you considered to be so much more important than her. Those are the thoughts that went through her head when the bomb beside her ticked down to zero. As she sat there and died alone."

Jordan's knees didn't want to work anymore. Her legs felt as if they might drop out from under her, and she found herself leaning on the ledge of the safety wall, black smoke billowing up around her. Soot and grime thick in the hot air, filling her lungs with each breath. Her body fought to expel it, cough it back out, while her mind wanted nothing more than to inhale, suck it all in, let it choke her from the inside out and end all of this.

Another explosion shook the building.

The 19th floor. One above where Charlotte had been.

Gone now.

Through the haze, the increasing smoke, she watched Jules Goldblatt and one of her interns helping others into parachutes. She watched as they stepped up onto the very ledge she now rested against, and hesitantly jumped over the side, vanishing as the senator had. One by one, they were gone too. All of them leaving, deserting her.

"They don't care about you, Ms. Briggs. Not a single one of them. You may have provided them with an income over the years, but you never garnered their respect, their love, their friendship. At best, they tolerated you. The only one to even offer you a parachute was Jules Goldblatt, the man you probably treated worst of them all, and he probably did it more out of some sense of obligation than a need to help you as a person. Like all the others, he doesn't care about you."

"How are you still watching us?"

Jordan looked over the few remaining faces, and her eyes landed on Billy. He was about ten feet from her, two parachutes in his hands. He faced her, his expression unreadable. She half-expected to see his lips move as Bernie spoke, some final trick, but they didn't. When Bernie spoke again, Billy only stepped closer to her, holding out one of the parachutes.

Bernie said, "He may be the only one who deserves your trust, and yet you still look at him as an outsider. So self-centered, you've never allowed anyone into your bubble—not your ex-husband, your child, or Billy, the man who has been by your side longer than any of them."

The guilt swelled within her, this balloon within her chest threatening to burst, because she knew he was right. She'd kept them at arms-length. Not just Billy and her staff, but her husband and her daughter. She'd been too focused on her career. She was as alone as she had left Charlotte. She was—

"These are the people you chose to help as your daughter died alone in a closet. People who wouldn't blink an eye if you were dead."

"Charlotte's not dead. I would know," Jordan said again, unsure if the words were meant to convince him or herself.

"Jordie? What's he saying to you?" Billy held out one of the parachutes. "Take one of these, and step back from the ledge. I'll help you get it on. You're scaring me."

"You don't think Charlotte's dead because Detective Cole and your ex-husband went back for her. You're willing to hang yourself with that thin piece of thread, that feeble belief, because it's better than accepting the truth—I'm in control, not you. I've prepared for every possible outcome. If they somehow managed to get to her before her bomb exploded, if they're on their way back,

I won't allow her to reach that roof. I'll just blow the remaining floors. I'll kill them all."

Another minute had ticked by, and the building shook again. The 20th floor now.

"What if..." Jordan heard herself say.

"What if, what?"

"What if *I* offered *you* a choice."

Bernie's voice managed to slip even lower. "What do you have in mind?"

Jordan knew it was the only choice that remained, the only thing she had left to give. She looked up again. Her eyes found Billy's. He was still standing there, his parachute on, hers in his hand. Silently, she mouthed *I'm sorry* to him.

To Bernie, she said, "My life for theirs. You allow them to live, and I'll climb up on this ledge and jump."

76

Cole

Three more bombs went off before Cole and Nick managed to pry open the elevator doors with Charlotte watching them both from the confines of her chair, the metal box resting in her lap. Whether due to the bombs, the fires below, or some other act by Bernie, the power in the elevator was completely off. So was the power on whatever floor they found themselves. No emergency power, either. They were in complete darkness.

Cole took out his phone and switched on the flashlight. "We're on 45."

"That's higher than I thought we got."

Nick coughed again, and the wetness that came with it was worse than only a few minutes earlier.

"How bad are your ribs?" Cole asked him. "Are you sure they didn't puncture one of your lungs? Can you breathe okay?"

"It doesn't matter. We gotta keep moving."

The elevator had stopped about two feet above the floor. Cole eased himself out, got his feet planted on the ground, as another bomb went off. He glanced at his watch and did the math in his head. "I think that was the 22nd floor."

Without the fire suppression systems running, the air was heavy with smoke. Even twenty floors above, it was barely breathable. He couldn't imagine what the fire and heat was doing to the structure below. Many changes had been made to building codes after the Twin Towers fell, but Cole was fairly certain this particular building had gone up long before that. Most of the high-rises in this part of the city were built in the sixties, *before* the original World Trade Center went up. With twenty-two floors on fire and more to come, it wasn't a matter of *if* the building would fall but *when*.

Cole set his phone on the floor, illuminating the hall with dim light, then reached back into the elevator. "Can you slide her over to me?"

Nick nodded and gently rolled Charlotte over to the edge. He held the back of the chair and kept it steady as Cole grabbed at the seat and lifted it down. He figured Charlotte weighed around seventy-or eighty pounds, and the chair was at least thirty. He watched Nick's face carefully as he lowered his daughter down, the strain there.

Nick must have known what was going through Cole's head, because he quickly insisted, "I'll be fine."

Cole was thinking they were on the 45th floor. Five stories from the roof, and without an elevator, that meant they'd have to carry Charlotte in the chair up ten flights of steps—a difficult task for two healthy men.

"We will do this," Nick said again before climbing down out of the elevator.

To prove his point, he scooped up Cole's phone and handed it to Charlotte. "You're in charge of the light." He began wheeling her toward the stairwell at the end of the hall.

When Nick opened the door, a rush of black smoke belched out and filled the hallway, hot and dry. He twisted his head away from it. He looked back at Cole, his worried gaze saying all that needed to be said. They had no other choice.

He pushed Charlotte's chair over the threshold, and both men were positioning themselves, preparing to lift, when the next bomb went off.

Dust dropped down from above, bits of plaster and concrete.

"Is it just me or did that one come faster than the others?" Nick asked.

Cole looked down at his watch. "You're right; that was only thirty seconds. He's speeding up."

"Get her feet," Nick said. "I've got the back."

The stairwell wasn't wide enough for them both to walk sideways, so Nick went backward with Cole taking the bulk of the weight below. They made it to the 46th floor before Nick asked to switch positions. 47th before he had to stop and rest.

Cole lost count of the bombs going off down below, but he could feel them quickly gaining ground. The air had grown thick with smoke, the bubble of light created by the flashlight quickly shrinking. Each time he sucked in a breath, his lungs fought him and tried to expel the tainted air back out.

Charlotte had grown uncharacteristically silent. They'd pulled the collar of her shirt up over her mouth in an attempt to block the smoke but it was doing little good.

"Keep going," Nick muttered between clenched teeth, stifling a cough. It was clear his body would give out long before his will.

77

Jordan

"I'll jump," Jordan repeated.

"You'll what?" Billy said, stepping closer, trying to grab her.

"Tell him to stay back," Bernie insisted.

Jordan held her hand out. "Don't, Billy. Don't come any closer."
Billy froze.

"He tries to stop you, I'll blow the rest of the floors."

"Does that mean you accept?"

"Their lives for yours?"

"Yes," she heard herself say.

"Okay."

She quickly told Billy what Bernie agreed to.

Billy went white. "You can't do that. What if he's lying?"

"What if he's *not?*"

In her headphones, Bernie said, "You have my word, Ms. Briggs. They'll get out safe. I'll see to it."

Jordan's heart fluttered. "So she is still alive! Where is she now?"
Bernie didn't answer.

"Bernie, this is a two-way street. You want me to trust you, to believe you, you need to give me proof that my daughter is still alive."

Another explosion.

The last of her staff, the last of the people from the building went over the side, leaving only Jules Goldblatt, Billy, and herself. Goldblatt came over and nodded at the two parachutes on the ground at Billy's feet. His was already on. "That's the last of them."

"Boom," Bernie said a moment before the next bomb went off.

"That's not enough," Jordan said more to herself than anyone else.

Goldblatt frowned. "What do you mean?"

"It's exactly enough," Bernie replied. "If you jump."

"What's he saying?" Billy asked.

"You need to get up on the ledge, Ms. Briggs."

"We need three more chutes, not two. Nick, Cole, and Charlotte are still alive...somewhere on the stairs," Jordan told Billy. "Bernie said if I jump, he'll make sure they get up here safely. There's enough for them, not all of us...I don't need one."

"You're not jumping," Billy told her. "That wasn't the deal."

Bernie said, "It's time. I'll detonate the bombs even faster if I have to. I'll snatch her from below."

Jordan could hear the fire now. She told herself it was just her imagination twisting the growl of high winds weighed down with smoke, the hiss of it between buildings, not flames eating away at the lower floors, slowly reaching up for her and the others, but every time her eyes blinked shut she saw deep red curling through black hallways, she saw her daughter stumbling through it in the dark, her lungs choked with foul air, one hand groping for the wall, the other searching frantically for a way out, as she called out to her, the mother who left her behind, as she called out to the one person who was supposed to keep her safe.

Jordan braced herself on the concrete ledge of the wall surrounding the building's roof and climbed up. First on her knees, then to her feet, she forced herself to stand.

Billy was shaking his head, but when he tried to step closer, she told him to stop. She held her palms out to him and inched closer to the edge.

"I have to, Billy."

Although she was only a few feet above the rooftop, the wind was far stronger. It didn't seem to blow in any particular direction, the heat from below, the walls of the surrounding buildings, all of that funneling the harsh air. It smacked against her from all sides, with the sharpness of a hefty blade.

Another bomb detonated.

Jordan felt the wall roll out from beneath her, felt the weight of her shoulders and upper half twist over the side as her legs struggled to regain some kind of balance. She bent at the waist, back toward Billy, Goldblatt, and the rooftop, held her arms out, and somehow managed to find a center and steady herself. All of this took less than a second but felt like another full minute, and she knew another bomb would go off soon, each closer to her daughter than the last.

Bernie said, "Jumping will be the only caring thing you've really done as a mother, Ms. Briggs. The only selfless act of your life. Your daughter will grow up knowing what you sacrificed for her, what you gave."

The building let out a loud groan. This was followed by a shudder, and Jordan knew something deep down in the structure had finally given way.

From the ledge, her eyes found Billy's again, and for one brief second, every moment they spent together played in her mind.

Rather than trying to grab her again, he was backing up, mumbling, talking to himself.

That wasn't the deal.

Is that what he said?

He looked first to her, then back at the stairwell, dark smoke bellowing from there too. Before she could object, he dodged around Goldblatt, ran across the roof, and disappeared back down into the burning building.

78

Cole

They were half a flight above 48 when Nick nearly dropped Charlotte. He crumpled more than fell—first his right knee buckled, then his body twisted awkwardly to the left as he attempted to pinch back his damaged ribs with his elbow rather than let go of her chair. His left knee came down hard on the edge of the concrete step, and he managed to set his side of the chair down before rolling out from beneath it.

Cole wasn't faring much better.

With each breath of acrid smoke, he became weaker, his vision grew cloudy, and he found his muscles quivering. When Nick collapsed, a part of himself he didn't want to acknowledge was secretly grateful, not because the man was hurting, but because it meant they could take a break, and he wanted nothing more than to sit and try and catch his breath. As this thought worked through his brain, the other half argued that sitting, stopping for any length of time, meant death, and while he hoped that revelation would provide a quick boost of energy, none came. He dropped down onto the steps a few feet from Nick.

"We're almost there," Charlotte told them both before launching into a coughing fit that lasted nearly a minute. Cole only knew this because two more bombs went off. When he tried to get back to his feet, his legs fell out from under him, and he found himself coughing too.

Nick *wasn't* coughing, and it was that realization that finally broke through the haze engulfing his thoughts, and when Cole looked over at him, he saw that Nick's eyes were closed. Not completely, only about three-quarters of the way, and for a moment Cole thought he was dead. Then his body spasmed as some involuntary function drew in smoke-filled air, whether he wanted it or not. A cringe drew across the other man's face, and his eyes snapped back open, darted around, realized where he was.

Nick looked up at his daughter, then reached for her hand, took her fingers in his own. "I'm sorry, sweetie."

A deep rumble rolled up from somewhere down below as another bomb detonated. Cole looked at his watch, tried to do the math and figure out what floor that was, but the numbers all jumbled together without making sense. He knew that was from the smoke, the thinning oxygen, but knowing these things didn't make his thoughts any more clear.

"People are supposed to go down in a fire, not up," he muttered. "Smoke's worse at the top."

He wasn't sure who exactly he was talking to, but it felt good to get the words out there. Felt like he had accomplished something.

Somebody hit him then.

A hard smack across his face.

He didn't realize his own eyes had closed, but they had, and when he opened them, Jordan Briggs's producer Billy was kneeling next to him, ready to hit him again.

79

Jordan

With every sound, the wind and fire wrenched up from the building, every creak, pop and rattle, the building felt like it was swaying, tilting. A tower of blocks placed precariously by a two-year-old ready to tumble. More explosions came, and with each Jordan knew the building itself was Bernie's final bomb; its fall would be the loudest of them all and would most likely take out buildings around them.

Jordan stood there, on the ledge, swaying with the injured structure on legs she could barely feel, Jules Goldblatt was still standing beside the remaining parachutes, his mouth hanging open, his gaze on the stairwell door. When he finally turned back to Jordan, when their eyes met, she told him the only thing she could, the only thing that felt right. "I'm sorry, Jules."

This seemed to puzzle him. "For what?"

"For the way I've treated you. The lack of respect. The pain I've put you through, the—"

"Jordan, you don't have to—"

"Yes, I do."

He shook his head. "No, you don't, because you're not jumping. Not without a chute. Someone will send help. They'll send a helicopter, or the fire department will—"

From her headphones, Bernie said softly, "He's got his parachute. Tell him to jump, Ms. Briggs. Tell him to go, or I'll take him too."

Jordan lowered her head. "Nobody's coming, Jules. There is only one way this can end. That's with me dying. An eye for an eye. I get that now. That's the only way the rest of you will be spared. That's how Charlotte and Nick survive." When another floor exploded down below, Jordan didn't pull away from the ledge, but instead edged closer. She tried to look out over the side but could see nothing through all the black smoke. "You've got a family, Jules—a wife, two boys. You need to go. Get out of here while you still can. When you get down there, find Detective Tresler. Tell him everything that happened—fill in the blanks for them."

Jules reached out, as if to take Jordan's hand, and she shrunk away from him. "Go."

Finally, he nodded. With one last check of the buckles on his parachute, he climbed up onto the ledge several feet down from Jordan, gave her a final weak smile, and disappeared over the side.

"Just us now, Ms. Briggs."

"Just us."

"I like to think we have an agreement, that I can trust you, but I think it's important we spell out the rules. I'd hate to see something happen because of a misunderstanding between the two of us. In our remaining time together."

"What kind of misunderstanding?"

"Charlotte will be there soon, and when she gets to the roof, you may think she's safe and you don't have to jump, but I assure you, that's not the case. If you don't jump, if you make any attempt to get her off that roof before you *do* jump, I'll take out what's left of that building, and everyone dies. Every remaining bomb, all at once. Do you understand?"

"Yes."

As she said this, Billy appeared at the open stairwell doorway, hunched over, holding the back of an office chair. Detective Cole was on the other side, carrying the chair by the base, and sitting between them both, somehow fastened to the chair, was her daughter, her Charlotte.

Jordan felt her next breath catch in her throat as relief washed over her, flooded every ounce of her being.

Several moments after Billy and Cole came through the door and set Charlotte down, Nick followed. Horribly pale, his beaten and bruised face a mix of white, purple, and blue under a dark layer of soot. He looked like he was about to collapse, like he *should* collapse, but instead he stumbled over to her. "What are you doing up there?"

"Not too close," Jordan warned him.

She quickly told him what Bernie said and saw what little life still filled his eyes vanish.

Bent at the waist, both hands on his knees, Nick eyed the remaining parachutes. "One of us could probably hold Charlotte, but she's fastened to that chair with a cable and lock, some kind of box. We gotta get it all off, or there's no way."

Coughing, Billy stumbled over to the two remaining parachutes. He tossed one toward Nick, another toward Cole, and double-checked the straps and clasps on his own. There wasn't much to them. They were like backpacks with two additional straps around the legs.

The building roiled with another explosion.

"What kind of lock?" Jordan asked.

Nick told her.

Jordan remember the key, the one she found in the doll. "Billy, where's that key?"

Billy fished the key from his pocket and handed it to Nick.

Nobody asked where they'd gotten it. There was no time for that.

"You should say good-bye to her, Ms. Briggs. I never got the chance to say good-bye to my wife or daughter. It may be hard now, but I'm sure she'll appreciate it when she gets older."

Charlotte was facing away from her, and Jordan was thankful for that. She wasn't sure she could look into her daughter's eyes and do what she needed to do. "I can't."

"You should, though. For her."

Nick fumbled the key into the lock and twisted.

The lock, the cable, the box, fell away.

Nick scooped Charlotte into his arms and pulled her to his chest, buried her in a deep hug. He was obviously in a lot of pain and didn't care. Jordan wanted nothing more than to be a part of that hug.

Another blast from below. They were getting close now.

Cole had the metal box that had been secured around Charlotte. He placed it gently down on the rooftop and thumbed open the latches. He studied the contents for a moment, then reached in and carefully took out a stack of folded pages, opened them, and scanned the text. He quickly looked up, alarmed.

"What is it?" Jordan asked him. "What are those?"

Several of the pages fell from Cole's hand. "They're visitors' logs from Rikers. Nearly a decade."

Bernie said, "You should ask Billy how well he knows Marissa Chapman."

80

Jordan

Billy pressed a hand to his ear and shook his head. "Christ, Bernie. Why did you have to—"

"Cole, stop him!" Jordan shouted out.

Cole was on his feet, reaching for the gun tucked under his belt, but Billy was faster. Jordan had no idea where he had concealed it, or how he managed to get it out so fast, but he was pointing a small pistol at her.

He shook his head at Cole. "Don't, man, don't."

Cole froze.

"Take it out with two fingers and throw it over the side of the building. You do anything else, and he'll make me shoot her. I don't want to. I don't want to hurt anybody."

Cole did as he was told, and the 9mm vanished in the black smoke.

To Nick, Billy said, "Do you have any weapons?"

Nick moved closer to Charlotte, got between her and Billy, and shook his head.

Jordan glared at her producer, this man she'd know for so long. "Billy, put the gun down. Give it to Cole."

When he looked back at Jordan, his eyes welled up with tears. "He said he'd kill her, Jordie. I couldn't...I had to help."

"He's been visiting Marisa Chapman for years," Bernie said. "Unlike you, Ms. Briggs, Billy has a conscience. He understood what the two of you did was wrong, and he tried to make amends. Apparently, somewhere along the line, he fell for Ms. Chapman."

Jordan saw it then, clipped to the pocket of his jeans, no bigger than a pen cap—what had to be a small camera. He was wearing a tiny earbud, too.

"You've been helping this monster the whole time?"

"Oh, he's been instrumental," Bernie said. "I think he saw this as a way to take your ratings to the next level."

Billy sniffed. "That's bullshit, Bernie, and you know it. I don't give a shit about ratings. I just wanted to keep Marissa safe. Draw some attention to her case and maybe help get her out. You took this way too far. I didn't agree to any of this. It was supposed to be a couple of mailboxes, empty cars. Nobody was supposed to get hurt."

"Now's not the time to lose your spine, Mr. Glueck."

"Why would you even go to see her?" Jordan cut in.

Billy turned on her. "Because we did that! We put her there! Unlike you, I have a conscience, Jordie. I couldn't pretend what happened to her wasn't our fault and just move on like you did. We ruined that girl's life! People died! I wrote letters. I called the governor's office. I spoke to her family. None of that mattered, though, because I couldn't do a damn thing to make it right. In the end, all I could do was see her. Visit. Offer her that little bit of comfort. Bring her books. Make her laugh. That's all I could do. And you know what? After a while, that became enough for her. She's a better person than either of us, that's for damn sure. She forgave me. Hell, she even tried to forgive you in those early years. Maybe if you'd pulled your head out of your ass long enough to go and see her, apologize, maybe she would have. Who knows. I'm not going to tell you I'm sorry for visiting that girl in prison. That might be the only righteous thing I've done with my life. I had to try and get her out."

He took several steps toward the ledge and attempted to peer over the side, but the smoke and heat was too much. He leaned back. "That piece-of-shit senator fought me every step of the way. Every letter I wrote to help her, his office wrote a goddamn novel to keep her in there. Called her a murderer, a terrorist, a heartless killer. He didn't even know her! I don't think he even took the time to review her case. All he ever cared about was advancing his own agenda, using her to set an example." He scratched the side of his head with the gun. "Christ, Jordie, why didn't you just shoot that prick? This would have all been over. It didn't need to go this far."

Billy pressed the earbud again. "I do this, Bernie, and you keep her safe. That was your promise. I expect you to keep it."

"Of course. You have my word."

"Yeah, your fucking word."

Another bomb went off, and the roof shook with such force Jordan nearly lost her balance. She took several steps, held an arm out, and somehow managed to regain her footing before a secondary explosion rattled the rooftop. The ledge felt as if it were tipping to the side, ready to break from the building, and she stumbled again, almost jumped down to the roof, but caught herself.

"Stay on the ledge or go over the side, but *do not* set foot back on the roof," Bernie said in Jordan's headphones. "That was the 39th floor. Tell everyone they can either do as Billy tells them or wait for the bombs to come. I'm fine either way." He paused for a second, then added, "Detective Cole is also carrying a second firearm. This one is on his ankle. Tell him to throw that over the side like the first gun."

Jordan's legs were still quivering, and she wasn't sure if it was nerves, the building, or a combination of both. She told Cole, "He knows about your other gun. You need to throw it away."

Cole nodded reluctantly, then took the smaller gun from the holster on his leg and tossed it across the roof.

"You know what to do, Billy," Bernie said. "Just as we discussed. You might want to pick up the pace, though."

Billy pinched his eyes shut for a second, rubbed his temple, then turned back to Nick. "Put on your parachute, then use the cable and lock to secure Charlotte to you." He waved the gun at Cole. "Help him, then put your own chute on. Hurry up."

The remaining pages from Rikers fell from Cole's fingers and caught the wind. They fluttered up and over the side of the building. His gaze flickered over to Jordan, then Nick. He knew none of them had a choice. He reached for Charlotte.

When Nick tried to release her, she only grasped him tighter. Cole had to peel her away.

"We're going to get you down, your mommy and daddy too," Jordan heard Cole tell her.

Nick carefully shrugged into the parachute and fastened the clasps, then took Charlotte back, trying his best to hide the pain and failing. Like a vice grip, Charlotte wrapped her arms around his neck and her legs around his waist. Cole wound the cable around them, circled both their legs, then back around her small body twice, until there was no slack. He then used the lock to fasten the ends of the cable to one of the parachute's metal rings.

Another bomb went off, and they all waited until the aftershocks died away before anyone spoke again.

"Eye for an eye, Ms. Briggs," Bernie said over the rumble. "You took my daughter from me. It's time you say good-bye to yours. Tell Nick to jump."

Jordan's eyes were filled with tears. "I can't."

"Billy…"

Billy waved the gun at the wall of smoke rising beside the ledge. "You need to jump, Nick…hurry, while you still can."

Both arms around Charlotte, Nick looked up at Jordan and she saw something there she hadn't seen in so long. The last year of animosity had washed away, and the man she had fallen in love with was looking back at her, his eyes deep and warm, filled with this tenderness she thought had died. He must have sensed something too, because even through the pain, the harsh lines of his face softened and the corner of his mouth managed a brief smile.

"Take care of our baby," she managed to say.

Carefully balancing his weight and Charlotte's, Nick climbed up on the ledge and faced her again. "I love you, Jordie. I always will."

She wanted to reach for them both, become part of their embrace, smell her daughter's hair. She wanted to tell Charlotte everything would be okay, and she found herself taking a step toward them.

"No," Bernie said defiantly.

And then they were gone, dropping over the side, lost to the smoke.

81

Jordan

"Now you," Billy said, pointing the gun at Cole and eyeing the parachute still in his hand. Something shifted in his eyes, though. His voice wavered when he spoke, cracked. He looked back at the edge, the spot where Nick and Charlotte had been only moments earlier. He seemed to be trying to see through the wall of black smoke, thick enough to appear solid now.

Cole slipped his arms through the shoulder straps of his parachute and fastened the other two around his legs. "I'm not going anywhere unless I know Jordan is safe," he said when he finished.

"Now you," Billy said again, as if he didn't hear him or remember saying it the first time. Something was wrong. He waved the gun, his face flustered. "Jump, dammit!"

When Cole didn't move, Billy sank to the ground, his back against the small safety wall. He looked down at the gun in his hand. "Now you," he muttered for a third time, the words barely audible. "Oh, fuck. What did I do?"

Cole exchanged a quick look with Jordan, then took several steps toward Billy, got between him and Jordan. "How about you put the gun down, and we all jump? We figure this out on the ground."

Billy laughed at this. A quick chuckle. "You lied about the helicopter, didn't you, Bernie? Nobody's coming. You fucking lied to me too."

"What helicopter?" Jordan said.

Cole edged closer, eying the gun. "Helicopter won't work for the same reasons they couldn't use them on 9/11. The smoke is too thick, and the heat from the fire creates an updraft. The thermal pockets mixed with cold air would cause the chopper to either drop or rise, maybe fifty to a hundred feet in a clip. It's too dangerous. They wouldn't be able to get close enough. You want to get down, you need to jump."

Billy only half heard this. "How could I fucking trust you? Are you even going to help Marisa get out, or was that all bullshit too?"

Bernie replied, "Marisa is as much a victim in all this as my wife was, my daughter. I didn't lie about that. I've got no power to get her out, but the whole world knows what happened now. Public opinion will be Marisa's savior. That burden is no longer on your shoulders. You should have never been in that car with her. You're as responsible as Ms. Briggs and all the others from her show. Your death will set things right. All your deaths."

Billy's face was horribly white. With his free hand, he reached up and unsnapped the buckles on his parachute. He looked like he might pass out.

Jordan felt her chest tighten. "Billy, what is it?"

"I wish I could see him, the poor, gullible shit. I hope you find each other in hell."

Half off, Billy's parachute fell to his side.

The gun dropped from his other hand.

Jordan opened her mouth to ask the next question but couldn't get it out. A lump was growing in her throat. She didn't have to say it aloud. Bernie confirmed the thought that had crept into her head before she could find the words.

"Billy knows it took the better part of a day to get through all of the parachutes. A cut string here, a torn strap there. Nylon is durable until you take a knife to it. Then it cuts up pretty easy. That was part of the deal, that was *his* choice. If he wanted Marisa to finally receive justice, everyone else needed to jump. Everyone associated with that damn show of yours." He paused for a beat.

"Jordan, everyone who jumped is dead."

Jordan's blood thumped so loud in her ears she only half heard him. Her eyes pinched shut, and she saw Charlotte strapped to Nick going over the side. She saw her staff, dropping, one by one. She saw them falling, arms and legs flailing as they screamed all the way down, silenced only as their bodies thumped against the sidewalks, the street, the cars below.

Dead.

All dead.

Because of her.

"Your debt to me is finally settled, Ms. Briggs. You owe me nothing else. Thank you for giving me your daughter and making things right."

Jordan felt her legs vanish from beneath her, replaced with a nothingness as the world began to spin. She heard Charlotte's name slip from her lips in a voice that did not belong to her, and that fell too, so soft it dropped and vanished behind the deep rumble of the fire below.

"There's only one way to end your own pain. Only one way to ever see your daughter again."

When the next explosion came, when it threw Jordan completely off balance, when the ledge pulled out from under her, she made no effort to recover. Instead, she leaned into it, wanting it all to be over. She fell back into the wall of smoke and tumbled over the side of the building.

82

Jordan

Jordan hadn't noticed how close Cole had gotten, but even before the rooftop vanished from beneath her feet, Cole lunged up at her, over the wall. He dove through the air, both arms outstretched, reaching. He punched under her arms with his, forced his legs between hers, and squeezed her in this awkward embrace she found herself returning as another explosion thundered.

She expected to feel as if they were falling, but there was only wind—smoke so thick there was no point of reference. Jordan couldn't see anything but Cole's hair. Unlike the other explosions, this one didn't come from below but *beside* them as they dropped. 40th floor? 41st? The heat of it hit them like a wall, and that was followed by a million shards of glass as she caught a glimpse of the windows bowing out and shattering in some adrenaline-fueled slow-motion vision. She was certain that explosion would kill them, and it might have if Cole's parachute hadn't opened and yanked them away.

Cole's arms jerked under her shoulders with such force she was certain one or both had dislocated. Then they were rising, not falling. Or at least it felt that way, their two bodies entwined so close they might have been one.

The world grew incredibly quiet.

"Hold your breath!" Cole shouted out.

But the warning came too late. Jordan's lungs filled with noxious fire-tainted fumes. Her body heaved and expelled the poison only to gulp down more—she'd drown in it, they both would, Cole was coughing too—each breath worse than the last as they dropped and the flames intensified. Jordan didn't realize their parachute was on fire until she looked up to try and get some semblance of bearings. The canopy was white with red stripes, rectangular in shape. While it had opened, the center was gone. Flames crawled across the nylon, fueled by the wind, reaching for the outer edges. She spotted two cords hanging down, both with handles, meant for steering, but neither of them could grab them without risk of—

They came down hard on top of a white laundry van.

Jordan's right leg hit first, buckled, then her left. She rolled to the side, Cole on top of her. The wind caught part of the canopy and yanked him over the side, and she tumbled over too, falling the last seven feet and hitting the pavement between the van and a Toyota. The wind caught the canopy again, started to drag Cole down the street, snagged on something, and went still.

Jordan found herself on her back, not exactly sure how she got there, tangled in chords and nylon. She was looking up the front of her building from somewhere on 49th Avenue. The structure itself wasn't visible. There was only this living, breathing monster of flames wearing a writhing coat of black, gray, and white. For one brief second, she wondered if her car was still parked out on the street nearby—she thought about the ticket *that* would get her, and the world went dark.

"It's her! It's Briggs!"

Male Voice. Accent. North Carolina?

"Don't move. Your leg's broken. The two of you came down hard."

The moment she heard this, an excruciating pain radiated out from her right leg, just below her knee. It raced up her thigh to her back and crossed every inch—every bone and muscle—to her fingertips, as if looking for a way out.

"Gunshot wound too, right shoulder. Superficial. Treated within the past several hours, but it will need some stitches. Numerous cuts and abrasions. Embedded glass. Ms. Briggs, can you hear me? I need you to open your eyes."

Jordan hadn't realized her eyes were closed. When she tried to open them, it felt like someone taped sandpaper under the lids. Someone pried them open with two fingers, and eye drops splashed down on her corneas.

She blinked several times.

"You've got windburn from the heat. That will help with the dryness." To someone else, "Cut that parachute off him!"

"…Charlotte."

Jordan managed to get her name out, surprised by how strange her voice sounded. That same dryness in her mouth, throat.

She coughed.

Water then.

A bottle at her lips.

A lot of voices now.

All around her.

Near.

Far.

Everywhere.

A needle prick in her thigh.

"That was for the pain. We're putting an inflatable split on your leg so we can transport you. It may feel cold." Jordan only got a glimpse of him—dark hair, short. Thin beard peppered with gray. He seemed too young for gray, his face unlined beneath the hair. He looked off to the side. "How's he?"

"Nothing visibly broken. Appears responsive. Sir, can you hear me?"

Jordan heard Cole cough several times, then, "Yeah. Get Detective Tresler. I'm a cop."

A blast of icy air raced up Jordan's leg and met the numbness growing at her thigh from the injection. She felt pressure, and her entire leg went stiff.

Jordan tried to look down at it.

"Don't move your head, ma'am. I want to get a brace on you until we can get an X-ray."

Even before he finished saying this, another pair of hands slipped something around her neck and fastened it.

"Move her to the stretcher on three. Ready?"

Jordan cleared her throat. "Did my daughter's parachute open? She's with my husband? Did you see them come down before us?"

"One, two—"

Several hands lifted her, moved her to the right, and set her down on a stretcher with practiced skill.

Female voice. "All right, strap her in and get her over to number twelve—"

Jordan quickly sat up. Swooned as her vision briefly went white, then rolled off the side of the stretcher.

"What the hell are you—"

She tried to land on her good leg, but the broken one came down too, and the moment she put pressure on it the pain came back tenfold. Jordan winced, willed herself not to pass out. She grabbed someone's jacket with one hand, got the mirror of the Toyota with her other, and managed to get to a standing position.

"Charlotte!"

Although the police had blockades up everywhere, they were far outnumbered by the spectators, the large crowd that had gathered up and down the block. They spotted Jordan a moment after she saw them, and voices started calling out her name. Hands were in the air, holding up cell phones taking pictures and recording video.

The two paramedics tried to pull her back down to the stretcher, but Jordan ripped the neck brace off and pulled away from them, turning in a slow circle.

She was in a war zone.

49th Avenue was packed tight with abandoned vehicles, the burned-out husk of a taxi still smoldering no more than twenty feet away. From above, ash and soot rained down, the air filled with an acidic haze. Several feet to her left, Cole struggled to his feet as a female paramedic tried to keep him on the ground.

Jordan continued turning, hopping on her good leg, scanning the street. "Charlotte!" she screamed out again.

Jordan finally spotted Nick, near the corner of 49th and 7th Avenue.

Untangling himself from his parachute.

Alone.

83

Jordan

"Get off me!" Two of the paramedics tried to hold her back, but Jordan used the Toyota as leverage and pulled out of their grasp. "Nick!"

She heard Bernie's voice then, not thin and small in her ears, but big, blaring, coming from all around her, and she realized it was all the radios. All the people in the crowd, all of them holding up their phones. The cars too, all the abandoned cars tuned to her show. His voice amplified a thousand times from every speaker. "Oh, Ms. Briggs. How the mighty have fallen."

Her headphones were on the ground near where she came down. One of the paramedics had picked them up, and she snatched them from his hand and put them on. "Where the fuck are you?"

"Close enough to smell your sweat."

"But still hiding, you spineless shit."

Her voice was amplified too, rebroadcast and echoing right along with his, and Jordan didn't care. She kept moving toward Nick, heaving herself forward on her good leg, balancing with the cars. Every step took all the energy she could muster, and speaking was nearly impossible against the pain. She was soaked with perspiration and getting light-headed. She sucked in a breath and went on anyway.

From behind the barricades, people shouted at her, took photos. Some cheered.

Why were they even here?

Was this just some kind of spectacle to them? Entertainment? Is that all she was to them? Her family?

There were television cameras too. At least a dozen of them, all shuffling around on the sidewalk trying to get some kind of shot of her.

How many dead now? And these people couldn't get enough.

Some asshole actually had a sign that read: *Bernie's the bomb!*

Just a few hours earlier, when the taxies had exploded, she had wanted to take a crew down to the street. She was no better than any of them.

This was her spectacle. She was responsible.

On you, Jordan.

All of this was, all on her. Every second of it.

As she neared him, Nick glanced up.

Hunched over, one hand on his knees, the other pressing against his ribs. Out of breath. Exhausted. His parachute was bunched up around his feet. The metal cable they had used to secure Charlotte was lying in the street, discarded.

Jordan frantically looked around. "Where is she? Where's my baby!?"

Nick nodded toward an ambulance no more than twenty feet away.

"Oh, my God!" Jordan gasped.

He raised a hand to calm her. "She's okay. We came down hard, but I took the brunt of it. The paramedic just wanted to get her off the street and check her out. He said he'd—"

Jordan didn't hear the rest. She was making her way to the ambulance, scrambling as best she could, the broken bones in her leg grinding against each other with each step, causing her vision to go white, then red. Through the haze, she saw Charlotte sitting inside looking out. A gurney covered with a sheet beside her, a paramedic between them leaning out with a gun in one hand and some kind of switch in the other, a trigger, identical to the one Daly had held.

Bernie.

God, that was Bernie.

He had Charlotte.

Their eyes met and Bernie held her gaze for what seemed the longest time. He watched her hobble closer before tugging the back door of the ambulance closed between them.

His every word cut into her like a nail. His voice amplified by every phone, every speaker, her own headphones. He was everywhere.

"After the accident," he said calmly, "when Kourtney died on the way to the hospital, they managed to get my daughter out. Kimberly lived for almost nine minutes. Nine minutes, and she saw only her mother's dead face and the inside of an ambulance, just like this one. Your daughter won't see your face in these final moments, but she will hear your voice. I suppose there's some comfort in that."

Jordan reached the back of the ambulance and yanked on the door handle.

Locked.

She beat on the back of the door, and for a brief second, she thought she heard Charlotte scream her name from inside.

Her small voice was cut off by the gunshot.

84

Jordan

The bullet tore through the back door about five inches above the bumper and less than three from Jordan's thigh. It cracked against the blacktop and vanished in a plume of dust. "This is no different from the building, Ms. Briggs. Tell the officers gathering around you not to come any closer. Anyone attempts to breach, and I'll detonate this last bomb manually. You'll lose those nine minutes with Charlotte. Well, eight minutes, twelve seconds now."

Cole came up behind her with another detective. When the second man spoke into his phone, she recognized his voice.

Tresler.

Tresler spoke softly, but Jordan's microphone still picked him up. "He's in an ambulance on the corner of 47th and 6th. I want all exits blocked. Set up a perimeter. He doesn't move from that spot. Get sharpshooters in position. All surrounding buildings."

"That's a North Bergen ambulance," Cole pointed out. "That's how he got away from the bombing in Jersey this morning."

"It's how I got *everywhere* this morning," Bernie replied. "No need for sharpshooters or roadblocks. I won't be leaving. This is the last stop for me. You may want to tell everyone to get back, though. You're all way too close. Seven minutes, twenty-three seconds."

"I did everything you asked of me, Bernie. Everything!" Jordan said, her voice booming as loud as his.

"You didn't kill the senator. You didn't even kill yourself. All you've proved to me is that you're not above cheating. That's okay, though. I thought I'd be alone when we finished the game. It's nice to have some company in these final moments."

Tresler stepped closer. "Bernie, this is over. The senator is dead. Most of the chutes opened just fine, but not his. He caught on something, tore it wide open. Fifty stories down, nothing to slow him. I don't think there's a single bone in that man that didn't break. I can get you proof. Open the door so we can speak face-to-face, and I'll—"

"It's too late for that. Ms. Briggs didn't follow the rules."

Jordan said, "You didn't damage all the parachutes, though. You didn't kill everyone like you said."

"I'm not sure any of the parachutes were damaged," Tresler pointed out. "We haven't seen any indication lines were cut. The ones like the senator, the couple that didn't deploy properly, it was due to external factors—jumping too close to the building, caught in the updraft, tangling, things like that, not sabotage."

"So you didn't kill any of my staff, did you, Bernie?"

Jordan wanted to pace, but her broken leg held her still. Her mind was working, though, her mind was churning.

"Everyone who deserved to die, has. All but you," Bernie replied. "I spared the rest."

"Well, I'm right here. Let me trade places with Charlotte."

"No."

"Why not? I'm the one you really want to punish, right?"

"You living, knowing Charlotte died because of you, you living with that knowledge, that was the original game. I changed the rules for you, and you lied to me, you broke them. Fool me once…maybe…but not again. Original game. Original rules. Six minutes and eight seconds."

"Killing the judge in my case, the jurors. That's one thing. You're a twisted fuck, and in a twisted way, killing them probably makes perfect sense to your twisted fuck brain. But you couldn't bring yourself to kill my staff, even though you had the opportunity. It would have been so easy, damage the chutes, just like you said, but you didn't…"

Jordan let that last sentence hang, hoping he'd take the bait and speak, but he didn't. He didn't say anything. When she went on, she lowered her voice. She looked directly at the back of the ambulance as if she could see right through it to his eyes. "I don't think you could kill an innocent child any more than you could kill my staff."

"Five minutes, eighteen seconds."

"If your daughter had lived, how old would she be, Bernie?"

Again, he didn't answer.

Jordan answered for him. "She'd be nearly eleven. The same age as the little girl next to you. The little girl no doubt watching you with horribly frightened eyes. Imagine she's yours, Bernie. For one second, just look over at her and pretend she's your daughter. That precious child. Imagine that's Kimberly sitting next to you, wondering why daddy wants to kill her. Could you look your own daughter in her eyes and tell her why you planned to take her life?"

"Four minutes. Twenty-one seconds. My daughter's eyes were blue, Ms. Briggs. I only know that because I read it on her death certificate. I never once got to look in them. I never got to hear her laugh or cry or see her smile."

"Yes, you did. You saw all those things whenever you looked at your wife, when you looked in the mirror. Because, trust me, they're the same. Children are us. They're the best pieces of us. When Charlotte tells me a joke, I see her father. When she pouts and plants her feet, I see myself. When she argues, I sure as hell hear myself."

All around her, the police were moving people back, creating this vacant, empty place around the ambulance. Several times, someone tugged on her arm, tried to move her too, but she wouldn't budge. Cole was still behind her. She felt his hand on her shoulder.

"I'll never know any of those things, because of you. Three minutes."

"Your daughter is still alive, Bernie. You know how I know that? Because of those letters she sent me every year. You may have written them, but they came from her. Her heart, her words. And she's a special little girl. I want more of those. I want to know what she's like in high school. I want to hear about her first boyfriend. Her wedding, her own children. That accident, and it *was* an accident, may have taken her body, but her spirit lives in you."

Cole handed her a tablet. She wasn't sure where he'd gotten it. There were a series of photographs. She quickly scrolled through and understood. "I'm looking at pictures of your apartment, Bernie. Your daughter's bedroom, her crib. All the toys and stuffed animals. It's a place of love, every inch of it. That's why you left those things at crime scenes. To remind people of that love. There are pictures of you and Kourtney here too. In this one, the way she's looking up at you... Is that the art museum near the park? It is, isn't it? Wow, the way she's looking at you, it's obvious she loved you so much. Nobody should ever know your pain, Bernie. Nobody. But everyone listening today, they all do. Every mother, father, brother, sister, daughter...they all understand your loss, your heartache. They all know what I did, and I'm sorry, Bernie. I know me saying that doesn't make it right. Nothing I can do will ever make it right, but I want to try. Work with me, Bernie. Come out of there. End this. Let's figure out a way to honor the memory of your wife and daughter. You don't want their legacy to be what you created today, not all this death. Let's create something special. I can't bring them back, but if you work with me, we can keep them alive."

Bernie said nothing.

Jordan had nothing else to say.

The ambulance sat there in the middle of the street, and all voices in the crowd had gone silent.

Nearly another minute ticked by before Bernie broke that silence.

"Tell the shooters to stand down. I want everyone to get back, we're coming out."

Cole and Tresler had already edged Jordan back at least ten feet from the ambulance, but when Bernie said that she wanted to go back. If the two of them hadn't been holding her, she might have done just that. But when the door to the ambulance opened, both of them held her tighter, refused to let her go. Even when Charlotte crawled out the back and jumped down to the pavement.

Charlotte stood there for a moment, confused, dazed. Then she spotted Jordan and closed the distance in a second. She crashed into Jordan so hard, she nearly knocked all of them over.

Snot dripped from Charlotte's nose. Her eyes were red and puffy with tears. They almost didn't hear her when she spoke, her voice so thin. "Mommy, he said to run."

Jordan looked up at the ambulance then, her gaze locked with Bernie, still sitting inside.

Tresler scooped up Charlotte, and Cole's arm tightened around Jordan's waist—he yanked her back, and the four of them dove behind a carpet delivery van stuck in the surrounding gridlock as the ambulance exploded in a thundering fireball behind them—a deep boom rivaled only by the explosion of the final floor of her building half a block away.

One Week Later

85

Cole

Mac's Tavern wasn't large. It only held about seventy-five people, but it had been a staple in Queens going on ninety-eight years now, first as a mob hangout shortly after the end of Prohibition, then taken over by members of NYPD in the sixties, commandeered as a cop bar. It had survived two fires, three recessions, one riot, and a flood that destroyed a kitchen already in desperate need of repair about the same time the wall came down in Berlin. The kitchen had been replaced, and now, thirty years later, needed another flood to wash it clean.

The walls were covered in dark paneling nobody wanted to see with the lights on and a tin ceiling stained gray from years of cigarette and cigar smoke caked on thick enough to flake off and fall during the colder months of the year, like a poor man's snow.

Mac's Tavern had also been the preferred gathering place for six generations of Gaffs in law enforcement. Their pictures lined the walls, along with dozens of citations received over the years, framed and hung haphazardly about. Mugs engraved with their names were mounted above the bar. A booth in the back corner was reserved for the highest-ranking member of the Gaff family. Nobody else was permitted to sit there.

As Cole entered Mac's, already crowded for six o'clock on a

Tuesday, voices dropped to a low murmur. Several people stepped aside, and Cole's eyes landed on that booth.

There were three occupants.

His lieutenant and commanding officer, Mitch Gaff.

Joseph Daggett, the warden at Rikers Island.

Milton Gaff, Mitch's father and former NY Chief of Police (1989-1993).

Each had a beer in front of them, no doubt Sam Adams, and each had drunk about half. Under normal circumstances, there would have been a bowl of potato chips shared between them, but he wasn't here under normal circumstances. In fact, Cole had spent the last ten minutes outside trying to decide if he wanted to enter at all.

Milton Gaff was first to look up and notice him standing there by the door. He nudged his son and Daggett under the table, and they looked up too.

That was when Cole knew he'd made a mistake by coming here. He considered leaving, but he could feel bodies closing the space between him and the door. From the corner of his eye, he spotted Trey and Darin, the Gaff twins, easing behind him too.

He wouldn't be leaving until they were ready to let him go.

Without looking him in the eye, the bartender poured another beer from the tap and carried it over to the Gaff table. He set it in an empty spot facing the other three men, then returned to the sink.

"Now or never, Cole," he said more to himself than anyone else and went over to the table, slipped into the empty seat.

"You look like a mule kicked the shit out of you," Milton said, taking a sip of his beer. "Not an inch on you not cut, scraped, or bruised."

"Traffic duty can be rough," Cole replied, eyeing his lieutenant, who said nothing.

Milton smirked, easing back in the torn red pleather seat. He tapped the lip of his mug. "Bernie left a list. All those people in the senator's pocket. Bad people trying to grease his bill. You know I'm not on it, right?"

"I've seen it."

"I'm not on it. Your partner's not on it."

"A lot of people are, though."

"Nobody at this table. Nobody in this bar."

Lieutenant Gaff leaned forward. "Everyone on that list is either in custody or under investigation. I hear they've got Moretti's partner on the bill, Mercer, in a safe-house upstate somewhere while the feds grill him. To me it seems like the Sentinels used all this as an excuse to flex their muscle. Moretti lit the flame to juice his own cause. Bernie played 'em all. Bunch of assholes all using each other to get what they want and half of them ending up dead. This will shake out, always does."

Milton interrupted him. "The point is, those of us on the right side of things will come out on top, always do in the end. Always will. The ones backing this thing, they'll hang themselves."

"The feds raided the Sentinel camp, and it was empty," Daggett said. "They cleared out. In the wind."

Milton took another sip of beer. "They'll hang themselves," he repeated. "Give 'em enough time. Every last one of them will turn up."

Cole twisted the mug in his hands and looked at Daggett. "How's Marisa Chapman?"

"We've got her in isolation," he replied. "I'll keep her there until things cool down. I've been talking to the warden up at Wilcox. We might transfer her. Put some distance out there. Haven't decided yet. Either way, she's safe. I'll keep her that way. There's a grand jury looking into her case, thanks to all this. Maybe she'll get a little justice too."

Lieutenant Gaff looked at his father for a moment, then into his beer. "You asked for my daughter's hand in marriage. I told you no. You understand why, right?"

"You don't want her married to a cop."

"I don't want her married to a cop," he repeated.

"You almost died, son," Milton said.

The lieutenant placed a hand on his father's wrist, silenced him, then looked back at Cole. "What do you think Gracie sees in you? She sees the men who raised her. The men who protected her, kept her safe her entire life. I know you, Cole. You're me. You're the men at this table. The men in this bar. You see a fire, you run in. You hear a scream, you help. You put all others before yourself, and that's a damn good quality to have, but—"

"But not in the man who marries your daughter."

"No. I can't have my daughter wondering if you're coming home at night. I don't want her jumping whenever the phone rings. Whenever there's a knock at the door."

"All due respect, sir, that's not your decision to make. It's hers."

"She's my baby. My little girl. One day, you'll understand that."

"She's a grown woman. Probably tougher than all of us."

Cole hadn't realized how quiet the bar had gotten. Nobody else was talking. All eyes were on them. He took a sip of his beer, weighed his words carefully. "I love Gracie with every ounce of my being. She's my first thought in the morning and my last at night. When I was in that building. When things were at their worst, I closed my eyes and thought of her. I thought of her smile, her laugh, the little crinkle in the corner of her left eye when she giggles. I thought about the warmth of her hand in mine, the feel of her in my arms, and how, more than anything, I wanted to get back to her. She kept me safe. She pulled me off that roof and out of the fire. There is not a moment when anything else became more important to me. She will always come first." Cole looked him in the eyes. "I would love to have your blessing, all of you, everyone in this room, but not having your blessing isn't going to keep the two of us from each other. Some things are too strong. The love I have for your daughter is too strong."

The three men at the table looked back at him but said nothing.

Several minutes passed before anyone spoke at all.

Lieutenant Gaff was first. He finally said, "You ever hurt her, and the people in this room will make you disappear. You know that, right?"

This brought up a soft murmur around the room.

Cole nodded.

The lieutenant glanced at his father and Gracie's godfather, then reached across the table and offered his hand to Cole. "Welcome to the family, son."

Two-and-a-half hours, six beers, and numerous shots later, Cole stepped out of Mac's Tavern into the chilly night air. He stood on the corner for a moment, located Gracie's 1984 black Firebird across the street, and shuffled over, doing his best to walk in a straight line and failing miserably.

Gracie was leaning against the driver's door in jeans, a white tank top, and a brown leather jacket. She smiled at him as he approached, did her best to stifle a laugh, and failed. "Oh, they did a number on you. Didn't they?"

"I'm fine. I'll be just fine."

The words didn't come out quite like that but weren't as slurred as he expected. He wrapped his arms around her and squeezed, always amazed at just how perfectly she fit. "I love you more than anything, you know that, right?"

"I love you too, Detective Hundley."

"I love you more than peanut butter."

She giggled. "Oh boy, I need to get you home."

"We need to make one stop." Cole took out his phone and showed her the text at the top of the screen.

She nodded. "Okay, but then home."

They climbed into the car, and Gracie leaned over and kissed him on the cheek. "Did you tell my dad we eloped yesterday?"

"Oh, hell no."

86

Jordan

Jordan heard him approach but didn't turn. Instead, she shifted her weight to the crutch under her right shoulder and pulled the tip of the other one out of the dirt. She'd been standing still long enough for it to sink nearly two inches into the grass. It made a sucking sound as she pulled it out. "For a detective, you're not very good at sneaking up on people."

"The bad guys usually do the sneaking," Cole said. "I've never been good at it."

When she finally turned toward him, her eyes narrowed and a thin smile found her lips. "You've been drinking."

Cole held up his thumb and index finger and pinched them together. "Little bit."

"Celebrating?"

"Little bit."

"I'm sorry, I didn't mean to interrupt."

Cole looked down at the fresh dirt, the temporary marker where a tombstone would eventually rest. "Wasn't the funeral this afternoon? Have you been here the entire time?"

"What time is it?"

"A little after nine."

"Wow, I guess I have." She looked back toward the entrance

to Holy Cross Cemetery. *When had it gotten dark?* "I had a lot to think about, and it's quiet here. I guess the time just got away from me."

"It was good of you to pay for it."

Jordan looked over at the tombstones next to Bernie's final resting place.

Kourtney Bretz on the far left, and their daughter's grave between them.

She'd cleaned them when she first arrived and put a bouquet of flowers in the metal vase attached to the side. "The groundskeeper told me Bernie came out here three, sometimes four times a week. He must have stopped every time he was in the area. He sat and talked to her for hours. Just the two of them. For nearly ten years. It seemed important they were together. If I hadn't bought him a plot, the state would have cremated him. Done who-knows-what with the ashes."

"It was good of you," Cole repeated.

"Well, don't tell anyone. I'd hate for the world to realize I have a heart."

He nodded at her leg. "Is that itching yet?"

The cast ran from her upper thigh to the toes of her left foot. Charlotte had covered it with sketches of characters from *The Simpsons*.

"Not yet. I hear I've got that to look forward to, though, in a few weeks. Right now, it just feels heavy and awkward."

"How do you get around? You can't drive, right?"

She pointed toward a black town car parked at the crest of the hill. Frank was leaning on the front fender, his face buried in the light of a phone screen. "That lucky gentleman gets to drive Ms. Daisy around for the foreseeable future."

She saw the question enter his eyes only a few had had the courage to ask her, so she just said it. "Nick and I aren't broke. That was just something those people said to try and get a rise out of me on the air. The documents were all fakes."

"You and Nick? Does that mean…"

She let out a soft sigh. "We're not back together. Not really. We're sort of dating, but I don't really see it going anywhere. I think we want things to work, primarily for Charlotte, but the truth is the problems we had before all this happened haven't changed. They're still there. We talked about moving back in together or maybe taking a family trip, but that just seems like a way to postpone the inevitable. Neither of us want to give Charlotte a sense of false hope. There was a time when Nick and I belonged together. I think now we've entered a new phase, one where we belong apart." With the tip of her crutch, she pushed a divot of grass back into place. "We're finally taking that trip to the Hamptons tomorrow to visit with my mother."

"Charlotte's first time?"

Jordan nodded. "All those years I kept her at arm's length for no reason other than her being as pigheaded as me. I guess I realized just how silly that all was. Charlotte deserves to have a grandmother, and my mother should know my child. Everything else seems so minor at this point it's not worth considering anymore."

"A lot of life's problems feel that way after something like this," he agreed. "I'm glad to hear you're working things out."

Neither spoke for about a minute. A cool breeze drifted across the cemetery as night took hold.

Jordan broke the silence. "I've been to see Billy."

"Is he still unconscious?"

She nodded. "They still don't know if he jumped or fell. The doctors told me the smoke would have killed him if he didn't get off that roof when he did. Maybe another minute or two at the most. Whatever he hit on the way down caused severe swelling in his brain, so they're keeping him in a medically induced coma. It's too early to tell if there's permanent damage."

"He put his parachute back on," Cole pointed out. "He jumped. Must have."

She thought about this next part carefully. If she didn't spit it out now, she probably never would. "The things he did up there, why he did them, what he told us… I've known Billy a very long time, longer than nearly anyone else in my life, and he's not a bad guy. In fact, he's a really great guy. He was manipulated, just like the rest of us. He was tricked. He doesn't deserve to be punished for it. I don't want him to go to jail." She was pleading now, didn't really care. "You, me, Nick, Charlotte…nobody else heard all of it. They just caught pieces over the air. If we don't say anything, then…"

Cole was already shaking his head.

"It's too late for that, isn't it?"

"I already filed my report," he told her. "I've been interviewed by more government agencies than I can count. I couldn't hold back at this point even if I wanted to. A lot of people lost their lives. The city suffered billions in damage, and it could take years to fully recover. The part he played, even if it was relatively minor, was a piece of the entire puzzle. It's not my job to determine who gets punished and who doesn't."

"Always the Boy Scout," she said softly.

They both fell silent for several moments. Cole shuffled his feet, and she caught him looking back over his shoulder at a Firebird parked at the curb. "Is that why you called me out here? To ask about Billy?"

She shook her head. "They want me to come back to work."

She saw the puzzled expression wash across his face. "Not here. SiriusXM has studios in Los Angeles."

Nobody would be returning to work here for a long time. While her building hadn't come down, there was nothing salvageable after the fires were finally put out. Most likely it would be imploded and eventually rebuilt. That was for the best. She had no desire to step foot in there again.

"Do you want to go back to work?"

She'd asked herself that same question so many times. "I feel I still have something to say. But I'm not sure I'm ready to say it just yet. I'd like to get better at listening. Charlotte told me if every word I ever said went into a bucket, I should have another bucket filled with all the words told to me, and both of those buckets should be the same. She said my talking bucket always overflows, and the other one is empty."

"She's a wise little girl."

Jordan sighed. "I'm not sure anyone wants to hear from me, not anymore."

"I don't know about that. I think you'd be surprised."

"I'm not the person I was before."

"That may be exactly why they need to hear from you."

Jordan let out a soft laugh. "God, I sound sad. You're not my therapist. I shouldn't be burdening you with all this."

"You sound like someone with a lot of decisions to make."

She smiled at him. "You're one of the good guys, Officer Detective Cole of the NYPD. Your fiancée is a lucky girl."

He nodded back toward the Firebird. "Would you like to meet her?"

"I think I would, yeah. In fact, if you'll let me, I think I'd like to pay for your wedding as a thank-you for everything you did. Have you set a date yet?"

Cole laughed and kicked at the dirt. "About that…"

Author's Note

As I write this, the date is March 25, 2020. It's about twenty past eight in the morning. A Wednesday. I'm in our home in New Castle, New Hampshire, a small island off the coast. Because the trees are still bare and haven't yet been told spring arrived early this year, I can see a peek of the ocean through my office window. A large cargo vessel just sailed by, heading toward the shipyard in Portsmouth, thin wisps of smoke coming from its stacks. I can hear my daughter in the other room (two-and-a-half now) yelling at Alexa, trying to get that little box from Amazon to understand her well enough to follow her instructions. It sounds something like, "Lexa, turns on the vee, please!" and it's not working. The TV is still off. My wife is cooking up some kind of breakfast in the kitchen. Smells like French toast.

Normally our house would be crawling with contractors. We're deep into a renovation. When we bought this place, not a single surface had been touched since Reagan was president. Red tile bathrooms, a once custom kitchen in complete disarray. A hot tub—yes, a hot tub—in the living room surrounded by green shag carpet. Not just a little hot tub, but a twelve-seater. I refuse to think about the things that have happened in that room over the years. I imagine there's video floating around somewhere, or maybe they used film back then. I've dared my wife to go in there with a blacklight, but she has yet to take me up on it.

Normally our house would be crawling with contractors, but nobody is here today. We sent them all home a few days back with instructions to sit tight for a bit. We'll reach out when we're ready to let them back into our lives, our home.

As of this morning, 54,968 people have the coronavirus in the United States. 435,374 worldwide. 108 cases here in New Hampshire. Nearly 30,000 in the state of New York, where many of my friends live. 1,467 in Florida, where our families live. Much of the world is in some kind of lockdown with the few places still lagging seriously considering heading in that direction. Most believe this ride is just getting started. The roller coaster is still clicking on its way up the first steep hill.

When you read this, some time will have passed. That's the nature of the publishing world. It takes a long time to write a book, far longer to get it out into the world. If I had to guess, it's mid-2021, maybe coming up on fall. Am I close? I'd like to believe the virus is in your rear view mirror and you know how this whole thing turned out. For better or worse, knowing the outcome is far better than sitting on this side of the keyboard, wondering where this whole mess is heading.

Being an author, it's my job to wonder "what if," to take a relatively normal scenario and spin it on its head. Find the crazy in the world, and throw a spotlight on it. Find the scary and turn down the lights, give it a chance to breathe on you from some dark, wet place. That's all fine and dandy when I'm able to get up from my desk, when I'm through and can head outside into the sunshine for my daily five-mile walk/run, maybe wave at the neighbors out on their porches or working in their yards. It's not such a good thing when the real world is more frightening than the fictitious one on my virtual paper. And that's where we are today.

I can't turn off the *What If* gene.

My brain wants to play that game whether I want to participate or not, and when real-world events such as these are feeding the machine, the output can go dark.

Really dark.

I woke last night around 2:30, firmly believing my wife and daughter were gone.

Our neighbor's house had a big red X on the door. They were gone too.

I wasn't in my own time anymore, I was in yours. A year or so into the future, looking back with thoughts like—

Why didn't we all wear masks?

Gloves?

When my wife said she was going to get the mail at our little post office, why didn't I tell her to skip it?

When she said she wanted to take our daughter with her, get her out of the house for a minute, why didn't I object?

Mail isn't delivered here. You have to pick it up. And our daughter loves going to the post office. She says hello to everyone (when you live on a small island, the post office is the local gathering spot and is regularly crowded). The building itself is several hundred years old, filled with ancient reminders of our little island's past. She loves to play with all shiny metal knobs on the antique boxes, peer through each tiny window, nose the glass, look inside. The coronavirus (COVID-19, as they're now calling it) likes those things too—it can live a long time on any one of them.

I woke at 2:30 believing my wife and daughter took the quarter-mile walk to our post office with their little red wagon in tow and brought something back to the house with them, something bad.

Something that took both of them away from me.

That didn't happen.

My wife *did* go to the post office and pick up the mail yesterday, but she wore gloves, a mask, and took a Purell bath the moment she was back outside. She sprayed every letter and package with disinfectant before it came into the house. Our daughter stayed home with me. Nobody got sick.

But that damn *What If* gene...

At times like these, I think we all start to realize what's really important to us. What really matters. I've been fortunate in life, and if I lost absolutely everything, I'd be okay with that.

But I could not lose them.

My love for them, their love for me, it's all far too precious.

There's no me without them.

As you're reading this, sometime in our collective future, you know what happened. You know if I got sick, my family, your family, the family next door. You've read the last page of that particular book while I'm still somewhere in the middle of the story. I envy you for that. The optimist in me wants to believe we all made the right choices and nipped this thing.

But that damn *What If* gene...

The What If gene keeps whispering about all the other ways it could go.

Well, time will tell.

In your world, time already has.

I'm supposed to be talking about the book you just read. That's why my publisher graciously grants me these last couple pages. They know I like to check in with you and dot the last few *i*'s and cross the remaining *t*'s before we part ways for a few months. There's no real easy way to go from what I just said to what I planned to say, so I'm going to just go right into it. How about we just do this?

[INSERT AWKWARD TRANSITION HERE]

Does that work for you?

If not, maybe take a quick break. Go grab a beverage, visit the little boy's room or the little girl's room, or maybe put together a snack in the kitchen, then come back. I don't mind, I'll wait for you.

All good? Cool. Here we go—

I've been told I write literary popcorn, and I'm fine with that. I always have been. When you read one of my books, you're never going to find some deep-seated social message or moral code. You're not going to get to page 237 and discover the meaning of life glaring at you from the text. When I write a story, when I share it with you, my sole purpose is to entertain you. Distract you for a little bit from all the goings-on in the world. Help you forget your own *What Ifs* for a little while. You'll never catch me sharing my personal views on politics or religion any more than I would tell you how to perform an appendectomy. I prefer to leave those things to the experts. I'm not an expert at anything. I literally get paid to make shit up. Do you really want to take advice from me?

This book, more than anything I've written in the past, may feel like it leans a little political in one direction or another. None of the views or thoughts expressed are really my own. They belong solely to the characters.

Jordan Briggs is strong-willed, opinionated. She's not afraid to tell you what she thinks or what she thinks you should think. That doesn't make her right, nor does it make her me. As with all my books, the characters told me their story, and I put it all down on paper. Sometimes they aggravated me, sometimes they downright pissed me off, but I'd never censor them. If I did that, I wouldn't be doing my job.

You're probably wondering how that even works, right? After all, the words did come out of my head.

This is tough to explain to anyone who hasn't tried their hand at writing fiction, but I'm going to give it a shot. When it's working, when I'm *in the zone*, when the words are flowing, I see the story play out like a movie in my mind. The characters are as real to me as you are. I write it all down and look up an hour later, amazed at all the words on the page and how they got there. That's partly why I don't outline. When I try to write a book based on an outline, the characters get frustrated. The story stops flowing, and someone like Jordan Briggs might shake the outline in my face and say, "That's not how it happened. I'll *tell you how it happened!*" In the end, I've got to listen to them. If I don't, the story becomes forced, fragile, fake. A good story is *character-driven*, not *author-driven*. If it's author-driven, it becomes commentary, and nobody really wants to hear from me. I'm frankly not that interesting.

I certainly wouldn't do the things Bernie did, and while Jordan and I might see eye-to-eye on some topics, there are plenty where we disagree. A conversation with her would be equal parts frustrating and fascinating. That's what makes her real (at least, to me). And if she wasn't real, there would be no story to tell. What would be the point?

So yeah, Jordan said some things.

So did Bernie, Billy, Senator Moretti, Charlotte. They all graciously told me their story so I could share it with you. They provided us all with literary popcorn, let us gobble it up. That doesn't make their *what-ifs* any more real than our own. But they did distract us. And in the end, isn't that all a good book should really be about? Particularly now.

I'll end this as I've been ending all my e-mails and letters lately, with *stay safe*. If you're reading this, a year and a half or so in the future, you clearly did *stay safe*, and I'm glad to hear it.

Until next time,
jd

New Castle, NH
March 25, 2020